ENGAGING DECEPTION

Books by Regina Jennings

THE JOPLIN CHRONICLES

Courting Misfortune
Proposing Mischief
Engaging Deception

THE FORT RENO SERIES

Holding the Fort
The Lieutenant's Bargain
The Major's Daughter

OZARK MOUNTAIN ROMANCE SERIES

A Most Inconvenient Marriage
At Love's Bidding
For the Record

LADIES OF CALDWELL COUNTY

Sixty Acres and a Bride
Love in the Balance
Caught in the Middle

NOVELLAS

An Unforeseen Match (from the collection *A Match Made in Texas*)
Her Dearly Unintended (from the collection *With This Ring?*)
Bound and Determined (from the collection *Hearts Entwined*)
Intrigue a la Mode (from the collection *Serving Up Love*)
Broken Limbs, Mended Hearts (from the collection *The Kissing Tree*)

ENGAGING DECEPTION

REGINA JENNINGS

BETHANYHOUSE
a division of Baker Publishing Group
Minneapolis, Minnesota

© 2022 by Regina Jennings

Published by Bethany House Publishers
11400 Hampshire Avenue South
Minneapolis, Minnesota 55438
www.bethanyhouse.com

Bethany House Publishers is a division of
Baker Publishing Group, Grand Rapids, Michigan

Printed in the United States of America

Library of Congress Cataloging-in-Publication Data
Names: Jennings, Regina (Regina Lea), author.
Title: Engaging deception / Regina Jennings.
Description: Minneapolis, Minnesota : Bethany House Publishers, a division of
    Baker Publishing Group, [2022] | Series: The Joplin chronicles ; 3
Identifiers: LCCN 2022022024 | ISBN 9780764235368 (paperback) | ISBN
    9780764240867 (casebound) | ISBN 9781493439089 (ebook)
Subjects: LCGFT: Romance fiction. | Christian fiction. | Novels.
Classification: LCC PS3610.E5614 E54 2022 | DDC 813/.6—dc23/eng/20220513
LC record available at https://lccn.loc.gov/2022022024

Scripture quotations are from the King James Version of the Bible.

Poem in chapter 13 is from William Shakespeare's *Measure for Measure*.

This is a work of historical reconstruction; the appearances of certain historical figures are therefore inevitable. All other characters, however, are products of the author's imagination, and any resemblance to actual persons, living or dead, is coincidental.

Cover design by Dan Thornberg, Design Source Creative Services

Baker Publishing Group publications use paper produced from sustainable forestry practices and post-consumer waste whenever possible.

22 23 24 25 26 27 28   7 6 5 4 3 2 1

To Lori,
the co-founder of our mutual admiration society,
the genius behind our mutually assured destruction compact,
and the best second double-cousin a girl could hope to have.
(I expect a dedication in return.)

The Kentworth Family

Albert & Laura Kentworth

Children
— Bill —m June
    - Finn Amos Maisie

— Oscar —m Myra
    - Willow Olive

— Pauline (Polly) —m Richard York
    - Corban Calista Evangelina

Calbert Kentworth —m Gretchen
(Grandpa Albert's Twin Brother)
    - Hannah Hilda Hank

Oh, the indignities of death.

Olive Kentworth dipped her horsehair brush into the jar of water and scrubbed the cold granite of the tombstone. Her mother had been gone for nearly a year, but Olive was still plagued by the emptiness in her days, in her home, in her heart. She tried to keep busy, and today that meant coming to the cemetery to wash away the bird droppings that marred her mother's gravestone. After rearranging her skirt to better pad her knees, she scrubbed with vigor. If only the birds would stop eating the mulberries. The purple was nearly impossible to erase, but she couldn't abide the idea that her mother's headstone looked untended. Not when she'd tended her so well in life.

"I thought I'd find you here," Maisie called from the far side of the shortleaf pine that shaded the family plot.

"Shh . . ." Olive said. "You're in a graveyard. You shouldn't be so buoyant."

But Maisie was striding toward her, swinging a berry basket high with a hatchet tucked into her waistband. Her cousin Maisie was buoyant wherever she went, just like Olive was cautious.

"Aunt Myra was an admirer of my spirit. She wouldn't mind." Maisie spotted a hard-shelled bug climbing up the tombstone and flicked it away. "What would bother her is her daughter spending too much time alone at her grave."

"Of course I'm alone. Mother's gone. Who else am I supposed to take care of?" Olive started in on another blotch of purple.

"Take care of yourself." Maisie said it like it was a reasonable course of action.

"I do take care of myself." Olive glared at her over the gravestone. "I have a lot of things planned. In fact, Willow invited me to go traveling with her and Graham to see the country."

"Welp, are you going?"

Olive dropped her gaze back to her work. "I would if it wasn't for Father. It's too soon to leave him alone."

"You spent the last eight years looking after your mother. Now you're going to look after your father?" Maisie set her basket down with force. "I'll tell you what you're doing. You're hiding from life, Olive, and that's why I'm here. I'm going to break you free."

Putting one hand to her side, Maisie extracted the hatchet from her waistband. This wasn't done easily, with the handle getting twisted in her skirt and requiring tugging and squirming to free it. Olive had time to pick up her jar and take a step back, as one could never be sure what her farm cousins were capable of. When Maisie grabbed the finial atop the grave marker and propped her foot against it, Olive gasped.

"Get down from there." She looked around, afraid someone in Fairview Cemetery would observe Maisie's outrageous behavior. "This isn't the place for climbing."

"I've come to free you, and that's what I'm going to do." Standing on Myra Kentworth's grave and stretching to her full height, Maisie caught the branch of the pine above her. With skill, she pulled it closer, then began hacking at it. "This tree looks mighty pretty, but you ain't going to keep the tombstone clean as long as the birds can sit above it."

"We chose this site because of the shade," Olive protested. "It's a pretty spot."

"Ain't nothing pretty about those bird droppings. The only thing worse is a smart girl like you hiding her light under a bushel." Maisie grunted with each strike. The bend in the branch showed that it was nearly cut through. Maisie dropped her hatchet, took the branch in both hands, and worked it until it snapped. She tossed the branch down, then hopped to the ground. "Olive Kentworth, your ma is dead, but you ain't. It's time to get to moving."

Leave it to Maisie to boil down all life's problems to a matter of will. "Moving for the sake of moving without any purpose or intent is futility. Maybe Granny Laura will put me on the board of some rich miner. Then my life would meet your qualifications." Newlywed Maisie couldn't expect everyone to up and marry a complete stranger, could she?

"I don't recommend doing what I did, but how about Willow? She would've never met Graham if she'd stayed home and not been a Harvey Girl. Or Calista? She went and became a Pinkerton agent. Look what come of that."

Olive did not possess Calista's love of adventure or her sister Willow's steely determination. Olive wanted to be safe at home with her drafting pencils, architect books, and her birdhouses. The challenges she sought were figuring out a floor plan or how to support a balcony. Something the other Kentworths didn't understand. They expected everyone to be brave and outgoing. Olive was a disappointment.

But she'd come to do a job, and she was going to finish it. Despite Maisie's groan of disapproval, Olive knelt and resumed scrubbing.

"You can't ignore me forever." Maisie snacked on some blackberries from her basket. "I think we should enlist Calista's help. She's always matching up jobs with the people who need them. Don't you reckon she can do the same for you?"

"What if I don't want a job?" Olive asked. "What if I'd be happier at home?" Or what if she didn't have a choice, because no one would trust a woman in architecture?

There were two buildings in Joplin that bore her designs though not her name—the Lighthouse Center for Miners and the visitors' center at the Crystal Cave. Because of her bedside vigil, she'd been unable to spend much time at the construction sites when they were built. Instead, Maisie's brother Amos had been her representative. In fact, Amos, with his gift for gab, had convinced everyone that he was the designer behind the plans. Which was fine with Olive. She wasn't looking for credit.

"You stop it, Olive. You used to be the most courageous one of us. You were so brave that you tossed everything aside to take care of your ma. That took gumption. But now you're stuck in a rut." Maisie twisted her mouth to the side as she sized Olive up. "If you want to stay cozy at home, we can go that route. Calista will get you gussied up while I corral a herd of eligible bachelors for your inspection. Either way, we aim to get you some prospects before suppertime."

If Olive wasn't kneeling by her mother's grave, she would've laughed. Her with a herd of eligible bachelors? She touched her messy blond hair pulled into an uneven knot and tried to imagine what Calista would have to do to get her up to snuff. But it didn't matter. Maisie wouldn't understand. Olive's insistence that she enjoyed solitude was mocked, her guarantee that she wouldn't regret staying home rejected, and her demand that Maisie mind her own business ignored.

As Maisie continued on with her arguments and plans, one thing was becoming clear—according to her family, the only unacceptable thing was for Olive to remain as she was.

Olive was home from the cemetery with plenty of time to clean up and make her father's dinner.

Time, she had plenty.

Early on, when her mother required tending, passing the time had been difficult. As she listened to her mother's wracking cough, trying to keep up a brave face so her mother wouldn't see how much her illness troubled her daughters, the hands of the clock seemed permanently set in place. When her sister, Willow, took her turn to spell her, Olive felt like a prisoner released from her sentence.

But over the months, time became something that slipped by unnoticed. Olive found herself acclimated to the bedside watch. When Willow left for employment to help pay for her mother's treatments and medicine, the full responsibility for her mother's care fell on Olive. By then, she preferred the solitary but predictable routine.

She never thought about what came next.

The roast that was stewing on the stove was left over from the night before. So were the rolls. With only two of them eating, there wasn't a reason to cook every night. Olive rinsed some blackberries and set them aside for after dinner. She stepped into the parlor to look at the clock hanging on the wall. Still time to kill.

The pendulum wagged its finger at her. Waste was a sin. Having grown up with a chronically ill parent who required expensive treatments, Olive had learned thrift from an early age. You didn't throw out something that had a use. You saved what you could in case you needed it tomorrow. But time got spent whether you used it wisely or not. You couldn't wrap it up in paper and set it in the icebox. It expired immediately, whether for good or ill.

Olive turned the corner and opened the door of the room that she used to share with her sister. Now Willow's bed held a straight-edge, protractor, and right angle nestled among the wadded-up papers full of her mistakes. On the floor were hatboxes full of receipts from her two building projects. She knew the records were important to keep but didn't have anywhere to file them. As long as the amount in her father's checking account—which is where she cleared all expenses and income—continued to go up, she knew she was doing well.

Olive opened her notebook to a blank page and fished around in the wrinkled quilt to find a pencil. Her daily walks to the cemetery carried her through the newest neighborhoods being built. Joplin's mining boom had hit the region like a wildcat, but it took time for fortunes to accumulate and for the first seeds of society to bloom. Now the city was filling up with beautiful buildings for every industry, every organization, and every family. And just like someone might walk through a flower garden, drawing peace from the lovely scents, Olive walked the city streets, absorbing the beautiful intricacies that were going up around her.

After wetting the pencil tip with her tongue, she started to sketch the west elevation of the house that James Dennis was constructing. Dennis was newly come to Joplin, having already earned his fortune elsewhere. From the frame that was going up, it looked to Olive as if the house would have a *porte cochere*. Her pencil moved swiftly as she allowed her imagination to fill in the gaps between what already existed and what she'd want to place on that lot.

As if anyone would ever give her, a woman with no formal training, a chance at building a home.

The curtains on Olive's opened window swayed when the front door opened. Olive dropped her sketchbook and tidied her hair. Despite it only being herself and her father, she always felt that one should look their best at dinner.

"I didn't think you were home." Her father hung his suit coat on the rack beneath his hat.

"Where else would I be?" Olive lifted on her toes to give him his daily kiss on the cheek. Her father had suffered terribly at her mother's death—a death he'd known was pending even before he married her. But now, day by day, Olive was seeing his strength return. In a way, he seemed less burdened than the father she'd known her whole life.

"I don't know. Somewhere." He smiled. "Surely you have places you'd rather be than sitting here in this empty house."

Her gaze darted to the floor as his words stung. She spun toward the kitchen to flee from answering. He didn't understand. It'd been so long, she didn't want to change now. She felt comfortable where she was.

The stovetop rattled as she dragged the pot off. After setting the roast on the table, she reached in the warmer for the rolls. Maybe the pots were clattering more than normal, for rather than coming in and taking his seat, Oscar Kentworth leaned against the doorway and watched her with a father's concern.

"You take such good care of me without complaining, without fuss. Most young women your age are looking ahead."

Olive wiped her hands on a dish towel before motioning her father to his seat. "I only made leftovers. I should've made something fresh, but I was at the cemetery. I went to wash Mother's headstone. The birds keep befouling it, and I can't bear . . ." She sniffled. "We have blackberries for dessert. Maisie brought them from the farm."

He looked her offering over before saying, "I brought you something too."

"For supper?" Olive took her seat, crossing her ankles beneath the chair.

"It's not berries, but maybe an opportunity. Let's pray first." Her father bowed his head and spoke simple but sincere words over her, himself, and their food. Then he started eating. Just as Olive had begun chewing a mouthful of roast, he said, "Mr. Blount has decided to make an addition to his house. He's looking for an architect."

Olive's jaw stopped. "Clydell Blount?" She spoke around the chunk of meat despite her training. Chomping it quickly, and washing it down with milk, she dropped both hands on the table and leaned over her plate. "His house is only a few years old. What could he possibly want to change?"

"Far be it from me to try to read the mind of a man like Mr. Blount. All I know is that he wants a sizeable addition and is going to request plans from different architects in the area."

"That's nonsense. He has a Maxfield Scott house. How could

he want anything else?" Olive drummed her fingers against the table. Making an addition to a Maxfield Scott house would be like painting another smile on the Mona Lisa. One didn't mess with perfection. Being that Clydell Blount was her father's boss, she'd watched the house's construction with interest. In fact, she'd attended the company Christmas party there as her father's guest when her mother had been too ill to do the honors. Walking through the halls, appreciating the flow of the floor plan, being delighted with unexpected nooks was the best Christmas present she could've received. And now, scarcely two years later, Blount wanted to change it?

Who would work for a madman like that?

Olive speared another piece of roast with her fork. "How was work today? Did you find hires for the ore jiggers?"

Her father began his answer. Olive tilted her head and listened as well as she was able, but beneath her messy blond bun, other thoughts intruded.

Who would Blount hire? Obviously Mr. Scott wasn't an option. Not if Blount wanted to tamper with his work. Austin Allen? He was another skilled architect in the area, but Olive doubted he had the time to take on home additions. Not when he could be constructing another church or apartment building. Besides, taking this job would probably put him at odds with Maxfield Scott. Professionally, it would be a bad idea.

Mr. Blount's best option might be an unknown designer with nothing to lose.

"Dan Campbell's claim is starting to produce," her father continued. "We're having trouble finding cokeys because he's hiring the newcomers. I've had to send word to a few that we've laid off before. Of course, it's nice to give a man a second chance, but it's not . . ."

But who was she to challenge Joplin's premier architect? Just thinking about any sort of confrontation made her feel sick to her stomach. Educated on the East Coast, trained in Paris, Milan, Florence, celebrated for his classical sensibilities and flawless balance—that was Maxfield Scott. Comparing Olive Kentworth—who had bought some architectural books at a rummage sale, read by her mother's bedside, traveled to nearby Carthage, Missouri, to look at houses, and built birdhouses—to Scott was like comparing the train depot's water fountain to Bernini's. She felt ashamed that she even picked up a pencil with the same right hand he did. Or maybe he wasn't right-handed at all.

"Matthew assured me that Irvin has stopped drinking, so I signed him, but no sooner than I did, Irvin came back to tell me he had a change of heart and was going to work for Dan Campbell. Isn't that something?"

And yet . . . Olive conjured the memory of Blount's house. She'd passed it often and knew it from every angle. If Blount wanted to add on another room, the east side was rather bland. She couldn't remember the layout exactly, but for such an elaborate design, it had one blank canvas to work with. Not that she would dare . . .

Her father, God love him, was still talking in his quiet, steady way. "He's proud of that miners' center, and he ought to be, but he doesn't know it was you who drew up the plans. Let's tell him and see what he says. Seems like he should at least give you a chance."

"Tell whom?" Olive touched her hand to her lips. Had she been thinking aloud? "I don't know what you're talking about, but . . ."

"I'm talking about Mr. Blount and the work he wants done on his house. I know how much you enjoy coming up with building plans. It wouldn't hurt to see what you could design to help him."

Suddenly the roast was unappetizing. "You don't understand how it works. Someone like me can't insert herself into a project like that."

"Why not? You've done it before."

"Both of my buildings were done for family. Simple, practical structures. And they were from scratch. Building for Mr. and Mrs. Blount is on another level. Besides, trying to add on to something built by Maxfield Scott . . . it isn't done."

"Don't tell me you weren't thinking about it. I could see the wheels turning."

Olive stood and took her plate to the sink. "All these dishes to clean. That's what I need to do today. And then tomorrow I'll be busy . . ." What was she going to do tomorrow? Maisie had solved her problem with the birds. ". . . I'll need to go to the market."

"And tonight you'll stay up late sketching the perfect addition to Blount's house, but you'll never show it to a soul."

Without a word, Olive marched to her room. She riffled through the spare bed's coverlet, pulling out every notebook, sketchbook, and pad of paper. She dropped to her knees and reached beneath the bed to retrieve a dust-covered collection of plans. Then, pulling a stack of paper from the bottom of her washstand, she gathered all the paper together and hauled it into the kitchen.

The books dropped on the kitchen table and rattled the serving fork in the pot of roast.

"There," she said. "These are all my notebooks, Father, so you don't have to worry about me drafting a design for Mr. Blount tonight. I'll clean the kitchen in the morning. Good night." She kissed her father on the cheek, then turned on her heel and made a beeline for her bedroom.

It was too early to sleep, but that was fine. She didn't need paper to imagine all the possibilities for the Blounts' home. What she needed was for her family to stop pestering her and leave her in peace. That was the only way she would be happy.

CHAPTER

2

Tightening his roll of plans and dropping them into the leather-covered tube, Maxfield Scott watched as James Dennis approached, walking past the bricklayers and up the newly set steps of the porch of his Second Empire mansion.

Mr. Dennis paused in the framed doorway as if unsure it was safe to continue through the construction materials. "How are things progressing?" he asked as he tapped his cane against the threshold.

"Beautifully!" Maxfield said. "Mrs. Dennis will be pleased to hear that this will be her last month in the hotel." Despite her complaints, Maxfield didn't feel sorry for anyone living in the Keystone Hotel. It was a beautiful building that perfectly balanced space and structure. Other than the massive fish tank in the lobby, an unfortunate misstep, the decor came as near perfection as any lodging in the area.

Besides his own, naturally.

"That's capital." James leaned against his cane to catch his breath. "Our apartments are beginning to feel cramped with the three of us."

"Ruby and I have plans tonight, so that'll give you some temporary relief." Maxfield had an hour to see his children, get dressed for the evening, and then pick up Mr. Dennis's daughter for a night at the theater. It had the potential to be a phenomenal evening. After hours of working with plans, draftsmen, builders, and prospective new clients, he was starved for the joy and laughter that was ahead with Ruby. Balm to his soul.

"Before you go . . ." Mr. Dennis gave him a tired smile that caused Maxfield to rest on his heels. Mr. Dennis was never in a hurry, unless it was a hurry to slow him down. "I'd like for you to double-check the square footage of this house again. I know you mapped it all out, but when I look at the footprint here, and I compare it to Clydell Blount's place, I'm not sure it really is bigger."

Maxfield pushed back the brim of his hat. "Mr. Dennis, I've gone over the figures with you a dozen times. When this house is finished, it will be the biggest house in Joplin."

"But if there was a way you could remeasure Blount's house, in case there's a mistake—"

"There's no mistake. I built Blount's house myself. I have the blueprints. I know every joint and every nail hole in that house, and your house will be one hundred square feet larger, making it the biggest. I guarantee it." Maxfield shoved a stray piece of lumber with his foot, clearing the way out of the house. Taking Mr. Dennis by the arm, he walked him down the steps. "There will be many things for you to worry about in the upcoming days—which view from the windows is your favorite, how often you want to entertain in your glorious dining room, how jealous others will be when this is completed—but one thought that must not trouble you is the question, 'Is this the biggest house in Joplin?' Because that question is settled. There will be no dispute. The James Dennis house will be the largest."

He'd managed to walk Mr. Dennis to the lawn before the man realized he was leaving. "It's your project, so I'm trusting you with the outcome, but don't let me down. I'd rather it have an outhouse than fail in this contest. It's about time someone knocked Blount off his perch."

Knocking another man off his perch? That wasn't why you built a house. You built for the beauty of it, for the artistry. You built to have something that would outlive you, that people would appreciate long after you were gone. Maxfield squinted into the sun. Life didn't last forever. He intended to do all that he could with the days he was allotted.

He moderated his pace to keep step with Mr. Dennis until their paths diverged. Only then could Maxfield ramble ahead without thought beyond holding his children, then spending the rest of the evening in the sparkling company of Ruby.

Maxfield hadn't built his own house. When he and Georgia moved to Joplin, his first priority had been acquiring clients. He needed to be building for other people. At the beginning, the new houses in Joplin had been modest, but when the luck in the mines had increased, so did the fortunes of the mine owners. Suddenly merely functional houses were not enough. Everyone needed a home that made a statement, and that was how Maxfield had managed to snatch up his practical home nearly new and for a reasonable price. The Stick Style cottage avoided the fussy curlicues that were so popular, while still boasting ample embellishments. It was modest compared to the structures he was building now, but that didn't bother Maxfield. Ever since Georgia had passed away, it was not a place where he wanted to linger.

But coming home to Leo and Stella was his favorite time of day, with the possible exception of waking up, meeting clients, midday meals, drafting, and bedtime.

"I'm home." Maxfield's voice echoed through the entry hall and up the staircase. He hung his hat and coat while stepping out of his shoes. If he was going to get dinner before the theatrical, he had to hurry. From the looks of the staircase, Leo had been throwing blocks from the balcony again. Maxfield swooped down, scooping blocks with one hand as he made his way up the stairs.

"Leo? Stella? Mrs. Wester?" The children weren't already in bed, were they?

"Mr. Scott," Mrs. Wester called from down below. "We're in the kitchen."

Dinnertime. That was good. He and Ruby were eating on the town, but he'd have a seat at the table with the children. Mrs. Wester met him at the kitchen door, her coat and reticule in hand.

"They have been bathed and started their supper. You can expect me late tomorrow, since I've worked past hours tonight."

"Past hours?" Maxfield craned his neck to look at the clock hanging on the parlor wall but couldn't see it. "How late is it?"

"Later than we agreed to. This has to stop. I've got my own family waiting for me at home."

"But I thought you were going to stay. I have plans tonight."

"You asked me yesterday, and I said I would check with my husband. I did check, and he said no."

Maxfield couldn't believe his ears. "You never told me you couldn't. Why didn't you say something this morning?"

Mrs. Wester dropped her hat on her head and lowered her chin. "You are a very difficult person to say no to, Mr. Scott. I'm sure you'll have a wonderful evening without me. See you tomorrow."

Maxfield rubbed the back of his neck. No one to watch the children for the night? He'd barely gotten home, but already he was raring to get back out there. See people, do things, spend time with Ruby. Well, no answer for it but to take Leo and Stella with them. Yes, they would enjoy themselves. The evening would be delightful.

His stockinged feet slipped a bit on the hickory wood floor, which had been sanded until it was as smooth as a gunstock. Once he made it around the corner, he darted straight into the kitchen. Both children were as motionless as caryatids as they listened for his approach, but when he appeared in the room, they sprang to life. Four-year-old Leo shot both his arms into the air while two-year-old Stella threw her spoon of oatmeal across the room.

"Dada home," Stella squealed as she squirmed in vain to get out of her children's chair.

Leo was not similarly restrained. He got to his feet and stood in his chair.

"How are my two best works of art?" Maxfield's spirits were lifted every time he saw them. Stella had her father's fine features while Georgia's generous smile and broad brow were more evident on Leo. Their glee was so like their mother's . . . and his own.

"I made cookies," Leo said. "Mrs. Wester helped me. Stella tried to help but she only made a mess."

"Cookies!" Stella cheered. "Make cookies!"

Maxfield took stock of the room as he patted Stella's pecan-colored locks. Both children were in their pajamas. That was a problem. And they hadn't finished their dinner. Well, he hoped that they'd eaten enough to tide them over. Cleaning the mess they'd made at the table, that could wait for another day.

"C'mon," he said. "I have a surprise for you." He reached beneath the tray of her chair and unlatched the belt holding Stella down. Then he lifted her chunky form and held her back against his chest with one hand while wiping her face with a napkin in the other. "Run upstairs, Leo, and put on a nice suit of clothes. We're going to the theater tonight."

"We are?" Leo jumped off the chair, pounding his feet against the floor at the perfect time to maximize the noise. "Is it a puppet show?"

"No, it's . . ." What was the play? Maxfield couldn't remember. All he'd cared about was that he was going with Ruby. "We're going to eat first, so don't worry about your food. You'll get something else."

"Yee-haw, I get to eat at a restaurant!"

Maxfield shared his excitement. This would be fun. Ruby would love it.

He laid out clothes for Leo, then helped Stella into a dress, stockings, and shoes. He ran a brush through her thin curls but didn't have time to add any bows. Not when he himself wasn't ready.

Under normal circumstances, he would've shaved again, but

he'd just hope Ruby didn't notice. He washed quickly, dabbed on some cologne, then jumped into his trousers while Stella played with his shoe stretchers.

"Are you ready, Leo?" Maxfield called as he pulled on his dress shoes. At least the children had been bathed. That was one thing working in his favor.

"I am *soooo* handsome," Leo called back.

Maxfield tied his tie. "Let me see."

Leo walked into the room with the buttons to his suit coat buttoned askance and his shirt untucked, but he'd tried valiantly.

Maxfield knelt and tidied the oversights. "You *are* so handsome. Miss Ruby is going to be impressed."

"I like Miss Ruby." Leo dug his finger into his ear, then pulled it out and inspected it. "She's giddy."

"Don't wipe that on me." Maxfield grabbed a crumpled handkerchief and cleaned his son's finger, wondering where in the world Leo had heard Miss Dennis described as giddy. "We're going to have fun together. Let's go."

Ruby was surprised to see him with the children when she opened her apartment door at the Keystone. Her blue eyes widened, and her lovely smile broadened. "My goodness," she exclaimed. "You brought everyone, and how lovely they look."

"I apologize, but Mrs. Wester had an emergency at home." Or he had an emergency. His emergency was that Mrs. Wester went home.

"I don't mind. We'll have a smashing time."

Maxfield checked his watch, then smoothed the sleeves of his worsted suit. "We need to hurry if we want to eat before the show starts."

"We can eat after," Ruby said. "I don't want to miss the beginning of the play."

Leo and Stella raced up and down the hallway of the hotel, delighted by the long stretch of flooring. They didn't look hungry. Surely they'd be fine. They'd already eaten a little.

The Joplin Opera House awed Stella. Her little hand tightened in his as they passed inside the double doors. The ceiling was molded extravagantly, and crystal chandeliers hung from the center of medallions. Brass wall sconces shaped like flower bouquets lit velvet-draped walls. Maxfield shared her amazement at the sparkling lights and elaborate balustrade along the main staircase. Who would've thought that little Joplin, Missouri, would aspire to such a level? He was proud to be a part of it.

Before the children were born, Georgia and he had loved leaving the opera house late in the evening, still hearing the music echoing in their memory for hours. At times, Joplin reminded him of Paris—the street lighting, the picturesque streets, the live music—yet the town was small enough that you knew the people sharing the sidewalk. New enough that there was unlimited potential for a young and upcoming couple, but then everything had changed in a second.

But if he'd wanted to dwell on those sad thoughts, he would've stayed in the house, trying to keep his eyes from straying to Georgia's musical roller organ. He would've spent the evening trying to forget how she would chatter happily as she installed a new cylinder, and how she would sway and hum along with the music until she knew every note.

Quickly, before that dark blot in the pit of his stomach could grow, Maxfield picked up Stella and swung her in the air, producing peals of laughter and startling the matron walking next to him.

"I beg your pardon," he said as he shifted Stella to one arm. "I was overcome." But with what? Joy? That's how he acted. It was the only way he could act to push away the despair.

The woman looked into Stella's impossibly blue eyes, then again at Maxfield's debonair smile. "I wish all fathers were as enthusiastic as you." She adjusted her shawl, then proceeded to the staircase.

Ruby threaded her arm through his and leaned against him.

"Must you wrap all the ladies around your little finger?" She poked Stella's round belly. "Every lady from two years old to one hundred?"

Had they not been in public, Maxfield would have kissed Ruby on the cheek for her sweetness. Instead, he tried to convey his gratitude with a look to inform her of how much he appreciated her rescuing him from a night of brooding.

"Leo, we shouldn't keep Miss Ruby waiting. Let's find our seats," Maxfield said. "Follow me."

Being among the joyous raised his spirits. Compared to sitting alone in his library after the children went to sleep, this was life, it was oxygen to him. After showing his tickets to the usher, Maxfield and Ruby were directed down the sloped auditorium toward the front. While Maxfield was excited to have the children near the front, it occurred to him that he only had two tickets. Stella would fit on his lap, but Leo might be less comfortable.

They came to their row and Maxfield stepped aside to allow Ruby and the children to enter before him. As luck would have it, they were situated in the middle of the row. Mr. and Mrs. Landauer, who owned several successful mines, had to stand so they could pass.

"Bringing young children to the theater? They must be very well behaved," Mrs. Landauer said.

"Not particularly," Maxfield said, "but they're young. They have time to learn."

"Before the first act begins?" Mr. Landauer raised his eyebrows at his wife. With a small shake of her head, she shushed him and smiled at Leo as he passed.

Once they were seated, Ruby lifted Stella to her lap. "Can you see from here?"

Stella pointed as the curtain rose and clapped her hands.

Maxfield beamed and shifted Leo back so he was leaning against his chest. Being harder to impress than his little sister, Leo's questions began as soon as the drama did.

"What did he say? Why is she crying? Is that man a villain?"

He really was a clever boy to understand everything that was going on, but what would Ruby think? Would Leo's constant questions annoy her? Maxfield looked at his companion, who held his daughter on her knee, bouncing her a little too exuberantly as she watched the play.

Leave it to Ruby to have fun no matter the situation. Judging by the intensity of the audience, the play was very compelling, but Maxfield had trouble following it. He was there because it was the place to be, not because of the story. In fact, he looked forward to the intermission when he could visit with the friends he was spotting from his seat.

"Father, I'm hungry. Mrs. Wester made me oatmeal."

"We'll eat after the show," Maxfield whispered. "Just watch the play."

Leo leaned forward, then flopped backwards against Maxfield. "I'm hungry now."

Ruby didn't act like she'd noticed, but the Geddeses in front of them did. The man turned his head just enough to catch sight of them with his peripheral vision and let them know that they were disturbing him.

"Want food." Stella's voice had never reached those clear tones before, but now it carried as only sound in a perfectly designed acoustic theater could. "Want food, Dada."

Ruby patted her leg. "Here, play with my bracelet." She slid the thick silver band off her wrist and held it until Stella had it in her soft hands. Stella put it in her mouth.

"I want it." Before Maxfield could stop him, Leo had snatched it from Stella.

Stella squealed in protest. Now several in the row in front of them turned to stare. A man behind them cleared his throat.

"Give it back to her." Maxfield took the bracelet from Leo. At the same time, Ruby leaned over and set Stella on the floor. Maxfield's brow lowered. What was Ruby doing? Leaning forward in her seat, Ruby was one hundred percent engaged in the story and oblivious to Stella, who was trying to push her way past the Landauers and into the aisle.

"I'm hun . . . gry!" Leo tilted his head and fell against Maxfield again.

Mrs. Landauer had trapped Stella and wasn't letting her pass, but Stella wasn't giving up. Her little hands were full of Mrs. Landauer's skirt. Her whining grew louder with her frustration as she tried to squeeze between Mrs. Landauer and the seat in front of her. Ruby's eyes were moist as the actress on the stage comforted her dying father, but she showed no concern for Mrs. Landauer, who was trying to politely get Ruby's attention. Maxfield handed the bracelet to Leo. He'd have to reach over Ruby and . . .

Stella buried her face into Mrs. Landauer's knee. The next thing Maxfield knew, Mrs. Landauer bolted out of her seat with a scream.

"That child . . . she bit me!" Her powdered chin quivered in outrage. Mr. Landauer stood, ready to defend her against the two-year-old attacker. The dying father on the stage lifted his head to see what was happening in the audience. Only Ruby seemed unaffected. Without a word, she took the bracelet out of Maxfield's hand and passed it to Stella, who promptly threw it behind them.

"C'mon." Maxfield set Leo on his feet and stood. "My apologies. This was a bad idea. I'm sorry." There were people aplenty who needed apologizing to, but it'd be better to save the apology for another time. Stella was pounding on the back of the chair in front of her, bouncing Mrs. Geddes' earrings.

Finally, after what seemed like an eternity, Ruby stood, but instead of gathering her things, she smiled sweetly. "I'll meet you at the east doors when it's over. You all have fun." Then she flattened herself against her seat so Maxfield could slide past her.

He picked up Stella, then with a final apology to the Landauers as he passed, he dragged his errant children through the now-silent theater. Maxfield usually enjoyed every eye on him, but not tonight. Was he expected to wait on Ruby while she finished the play? What could he do to entertain the children?

Leo answered that question. "I'm hungry."

Maxfield got the door to the theater closed behind them just as Stella joined in the chorus. "Hungwy, hungwy."

"Food. Of course." He had failed. It was his fault, and he knew that. He should've known not to take them to the theater. A better father wouldn't have made that mistake. Maxfield knew just the restaurant for their wait. If he got a table by the window, he'd be able to see when the performance was over.

They were the only children at the restaurant and keeping them in their seats was a challenge. He told the waiter to bring whatever was already cooked, and Stella barely had time to drop her silverware on the floor before their food arrived.

Content with grazing on the dinner rolls left on the table, Maxfield was gratified to watch the children's tension melting. They weren't bad children. He tended to get cranky himself when he was hungry. After checking Leo's fish for bones, he took Stella on his knee and fed her the green beans. If he thought the opera house had been a disaster, he could only imagine how messy it could be if Stella tried to feed herself.

Maxfield hoped that Ruby didn't mind too much that he'd left her. He hadn't planned the evening this way. He'd been optimistic to think they would enjoy an evening at the theater. Or maybe he wasn't optimistic. Maybe he was willfully obtuse. Maybe he knew it was a bad idea but had wanted to avoid another evening alone and was willing to try anything to avoid it.

Now fed, Stella's eyes were drooping. He pulled the napkin from her collar and turned her around so her head rested on his shoulder. Lifting his hand, he motioned to the waiter for the bill.

"Are we going home now?" Leo kicked his leg against the leg of the table.

Taking Leo and Stella home was the next logical step, but it was impossible. He couldn't leave Ruby to cross wicked Joplin alone.

As beautiful as the fine neighborhoods were, they weren't free from the rough miners and the crime that followed them. He was the one who had brought her to the theater. He was responsible for taking her home. What would Mr. Dennis think of him if he did anything less?

But entertaining two sleepy children for another hour in downtown Joplin would not be an easy task. Maxfield would persevere, but he wasn't the only one who'd been inconvenienced. He owed several acquaintances an apology, and a promise that he wouldn't allow the same mistake to happen again. The problem was that without Mrs. Wester's help, he didn't know what he could do to prevent it.

CHAPTER
3

Hopping up on her toes to gain leverage, Olive kneaded out the bread dough with the heel of her hand, doubled it over on itself, and kneaded it again. In the interest of tidiness, she'd moved her stack of notebooks and sketch pads off the table and onto the kitchen cabinet earlier that week, but she wanted them within sight for her father. He mustn't forget that she was content and was not striving for something more than she'd been allotted. Being pushed into the limelight was the last thing she wanted.

Her cat was stretched on the floor, relaxing in the sunlight as she watched the birds who roosted in Olive's birdhouses. Her last birdhouse, which was done in the Italianate style with a belvedere, wide cornices, and brackets, had been inhabited by some finches. Knowing the probable residents, Olive had narrowed the doorway and added a slant to keep predators from reaching inside. She'd rather be designing staircases with fretwork and wainscoting, but she wanted the residents of all her creations to be happy.

The cat's ears twitched, and her attention was drawn away from the window by the sound of someone on the front steps. The door opened, and Olive looked at the clock. He was home early. What was wrong?

"Olive, I have a surprise." It was her father, his long, angular frame twitching with excitement. "Clean yourself up and come with me."

"It's not time for you to be home." Olive picked at the dough that flecked her palms. "What's happened?"

"I've got an important meeting and I need your help." He looked her over from head to toe and even Olive couldn't miss the pride in his eyes. "Wash the flour off your hands and leave the apron here. You won't need it where we're going."

"Which is . . . ?" She turned on the faucet and scrubbed her hands.

He shook his head. "Not telling. I'm just happy I have a chance to show off my daughter." He passed her a hand towel, barely containing his excitement.

She tidied her hair the best she could and checked in the hall mirror to see that no flour smudged her face. Perhaps her vanity wasn't completely extinguished, because she noticed how her flushed cheeks enhanced her hazel eyes, but she didn't worry whether anyone else would notice. "When someone doesn't want to tell me what we're doing, it's usually safe to assume I wouldn't approve," she said.

"You'll have to wait and see."

They left the house on foot and her father led her to the far side of town toward the Fox-Berry Mine where he worked. Perhaps Calista and her husband, Matthew, needed something? Matthew was a pastor who worked at the miners' center on the mine's property. He helped the men with educational pursuits and health concerns and counseled them concerning their alcohol consumption and gambling. He was always busy, but he always had time for a visit from Olive or anyone else.

The thought of her work on the miners' center filled her with pride and anxiety. Despite the fact that Mr. Blount had donated the funds and the land to build the Lighthouse Center for Miners, she still didn't want him to know she'd built it.

Her father had kept her secret from his boss, so why did he have one of her sketchbooks tucked under his arm as they hurried toward the mine? He was going to betray her.

Olive spun on him, grabbing for the sketchbook. He pulled it away at the last moment.

"What is that for? Why did you bring it?" He must have taken it off the top of the stack while they were in the kitchen. She tried to remember which sketches it held, but the memory escaped her. When her father refused to answer, Olive stopped in her tracks. "I'm not going any further until you tell me what's going on."

"Fine, fine. Mr. Blount is having a meeting with some builders to see who he wants to hire for the addition to his house. I know you have the skill. You should be there."

Olive pressed her hand against her forehead. Her father thought that she was smart because she could draft plans. Well, she did a decent job of estimating costs too, but she hadn't studied design like a real architect. She'd checked out every book on the subject at the Joplin Carnegie Library, and she'd purchased any book that had come across her path, but she had difficulty keeping up with the latest trends. While she appreciated her father's faith in her, she would not expose herself to the ridicule she'd most heartily deserve if she threw her hat into the ring.

"At least see what he's looking for. Maybe it's a project you wouldn't be interested in. Then you would know that it wasn't the right time, but if you don't listen to his request, you'll always wonder."

Olive dropped her gaze to the ground. Walking into a room full of men and pretending that she knew what she was doing? Never. But didn't she love any chance to work on a project? Who was going to give her a project without her fighting for it? She couldn't rely on her family to keep constructing buildings. If she wanted her designs to ever take form, sooner or later she would have to work with strangers. That was the only way.

She could feel the world tightening in on her. Her chest felt heavy, her breath short. Not today. She couldn't do it today. She wasn't ready. If she'd known, she could've sent Amos in and let him present her plans, but it was too late. She'd have a fit of nerves.

"We can go home." Her father held her sketchbook in both hands, took a long look at it, then tucked it away beneath his arm.

She'd disappointed him, and he'd already lost so much. But he didn't understand the courage it took to present something she'd designed.

And here came another person who didn't understand. Calista was walking the wooden boardwalk toward the miners' center when she spotted Olive and her father.

"Olive! Just the person I was looking for! Are you busy?" Although married to a young pastor, Calista wore the latest fashions sent by her Kansas City mother.

Olive could feel her father's sad gaze on her. "According to Olive, we're headed home. What do you need?"

"Home or to the cemetery?" Calista and her impertinence. "From what Maisie says, those are the only places she goes anymore."

Had the newspaper printed a notice to everyone in Joplin that they were to start harassing Olive Kentworth? Olive balled up her fists. She wished she could prove Calista wrong, but she had nowhere to go besides home. She looked to the mining office, and then at her sketchbook. How wonderful it'd be to grab that sketchbook and march into Mr. Blount's office. That would show Calista.

But if Calista knew her thoughts, she'd have something else to pester her over. "I'm going home," Olive said. "What was your message?"

Calista produced a slip of paper. "You know I find employment for some of the unfortunate women in Joplin—"

"And I'm an unfortunate woman?"

Calista looked at her uncle. "She's out of sorts, I take it?"

"God bless your efforts," he said. "Mine were unsuccessful."

It was a conspiracy. Olive took the paper from Calista's hand

and opened it to see an address in her neighborhood. "What's this?"

"A family that is looking for help tonight. The Scott children need someone to mind them for the evening. I don't have any ladies qualified for this particular job, so I thought you might do them a favor. It pays."

"I don't need a job," she said. "I have everything I want."

"You like to help people," her father said. "What's it hurt?"

Olive looked again at the address. She didn't know any Scott family. Couldn't think of a Mrs. Scott in her acquaintances. "How many children?"

"Two. Aged four and two years old." Calista was holding something back. Olive could tell.

"What are you not telling me?" Olive asked. "Are they monsters?"

Calista touched her glossy dark hair and feigned indifference. "Don't be ridiculous. I'm just wondering if your self-imposed exile excludes you from going to private homes and keeping the company of children."

To tell the truth, Olive did enjoy children, but she hadn't been considering what she enjoyed lately. Not when everyone was so determined that she find something to enjoy. But if they needed help, how could she refuse?

"I'll do it, but only because you need help. Otherwise, I'd be quite content at home."

Besides, if she was busy with the Scott children, then maybe she wouldn't have time to wish that she was designing the addition to Mr. Blount's house.

This was the house. Not far from her own house actually, and built by the same builder, if she had to guess. Olive admired how crisp and cool the cream board-and-batten siding looked behind the green landscaping. And instead of multicolored gingerbread and shingles, the tan stick work showcased the clean lines of the home—a choice that showed restraint and confidence. The lady of the home had a good eye for design.

Olive tucked the slip of paper into her bag and mounted the front steps. Since she didn't know the family, she'd brought along a few children's books from home, a top, and one of Willow's old rag dolls, and if one of her sketchbooks accidentally fell in with the other items, then whose business was it what she did with her time once the children were abed?

She rang the bell and heard a clamor inside. Through the glass she could see the top of a child's head approaching. The doorknob turned, but not completely. The door rattled, then a small voice called for help. Olive smiled. Hopefully the children would think it a treat to have her there. Hopefully they wouldn't cry for their mother all night.

A taller figure approached, and the door was opened. Olive was already smiling, anticipating the smaller version, but what met her at the door was confusing.

"Mister . . . Mister Scott?" She stuttered, then bit her lip to keep from saying anything more. Not only did the man standing before her possess the most interesting eyes she'd ever seen, he was someone she knew. She couldn't place him, but there was a familiarity that chilled her. He was a danger, a threat to her, but she couldn't remember why.

"You must be Miss Kentworth. Come in, come in." He stepped aside as he pulled the door open wider. "Look, Leo, it's our friend Miss Kentworth come to visit."

How could such a charming man be a threat? Olive released a long breath to steady herself. Whatever their connection, he didn't recognize her. If only she could place him. Maybe his wife would be familiar.

Mr. Scott closed the door behind her as she racked her brain. Had he been a miner that her father had fired from the Fox-Berry? Sometimes they held a grudge. But, no, his features looked more like a scholar's, and his slim build didn't look like that of a miner. Maybe a doctor, then. Someone who had given her mother no hope? Could that be the association? She listened as he calmed his son and instructed him to be patient. His voice didn't sound familiar. She couldn't place him at any of the many appointments they'd attended.

She tightened her grip on her bag. Had she become such a recluse that she lost her marbles in the presence of a man? And a married man at that?

With a stilling hand on his son's shoulder, the man turned his smiling eyes on her again. "I do apologize for the interruption. The children are quite excited to meet you, as am I. I'm Maxfield Scott, by the way. Thank you for coming. And this is my son, Leo."

Maxfield Scott? There was only one Maxfield in Joplin, and he was the architect. A real, lauded, professional architect, so of course she knew him. She'd studied his work. She'd followed his career, and at some time or another, she must have seen him from afar. But he wasn't afar now. She was standing in his house, talking to him. Or he was talking to her, rather, and she wasn't attending.

"May I take your bag?" he repeated.

Olive hadn't realized that she was holding it with both hands until she tried to pass it to him. Then she remembered her sketchbook. "No, thank you. I'd rather keep it with me."

His eyebrow rose and his lips pursed. Even his son looked puzzled. "I realize that we've just met, but I assure you that I have no interest in absconding with your belongings." He turned and picked up the little girl who had come in the room, but Olive still heard his whispered jest, ". . . this time."

She shuddered, trying to shake herself out of her fog. He was just a man, and she was just the help. He had no way of knowing of her aspirations. He wouldn't remember her past this night. Not unless she acted bizarre and caused notice. Olive used to be an expert at avoiding notice. She had to get herself under control.

"Leo is your name, and who is this young lady?" Olive smiled at the girl who was watching her closely from her father's arms.

"This is Stella. She likes warm milk, shortbread cookies, and playing with her dollies." Mr. Scott smacked a kiss on her cheek, causing the girl to giggle. He buried his face into Stella's neck, making her squeal and push against him.

Olive looked away, not sure that she understood why. Mr. Scott was so easy with his smiles, with his affection. She was uncomfortable being a witness to it, but he obviously wasn't embarrassed. He looked totally at ease in his clean suit, ready for a night on the town with his wife.

Where was his wife?

"I'll show you around the house," he said. "Follow me."

To her distress, she realized that there was no chance he would forget her. His gaze was too curious. He pointed out the kitchen and opened the pantry. Olive's heart began to pound as they strolled through the library. The built-in bookcases on the sides of the fireplace were full of books, and even from a cursory glance, she could tell that they were books on architecture. More books on architecture than the Joplin library had. Many more.

He was watching her and had noticed her interest. Olive shifted her bag around as if she could hide behind it.

"Feel free to avail yourself of a book once the children are asleep. They should go to bed around eight. I'm afraid you won't find any interesting novels on the shelves, but there are some books of poetry."

Poetry? He had no idea. Olive felt her confidence returning. "That would be delightful. I just might."

He walked her through the downstairs, and all the while she was keeping an eye open for Mrs. Scott. No doubt she was dressing for their evening out. Whatever her reason for not greeting Olive, Mr. Scott surprised her with his knowledge. For such a busy man, he took an unusual amount of responsibility for the children's care.

"Do you live nearby?" he asked as he led her upstairs.

"Just around the corner." She stepped aside to let Leo run past.

"I've heard the name Kentworth. Do I know your family?"

"I have a lot of family around town, but my father is a manager at the Fox-Berry Mine. He works for Mr. Blount."

"I know Mr. Blount. I've worked with him before." If this was a normal situation, perhaps Olive would ask about his work, but Olive knew all about his work for Mr. Blount, and wasn't going to wade into those dangerous waters. Thankfully the gregarious Mr. Scott didn't need any inducement. "I designed his house."

Oh, it was torture to be in the presence of a man who had all the knowledge she desired and not to be able to learn anything from him. Olive wanted to cry. Instead, she said, "You design houses? I thought I'd heard your name before."

"Very kind of you. Architects don't get to sign their works like an artist, so one never knows if it's recognized or not."

And that was the only reason Olive thought she could ever stand to be an architect.

Their tour took them to the children's room upstairs. This was the entire house, and despite Mr. Scott's instructions and the children's chatter, the house was strangely silent. No noises coming from behind the closed bedroom door. No woman hurrying out to say goodbye to the children.

"So, that's everything." Mr. Scott led her downstairs with the children following. "If I've forgotten something, make do the best you can. Feel free to help yourself to anything in the icebox." His buoyancy was increasing as he neared the door. "I'll return around eleven, and—"

"And Mrs. Scott?" Olive looked up the staircase. Clearly she wasn't home. Would she be returning before him or was she out of town?

Mr. Scott reached for his suit coat. "I am a widower, Miss Kentworth. My wife passed away two years ago."

"I'm sorry." The room had gone quiet, but Olive knew better than to offer empty words, even to fill the silence.

He looked around the room as he pulled on his coat. His eyes traveled the breadth of it as if it were a trap closing in on him. "You can see why your help is needed." Then he flashed that engaging smile. "Good luck, Miss Kentworth," he said and walked out the door.

4

As much as he loved his children, Maxfield was eager to escape. After stopping at Trochet's Flower Shop to buy Ruby a bouquet, he hurried to the Keystone Hotel.

When he'd asked Pastor Cook's wife for a recommendation, he'd expected she'd send someone older and more experienced. Miss Kentworth was charming. Despite her efforts to avoid notice, she couldn't hide the emotions that played across her expressive face. She'd been so nervous when she'd first arrived, but after a bit she managed to control it. It wasn't until he told her about Georgia that her mask slipped again, and that time it exposed a deep sorrow. Perhaps she had experienced her own?

Maxfield shuddered. He'd had enough sorrow. He didn't need to carry someone else's.

Besides, she seemed like a sweet girl. He only hoped Leo and Stella wouldn't take advantage of her naivety. Either way, he and Ruby would have a marvelous time together. Well, Ruby always had a marvelous time but, finally, he'd be able to join in.

Ruby answered the door, wearing her namesake color. She grabbed him by the wrist and dragged him inside. "Papa, look who has come to see us."

"I didn't come to see your father." Maxfield felt carefree and reckless. He winked at Mr. Dennis before saying, "I see him every day. This time I came to see his daughter."

"Because it's been nearly a week." She pursed her lips up into a pout but couldn't hold it longer than a heartbeat. "Did you find someone to watch the children, or did you leave Leo in charge of tending Stella?"

"I found someone to watch them. We can stay for the whole concert." It was impossible to be morose with Ruby around. That's why she was essential. Even if Maxfield didn't love the orchestra or theater, he needed something to distract him. He couldn't work around the clock.

"No need to hurry away." Mrs. Dennis was as severe as Ruby was lenient. "You've only arrived."

"Thank you for the offer, but the concert starts in half an hour." He didn't leave his own home to stay in the Dennises'. "I don't want to rush Miss Dennis along the way."

"Bye, Papa." Ruby smacked a quick kiss on her father's cheek. She snagged her reticule off a side table without slowing down in her path to the doorway.

She'd never kissed Max on the cheek, or anywhere else. Maxfield tipped his hat to Mr. Dennis, then followed his daughter. What would Ruby think if he kissed her? She was so full of life and affection, Maxfield couldn't imagine that she'd take offense. She'd probably laugh at him and forget all about it. He might as well forget all about it. They had a concert to attend.

The best part of these outings with Ruby was when they approached the venue. Maxfield loved being in the crush of the crowd. He loved the greetings and acknowledgments, and for him there were plenty. Ruby was patient while he worked his way through the people he wanted to visit. Even when surrounded by strangers, their greetings and good cheer strengthened Maxfield. He felt shored up, supported, knowing that there was a community around him and that life hadn't stopped when Georgia's did.

"Maxfield, glad to see you out and about." Eric Vogel slapped him on the back. "How'd you get Mrs. Wester to stay?"

"I found someone else to watch them this evening. She seems competent." Eric was Maxfield's draftsman. He and his wife had grown up with Georgia and were the Scotts' closest friends in Joplin. Any day now, Maxfield expected to hear that Eric was opening his own office. He'd be happy for him when that day came, even though he'd miss his help.

Eric's wife, Elaine, turned to Ruby. "I imagine you're anxious to get in your new house. I rode by it today, and it looks nearly finished."

Maxfield tried not to think about how Elaine mourned when they lost Georgia. Or how difficult it might be for her to see him with another woman.

"That's what Papa told me. It'll be nice having some room and privacy. If only Maxfield would hurry up and finish the house." Ruby turned as the ushers began closing up the doors to the auditorium. "It's time to go in, Maxfield. We can't be late."

Maxfield would rather visit with Eric, but she was right. On this trip to the theater, it was easy getting to their seats. Maxfield made an extra effort to greet the Landauers and show his contrition for last time. So intent was she on getting to her seat, Ruby didn't notice them as she squeezed by.

The music started and Maxfield grew drowsy. He shouldn't expect to be entertained. He didn't know enough of music to appreciate the intricacies of the arrangement. Enjoying the company of a beautiful lady and having a reprieve from the oppression of his lonely house was all he could expect. It was enough.

Ruby sat on the edge of her seat, enthralled. Occasionally she would grab his wrist with a fierce grip, as if she were in danger of being carried away by the music. He doubted she knew that she did it, but it was appealing.

His mind drifted to Miss Kentworth again. He hoped she was faring well. Leo could be rebellious and Stella whiny. Surely someone like Miss Kentworth knew what she had volunteered for. She'd be fine.

It seemed the concert lasted forever. Then a rush of greetings as they found a table at the restaurant, a rapid recitation of Ruby's favorite movements in the concert over her flounder, a romantic stroll to the Keystone, and the night was over.

Maxfield found himself walking back along the sidewalk alone beneath the streetlights. It was Tuesday, and he had to work the next day. He shouldn't linger in town. Surely this late, he'd be able to fall asleep quickly and soundly.

Not wanting to wake the children, Maxfield closed the door gently. The house was still and settled. He followed the light shining from the library, and there he found Miss Kentworth sitting on the fireplace hearth with one of his thick architectural books. It was on her lap, and she was sitting on a tattered notebook, twirling a pencil between her fingers.

She was daydreaming, no doubt. So bored with the book that she hadn't heard him come inside.

Maxfield cleared his throat. Miss Kentworth jumped. She slapped the book closed, then hopped to the bookcase and slid it in its place.

He'd told her he didn't mind sharing his books, but she acted as guilty as Cain. Maxfield walked to the hearth, picked up her notebook, and held it out to her. "How did Leo and Stella do?" he asked.

Miss Kentworth reached for the book. Her eyes never broke contact with his as she eased it from his hand. "Fine. They were fine." Once the notebook was in her possession, she swiftly stuffed it in her bag. "They had dinner, played, and bathed, and they went to sleep. The night was perfect."

It had been perfect, Maxfield thought. Or was it? He watched as she gathered her things. Perhaps the night had only been satisfactory. Ruby was lovely, the music was endurable, and he'd laughed and smiled and kept hurtful thoughts at bay for another day. Satisfactory was all he was aiming for.

"You shouldn't walk home unescorted," he said. "Let me walk with you."

"You can't leave the children in the house alone." She blinked as she looked toward the staircase. "What if they wake?"

"It's just around the corner, right?" He opened the door. "They're sound sleepers, and they'll never know I'm gone."

"They're your children," she said. "If it doesn't bother you . . ."

He took her book bag from her arm and slung it over his shoulder. She hesitated only a moment before gliding out the door.

"How was your evening?" Miss Kentworth asked.

"Perfect," he answered, even though he knew now that was a lie. "We went to the symphony and dinner, and then I escorted Miss Dennis home."

"Escorting two ladies in the same night? How debonair." Miss Kentworth ducked her head, but he'd heard her nonetheless.

"Whenever my services are required, I'm pleased to be of use." The night was still. Although clouds covered the sky, the moon shone brightly through, lighting the street indirectly.

"Is this Miss Dennis any relation to the man whose house you are building?" she asked.

"His daughter."

"Hmm. . . ." She kept her eyes on the sidewalk.

"Hmm, what?" Maxfield asked, finding it interesting that she found it interesting.

"That could be a lot of pressure to do well, or maybe they'll go easy on you because of the relationship. It could go either way."

Maxfield felt his chin rise. "I am my own motivation. I don't need incentive from anyone else to do my best."

She looked up, startled. "I didn't mean to suggest any such thing. I was musing on the fact that such a relationship could come with complications. That's all."

Now he felt like a brute. "No harm done," he said. "You are correct in your assumption. It could come with complications, but so far we've avoided that pitfall." Then to change the subject, he asked, "We turn here? I always avoid this street. It offends my sensibilities to walk by that house."

She slowed in front of it. "What is it about this house that bothers you?"

Maxfield knew better than to talk about his work to ladies. They inevitably had things they'd rather discuss, but he didn't know Miss Kentworth well enough to know what topics those might be. Hopefully he wouldn't bore her too thoroughly. "The proportions are awry. The roof of the porch hulks over the foundation. The supports on the porch are too spindly. It looks ready to topple over." He smiled. "I hope that's not your house."

For the first time that he'd observed, Miss Kentworth looked pleased. "It's not. But let's say you were given the opportunity to fix it? What would you do?"

"Good question." He adjusted her bag on his shoulder as he considered the structure. "I've never added onto another's work. I wouldn't want to dilute their vision for the project."

"Even if their vision needed diluting?"

As distasteful as the house was, she'd asked him an intelligent question. He didn't want to disappoint. "If I were going to correct this house, without structurally changing it . . ." He stepped off ten yards to get a view from the side of the place, then returned to her. "First the porch needs to be resized. I would extend the deck farther and make the columns thicker. That would help with the balance. Then I'd change the color of the shingles on the second story. Go from the dark green to a neutral gray so it doesn't interrupt the flow of this elevation. And see that chimney?" Maxfield bent so he was at her eye level. He put a hand on her shoulder and pointed to direct her view. "That chimney there. It's too thick. I'd demolish it and have it reconstructed thinner. Those changes wouldn't make it a house I'd be proud of," he said, "but at least one I could tolerate."

He turned his head to judge her response and found that he was too close. Closer than he'd been to Ruby that evening. Removing his hand, he straightened, took a step away, and directed his attention to the house as if he were considering what else could be done.

If he expected some flattering remark about how intelligent he was, he was disappointed. Instead, she quietly considered the house as if she'd understood every word he said.

"I don't blame you for limiting your efforts to new construction," Miss Kentworth said. "It must be easier to start with a fresh canvas." With a nod, she signaled that she was ready to resume their progress.

Max shoved his hands into his pockets as he ambled forward. "I find it so, although sometimes there are so many decisions to make, it feels like drudgery."

"I hope not!" she blurted. Then she stopped in front of a modest house, similar to but smaller than his own. "No need to evaluate it," she said. "We wouldn't be able to afford a renowned architect to improve it."

Ah, there was the expected compliment. He'd return it with one of his own. "I don't see any improvement necessary. Much like my house, it achieves what was expected of it with no pretense or vulgarity." He took her bag off his shoulder and handed it to her. "Thank you again for your time this evening. I'm in your debt."

"Actually you are." Her throat bounced as she swallowed, then added, "You never paid me. . . ."

"A million apologies!" Maxfield fumbled for his wallet. He felt like a cad for putting her in such a position. He should've paid her before he'd ever left for the night, because handing her a few folded bills felt odd after their stroll, but he was glad that she wasn't afraid to speak up for herself. "I hope you'll forgive me. I didn't mean to put the burden of collection on you."

She shoved the bills into her bag, then dusted off her hands. "I'm not offended," she said. "I enjoyed the evening. Have a good night, Mr. Scott." She braved a quick smile, then went to her door.

"You too." He remained standing on the quiet sidewalk until she'd gone inside and the lamplight from the window faded as it was carried away. The calm coolness of the night was welcome after the crowded, noisy concert hall. This walk was exactly what he needed to help him sleep tonight.

Perhaps the evening had been perfect after all. There was no electricity to her room but, as late as it was, Olive had to have light. She set the lamp next to her bed, pulled out her sketchbook, and flipped quickly past the notes she'd taken that night to find a blank page. Lying on her bed, supported by her elbows, she drafted the neighbor's house as it was. She'd walked by it a dozen times and never thought to look at it like Mr. Scott did. Once she'd drawn it to her satisfaction, she started again, but this time with the changes he'd suggested.

It was heady, this feeling of partnership with a man like him. When he'd shared his ideas for the house, Olive felt like sitting on the ground and catching every word in her notebook. Naturally she couldn't do that, so here she was, jotting down everything she could recall before sleep erased the memory.

Changing the color of the shingles. Ingenious. Thinning the chimney to help with balance. Olive hadn't considered the width of a chimney to be an important factor, but she would from now on. Oh, to have the training that he'd had. It had come to her that she should pay him for lessons. That's when she remembered that actually he was supposed to be paying her, and why wouldn't she take his money? That had been the deal they'd struck from the beginning.

Olive held the sketch before her. Someday she'd have the confidence to take credit for her work. Someday she'd show people what she could do. Never to someone with training like Mr. Scott, but to people she knew that wanted something built. Maybe for people who wanted the look of their houses updated. If important men didn't have time to remodel, then there was a niche for Olive, perhaps. Houses aged. The families outgrew them. There were a dozen reasons someone would want an addition to their home.

Just ask Mr. Blount.

Olive flipped back through her notebook to the pages of notes she'd taken before Mr. Scott had returned home. She'd never heard of a living hall before seeing one in Mr. Scott's publications, but the uses seemed practical, especially for someone as concerned with appearances as Mr. Blount. Designed to resemble the great halls of medieval castles, the living hall was a cozy, masculine room that encompassed the central fireplace and staircase and replaced a more formal parlor. With Mr. Blount's house, one could open up the way between the parlor and the music room, then add a room on the west side of the house as a ladies' parlor. Instead of a parlor for everyone, the men would have their living hall, while the ladies' parlor would be decidedly more feminine, with wide windows overlooking the garden.

She drew the existing floor plan from memory the best she was able, then struck out walls and dashed in new construction. This was what she loved—the planning, the possibilities, the perfection of an idea before it was tried and the flaws were exposed. And that's why she never wanted to be at the forefront. She couldn't imagine being called to account by an angry client for a mistake or a delay. She couldn't imagine walking downtown and people looking at her and knowing who she was, just as they must know Maxfield Scott.

And that's why this design would exist only on paper. Olive smoothed the page and thought again of Mr. Scott and what she might want out of life. Her mother had been a big part of her life, and with her gone, Olive was missing a piece of the puzzle. Tending children was a role she could fill comfortably. Caring over those who couldn't care for themselves came naturally for Olive and it didn't force her into any uncomfortable situations. And if she could watch children in the finest architectural library in the state, then she'd be a fool not to.

She pushed her paper aside and blew out the light. It was too late to change into her nightgown, too late to work anymore, and too late to change who she was. Olive Kentworth would go on being Olive Kentworth, and that's how God designed it.

But that didn't mean that she couldn't do some designing of her own. Even if no one ever knew about it. With thoughts of living halls and ladies' parlors in her mind, Olive drifted to sleep.

CHAPTER
5

"Olive, you got any buildings that need building?" Amos Kent-worth unwrapped his sandwich from his bandanna and kicked his feet up on the back of a nearby chair.

After church it had always been the Kentworths' practice to stay and visit with neighbors and friends until bellies rumbled and the pastor herded them out the doors. Now that they were attending services led by Calista's husband, Matthew, they were likely to bring food and throw together a dinner.

"Why would you ask that?" Olive passed him a basket of rolls. Was it obvious to everyone that she had big designs in her head?

"Welp, we did a fine job on this place and Maisie's crystal cave. It's about time our partnership got to rolling again. The fields are planted, and I'm ready for a diversion."

So was she, actually. While Amos didn't know the first thing about architecture, his gift of gab, his confidence, and his basic understanding of construction had allowed him to take credit for Olive's designs and work with her builder, Mr. Flowers, while she stayed in the background. It was a unique partnership, but one both cousins enjoyed.

"We need you doing tours if you're finished with planting."

Maisie folded a chair, then carried it to the table where the family was gathering. "Although that visitors' center at the Crystal Cave is doing a humdinger of a job. People exclaim over the jagged rock walls and the open-air cafe. I don't know where you get your ideas, Olive, but you have a knack for it."

One place to get ideas was from Maxfield Scott's books, but Olive hadn't been invited to his house again. She supposed it wasn't surprising. The children had a regular nanny, and the man surely didn't go to a concert every evening. He'd gone on Tuesday night, and here it was Sunday. Nearly a week. If he really cared for this lady, wouldn't he want to see her more?

Her father took a seat next to Amos. "You know, Mr. Blount never did accept any of the proposals he had on his house. He spent the better part of the afternoon telling them what he wanted, but when they submitted their drafts, Mrs. Blount refused them all."

"Not surprising since their house is beautiful," said Calista. "Why does he want to change it?"

Matthew shrugged. "People are never content."

Boone Bragg, Maisie's husband, walked to the table with two hot lunches he'd purchased at the miners' cafe. "I'd imagine that Mr. Blount doesn't know what Mrs. Blount wants. It'll be hard to do as he's asking and please her, if she doesn't agree to the premise."

What if the problem lay in a difference of opinion between the spouses? What if Olive still had a chance? She looked at Amos happily munching on a cold sandwich. Could he play the role again? Mr. Blount already thought he was responsible for this miners' center. He would trust Amos with something as simple as adding a room. How would this be any different from her other projects?

First off, it wasn't for family. Second, she would be working on a house, not a commercial building. Third, and this terrified her the most, she would be changing a Maxfield Scott home.

And yet, Olive was convinced that she had a perfect design in mind. There were a few details that she hadn't drafted to her liking, but she felt the solution was at hand. If only she could take another gander at Mr. Scott's library. How could she secure an invitation?

Leaving the table, Olive grabbed a chair used for Sunday service, folded it up, and carried it to where Maisie was stacking them. "Say, Maisie. I have a favor to ask."

"I'm not watching someone's kids," Maisie said. "You can forget about that."

"No one wants you to watch their kids," Olive said. Maisie was more likely to break something or get into mischief than most children. "I was wondering if I could get some tickets to the Crystal Cave."

"Sure you can. We'll let you inside whenever you want. No need to buy tickets."

"Well, there is. I want tickets so I can give them to some friends, on the quiet. I don't want them to know who gave them the tickets. It's going to be a surprise."

"You taking a fellow there?" Maisie smiled wide. "Look at you blush. You are, ain't you?"

"I'm sending a fellow and his girlfriend. Don't worry about it, Maisie. Just get me two tickets, and hurry. There's not much time."

Not if she was going to get some books, study them, and get her blueprints to the Blounts before they found someone to do their bidding.

"Stop by the office on your way home. Boone's got some in his desk. I'm mighty curious, though. I can't think of who you're trying to get to go to the cave." Maisie scanned the meeting room that served as a church. "Is it Amos? You got someone that you're trying to hitch with Amos?"

It was as good an excuse as any. Olive bounced her eyebrows and tried to look mysterious. She wasn't used to orchestrating events to get her way, but she had begun to think she might be good at it.

"If you want ceramic tiles in the foyer, it's time to choose them. They should be installed before the baseboards go in." Maxfield straightened the delft blue painted tile on the showroom table as Mrs. Dennis fretted.

"I can't decide without seeing it there. Why can't I go to the house?"

"It's a construction site and not safe for ladies. As soon as the scaffolding comes down and the debris is cleared, I'll let you know." He answered smoothly, but his heart raced at the thought of the ladies exposed to danger.

Ruby patted her mother's hand. "Who cares how the entryway looks? Just pick the tile you like best. Then Mr. Scott can get back to work."

"This *is* my work," he said. "Your mother is my client, and I want her to be pleased with her house." As long as she didn't visit until the dangerous construction was completed. That rule was nonnegotiable.

"Well, hello, Mrs. Dennis, Miss Dennis." It was Eric coming in the door from his lunch break. He hung his hat on the hat rack. "How are you ladies doing today?"

"We're trying to choose tile," Ruby said. "So many decisions."

"Yes, ma'am." Eric waved a handful of mail at Max. "Do you have a minute?"

"Excuse me," Max said to the ladies and followed Eric into his office. He eased the door closed, knowing there was a reason Eric had asked for privacy.

Eric tossed the mail on the desk. "You couldn't pass off those detail decisions to some underling? Like me?"

"Not when it's Ruby's family."

"That's what I wanted to speak to you about. Elaine is inviting you, Miss Dennis, and the children to come over for dinner on Friday. The little ones miss their friends."

"Count us in." Maxfield flipped through the envelopes containing bills and payments. "Should I bring anything?"

"Are you going to cook something?" Eric laughed. "Please don't. Just bring your usual charming company."

One envelope caught Maxfield's attention. The script was feminine, tidy, and unfamiliar. He picked the edge of the seal open and pulled out a folded paper.

"What's that?" Eric asked.

The paper only had one line of print. *A gift from a satisfied client*, it read. Maxfield held up two slips of paper. "Tickets to the Crystal Cave." He turned them front and back. Who had sent them? He couldn't think why one of his former clients would've wanted to send them anonymously.

"Elaine and I went a few months ago," Eric said. "It's unbelievable. Your kids will love it."

"But it says *Adult Ticket Only*." Maxfield looked closer. Written in ink over the printing was the specification that the tickets were only for adults and they were only valid for this Monday and Tuesday nights. "My secret appreciative customer is rather impatient," he said. Would Ruby want to go? It sounded like more fun than another concert.

"Go tonight. Elaine and I will keep the kids. I've heard the cave is a very romantic place."

Maxfield hesitated. The more he thought about it, the more he wanted to go. Seeing a cave completely covered in crystals interested him, and Ruby would love it. He could send the children to the Vogels'. Or even better, he could hire Miss Kentworth. He felt good about her watching them.

"Sometimes Mrs. Wester can stay late and watch them, but I'll figure it out. Let me ask around and see if I can enlist help. Then we'll plan on visiting with you on Friday."

"Whatever you think best. If I don't hear from you, I'll assume you have it covered."

"Thank you, Eric," Maxfield said.

The simple gift in the envelope had completely changed his day. He might not have planned to go to the Crystal Cave, but now he couldn't think of anything he'd rather do. Walking back into his showroom, he held up the two tickets. "What do you say we go see the Crystal Cave tonight?"

Ruby clapped her hands together. "Do you mean it? I've wanted to go forever."

"Of course I mean it. I'll have to find someone to watch the children, but that shouldn't take long."

"They can't go with us? I bet they would love it."

"No," Maxfield said. "They need to stay home. It won't take much to find someone on a Monday night, I'd imagine. In fact, I'd better get started right now."

"What time does the cave close?" Ruby asked.

He consulted the tickets. "Six o'clock. We'll need to hurry."

"You know where to find me." Her eyelashes fluttered with her smile.

Six o'clock. Mrs. Wester usually stayed until six o'clock anyway. She probably wouldn't mind staying a little over. Then again, he didn't know how long it would take to walk home from the cave. And Ruby and he might as well get dinner. There was no reason to hurry back. Not if he could get Miss Kentworth's help.

That was his reasoning as he made his way to her house. A less confident man might dread asking for a last-minute favor, but Maxfield trusted that Miss Kentworth knew her own mind well enough to refuse if she wanted. He knocked at the door, still surprised at the turn the day had taken. This hadn't been in his plans, but he couldn't have planned anything better.

"Mr. Scott." She certainly seemed pleased to see him. "To what do I owe this honor?"

"Miss Kentworth, the most extraordinary thing has happened. I have the opportunity to tour a local attraction tonight, but I find myself in need of your services for the children. Would you be able to assist me?"

She looked over her shoulder at the clock on the mantel. "What time? I'd like to tidy up first."

In his opinion, she looked tidy enough, but he nodded. "Naturally. I won't leave the house until 3:30."

"It's three o'clock now." The corners of her eyes tilted with a smile, daring him to press.

He loved a dare. "Then you have plenty of time." Looking inside, he spotted her heavy book bag that she'd brought last time. "I'll leave you to get ready, but would you like me to carry your tote? No use in you lugging it there by yourself."

"No! I can carry it. I'm quite strong." She pushed against the door, narrowing the gap, until only her face showed. "I don't need any help. Now, if you'll excuse me."

"Alright then. See you in half an hour." She didn't get to see him tip his hat before closing the door, but that was fine. He had no time to waste either.

Some people waited around for life to determine their course, while others took the reins in hand and forged their own journey. Instead of dithering about who sent the tickets or why, he'd jumped at the opportunity to enjoy a pleasurable evening with a charming lady. And he had Miss Kentworth to thank for making it possible.

6

Maxfield had graduated from the University of Illinois School of Architecture and then studied abroad in Florence, Rome, and Paris. He'd been all over the continent, but he'd never encountered a structure like this. The building was simple, really, but it so captured the spirit of Joplin that he couldn't help but be impressed.

Constructed with limestone, calcite, and other materials that had been excavated while gaining access to the cave, the exterior was as abrasive and rough as the piles of chat that littered the minefields in the Tri-State District. No smooth facade, no polished stone, these walls were rough and unashamed, just like the miners. But atop the exterior walls, the designer had crowned it with jagged stones, making it look like some medieval keep or fortress. This place might be young and primitive, but it had aspirations. Like Joplin, it reminded him of a young king, finding his way and testing his strength.

He'd heard about Boone Bragg, the mine owner, and the farm girl who'd discovered this treasure in his abandoned mine. Boone had married her, and now they hosted tours, parties, and even weddings in the mine. It was high time he saw it.

Maxfield presented his tickets to the dour man at the door.

The briefest twitch of his eyes told Max there was some question about the tickets.

"Wait here a second," he said, then lumbered inside.

"What if the tickets are no good?" Ruby asked, her eyes wide.

"Then I buy two tickets. We didn't come all this way for nothing." And he wouldn't go back home. Not yet.

He recognized Boone Bragg as he approached. Approximately the same age, the two had rubbed shoulders at countless events, but Maxfield didn't know that he'd ever had a conversation with him. It seemed that Boone was adept at disappearing during social gatherings.

"Mr. Scott, welcome to the Crystal Cave. Miss Dennis, if I remember correctly?"

"Nice to see you again, Boone." She shot a sideways glance at Maxfield, making him wonder how she knew Mr. Bragg.

"Is there some problem with my tickets?" Maxfield asked.

"No, surely not." But Boone looked them over, just the same. "It's odd that they have expiration dates on them. We don't sell tickets with expiration dates."

"That's how they came to me. They were a gift, although I don't know who bought them."

Boone turned the tickets over again, then looked from Max to Ruby. "Well, then, I'm glad you have a friend who wants you to see our little hole in the ground. I hope you're not disappointed. The next tour should start in about ten minutes."

"Before we go below, allow me to compliment you on your building. It's quite original. Who was the architect?"

The ticket-taker decided to speak up. "It was my cousin. She . . ."

"His name is Amos Kentworth," Boone corrected. "Amos designed this building. This here is Hank Kentworth. These woods are thick with Kentworth cousins. My wife is one of them."

"Would Olive Kentworth be another?" Maxfield couldn't see any family resemblance between Hank and Olive besides the widow's peak on his forehead.

"Who is Olive Kentworth?" Ruby asked. "I've never heard of her."

"She's the reason we're here. She's at my house watching Leo and Stella."

"Olive is part of the family." Boone chose his next words carefully. "She's tending your children this evening, you say? And you, a famous architect?"

"What does me being an architect have to do with anything?"

Hank cleared his throat with a deep cough that sounded like a foghorn. He leaned his elbows against the ticket counter and said, "Olive don't cotton to getting out of the house. She's a homebody. We're surprised she decided to work for you. That's all."

Boone nodded in agreement. "Nothing more than that."

Why didn't Miss Kentworth like to leave her house? He couldn't imagine. Not when he himself couldn't stand to stay at his.

A large door swung toward them, then was propped open by a man wearing a lit miner's hat. He stood to the side as a crowd poured into the room. "And that's our tour of the Crystal Cave. Be sure and stop by the gift shop and pick up a postcard to send to the folks back home. Or see my cousin Hilda in the cafe for a cup of coffee and a cookie. Best cookies in Jasper County."

"That's Amos," Hank said. "He does tours when he's not busy."

"Why is an architect doing cave tours?" Between all the cousins, Maxfield was confused.

Boone looked tired. "I'm headed to the mining side of this enterprise. Ore is much less complicated. Nice to see you, Mr. Scott, Miss Dennis. Amos will take good care of you."

Maxfield pinched Ruby's elbow, leaned in, and whispered, "I came for the cave tour, but all this family business might be more interesting."

Ruby scrunched up her face. "It's a family business. How is that interesting?"

So Ruby didn't share his curiosity about the Kentworths? Noted. But she hadn't met Olive. Perhaps then she'd understand. The crowd was dispersing and the people sitting in the waiting area were lining up before the door, ready for their turn.

Maxfield waved to Amos. "Excuse me. I'm Maxfield Scott and I understand that you built this building?"

Amos had a smile that involved his whole face. "I reckon I did. Ain't it a dandy?"

"I'm an architect myself, and I wanted to compliment you on your original design."

"Welp, I want to compliment you on your pretty sister." Amos tipped his hat to Ruby. "Amos Kentworth, ma'am. Pleased to meet you."

Ruby's eyelashes fluttered. "I'm not his sister."

"You're not?" Amos's mouth turned down. "That's a crying shame, but I hope you enjoy the tour nonetheless."

"Before you get started . . . the building? I'd love to hear about your training. What was your influence? I see Norman design, but with a frontier influence, perhaps?"

"I don't know anyone named Norman, but I have a tour to run. Let me get up front and we'll start your show." He winked at Ruby, then went to the front of the line and began his presentation.

"He's funny," Ruby said. "This is going to be entertaining."

"Much better than the symphony." When Ruby gasped, Maxfield patted her hand. "Don't act shocked. You know I only go to enjoy your company."

But this was something different. They were at the back of the line that moved deliberately down staircase after staircase. Maxfield could feel the excitement in their gathering growing. At every bend in the tunnel people paused, then laughed when they found only another staircase going down. This was something new, he kept telling himself. Something new. Something to keep the melancholy at bay.

Ruby turned to beam at him over her shoulder. "This is so exciting."

"I'm glad I get to see it with you."

When the line stopped, Maxfield reasoned that they must have reached their destination. Amos could be heard encouraging people to go on inside and to clear the way, but the line didn't move. It took repeated urging to get everyone inside, and once inside, Maxfield was awed.

According to Amos, this was a geode, just like so many children loved to collect. The only difference was the size. This geode was as big as a ballroom and even deeper. Maxfield stood stunned, unable to understand what he was seeing.

"Oooh, it's gorgeous!" Ruby covered her mouth but kept speaking. "Who would've thought this was under here? How many crystals are here? I'd love to have a number."

Who could think of numbers here? Without a word, Maxfield walked the wooden walkway so he could appreciate what he was seeing in silence. The only man-made construction Maxfield had ever seen that he could compare it to was the Hall of Mirrors at Versailles, but even that didn't have the effortless grandeur that was here. Just think, men worked, strove, and stressed to make something with a fraction of the beauty found here, while God effortlessly created this, and then allowed a farm girl to stumble upon it millennia later.

How could anyone question God's power or His beauty? And yet, Maxfield realized, he had been questioning His goodness. When Georgia died, Maxfield had gone into survival mode— suppressing his sorrow for the sake of the children, working for his clients, smiling for his friends. Whenever his heart was drawn back to his relationship with Christ, he felt pain again. The pain of abandonment, disappointment, betrayal. Maxfield knew that God loved him, and he knew he wasn't owed an explanation for Georgia's death, but it was easier to avoid any thought of God than to pretend that all was well.

When he came face-to-face with evidence of his Creator, he couldn't remember how to respond. He only prayed that God would continue to be patient with him and would show him the way back.

Maxfield didn't know how long they explored the cave. At every turn there was a new sight, a different reflection of the colored lights on the crystals, of the crystals on the water. An inspiring scene he wanted to remember forever. Whoever gave him these tickets knew exactly what he had needed that night.

⚘⚘⚘

This time, Olive was prepared for Mr. Scott's return. She'd sat on the stairs with her notes and the architectural book angled so she could see his form as it passed in front of the window. Since Mr. Scott and his lady would be done with the cave tour early in the evening, she didn't have much time after the children went to bed. Hopefully the restaurant would be slow to serve them.

All too soon, the shadow moved across the window. Olive sprang up, ran on tiptoe to the library, slid the book between two others, and dropped her notes into her bag. Then, grabbing the poetry book she'd set out for just this moment, she curled up in the armchair.

The door creaked, then the latch clicked. Mr. Scott came around the corner, knowing exactly where to look for her. Did everyone notice how he lightened a room, or was it her nerves that made her sensitive to his presence?

"How are the children?" He was more subdued than the last time she'd seen him. "Asleep now?"

"Barely. I just put them to bed." Feeling self-conscious, she stood and reached to put the poetry book back on the shelf.

"You can take that with you if you'd like," he said.

Olive paused. She turned the book over in her hands. "But I don't know when I'll be back." There were so many books she'd rather have, but if he approved of her reading poetry, that's what she'd pretend to do.

"I think it's safe to assume that you'll be back ere long."

So he and Miss Dennis were seeing each other frequently? If they got married, would they still need a part-time nanny? Olive dropped her gaze. No more interfering with his life. It wasn't right.

"Excuse me while I check on the children. Then I'll walk you home." He turned and eased up the staircase.

"It's fine. . . ." Protesting was polite, but her half-hearted attempt was short-lived. Of course, she wanted to spend more time with someone she could imagine as a mentor. Not that he was that much older, but in experience he was her senior, no question about it.

She waited for him by the door and smiled when he winked and nodded. They remained silent until they were outside. Wordlessly, she handed over her book bag and they set out.

"How was the . . . Where did you go again?" Olive couldn't remember if he'd told her about his tickets. It wouldn't do for her to mention them if he hadn't.

"We went to the Crystal Cave. It was incredible."

"I love going there," Olive said. "My cousin is the one who discovered it."

"I met several of your cousins." Maxfield tugged on the cuff of his sleeve, making it reach his wrist. "The one who most impressed me was Amos."

"Amos?" Olive dropped her hand against her chest. "Amos is a rounder. I can't imagine what he did that impressed you." Had she stressed the *you* too much?

"That building. I've never seen anything quite like it."

Olive's toe caught a seam in the sidewalk. She stumbled and would've fallen had Maxfield not caught her by the back of the arm.

"Whoa, there." He held her upright until she'd steadied. "This sidewalk is uneven in places."

"I'm sorry," she said. Maxfield Scott liked her building. He was impressed by her building. And he was holding her arm. "I'm so clumsy. What were you saying about the building?"

He slid his arm in hers and arranged her hand as was proper. "The structure is practical. There are no wasted materials or space, and yet it possesses a grandeur that's almost Norman in spirit."

Norman? She thought it might have Saxon traits, but not Norman.

"It's high praise coming from an architect of your stature." Olive was trying not to gush, but all she could hear was gush, gush, gush.

"You don't need to flatter me. My pride is strong enough as it is."

She tucked her chin to hide the satisfied grin she couldn't suppress. They walked in silence the length of another appropriately manicured yard. It was good that Olive had Mr. Scott's arm to steady her, because all she could concentrate on was reciting his praise endlessly, so she would never forget it. They were nearing home and then they would have to part. She wanted to hear more from Mr. Scott and she was nearly out of time.

"How about the Crystal Cave itself? What was your impression of that?" She watched closely as he struggled with his response.

"It's hard to describe how I felt. Obviously there's the beauty of the place. It's a natural phenomenon, and should be celebrated for its rarity and size, but it's more than that." His steps had slowed. Olive waited in the silence as he chose his words. "It reminded me that there's a designer, a God who moves planets, subterranean water, and even tragedy by His plan. It's an uncomfortable thought, isn't it?"

Her eyes slid closed, and her fingers tightened on his arm. This wasn't a conversational turn that she'd expected. He was speaking of his wife. She understood that. She also understood how loss could undermine faith. She wanted to ignore his observation, to keep the conversation on safer topics, but she couldn't leave him without an answer. She had to let him know that he wasn't the only person to struggle. If she could only find the words.

Thankfully he went on without her.

"It was so uncomfortable that I've avoided the thought of God altogether. Tonight was a reminder that He is everywhere. I must come to terms with it and come to terms with Him."

Olive's eyes were drawn to the end of the street where her house stood. She'd been so fixated on Mr. Blount's project and her opportunity with Mr. Scott that she'd allowed her sorrow to recede. Had she been wrong to do so?

"I'm sorry. I didn't mean to make you uncomfortable," he said. "You gave me no invitation to tread on such sensitive ground."

"Tragedy is always sensitive ground," Olive said, "but no one who has been there would fault you for your observation." Then, with all the courage she could muster, added, "It's ground I find myself wallowing in. Maybe I've spent too much time there already."

"I find it to be ground that I'm avoiding, but it keeps pulling me back like quicksand no matter how I fight."

Mr. Scott of the quick humor, the debonair manners, and the lively social life was beset with sorrow? Olive had only considered what he could offer her professionally. She'd never considered that she might have something to offer him in return.

"Do you have people who help you in the fight?" She was thinking of Maisie, Calista, her own father, and all those who thrust her into life when she wanted to hide.

"I have people that I have to fight for—Leo and Stella. And yet, I feel like I'm often leaving them behind." His gaze traveled past the rooflines of the houses along the street, then he sighed. "But it's ungallant of me to burden you with my troubles. Whatever it is that I need, I trust that God will guide me to the solution."

Did he tuck her hand tighter against his side as he walked her the rest of the way home or was Olive imagining it? Either way she didn't mind. Mourning people would reach for any comfort they could find. Come sunrise, Mr. Scott would probably have forgotten his melancholy. He'd wonder at his strange reaction to the cave and feel that his sorrow couldn't have been as strong as he'd imagined. Whatever his conclusion, Olive only hoped that he remembered her fondly enough to enlist her help with the children, so that she could make use of his wisdom and his library.

CHAPTER

7

Tuesday morning came too early, and even though Olive had nothing pressing scheduled for the day, she wouldn't sleep in when she could make her father breakfast.

"Good morning, sweetheart." Her father pulled her against his side for a friendly hug. "I saw your lamp last night. You were up late."

She had been up late, but she'd accomplished exactly what she'd needed. She'd created a design for an addition to Mr. Blount's house that she was proud of. But why had she bothered? It must be the same urge that compelled puzzle workers to spend hours on a puzzle. It was the satisfaction of completing a task and solving a problem. Puzzle solvers didn't take their completed puzzle to town and expect everyone to congratulate them. It was done for their own benefit. So why couldn't she keep her achievements private?

"I was up late, just thinking through some things." She spread some jelly on her toast.

"Anything you'd like to talk about?" he said over his coffee cup.

"No, sir. Nothing to worry you over."

"I noticed that your sketchbooks aren't in here anymore. Did this thinking have anything to do with Blount's house?"

Olive's eyes flew to the empty kitchen counter. Of course he'd noticed.

"I don't want to be in public as an architect or anything else," she said. "If I come up with a solution for Mr. Blount, it's for my satisfaction, not for acclaim and praise. I'm not selfish."

He thought this over. "There are some who would say it's selfish to keep a solution to yourself when sharing it would help others."

"I didn't find a cure for tuberculosis. I just figured out how Blount can add onto his house without ruining the design."

"Even so, why wouldn't you share it? It's been nearly a month. He hasn't hired anyone else. What if your design is the best?"

"What if it is?" She jabbed her knife into the jar of jelly. "Then everything might change. I'd have to pretend like I'm educated and knowledgeable. I'll have to stand with people like Austin Allen and Maxfield Scott, knowing that I don't have their training or skill."

"Both of those things come with time. They don't come with staying home and burying your dream." Her father set his cup down and leaned forward, urging her to look at him. "Your Grandma Laura was widowed young with a house full of us kids to provide for. There were a lot of people—men and women— who didn't think she was up to the challenge, but once she got that ranch in hand, she never looked back. You are gifted, just as she was."

"Grandma Laura and I are very different."

"The biggest difference I see is that she had to work out of necessity. She had no choice. And for years, you had to stay home with your mother. You had no choice then, but you do now. The time for sacrificing your dreams is over, but you are stuck. If I didn't know better, I'd think that maybe you're still hiding from the world."

Olive's face warmed. This wasn't fair. She'd gotten out of the house to sit with the Scott children. And what did she do while there? Studied architectural books. She knew what she wanted, but she didn't necessarily want everything that came along with her dream.

She couldn't believe she was doing this. She walked to her room and flipped open her sketchbook. She ripped the final draft from the book. Then she tore out the papers showing the house from the west and the south elevation. That should be enough. Hurrying so she would do it before she lost her nerve, she swept into the kitchen and set the papers on the table in front of her father.

"There. Take those to Mr. Blount and see what he says. Let him decide if he wants this kind of a design for his house, but please don't tell him they are my work."

"I'll tell him the same person who made his miners' center wants to make these changes to his house. He'll pick you. I know he will."

"If he doesn't, I'll be so relieved."

"You'll be devastated. Don't you worry. If it's not this project, it'll be another one. Pray that God opens the right doors for you, then trust Him. If He gets you this job, He's not going to leave you to finish it alone." He downed the rest of his coffee. "But I'm going to leave. I'm going before you have a chance to change your mind."

And with that her father, and her secret, scurried out the door.

"I'm playing with Norris, and Stella better leave us alone." Leo jumped over the crack in the sidewalk. "She's a baby. She doesn't know how to play."

"No baby." Stella slugged Leo on the leg, then held her hands up to Maxfield for him to carry her. Eric Vogel's house wasn't far from the Keystone Hotel, and Maxfield thought the exercise did the children good. He wasn't sure that Mrs. Wester gave them much exertion during the day, so anytime he could take them with him in the evening, he would. That way they could all breathe away from the house that held so many memories.

"How about me, Leo?" Ruby asked. "Can I play with you and Norris, or are all girls excluded?"

Leo rolled his eyes. "No girls. That's the rule. No girls."

Ruby smiled at Max. "I'm glad his daddy doesn't feel the same way."

"Definitely not." Having friends that were women had always been a joy in his life.

Eric's wife, Elaine, was no exception.

They arrived at the Vogels' home to shouts of greeting and the mad scamper of the children to the bedrooms.

"It's so nice to see you again, Ruby." Elaine held open the door. Max appreciated her gracious manner toward Ruby, knowing that this evening could be emotional for her. "I'd been looking forward to getting to know you."

"It's so nice of you to invite us over. Maxfield gets irritable when he can't talk during performances."

Eric roared. "He doesn't talk? That's a change. He's never let a performance stop him."

"I'm maturing," Maxfield said, although he wished he could forget the scene with the kids during the play. Stella ran in and jumped against Maxfield's knee. He lifted her to his lap. "What's wrong? Why aren't you playing with Lillian?"

"I want you." She buried her face against his neck.

"Were they rude to you?" Elaine shook her head. "I'll make those boys—"

"It's alright," Maxfield said. "She wants some reassurance, then she'll go back and play. Just spend some time with Daddy first."

"Has Mrs. Dennis chosen all the flooring for her house?" Eric moved the potted plant off the coffee table in preparation for Stella's release. She'd destroyed more than one in his house.

"She's getting closer," Maxfield said.

"That's exciting." Elaine turned in her seat to face Ruby. "I bet you can't wait to move in."

"I can't wait to see it, period. Maxfield is so unreasonable. He won't let me or my mother see it until it's completed." Ruby

70

laughed, oblivious to the shift of tone in the room. "Can you imagine anything so ridiculous?"

Maxfield saw the concern in Eric's eyes. He looked down and fussed with Stella to hide his reaction. "It's nearly finished," he said, "and it'll be worth the wait." He wished he could come up with something to say to change the topic, but he'd gone blank.

"Max is generally reasonable," Elaine said. "I'm sure he has his reasons."

"For not allowing me to go?" Ruby threw her hands in the air. "He lets my father go, and he walks with a cane. What's so dangerous that I can't go? Am I going to trip over a brick and fall to my death?"

His skin prickled like he'd stepped outside in the Scandinavian winter. Again he heard the crash. Again he heard his crew yelling and the mad dash of everyone as he watched from afar, wondering what had happened.

Eric put his hand on Elaine's arm. "She doesn't know."

Elaine was ashen. She stood and took Stella from Maxfield. "Excuse me. I'll check on the children." She walked out of the room with her back straight, leaving Ruby perplexed.

Max should say something. He should smooth over Ruby's gaffe. It wasn't her fault. She was high-spirited. She danced through topics when others tiptoed. And he hadn't warned her.

Uncrossing his legs, Eric leaned forward. "Miss Dennis, you're at a disadvantage, being a more recent friend of Maxfield's. It seems you aren't aware of why he would prefer it if you stayed away from the work site." With frequent pauses, Eric was giving Max ample opportunity to take over the narrative, but Max was unable. "I'm sure you will understand once Maxfield shares—"

Ruby got to her feet. "I wouldn't do anything to hurt Maxfield, and that includes forcing him to talk about things that make him sad. Why waste time mourning over what you can't change, when you can celebrate the day?" She pushed up her sleeves. "I'm going to play with the children. Call me when it's time to eat."

She left the room. His friend's parlor, which had always been a refuge, felt strange and unyielding. When Max was finally able to breathe, he said, "It's not her fault. She doesn't know."

"When are you going to tell her?" Eric asked. "You've been courting for months now."

"The time has never been right."

Elaine reentered. Maxfield knew she felt Georgia's absence nearly as keenly as he did. "She doesn't want him to talk about it," she whispered. "Didn't you hear what she said?"

Ruby's laughter could be heard mixed in with the children's, making Maxfield feel particularly old. "She's been a godsend to me," he said. "Without her, my life would be drab and lonely."

"But you can't ignore—" Eric's thought was interrupted by Elaine's raucous clearing of her throat.

Ruby came back inside with Stella on her back. "Somebody is getting hungry." She bounced as she walked, making Stella giggle.

"I forgot the bread." Elaine ran to the kitchen. The oven door creaked open, then slammed closed.

Rousing himself, Maxfield took Stella off Ruby's back and swung the child until her feet flew straight out. "Are you being a good girl?"

"She is," Ruby said. "We are having a lot of fun."

And that's why he'd brought Ruby. Because Ruby always had a lot of fun, and that's what Maxfield wanted. It was no crime to be happy. Change something, and his carefully balanced life might fall apart.

"Olive Kentworth, what have you gone and done?"

Olive dropped her straightedge and hurried to the front door at the sound of her cousin's voice coming up the walk. It was definitely Amos, and his voice carried like a shift-change whistle on the Fox-Berry Mine.

She opened the door. "I don't know what you're talking about, but come inside before the whole neighborhood finds out." Particularly Mr. Scott. She'd noticed him walking by occasionally. No telling what he'd think about her feral cousin raising a ruckus on the street.

Amos came inside and pulled the armchair away from the wall before dropping himself into it. "Girl, we aimed for the moon, and we hit it."

Olive crossed her arms over her chest. "Are you going to tell me what it is I'm supposed to have done, or continue with the riddles?"

Giving up a chance to annoy wasn't an easy decision for Amos. Olive turned to go to the kitchen, and he relented.

"Fine, it has to do with Mr. Blount. He sent a telegraph for me to come to his office. I went thinking he was likely to extol me for doing so fine a job on the cave tours, or something, but instead he blindsides me with plans for an addition to his house."

Olive's knees shook. She dropped into a chair. "Go on."

"He has me meet him in his high-dollar office at the mine and shoves some papers my way. Now, right from the get-go, I recognize your work. These are your papers, but he thinks they're mine."

"What did he say?"

"He said he wanted me to build the addition to his house."

Olive couldn't stay seated. She paced the room like a caged animal. "He liked the design?"

"He went on about giving instructions to builders, and they all came back with the same ideas, but I'd come up with something original. What's crazy is that I have no idea what he's talking about. What design? What plans?"

She'd done it. She had another project to work on. Only this time, instead of sketching plans that family members decided to work with, her design had won out over others. She'd been chosen. Or rather Amos had been chosen.

She took another look at her cousin, who reeked of orneriness and arrogance. Why had she thought that he was a fitting representative? Because he was the only one reckless enough to try it.

Olive grabbed a notebook and dropped on the sofa next to Amos. She flipped through her copy of the design and held a page open in front of him. "Does this look familiar?"

"Sure it does. That's what Mr. Blount showed me." He still wore his chaps from the farm and his boots smelled of manure.

"What did he say about it? Were there changes he wanted?"

"I reckon. He pointed at different things and said, 'This wall here,' and 'windows altered,' and 'Mrs. Blount prefers.'"

Her heart was going to tucker out. "What wall? Can you show me where he was pointing?"

"I was so caught unawares that I didn't have my wits about me."

"You didn't take any notes or anything?"

"Mr. Blount noticed that right off. He said he was impressed that I could retain all the alterations without putting it to paper."

"Did you retain it?"

He grinned. "Not a lick."

This would never do. On her two earlier projects, Olive had worked with her cousins and their husbands. She could talk to them about the plans and still send Amos to the construction site to work with Mr. Flowers and his workers. No one besides family knew she was the brain behind the project. The rest of town saw Amos. But Amos had never been involved in the actual planning of the project.

"Those sketches, they weren't the actual plans. I need measurements. I need specifics. I have to get inside and see the structure that's already there so I can know how to tie into it. And most importantly, I need to know what changes Blount wanted."

"I'd be glad to step aside and let you do this if you're going to get all picky."

"You have to help me."

He stretched his arms up and laced his fingers behind his head. "Being in high demand sure takes its toll on a body."

Olive was too worked into knots over a new sketch to mess with Amos. "I could redraw this with what I think he'll want, and you take it back and pay close attention this time . . ." No, that wouldn't work. It'd be a shot in the dark for the adjustments, and there was no guarantee that Amos would come back with better information than he did last time. Besides, it was too early in the project. If Mr. Blount got nervous or questioned Amos's skills, he might change his mind.

For a brief second, Olive imagined what it would be like to walk into Mr. Blount's office on her own and tell him that the plans he'd approved were her plans. The ease of not having to work through an imperfect vessel like Amos would be incredible. The embarrassment if she got something wrong, mortifying.

Fortune had smiled on her. She wouldn't push her luck. If things went wrong, which they surely would, then Amos wouldn't feel ashamed. He had nothing to lose. He'd go back to the farm and feel accomplished for having fooled people for as long as he had. Olive, on the other hand, would be crushed. So let Amos be the lightning rod. Let him attract the praise and the criticism. She wanted neither. But she did want the project to be successful, and they had to come up with a plan for that to be a possibility.

"I need accurate plans," she said. "I need to get in his house." Olive couldn't trust Amos to give her an accurate description of the construction. And if Blount would come too, maybe she could listen in without seeming too suspicious.

"I can get you in his house. I can jimmy a lock if no one's home."

"We are not breaking in. You're going to make an appointment to see the house. I'll go along and we'll tell them I'm there because . . . because . . . Oh, come on, Amos. Making up ridiculous excuses is your domain."

"You have to come with me to write down what I say. I'll strut around like an important architect, and I'll say whatever gibberish happens to come to mind, but you can write down what you need." If there was one thing Amos was serious about, it was being ornery. He gave pranks his best effort.

"That's not a bad idea. I'll come as the secretary, but the notes we use will be mine." Then she could hear the actual discussion going on as well. But no one would suspect that she was the one doing it. It'd be the best of both worlds, as long as her luck held out.

CHAPTER

8

It wasn't as if Olive had to worry about how to dress. Her wardrobe ran the gamut of uninteresting and dull to uninteresting and out-of-date. One cotton shirtwaist and a dark skirt was as good as the other.

When it came to picking which sketchbook she would carry, that's where distinctions had to be made.

This was a new project. A parable about old wineskins and new wine had her looking for a crisp, fresh sketchbook. You didn't commence on a new project with a sketchbook that had already been tainted by her aimless doodling. This was for real, and it deserved a professional start. After she wrote her notes on-site, she'd come back and create some real blueprints with the paper she'd been saving for legitimate projects like this one, but this book was important too.

After rejecting various crumpled sketchbooks, she found three that were untouched. One was tightly bound, which would require her to break the spine before it would lie flat. The other two were held together with staples, which would make for ease of drawing on the flat surface. Neither had lined paper and both covers were embossed. One cover was the red leather of law books and medical tomes. The other was green with leaves imprinted.

Leaves like an olive tree? Holding the journal in both hands and pressing it against her chin, she gathered her thoughts. Mr. Blount would pay scant attention to her. As the daughter of his manager, he knew her and had never shown more than minimal interest in her. As Amos's assistant, she wouldn't be expected to present anything. She grabbed the nicest gloves she had and her bonnet, then scurried out the door toward the Blounts' house.

Normally her path would've taken her past Mr. Scott's house, so she'd altered it. The less he saw of her coming and going from Blount's, the better. It seemed like he saw an awful lot of her as it was. She'd continued watching Leo and Stella a couple nights a week, enjoying the time with them but also making the most of her time alone with Mr. Scott's library. If Olive wasn't mistaken, Mr. Scott didn't stay out as late as he used to. Not only that, but he was never in a hurry to take her home once he'd returned. Less time with his ladylove meant less time that Olive had with his books, and now, with a project before her, her study had become urgent.

She grew more nervous as she approached Mr. Blount's street, unsure of what awaited her. If there were two men in Joplin more unpredictable than Mr. Blount and Amos, she'd yet to meet them. Trying to calm her nerves, she didn't see Mr. Scott until he called her name.

"Miss Kentworth? What brings you to this neighborhood?"

Olive blinked at the crew with horses pulling down a rotting sycamore in an empty lot. Maxfield Scott was supposed to be busy building James Dennis's house. She hadn't expected him to be at this lot, but here he was, jogging out to the street to meet her.

"I . . ." She caught herself checking the sketchbook in her hands, wondering what he could see. "I was on my way to meet my cousin." She tried to smile, forcing her mouth to stretch that way.

His smile was unencumbered. "The builder?" he asked.

"I have a lot of cousins," she answered, then nodded to the building site. "Is this a new project of yours?"

"No, I just came by to see what was going in. It's going to be a nice—"

"Miss Kentworth." Olive turned to see Dr. Stevenson, her mother's doctor, waving as he approached with his medical bag in hand. "It's good to see you out, dear. How are you faring?"

Olive winced at his concerned tone, which wasn't lost on Mr. Scott.

Mr. Scott's smile vanished. "I'm sorry, have you been unwell?" he asked.

"I'm never sick," she answered. Not her, but sickness had left its scars, just the same.

⸙

You never knew what a day would bring. Maxfield hadn't expected to see Miss Kentworth today, but he was pleased to encounter her on the street. He couldn't help the nervous tightening across his chest as she approached the lot being cleared, but he'd intercepted her before she'd come near harm's way.

Now that they were a safe distance away, he was free to notice her insecurities instead of battling his own. Who was this man with the doctor's bag, and what was it about Miss Kentworth that had him so concerned?

"My father and I are doing well." Her strained tone surprised Maxfield. He'd never heard his nanny speak so curtly. "I'll tell Father you send your regards."

If the doctor was taken aback, his reaction seemed cloaked in compassion. "Naturally," he said. "Tell him that I miss our visits, even if they were under sorrowful circumstances. But it's good to see you out and about. I guess there was no need for me to worry about you after all."

Olive's mouth tightened. Just when Maxfield expected her to

79

withdraw, she laid a gentle hand on the doctor's arm. "We appreciate all your efforts. I know you did all you could do."

The doctor's face softened. "Thank you, Olive. Enjoy the rest
of your day." His eyes flickered to Maxfield, then back to her. "And
enjoy the rest of your life."

With a tip of his hat, he left the two of them on the sidewalk.
Miss Kentworth fidgeted with her notebook. She turned as
if to follow the doctor's path, then spun to face the way she'd
come. When with his children, she was the epitome of maturity
and decorum. Now she was acting like Stella when she couldn't
settle down. He didn't think Miss Kentworth would allow a lul-
laby while being rocked in the rocking chair, so he offered the
next best thing.

"Would you like me to accompany you?" he asked, already de-
termining that it was exactly what he wanted.

"No. I'm going that way." She motioned toward the doctor's
path, still hesitant to follow him too closely.

"I see." Maxfield saw a lot, but he wished he understood more.
"So you've never been sick, but . . ."

"Tell me about the house that's going here." She looked past
him at the men working, her face calm, poised, and not revealing
anything more.

"My draftsman talked to the builder. It's to be an Italianate
residence. Marble, porticoes, and a fountain. All the elements required." He was preparing to tell her what color it would be, which
was usually what ladies primarily wanted to know, when she asked
him something else,

"How will it be situated on the lot?"

She'd stepped around him, before he'd recovered from the unexpected question. Taking her arm to prevent her from going any
closer to the men at work, he drew her across the street.

"I'm not sure, but I can tell you how I would do it," he said as
they took to the neighbor's yard across the street. "I would leave
the trees in the back. They'd make a good start for the landscaping

behind the house. Then I'd have the floor plan wrap around that dogwood in the front, but I'd have the rest removed or replaced."

He watched her closely, wondering if she really was interested. Obviously she was trying to distract him from asking about the doctor. Maybe her business with the doctor was none of his, but Maxfield felt a tug of kinship. No wonder he found her so interesting. She might be as skilled at diversion as he.

The last thing Olive wanted was for Amos to speak to Mr. Blount without her. While the project Mr. Scott was describing interested her, she had her own project to commence. There was no time to waste on Dr. Stevenson's compassion or on Mr. Scott's curiosity.

She tried to keep the conversation on benign topics until Dr. Stevenson had cleared away and she could walk unobserved.

"I'm sure it'll be fascinating once it's built," she said. "What type of marble did you say they were using?"

He raised an eyebrow. "It's going to be tan with gold stripes. It's mined in Missouri, and—"

"St. Genevieve's? Gold vein, I suppose."

"Actually you are correct. How are you familiar with different types of marble?"

And she'd thought she was keeping to benign topics.

"I read a lot." She shrugged. "It was nice visiting with you, Mr. Scott, but my cousin is waiting."

"We'll talk again soon. Actually I might need your help tonight. Are you available?"

"Yes. Tonight." Olive bit the inside of her cheek. Not tonight. She'd have all kinds of work to do, but she'd already agreed to it.

"Until then." He stood between her and the empty lot as if ready to intercept her if she walked toward it.

But she wasn't inspecting the lot. She had her own lot to worry about.

By the time Olive reached the Blount home, Amos was there

waiting. He'd washed up for the occasion, his tawny hair combed back and his cheeks flush with a recent scrubbing. He'd ridden in from the farm and had tied his horse to the birdbath in the front garden.

"You think that birdbath is strong enough to hold your horse? If it gets a notion to leave, it's taking that thing with it," Olive said.

"You reckon?" Amos walked to the stone birdbath and without a by-your-leave gave it a strong shove. The heavy bowl atop the pedestal got to tipping, and then gravity did its part. Seeing the bowl toppling, Amos's horse shied backwards, and as it did, it pulled the pedestal over onto the peonies, smashing the landscaping.

Olive winced as Amos sprinted to the horse's side to grab the reins and calm it.

"Welp, that was unfortunate," he said. "But who could've seen it coming?"

She could. She had. And the fact that Amos didn't was the reason that their plan would never work.

The front door opened. Mr. Blount's face screwed up in annoyance. "What in the Sam Hill happened to the missus's birdbath?"

As determined as Olive was to be the silent partner, she was used to being the more responsible of the cousins. But before she could apologize, Amos spoke.

"Mr. Blount, that birdbath was a hazard. I've never seen anything so poorly constructed. It's a wonder that it hadn't fallen on a guest ere this. I'll tell you what, when I build you something, it's not going to be rickety like that."

Olive rocked back on her heels. Amos had copious experience in talking his way out of situations. That was the one thing he excelled at. In these instances, she should let him ply his craft.

Mr. Blount had changed his tune. "It didn't frighten you, did it, Miss Kentworth?"

"No, sir. I was well out of the way but thank you for your inquiry."

"Then I guess no harm done. I'll add the construction of a new birdbath to the list of changes." He turned, then called over his shoulder, "Come inside."

Forgetting Olive, Amos followed right behind him. They should've met somewhere else first, where they could've gone over their plans together. Ignoring the beautiful wrapped porch that Mr. Scott had designed, she hurried along. More than likely, it wouldn't have mattered anyway. Amos would do what Amos would do. He would be just as surprised as she was when it happened.

"Here's the room I want extended." Blount stopped in a parlor on the west side of the house. "There's space on the lawn for it to be here, and this room isn't anyone's favorite. In fact, it's only used for the staircase. If I remember your plans, you wanted to turn this into a living hall, and I'd like to hear more about that."

Settling in on a footstool, Olive sketched the room as quickly and accurately as she could, while still keeping an ear open to what Mr. Blount was saying.

"It's not that I don't like this room, it's just that I need more space. I liked the idea on your sketch. Show me how you would change this room to make the new room look like it belongs."

Olive drew in a strong breath. With her eyes wide and directed at Amos, she willed him to look her way. The doorway to the new parlor should be where the left window was currently situated, but Amos was headed straight for the corner of the room. Olive cleared her throat. Amos looked at the floor as if the instructions were marked there instead of at her, who was trying to communicate with him.

"I'd fancy a door somewhere out of the way," he said. "It'd be best if it was around here." He'd nearly walked himself into a corner. It wasn't until he turned to Mr. Blount that he caught sight of Olive waving her hand in warning.

He took a big step sideways. "Or maybe it would look better here?"

Olive pointed her finger to the left. Amos narrowed his eyes. He wasn't much on reading, but surely he could read that sign?

She took both hands and, holding them horizontally, mimicked a windowpane opening and closing.

His eyes lit with understanding. "Here! Here, where the window is." He squared his shoulders and stood in the passageway.

"And could we put a fireplace along this wall?" Mr. Blount asked. "I don't remember if there was one on your proposal."

"I don't remember either," Amos laughed.

There wasn't. Olive looked the room over and tried to remember the second story. What was above this room? Would a chimney be obtrusive upstairs? She wrote her questions in the margin, then blocked in a fireplace. A door didn't need to be in the corner, but it was a good place for a fireplace, where it would cause the smallest annoyance upstairs. Set diagonally in the corner. She'd come back and perfect it later, but while she was here and they were busy, she wanted to get the basics on paper.

"Hey, Olive, did you get that written down?" Amos asked.

Olive lifted her head. The two men were watching her. "Get what written down?" she choked out.

"I'd like some Leghorn design in the spindle work here and some Dominique brick around these windows."

"Leghorn design and Dominique brick?" She tapped her pencil. "Got it." Obviously Mr. Blount had never raised chickens, or he'd wonder if Amos was turning his parlor into a hen house because, instead of architectural terms, Amos was bluffing with agricultural ones.

"And let's plan for an Angora-shaped window with a door that has Spanish Billy accents."

Now, he'd gone on to goat breeds. Olive needed to intervene. "I'm not sure what to write about that," she said. "Mr. Blount, could you explain in a way that's easier for me to understand? What exactly is it that you want in here?"

"I want it bigger," he said. "Amos's design mentioned a dark study in the center of the house that was reminiscent of a European great hall. I think that's a splendid idea. As for what the new room is, I don't have any idea. Since we're taking out a parlor, we should probably make the new room into another parlor, don't you think?"

Amos nodded. "Let's go outside and see what we're working with there."

"Certainly, but I hate to leave Miss Kentworth without entertainment."

Olive rose to her feet. "I'll go with—"

"Minnie, you have a guest," Blount bellowed.

No, she wasn't a guest. She had work to do. Olive flashed a warning at Amos.

"Actually my cousin is assisting me." He laced his fingers together and spun his thumbs. What was that? An imitation of an educated man?

Olive had to speak up or she'd be left out of the discussion. Remembering her father's challenge to be brave, she stretched her spine to its furthest limit and addressed Mr. Blount. "I play an integral part in Amos's work. It's important for me to hear exactly what it is that you're asking for."

But instead of showing any surprise at her demand, he ignored it. "Minnie, this here little lady is Oscar Kentworth's daughter. She's tagging along with her cousin. He's the one doing our house addition."

Mrs. Blount stepped into the room, dressed for a day on the town. "I had planned to go to the market," she said, but with another look at Olive, she changed her tune. "Please have a seat, I'll hurry back with some lemonade."

Olive sat. Her attempt to claim respect for herself had failed miserably. She was being left behind, but at least Mrs. Blount wasn't poor company. Despite her fine dress, Mrs. Blount reminded Olive of her Aunt June. Olive's father had told her that the Blounts came to Joplin around ten years ago, as broke as an eggshell in a throwing contest. One discovery of ore had led to all the riches they could ever imagine. Mr. Blount might be competitive and aggressive, but her father respected the man, and his wife seemed of the reasonable sort.

Amos followed Mr. Blount to the back of the house, leaving Olive with nothing to do except return to her seat on the footstool and finish her sketch of the room. Before they left, she'd have Amos take her to look around the garden. Hopefully he could remember everything Mr. Blount had said, and not dig them in too deep of a hole with his baseless promises.

"Here you go." Mrs. Blount handed Olive a glass and set her own on the floor. She went to an armchair next to the staircase and slid it over so she could sit closer to Olive. "How did you get the job with your cousin? Does architecture interest you, or are you only helping him out?"

Olive had been concerned with exposing her charade to Mr. Blount, but Mrs. Blount's first question had struck to the heart of their deception. She wasn't sure how to answer.

"It's fascinating, no doubt, but I'm sure he could find someone more capable than me if he searched." She slid her hand over the sketch on her notebook.

"My friend Matilda Weymann helped design her house over on Sergeant Avenue, so it's not unheard of for a woman to assist an architect."

But maybe for a woman to be an architect?

"You have a lovely house," Olive said. "I'm surprised Mr. Blount wants it changed."

"It is lovely, isn't it?" Mrs. Blount's mouth tightened as her eyes roved from the staircase behind them, to the massive beams overhead, and the glowing light that filtered through the windows. "It was designed and built by Maxfield Scott. He's the best, and Clydell wants nothing short of the best, which is why I don't understand having it changed."

"I wondered the same thing," Olive admitted.

"I'm not saying your cousin Amos isn't talented, but he has no education to speak of. Didn't train abroad. In fact, when I eavesdrop on him, it doesn't seem like he knows what he's talking about at all."

Olive had to agree, even though most of the description applied to her as well. "I think your house is lovely, but when Amos heard that your husband wanted to change it, there was one area he thought he could improve upon."

"That's what Clydell said, but I'm not convinced. He gets an itch to change for the sake of change, and I get dragged along with it." She looked into her lemonade. "When life gives you lemons . . ."

If she was smart, Olive would sit and commiserate with Mrs. Blount about the unfairness of men who spent their days at an office designing a house that they were too busy to rest in. If she was careful, she'd ask Mrs. Blount who she used as a dressmaker and where the inspiration for her gown came from. But Olive Kentworth had a daring streak that years of safety, dread, and protection hadn't quite been able to extinguish.

Flipping her notebook open to a blank page, she asked Mrs. Blount, "If you had a say in the design of the new addition, what improvements would you want?"

And she smiled as the lady shared her vision.

CHAPTER

9

Back home, Olive mused over the outcome of her serendipitous encounter with Mrs. Blount. The living hall plans that had captured Mr. Blount's imagination and secured the project for her would remain largely unchanged. Olive had been able to steer Mrs. Blount away from alterations to that, but the parlor he was tacking on would be another matter altogether. A ladies' parlor, they were calling it, full of large windows, light-colored wallpaper instead of heavy woodwork, and sheer drapes instead of brocade. Let the men retire to the living hall with exposed timbers and taxidermy. The ladies would have more delicate furnishings that they could arrange to enjoy the sun coming through the windows or to appreciate the view of the rose garden. It would be beautiful, and at least one of the inhabitants would like it.

Now that she had a specific design and measurements—Mrs. Blount had been most helpful in holding the measuring tape as they worked their way through the room—it was time to make a list of materials, estimate the cost, and enlist Mr. Flowers and his construction crew.

But not tonight, because she'd inadvertently committed to staying with the Scott children. Olive packed her notebooks, along with a few children's books in case she was ever questioned about the contents of her bag, and headed to the front door.

"You're working for Mr. Scott again tonight?" Her father lowered his newspaper.

"I'm either working on Mr. Blount's plans or I'm with Leo and Stella. You wanted me to be busy. I'd say you got what you wanted."

"And you've never been happier." His grin was contagious. "Admit it. Every morning you wake up looking forward to your work."

"Every morning I wake up scared to death that I'm going to make a mistake. I wonder how I'm going to get everything done, how I'm going to work without Mr. Blount knowing, and how I'm going to keep Amos under control. It's a lot of stress."

"But you don't regret it, do you? You're looking to the future, anticipating seeing your creation standing before you. The work is something you need."

He was right—she couldn't deny it. "As long as no one knows, then yes, you are right. I do enjoy the work. And I have another job I enjoy that I'd better get to. Don't want to make Mr. Scott late for his engagement."

At least Leo and Stella's bedtime was early. After dinner and baths, she could work on her estimate, although the time wouldn't be long. Some nights it seemed that Mr. Scott spent more time visiting with her than he spent away from the house, although he was taking his lady friend out more often. Olive had yet to meet her, but she could only imagine how sophisticated and knowledgeable she must be. Probably she sat around spellbound as he talked about his experiences and projects. Olive was jealous, but she knew there were some things you didn't even hope for.

When the sidewalk turned onto Mr. Scott's street, Olive was surprised to realize she was no longer nervous. Instead, she was eager to see the children's cheerful faces. Playing with Leo and cuddling with Stella was a break from the enormity of what she was trying to accomplish. She knocked, but she didn't expect Mr. Scott to open the door wearing his checked cassimere vest without a suit coat or tie.

"I'm sorry," she said. "Am I early?"

"Not at all. Come on in." He stepped aside to let her pass. "How's your father doing?"

Always the gentleman, was Maxfield Scott. Why he bothered charming his help, she couldn't guess. Unfortunately, no one was below his notice, and she was doing things she didn't want him to notice.

"He's doing well, thank you," and then because she felt like she should have some polite inquiry in return, "How is your work on the Dennis house?"

She tensed as she waited for his reply. Was that too much? Should she pretend to have no interest in his work? If she wasn't doing architecture, would she have asked that?

"It's coming along nicely. Soon I'll be ready to turn it over to the family to decorate and furnish, and in the meantime, I'm drafting a new design that's opened for bids."

"Which is?"

"Which is the reason we've got a change of plans tonight." He had leaned against the wall with one leg crossed over the other—an informal stance that showed no sign of urgency to see his love. "Peter Christman has asked me to make plans for a department store downtown. Since I'm working the residential projects during the day . . ."

Olive pulled her book bag hard against her side. "Then you don't need me. That's not a problem. I'll go home. I don't mind."

"No, I still need you." His languid pose hadn't changed, and he seemed to take it for a fact that she wanted to be needed.

She did, and especially by him, but there were practical considerations.

"What could I do to help?" Had he learned her secret? Did he suspect? Had Amos talked, or Mrs. Blount?

"The same thing you always do. Fix dinner, bathe the children, and entertain them while I get some much-needed work done."

"Oh, I see." She adjusted the strap of the book bag so it wasn't cutting into her shoulder. "You're going to your office?"

"I've spent enough time in the office. What I'd like is a dinner in my own kitchen and then to sit in my favorite chair in the library and work from there."

This was unexpected and unwelcome. Practically, Olive had planned to do her own work, and that would be impossible with Mr. Scott underfoot all evening. On the other hand, she was becoming increasingly reliant on his library. And those nuggets of wisdom he threw out about design and construction when he walked her home of the evening were worth her time.

She'd stay out of sight, busy herself with the children, and leave as soon as they were asleep. Their stroll home would give her an opportunity to ask about this department store he was building. Not ideal, but she was looking for a silver lining.

"While you're thinking it over, I'll check on the chops. Mrs. Wester put dinner in the oven before she left, and I picked up some rolls from the bakery. I work better after a good meal." He sauntered out of the room, leaving her to find a place to stash her bag. He said he was going to work in the library, so she wouldn't leave her notebooks hidden in there. Maybe they'd be safer by the front door. Olive set the heavy bag next to the parlor palm and pushed it with her foot until it was hidden behind the Chinese planter.

She had only been coming to the Scott house for a month, but there was already a noticeable change. Early in her employment, she'd gotten the impression that Mr. Scott was loath to stay home—that he was anxious to be out and about—but lately he'd taken to lingering more and more, and that was not in her plans.

"Miss Kentworth, I heared you." If everyone acted as delighted to see her as Leo did, she'd get out more often.

Olive grabbed him around the waist and swung him nearly upside down. "I didn't heared you. You are as quiet as a Bengal tiger sneaking through the Indian forest and jumping out to scare me."

Leo squirmed and laughed as she kept his feet off the ground. In another year, she wouldn't be able to handle him like this, but it was fun. Never having a little brother, Olive marveled at how much the physical roughhousing meant to the boy. And then there was Stella. Running to Olive, she grabbed her around the knees.

"Up, up, up." She pounded on Olive's skirt with her soft fists.

Careful to not let Leo kick Stella in the head, Olive switched Leo beneath one arm, then picked Stella up with the other arm. Although she always acted like she wanted to wrestle, Stella rarely kept up the act for long, preferring to be cuddled, causing Olive to wonder once again whether Mrs. Wester, their nursemaid during the day, gave them enough affection.

And what about Miss Dennis, Mr. Scott's beloved? Would she make a suitable mother for the children?

Enough of that. It was none of her business. Olive's musing would only breed discontent and covetousness. She wasn't Maisie to have her head turned by a handsome man or Willow to think a rich man would want a poor girl for a wife. She was satisfied. All she wanted out of life was to live quietly, be secure, and see her imagined creations constructed in real life. Was that too much?

But hearing children squeal with joy when they saw her was another blessing she hadn't expected.

"What did you do today?" she asked as she set them down. "Did you play outside? You smell like sunshine and sweat."

"We rode our hobbyhorses. Stella can't do it. She slings it around like this . . ." Leo waved his hand through the air. "She hit me on the head, right here." He pointed to a red welt near the corner of his eye.

"Let me give it love." Olive bent and placed a kiss on the owie.

"I didn't cry." He puffed his chest out before spinning and running to the kitchen. "I'm thirsty."

"Let's see if your daddy is still in the kitchen," she said, and took Stella's hand. Olive braced herself. While she felt very comfortable in this home with Leo and Stella, Mr. Scott's presence changed everything. They passed through the dining room, and she saw that the door to the library was closed. The kitchen was empty. A quick peek in the oven showed that the chops were nearly done.

Olive opened the cabinet door, took Leo's tin cup down, and filled it with water. There wasn't much preparation needed for supper. Stella had opened the cabinet door already and pulled out the metal measuring cups that Olive let her play with while she was cooking. Mr. Scott had said he'd gone to the bakery, but she didn't see any dessert. For some reason, she wanted him to see how busy she was and what good care she took with his children. Having them help her bake would keep them all busy and away from him.

"Can you help me make some sweets?"

Stella's eyes shone. "I can help," she said, while Leo showed his enthusiasm by jumping up and cheering.

What to make? Olive dug through the shelves and pantry, looking for inspiration. That's when she saw the loaf of bread. Upon inspection it was a little stiff and starting to go stale. "Do you have raisins? Yes, perfect. We'll make bread-and-butter pudding." A quick look at the spices in the pantry showed that either someone kept them stocked or no one had used them in years. Whichever it was, she had the ingredients on hand, and set Stella and Leo to ripping up pieces of bread and tossing them into a square baking dish.

He was in the library right now, designing a building out of thin air. Soon it would be something you could see on paper, and someday something you could touch with your hand. Something strong enough to protect its occupants from the elements. She felt good that she was contributing to his work. A partner, even if he didn't realize how well she could fill that role.

They had the bread torn into pieces. Stella's pieces were more wadded up than torn, but they would taste the same. Leo knew the basics of silverware placement, and soon the dining room table was set and dinner was ready with the dessert in the oven.

"Mmm . . . smells good." Mr. Scott walked in and picked up Stella. "Did you help?"

Olive looked at the table, embarrassed to see that she'd only set the table for three. "I'm sorry. I forgot. . . ."

Mr. Scott noticed too. "I can take my plate to the library . . . ?" He was so accommodating, so solicitous, that she almost missed the question in the statement.

"Please join us. The children. They'll want you at the table." Why did every second seem measured by her heartbeat? When it was just her and the children, the time flew. Having him underfoot made her jittery, second-guessing her every move.

"Since you insist." He got himself a plate and silverware and took his seat at the head of the table after Olive had seated herself. He hesitated, looking at each of his children. Leo clasped his hands and bowed his head. Mr. Scott caught her gaze with an almost apologetic expression.

"I'll say grace," he said.

His words were simple and earnest. Olive felt the tension in her shoulders lessen. He was a doting father and a conscientious host. With all his fine attributes, he wouldn't concern himself with her. Most people didn't notice her, anyway. Even if he learned that she was reading his material, he would know that she was no threat to his work. Her value watching the children would surely outweigh any annoyance at her dabbling in his industry. At least she hoped so.

"Thank you for allowing me to join you," he said with a wink at Stella. "I find the company in the kitchen superior to the potted plant in the library."

"Plants don't talk," Leo laughed.

"Oh yes they do. You just don't listen closely enough," he said. "Just now Ferny was telling me that he was thirsty. That Mrs. Wester forgot to water him this week."

Leo's face stretched in amazement while Stella screwed up her face with laughter. "Plants not drink," she giggled. "Her drink." She pointed at Olive.

"Miss Kentworth, have you been drinking in front of my children?" Mr. Scott asked, his eyes wide with feigned shock.

Olive inhaled, trying to decide whether to defend herself or laugh at the ridiculousness of his question, but her sudden gasp sent a piece of pork chop down her windpipe. The instant pain told her it'd lodged. She covered her mouth and stood to leave the room before she embarrassed herself with her choking. It was then she realized that she couldn't cough. She couldn't make a sound. Her feet seemed to move on their own, but with all her heaving, she couldn't budge the morsel.

Oh no. Just when Olive convinced herself that she could be unobtrusive and unobserved. She stumbled into the parlor and paced, pounding on her chest, to no avail. She could hear Leo asking about her and Mr. Scott telling him to eat his dinner. He didn't know the trouble she was in, but she'd rather die than have him see her in this distress. No air passed through her throat, not even enough to make a squeak. That would be just like her, dying without even a squeak.

Without intervention, dying was a possibility. Olive only hoped she didn't look horrible. She passed in front of a mirror and her appearance scared her. Her eyes looked wild, her face was cast with a tint of blue. She was seeing bright stars now. Maybe she should write a last note to her father, or maybe lie down and smooth her skirt so as not to scare the children when they saw her.

She heard him, felt him, enter the room. She couldn't make out his face, only the swiftness of his movements. He took one of her arms and yanked it upward. He was saying words calmly, but his actions were decisive. The first strike between her shoulder blades shocked her. Had he not had her by the arm, she would've slammed into the floor. Again her diaphragm tried to expand, but to no avail. The next strike nearly broke her in two. Was he trying to kill her? Her knees gave way, but as she fell, she was able to get a thin, searing gulp of air past the obstruction.

"That's right," he whispered. "Spit it out. Spit it out on the floor."

The little bit of air was in danger of being snuffed out again. He bent her forward and this time pounded her back rhythmically like he was burping a baby, although it was a wonder that his children survived when he was capable of striking with such force.

"What are you doing, Daddy?" Leo called.

"Stay in the kitchen," he answered with an edge. "Don't leave the table."

The piece of meat was coming up. Mr. Scott held his handkerchief to her mouth. "Don't you dare try to swallow that. In my hand. Now."

Olive was humiliated, but disobedience wasn't an option. She coughed and spat and gagged and breathed. Tears were now streaming down her face. He tossed the handkerchief aside and eased her off her knees and into a sitting position on the floor. Her throat burned as she hauled in deep, life-giving breaths.

He kept a hand on her back, then moved it to her shoulder. He couldn't stay still but seemed determined to keep some contact with her as he fidgeted.

"Shhh . . . shhh . . ." Each soothing noise he made was breathed out in unison with her as they gradually slowed together.

"I'll be right back," he whispered with a squeeze to her shoulder, and then jogged to the dining room.

Olive wished she could disappear. If she had the strength, she would've run out the door to home. How did one recover? And the most terrifying part hadn't been when she couldn't cough, but afterward when her strong coughs had sounded like her mother's.

Tears were running again, but this time from past memories instead of the present. The feeling of suffocation was so paralyzing, so terrifying, and her mother had died a slow death from it. Olive pressed her fingers against her cheekbones. She had to compose herself. She wasn't home in her bedroom, she was in Maxfield Scott's parlor. She couldn't fall apart now.

His handsome face was etched with concern as he carried her drink across the parlor. He knelt in front of her and handed her the glass. It took effort to swallow that first gulp. She expected it to be refreshing, but it burned like firewater and threatened to gurgle back up. He passed her a clean napkin, but she shook her head and forced the drink down. Only after gauging her recovery did he make himself comfortable next to her, stretching his legs out before him.

"The children are fine," he said, looking straight ahead. "They aren't aware of anything unusual."

She nodded, still not trusting her voice. "Thank you," she mouthed. She took another drink, grateful for his company, and even more grateful that he kept his eyes on the kitchen door, instead of her.

"As soon as you're ready, I'll send for the doctor. I pray that I didn't hurt you, but we need to make sure. I can't have it on my conscience—"

"Don't summon a doctor," Olive rasped. "I'll be fine."

"I'd be surprised if you don't have some bruising, maybe something broken. I was desperate, and considering your size, it'd be better—"

"No, please. I'm fine. I'll be sore, but I'd rather not worry the children."

"My apologies."

Olive gripped his forearm. Her words were slow coming, but necessary. "You saved me. Don't apologize."

At first she wondered if he understood what she'd said. His brow wrinkled and his face blanked as he said, "At least I accomplished one good thing in my life." Then, with a suddenness that startled her, he pulled her hard against him, pressed a firm kiss to her forehead, then returned to the kitchen.

The threat that another woman in his care could perish needlessly had almost undone Max. He'd thought that he'd offended her when she'd left the room after his tasteless joke. That had concerned him. Walking into the parlor, he'd been prepared to apologize, but when he saw her distress, fear had overwhelmed him. Ever since then, he hadn't stopped praying, but his prayers for help had turned to prayers of thanksgiving. Now, as he finished combing Stella's wet hair, the trembling in his fingers told him the drama of the ordeal was not yet behind him.

"There you go. All clean for bedtime," he said as Leo bounded onto Stella's little bed.

"Are you going to read us a story?" Leo crashed into Maxfield's shoulder and tumbled down his chest landing on top of Stella.

"Get under the covers on your own bed and I'll pick a book." With Miss Kentworth downstairs putting away the food, he didn't want to take too long. She might get impatient and go home on her own, but spending this time with his children was something he couldn't skip. Not after the scare that had raised so many painful memories.

As Leo jumped from Stella's bed to his own, accomplished with pride because he hadn't touched the floor, Maxfield reached for a slender book in the bookcase between the beds. First, he got Stella tucked in under her blankets, then scooted in next to her, putting up his feet and leaning his back against the wall so he'd be able to show both of them the pictures.

"*Chicken Little*," he began, as he flipped to the first page of his old children's book. When Max was little, he'd laughed just as Leo did about the acorn hitting Chicken Little on the head. What a silly bird to think that the whole world was ending just because an acorn had fallen.

But everyone believed Chicken Little. Henny Penny, Cocky Locky, Ducky Lucky, and Goosy Loosy were all convinced.

Stella laughed at each of the voices he created for the various comical characters. Maxfield felt his spirits ease as well. An acorn had caused all this trouble, but the world wasn't falling down. Everything would be fine. Tonight it hadn't been an acorn, it'd been a piece of meat that gave them a bad scare, but in the end, there'd been no harm done. In the end, Miss Kentworth and he were both fine.

His hands steadied as he recognized the irrationality of the fowls' fears. This had nothing to do with losing Georgia. Besides, Miss Kentworth was only the part-time nanny for the children. He shouldn't be this affected. She'd choked at the dinner table. It was a common occurrence with a simple remedy that he had performed speedily. So why could he not shake the dreadful thought that his life would be emptier without her?

Stella's eyelids were growing heavy. She'd stopped squirming and was cuddled up in a ball with her knees against him. Leo's laughs were growing huskier as Maxfield turned another page. The appearance of Foxy Coxy was where the story went from comical to didactic. Chicken Little and her friends' worry about the sky falling had blinded them to the danger that was stalking them. As the last of the friends were gobbled up, Chicken Little realized that she'd made a mistake and escaped.

Leo sighed contentedly. "I like that story, Daddy."

"You have a strange appreciation for literature." Maxfield eased off the bed, to not disturb sleeping Stella. He kissed her plump cheek before giving Leo a kiss in turn. "Your sky isn't falling," he said to Leo. "And there's no Foxy C."

The sky wasn't falling. It hadn't fallen, and Maxfield had the rest of the evening to work on a new project. The only thing that could interrupt him would be taking the time to walk Miss Kentworth home, but perhaps he didn't need to do that right away.

Instead of going into the kitchen where he knew she'd be, Maxfield went straight to his library. After pulling out the preliminary sketches he'd started, he spread a clean piece of paper across the drafting board. For the frontage, he'd sketched an Italianate roof with decorative cornices at the top. On the first floor, there'd be heavy Richardsonian arches made of local rock over all the entrances. Where this design differed from most of the commercial buildings in Joplin was that, instead of apartments or offices on the second floor, the second floor would consist only of small shopping areas along the exterior walls with the center being open to the ground floor below. This plan required a few supporting structures that wouldn't interfere with the openness that Mr. Christman was looking for.

Max picked up his straightedge and drafting pencil and sketched the dimensions of the building's footprint. He'd put small plain beams as supports—beams that wouldn't catch the eye—and scatter them throughout the showroom. Also, they would have a grand staircase in the center of the building. Hiding supports in that structure made sense and wouldn't be noticed. He'd love to find a way to have the support not be obvious. If there was a way, he'd disguise the staircase to look lighter than it was. A floating staircase that made people want to climb it and see what was upstairs. With a few swift strokes, he'd placed the staircase and was trying to determine how it would be supported.

Without realizing it, he'd had one ear tuned to Miss Kentworth's movements in the kitchen. Now he heard wisps of movement getting closer. Time to take her home? He glanced at the clock. It was early yet. The evening would stretch on for hours, silent besides the ticking of the clock. If the distraction of the quiet didn't interrupt his work, he might be productive. Or he might be more productive with company.

"How are you feeling, Miss Kentworth?" he asked as she stopped in the doorway. In the best of circumstances, she was more comfortable around the children than she was around him. Now she looked downright skittish.

"I'm fine. My throat is raw, but there's no damage done, I'm sure." Her voice was raspy and her neck showed strain as she swallowed. "Thank you for asking."

She waited in the doorway, leaning against one side as if clearing his way to the front door. Her blond hair was still ruffled from her earlier ordeal. Her eyes, having been recently filled with tears, were large and reflective, but she looked hardy enough, which was fortunate because he still had a task for her.

"If you don't mind, could I have some of your time?"

Putting on a brave face, she set her shoulders before nodding. "How can I help you?"

"I'm working on the design for this department store, and I wanted your opinion."

The look she gave him was hard to decipher—almost as if she were deciphering him. "How would my opinion help you?" she asked. "You've studied architecture in Europe. What would I know?"

He couldn't help the jolt of pride that she knew part of his résumé. Ruby and he often compared their time in Europe—the theaters visited, sights seen, ocean liners traveled on—but he didn't remember her ever acknowledging why he was there. She probably assumed he'd been there for a vacation like she had been.

"Since ladies are more likely to visit a department store, I thought it'd be helpful to have a lady's opinion."

Here her eyes shone with delight. With easy grace and surprising speed, she glided across the room. "What have you got so far?" She stood behind him and leaned forward to peer over his shoulder.

Maxfield usually didn't like people seeing his preliminary ideas, but these scratches would probably mean nothing to her. Still, it seemed to take her a long time to realize that what she was seeing was meaningless. He'd like to think she was trying to make sense of it. Trying really hard, because it was an eternity before she stepped to the side of the drafting board and smiled a sheepish smile at him.

"What's your question?" she asked.

No dancing around with Miss Kentworth. He'd asked her for help and that's what she was offering. She was so thoroughly practical that he couldn't help but be amused.

"When you are shopping, how much of the wares do you like to see at once? Do you want to enter and be able to immediately see the scope of the room, or would you rather wander through a maze-like path and be excited by discovery?"

She drummed her fingers against the board. Her eyes lifted to the ceiling. "Shopping? Well then, I suppose I like the secure feeling of aisles to get lost in." Her gaze fixed somewhere far away as if she were seeing herself there. "Discovery is the perfect word for it. I'm more comfortable taking in one section at a time. Seeing more can be overwhelming."

Maxfield didn't need to take notes. Once he learned something, he wouldn't forget. Since his clothes were sewn by a tailor and Mrs. Wester looked after the children's wardrobe, Maxfield hadn't spent much time in department stores. Miss Kentworth's insight was helpful.

"But along with narrow aisles come shadows," he said. "More lighting will be needed, which means more electric power. I'll have to make allowances for that. Also the airflow won't be as good. Fans from the ceiling would help in the summer."

"On the other hand," Miss Kentworth said, "while going on a journey through the store makes it a memorable event, if one already knows what they are looking for, then the needless delay would be frustrating. An open area would make shopping more efficient."

"But does my client, the retailer, want you to be efficient, or does he want you to linger among his wares? Isn't it in his interest to keep you wandering throughout his store?" Maxfield was trying to get a smile out of her, but instead she crossed her arms over her chest.

"Of all the manipulative nonsense," she huffed. "Father's celluloid collars are in the back of Herr's and every time I have to buy a new one, I have to walk past a rack of the most beautiful ribbons. I can't help but wonder over all the colors and the sheen. And every time I think, 'Why do they put the celluloid collars in the back of the store? Don't they know that they are more frequently purchased than ribbons?' And you're telling me that I've walked to the back of the store every month because they wanted to tempt me with the ribbons? That's outrageous."

Her full lips twisted to the side, and Max was enchanted. "Tempted, but have you ever given in?"

"I have ribbons at home that serve just fine," she said, "but the testing of my weakness rankles, just the same." Instead of outrage, now her eyes sparkled at her own folly. "I don't know how a story about ribbons is going to help you on your draft. I'm afraid I'm wasting your time."

"Quite the contrary." With pencil in hand, he started poking holes in the air between them. "What if you could see the section you were searching for from the front door, but you still had a pleasant walk through merchandise on the way there?"

"Signs hanging from the ceiling, perhaps? Wouldn't that interfere with the aesthetics?"

Max had to look again. For a moment, he'd forgotten that it was his children's nanny speaking. "Yes, and with the pressed tin ceiling, I wouldn't want anything covering it, so something more original and purposeful is required. What if there was a way to work the department identity into the permanent decor?"

"What do you have in mind?"

"Whatever it is, it mustn't block the open layout of the main floor. The view of the central staircase should be unobstructed."

Miss Kentworth scooted behind him again and angled herself so she could see the page from his perspective. Max felt a chill over his skin. Unlike Ruby, every move Miss Kentworth made was intentional. It raised his anticipation of what she had planned.

It took her bumping against his shoulder for him to push the draft higher on the board so she could view it better.

"Those are the support columns?" she asked.

"Ever since builders have been building with steel, support beams haven't been needed in the same quantity. It allows for a more open floor plan." He couldn't imagine boring Ruby with that information, but Miss Kentworth seemed genuinely interested. "That's why I can keep them narrow and unobtrusive."

"But without decorative columns, what's to keep this space from looking like one of the warehouses by the railroad docks? The room needs artistry and soul. What canvas are you using for that?"

"The ceiling and the electric lamps will be one venue for artistry, along with the staircase." For a man used to charming people, it was disconcerting to have a lady out of view as he was speaking. How was he to gauge her response?

"But all of that won't help shoppers find what they are looking for."

His chair moved slightly as she leaned against it. Why was it that he noticed her every move? Ruby flitted everywhere and he barely noticed. Maybe because things that are scarce are always more precious?

"What if you drew attention to the columns instead of minimizing them? Instead of merely being support, their design could reflect the department?"

"What do you mean?" Maybe she felt the same connection after the scare they'd shared that evening, because he couldn't imagine that she'd be interested in his work otherwise.

"It's probably a ridiculous suggestion, but maybe do the columns in the Corinthian style, but each capital at the top could have a different design. Instead of leaves, there'd be toys and butterflies for the children's section. Then a column with flowers and lace for the ladies. I don't know what you'd want shown to designate the gentlemen's department—snips and snails and puppy dog tails?" She stopped abruptly. The chair shifted again as she stepped away. "I'm rambling on, in front of you, of all people. It was fun to imagine with you, but it's just the blathering of the daughter of a mine operator."

Maxfield had to smile at her concern. True, people often thought they were helping by giving him fanciful ideas for designs and decor, but most of the time an odd notion didn't fit in with the overall design. A whimsical feature threw off the balance of the greater work. And the most common mistake was when people suggested features but had no understanding of the supports needed to construct them. One couldn't drop a fountain in the middle of a structure without considering the plumbing.

Olive's idea was a decent one, but he didn't feel obligated to humor her. She was too intelligent for flattery.

"In a perfect world where I had an unlimited budget to work with, I'd applaud the idea," he said, "but that would require that each column have an original design and be done by a craftsman. I don't think Mr. Christman will approve the expense."

She didn't argue or defend her idea. She merely shrugged and apologized that she wasn't more help. When she brushed the lock of hair off the back of her neck, he thought again about her choking and realized that she was due a break.

It wasn't until after he escorted her home, after Maxfield had wondered over the danger she'd been in, wondered over his role in saving her, and savored the evening they'd had together, that the thought occurred to him that her idea could work. If done correctly, the customized capitals would be the defining feature of the department store—one that people would make a special trip inside to see. And wasn't that what a retailer wanted? Austin Allen would probably borrow the idea and use it in Carthage, but everyone would know that it was Maxfield who had used it first. It might have been his untrained nanny who'd thought of the idea, but it would be Maxfield who was hailed as the genius who constructed it.

He was learning to value Miss Kentworth more with every encounter.

CHAPTER 10

Pulling her bonnet down tight on her head so she wouldn't be recognized, Olive walked the sidewalk that lined the Blounts' side yard. Amos had instructed his crew to remove the fence so they could get the materials in easily, but another benefit was that Olive could observe the work being done while looking like a pedestrian on a stroll.

And stroll by she did. Incessantly. The foundation was being dug and the siding on that side of the house was being dismantled. If the foreman, Mr. Flowers, guessed it was her calling the shots instead of Amos, he never revealed it. Even when she was standing in his office trying and failing to discreetly steer Amos toward the right answer, he kept his eyes resolutely on Amos, purposefully ignoring her. Whether he was doing her a favor or he was a misogynist mattered not. Olive could work with him, and he found ways to work around Amos's bad directives.

Olive stopped on this pass to watch all the activity. A trench was forming with each shovelful of dirt being tossed aside. Crowbars were plied against the cedar paneling, prying it off with protests of creaks and pops. Brick pavers were being pulled out of the dirt and set aside to be reused when the garden could be redesigned.

Mr. Blount hadn't thought twice about the changes that they'd put into the plans. According to Amos, he'd barely looked at what she and Mrs. Blount had decided, which raised many questions. Why would a man be so particular that he wanted to redo a Maxfield Scott design and yet not care what was built to replace it? It made no sense. Olive had to brace herself for the possibility that no matter how much thought she put into her design, in a few years he could be dissatisfied and want to tear it down as well. It'd break her heart to have her work destroyed, but at least she had an opportunity to build it in the first place.

Maybe her decorative columns in Mr. Scott's department store would have lasted longer. Olive stepped off the pavement to stand in the shade of the mimosa tree. What had she been thinking, offering Maxfield Scott advice? When he invited her to talk out his design, she'd panicked. What did he know? What did he suspect? But it soon became clear that he wanted the opinion of a lady, not another architect. That had been safe ground, although why she'd gone and started talking about columns and capitals, she couldn't fathom. The thing that she feared the most was him laughing at her aspirations to be an architect. The thing she desired the most was for him to see her work and approve of it. She was stuck between wishing and fearing the same discovery.

Tonight Mr. Scott was taking Miss Dennis to row at Lakeside Park. It'd been a week since he'd last asked for Olive's help with the children, and she'd worried that she'd overstepped her bounds with her opinion on his project. While she'd needed the time to look after her own work, she was relieved to hear from him again. Her plans on Blount's house might be completed, but she could learn things from Mr. Scott that would help her career in the future. That's why she looked forward to their time together—not because she found him fascinating.

She had to hurry, or she'd be late to his house. It was just so hard to drag herself away from work. With a sigh, she stepped back on the pavement, and that's when she saw Mr. Scott himself, standing at the corner with his jaw firm and uncompromising.

Quick as a hummingbird, Olive darted behind a tree and planned her escape.

What in the blazes? Maxfield couldn't believe his eyes. What was he seeing? He looked at the street sign once again to verify his location, but there could be no mistake. He knew the Blount house. He'd built it not five years ago, and it was being demolished.

His day had been filled with the satisfaction of seeing Mr. Dennis's house nearing completion. Every detail now was moving it closer and closer to the masterpiece he'd envisioned. Added to that was the very satisfying direction his plans for Christman's department store were taking. He'd been right to request Miss Kentworth's help last week. Just look at the breakthroughs he'd made with that one evening of uninterrupted work at home. He'd gotten so much accomplished that he'd taken Leo and Stella to the paddleboats at Lakeside Park last night, and tonight he was reliving the fun with Ruby. He'd hadn't been paying Ruby the attention she deserved lately and thought that he was in good enough spirits to entertain her this evening. Good enough spirits until he'd turned the corner and saw the unfolding tragedy before his eyes.

Maxfield stomped across the yard, tangling his foot in a wrought iron fence that had been laid on the ground. He shook himself loose, then found Mr. Flowers, who was undoubtedly the foreman on this project.

"What is going on here?" he demanded.

"Hey, Maxfield. It's a remodel. We're doing an addition."

"What needs adding?" Maxfield propped his fists against his waist and took in the beautiful balance of the building he'd created. "This design was perfection."

"Take it up with Mr. Blount," Flowers said. "I'm just following instructions." He directed a man with a wheelbarrow around the corner.

Mr. Blount. Why would he do this? He'd sung Maxfield's praises when the house was completed. What had gone wrong? If he wanted something changed, why wouldn't he have contacted Max?

Because Max would've told him that he was insane, and you couldn't improve on perfection. That's why Mr. Blount hadn't called him and wouldn't want to talk to him now.

"Who's the architect?" he asked Flowers.

"Amos Kentworth designed this. He's adding a lady's parlor."

Mr. Blount had never mentioned a lady's parlor to him. And who was Amos Kentworth? Where had he heard that name? Obviously it was some kin of his nanny's. Oh yes. The man who designed the Crystal Cave visitors' center. And then gave tours.

What was the world coming to?

"Is this Mr. Kentworth here?"

"No."

"Where's his office?"

"I don't think he has one. If he does, I've never been there."

Maxfield rubbed his forehead, trying to smooth out the knotted muscles beneath the skin. Ruby would be waiting for him. He didn't have time to explain the unexplainable. With his thanks to Mr. Flowers for the information, he headed home.

Before this, his week had been magical, but look how little it took to throw a man's balance out of whack.

He flung his front door open and called for the children. If anything could calm his roiling emotions, it was them. Leo hit his knees at full speed, but Stella came carried in the arms of Miss Kentworth.

"I hope you don't mind that I sent Mrs. Wester home. I didn't know how long you'd be, and she was anxious to leave." Miss Kentworth's fair face was flushed as if she'd run in the races.

Again Maxfield was hit with the strong emotion that had overcome him when Miss Kentworth had had her spell. He shook himself. He was planning an evening with Ruby. He couldn't second-guess his choice for a companion now.

"How inconvenient that Mrs. Wester has to have a family of her own." It'd been a weak attempt at humor, but he saw the pain cross Miss Kentworth's face. Did she yearn for a family? Again with the stray thoughts that served no purpose. Maxfield had to get control of his curiosity and his tongue.

"Thank you for relieving her. You made the right decision," he said. He reached for Stella, who dived into his arms.

"C'mon Leo," he said. "You two can help me get dressed. I'm taking Miss Dennis to the same place we went boating last night."

"I wanna go," Stella said.

"It's not your turn," Leo answered. The only way he'd not whine was if it gave him an excuse to correct his sister. "The boat isn't big enough for all of us."

There were boats that size, but Maxfield had already planned to have Miss Kentworth come over that night, and another trip to Lakeside Park gave him a reason to enlist her help.

And the builder on this project that was desecrating his design was a cousin of hers? Another complication in a relationship that was growing more complicated by the hour. Maxfield took the children upstairs with him to listen to their chatter while he dressed into something more casual. It'd be unchivalrous to hold Miss Kentworth accountable for her cousin's arrogance. He'd handle it man to man. In the meantime, he was running behind.

Pushing away his frustration, Max kept his focus on his children. He'd had so much fun with them the day before. Leo was growing out of his babyhood and becoming an astute child. Watching Leo try to match his pace, mimic his pose, filled Max with caution. Leo deserved the best. So did Stella. He was glad that he was spending more time with them, but he couldn't stay home every evening. The children went to bed early, and then what was he to do? A man with less imagination would reach for a bottle. Max was searching for escape, but he knew to avoid the pitfalls of oblivion. Instead, he chose to bury his pain with light, and fun, and entertainment, and Ruby.

And for now, with the joy his children brought him. After he'd cleaned up, he stopped by their room to help Stella dress her dolly and finish listening to Leo's intricate story of how he beat Mrs. Wester at jacks, even though she made him play on the table instead of the floor because her knees didn't allow her to get on the floor, and how the ball kept bouncing off the table and Leo had to crawl beneath it and get it.

Then it was time to go.

"Come downstairs and see me off," he said. Stella was proud of her ability to go on the stairs by herself, but he hovered at her side to prevent a fall just in case.

Did he hug them extra tight before he left them behind? Yes, he did. Miss Kentworth stood back against the balustrade to give him his time alone with his children. He checked himself at the desire to include her in the familial affection. Had he come to care for her? If so, it hadn't been intentional. Maxfield felt his jaw tighten. Was he becoming too skilled at denying his feelings? It was one thing to keep mourning at bay. Another thing to pretend he wasn't attracted . . .

. Attracted? How had he gone from familial affection to attraction?

Look at the time. Maxfield was too busy to ponder riddles.

"I'll be back late," he said to Miss Kentworth. "There'll be fireworks after dark."

"Yes, sir."

He looked twice, finding it funny that she was still *sirring* him after all their time together. "You can stay late? You don't have anything you need to leave for?"

"No. I can stay as late as required." Helpful as ever. Unflappable even though he was jittery.

112

"Your father won't be concerned?"

"As long as he knows I'm not walking home alone, he isn't inconvenienced." Her hair was flattened against her forehead as if she'd worn a bonnet much too small.

"And tomorrow? You wouldn't be too tired to go about your daily chores?"

Finally, he'd found a reaction. There was a concern about something that she might miss. "How late do you think you'll be?"

If he wasn't in such a foul mood, he might have assured her that he could return at her bidding, but instead he felt like prying. He was ignoring polite manners and being nosy to satisfy his own curiosity.

"Do you have an appointment?" he asked. "With whom are you meeting, Miss Kentworth? Is it a dressmaker? Or maybe it's a beau? Or maybe you have an interview for another position. One that pays more, and the employer doesn't ask prying questions."

Miss Kentworth pinned him with warning in her hazel eyes. She was not amused. Max shoved his hands in his pockets. He'd taken a bad day and made it worse. She'd done nothing to provoke him.

"I would like to be home by midnight," she said. "Can you arrange that?"

"I guarantee it." He had no more questions and no apology that would mean anything to her. He took his hat. "Thank you for the care you give my children. I appreciate it." He paused long enough to convey his sincerity then left for the Keystone Hotel and Ruby.

Ruby was in high spirits. Ruby was always in high spirits. So high that it was easy to hide his ill temper.

He couldn't stop mulling over the outrage. What was the purpose in spending weeks with the details and designs if someone was going to alter them willy-nilly? What would his legacy be if none of his original designs remained untouched? It was the grossest sort of insult, and Max didn't know how to respond.

"I hope the thunderclouds don't ruin our boating expedition." Ruby's eyes flashed at him from beneath the brim of her straw hat as they left the trolley.

Max looked at the sky. "There's a clear sky. Nothing to worry about."

"I wasn't talking about the weather. I was talking about you."

He'd thought he was being his usual charming self, but apparently not. "I can row, thunderclouds or not," he replied.

They'd entered the park and passed beneath the arbor. Max realized that he was walking too fast for the crowds this time of evening. People came to the park to slow down, not to race to their destinations. Families wandered off the crushed gravel and into the lawn. Lovers walked hand in hand, framed by the pines lining the path.

Without a word, Max took Ruby's hand. The primary reason he sought her company was her ability to chase away his darker moods. What good was this outing if he didn't allow her to play her role? Everything was going to be fine. What did it matter that the house he'd designed was going to be ruined? It was just a house, and he'd already been paid for his work. He should be able to let it go.

But it did matter because it was another thing that was out of his control.

Max had never wanted to be a widower. He never wanted his children to lose their mother. He never wanted to spend night after night in a quiet home with no companionship and no partner to help guide the children's future. That hadn't been the plan, but he had learned that you couldn't line out your life like an architect's blueprints and expect everything to work out. And now, even when he had the plans, he couldn't keep someone else from coming along and ruining them.

Maxfield paid the man with the boat, and the man motioned Maxfield to get in first. The boat rocked as he transferred his weight to it, then he reached back to help Ruby aboard.

"What a beautiful evening for a cruise." She fluffed her skirt around her and pulled her gloves tight against her fingers before taking up an oar. "Let's get out on the water where it's cooler."

Max took his seat opposite Ruby. There'd be time to straighten out the mess with the Blounts' house. This was an evening to enjoy the breeze, the lapping water, and the birdsong in the trees along the shore.

"Get to rowing," he said to Ruby with a smile. "It's about time you pull your weight around here."

She beamed at his change in mood and took both oars in hand. Max pushed off the dock to get them turned toward the middle of the lake, then lay back to enjoy himself. Bringing Leo and Stella had been fun. They'd rocked the boat from side to side as they leaned over the edges and exclaimed about the color of the water, the fish they saw, the occasional leaf floating by. Everything had been new and exciting. So much energy. But today, the energy was gone. He needed rest. He needed to be able to withdraw, lick his wounds, and prepare for the days ahead. With the sun's rays warming his skin and the cool breeze off the water, this was a good place to recover until he was fit company again.

"A penny for your thoughts." The cadence of Ruby's rowing had stopped, and he could feel her watching him.

Max opened his eyes. Sitting in the bow of the rowboat, leaning across the idle oars, Ruby was the epitome of elation. Everything lively, spirited, and encouraging.

"My thoughts are that I should be enjoying this lovely day with a lovely lady instead of being morose over a situation I can't control."

"Exactly. Why worry about something frivolous when you could be thinking about me?" She laughed as she always did after her outrageous statements. She was kind and giving and enjoyed playing the part of the giddy young girl, while mocking those girls at the same time. "Let's go farther. I enjoy the rowing, but you need to say something to help me pass the time if I'm going to work this hard."

Say something to pass the time? Max leaned forward, resting his elbows on his knees as the boat began moving again. There were few other crafts in this part of the lake. It was the middle of the week. People were probably going home to dinner with their families. Having a nice, quiet routine at home. Watching their children and sharing pride in them with the other parent. All things he couldn't do. Not now.

There he went again, his thoughts taking him down a shadowy path.

"Your house should be done soon," he said. "We're hanging the electric lamps and installing the gas stoves and water closets. As soon as all the heavy equipment is gone, then your mother will want to come in and direct us in the wallpaper choices and the flooring."

"Which she could do right now, but you refuse to let her." Ruby raised an eyebrow, but Max didn't fall for the challenge.

"Regardless, it won't be long before you can pack up your things and move out of the Keystone Hotel—"

"—And into the biggest house in Joplin." Ruby rolled her eyes. "If only my father was as concerned about aesthetics as he was about numbers."

Max's forehead wrinkled. "He is concerned about aesthetics. That's why he hired me."

"You know what I mean. He wants to be able to tell everyone he hired the best architect. That's what he wants to brag on. It doesn't matter what you design or how it looks, as long as he can impress people."

Max was stunned. "Of course it matters what I design. That's why I am the best, because of my designs. How else would I have my reputation? Do you think someone came along and said, 'Here, Maxfield Scott, your works are outrageous disasters, but we want to pay you for making them'? No, I am hired because I create beauty and balance and taste."

She tilted her chin like she was humoring a child. "Your designs might seem unique to you, but to the average person, it's just a house. We can tell how big the house is and whether it's decorated with taste, but most of the houses going up in the Murphysburg district look like littermates of each other. That's why Father needs to be able to tell people that it's the biggest. Otherwise, they wouldn't be impressed."

"That's not true," Max spluttered. "They aren't littermates." If he weren't stranded in the middle of a lake with her, he'd drag some of his peers over to support his case. "No one would confuse my designs for another's. And that's why a builder can't take one of my designs and add onto it. It's like trying to add another arm onto the human body. It throws everything off kilter." These were the words that he wanted to say to Blount, but Blount wasn't on the water.

"Calm down, Maxfield," Ruby said. "I don't like you when you're angry." Her forehead wrinkled as she stuck out her bottom lip.

But despite her beauty, he was seeing something spoiled beneath. "You don't like me when I'm sad either, or when I'm tired. You only like me when I'm happy and charming and don't have a care in the world. Isn't that right, Ruby?" Why couldn't she have a little compassion? Why couldn't she allow him to have a bad day occasionally?

Turning the oar so that it only skimmed the surface of the water, Ruby did a quick lunge backward, drenching him with a cold wave. "I came here to have fun. If you aren't going to be fun, then you shouldn't be here."

The water dripped down Maxfield's face, seeped through his clothes, and brought his rambling thoughts to a sudden point. "So if I'm not up to entertaining you today, you'd rather I leave?"

From the way she smiled, you'd think that this spat was exactly the type of entertainment she was after. "That's the story."

He'd had enough, and he wasn't going to take another minute of it. "You rowed your way here. I suppose you can row your way back." He stood, and the boat swayed.

"You are not going to leave me out here," she gasped. "You can't be serious."

Max pulled out his wallet and laid two bills on his empty seat. "Hire a cab to get home. Joplin's not safe to walk through alone." He stuffed his wallet deep in his pocket, took off his hat, and dipped his head. "Good evening, Miss Dennis."

Then he dived into the water.

When he came up, he heard her cross words, but he paid them no mind. He set his hat on his head and started swimming for the shore with strong strokes. Though he hadn't worn a suit jacket, his shirt and shoes slowed him down. Regardless, he reached the bank quickly, but not before a crowd could gather and gawk at him.

Getting his footing on the boulders at the edge, he scrambled past them and up the grassy bank, then took a minute to wring the water out of his necktie.

"What a refreshing swim," he said to a young fellow pointing at him. "Just what I needed."

The boy's parents would have trouble explaining to him what the crazy man at the park was doing, but that wasn't Max's concern. He was only worried about getting his squishy shoes home.

CHAPTER
11

Only by balancing the blocks perfectly was Olive able to construct the rickety arch. Leo had shown maturity past his years as he'd held his side motionless while she supported the other side with one hand and set the keystone with the other.

"Now, let's move our fingers away very slowly. So far, so good." Olive barely breathed. Leo held his breath with eyes wide as he withdrew his hand.

The arch swayed, then settled. Leo's mouth made an O. It was sturdy. Success! Afraid to clap, Olive beamed instead. "We did it. We got it to stay up this time."

"Father will be so proud." And that was obviously the most important thing to Leo.

What would be Mr. Scott's opinion of Olive's construction at the Blounts' house? From the look on his face when he saw the building, she didn't have to guess. Thankfully he'd been so stunned to see it that he hadn't noticed her slipping through the trees and out of the yard. This time she'd escaped his notice, but she would have to be more careful. Especially if she wanted access to the new architectural journal that had arrived in the mail. One more hour before the children would get their baths, their story, and then go to bed. Then she had until eleven o'clock to immerse herself in the fascinating article about Daniel Burnham and the work he was doing in Chicago.

Was that the door? Olive pushed off the floor, careful not to bump the structure, and went to the staircase. She stopped in her tracks, not sure if she could believe what she was seeing. Drenched from his dark hair to his leather shoes and all the white linen between, Mr. Scott was coming up the staircase.

Olive was dumbstruck. He might as well be in a bathing suit for all the protection his clothes provided. He was lean and long, she already knew that, but the fabric sticking to his shoulders and chest revealed strength she hadn't considered. She'd always been in awe of him because of who he was—Maxfield Scott, the architect. Now her awe came from something primal and heady.

He stopped on the steps in front of her. His hair was tousled and starting to curl. He didn't say a word, just held her gaze, much like Leo would've when pleading to be read one more story.

Olive clasped her shaking fingers. "You're home early," she said.

"I hope it's not an inconvenience." His eyelashes were dark and spiked with water.

"We were playing blocks." She stayed at the top of the stairs, holding her hands against her stomach to stop the fluttering. "Leo made a nice arch."

"He takes after his father."

Why wasn't he doing something besides standing there on the stairs dripping? Surely he wanted to change. Then she realized that she was blocking his way.

"Excuse me," she said. "I'll go downstairs."

"Stella, no!" Leo howled from the bedroom. "Stella kicked over my arch."

"Stay with the children," Mr. Scott said. "I'll just be a minute."

If only she could get her feet to move. Olive walked backward two steps before spinning around and throwing herself into Leo's room. Stella was sprawled across Leo, tossing every block within her short reach. Olive exhaled, grateful that this situation was one she knew how to handle.

"Stella, don't tear up Bubba's building." She lifted Stella off him and drew her to the side.

"Now I have to build it again." Sitting on the floor, Leo kicked out his leg and sent more blocks flying.

"Shhh, shhh. . . ." Olive was too discombobulated for words. Mr. Scott had shown up early. She hadn't expected him until eleven o'clock. It was a good thing she hadn't cracked open his new journal yet. Sopping wet. Why was he sopping wet?

She could hear drawers opening in the next room. A chair scraped across the floor. What was she doing upstairs while he was in his bedroom? Under different circumstances she might not have thought twice about it, but with the memory of him standing before her still in mind, she felt that she needed to go to the kitchen and stick her head in the icebox. Only then would the heat cool from her cheeks.

"We can build it again." Olive pulled aside a few blocks for Stella to stack, then pushed the rest back to Leo. "You start while I distract Stella." But she was the one distracted.

Her anxiety ratcheted up when she heard the rattle of his bedroom doorknob. Her heart accelerated at the sound of his footsteps. Evidently he'd had a boating accident with Miss Dennis and had only returned home to change clothes. Undoubtedly he'd return to his sweetheart as soon as he composed himself and could go back to her. Once this odd interlude was over, Olive would have a typical night with Leo and Stella and the journal she needed to study. She'd be home a little after eleven, as planned. Nothing out of the ordinary, if he'd just leave.

"We'll walk you home."

The tower of blocks crumpled as she dropped the last one on top. Olive looked up from her kneeling position on the braided rug. "Now? They haven't had supper yet, or their baths."

"I can do that myself." Although dressed casually in soft trousers and a white shirt, Mr. Scott was now every inch the genius that had so intimidated her. "The children would benefit from a stroll," he said, and then under his breath, "as would I."

No use in arguing. Olive got to her feet and lifted the bucket for the blocks. If only Mr. Scott would leave her to tidy unattended. As she helped Leo gather the blocks, she managed to keep facing Mr. Scott so her backside wasn't prominent, but that meant catching his gaze every time she glanced up, and she couldn't keep from looking his direction. Where was Miss Dennis? Why wasn't he returning to her? His behavior was puzzling, but none of her business.

"I'll get my book bag," she said as they made their way down the stairs.

"I don't mind if you leave it. There's no use in you hauling stories back and forth for the kids every time."

Reaching the ground floor, Olive headed to the door and grabbed the handle of the book bag. "I have a bookshelf full of favorites at home and I switch them out. It's not always the same stories," she said as she slung it over her shoulder.

"Have it your way." He held out his hand. There was no mocking good humor in his eyes, just the practical helpfulness required by gentlemen.

While her preference would be to keep the bag herself, she could tell that his tolerance would only go so far tonight. Olive handed it over, took Stella's hand, and walked outside.

The evening breeze had picked up, pulling dried blossoms from an apple tree and scattering them over the sidewalk. Leo picked up a flower and handed it to Olive. She stooped to give him a hug.

"Thank you, Mr. Leo. What a pretty gift." Then, not wanting to toss it to the ground with the boy watching, she tucked it behind her ear, feeling like a foolish girl. Leo skipped ahead, leaving her to wonder how to broach the obvious questions with Mr. Scott that any sane person would want answered. Under normal circumstances he was the most loquacious, most personable man of her acquaintance. Did whatever happen today change that? There was only one way to find out.

"Your clothes . . ." she said.

His chin rose as he scanned the top of the apple trees lining the road. "There was an accident in the boat."

"I hope Miss Dennis didn't come to harm."

His mouth tightened. "She did not. The accident was through a thoughtless conversation. My plunging into the lake to swim away was deliberate."

"Oh." He'd jumped into the lake to get away from Miss Dennis? Olive couldn't deny the tug of a smile pulling at her lips. This man never failed to surprise her.

"Forgive me," he said. "I should be clearer. Miss Dennis did nothing that deserves censure. I'm the one who is out of sorts."

Because of the Blounts' house? Or was there another reason? Normally Olive wouldn't dream of prying into his private life, but this might not be private. It might involve her work.

"If you'd like to unburden yourself, I'm willing to listen," Olive said. "I can lend a sympathetic ear."

Readjusting her bag on his shoulder, he looked straight ahead. "There's nothing to say. I wouldn't insult you by saying that you wouldn't understand, but this problem is uniquely mine."

Olive called Stella out of a yard and back onto the sidewalk. The cautious side of her wanted to ignore whatever it was that was troubling him, but she had already waded in too deep. She cared that he was hurt and wanted to offer her support, if it was something he could use.

"Sometimes the healing is in the telling of it," she said, "no matter who is listening. On the other hand, you can own a moment of grief or anger. It doesn't diminish your good name."

His steps slowed. "You can't imagine how refreshing that is to hear." He was looking at her anew, his intelligent gaze evaluating her in a way he hadn't before.

Olive fought the ridiculous urge to introduce herself—to say, "Now I'm Olive Kentworth. I don't think you've met *me* before"— as if some part of her was newly discovered. And this new part dearly wanted to touch him—to smooth his collar, to take his hand— anything to make contact and ground the sparks that seemed to jump between them.

But it was Leo jumping between them that broke the spell. "Is this your house, Miss Kentworth?" he asked.

As Olive was prone to do when Mr. Scott was with her, she looked at it with a critical eye. The flower beds were tidy, although not elaborate. The only signs of her skill were the intricate bird-houses she'd constructed. They were in the backyard, but Stella noticed them right away.

"Birdies." She pointed up at the Tudor house that the purple martins had made their home. "That's pretty."

"That is pretty." Mr. Scott walked to the fence and lifted Stella so she could see into Olive's backyard better. "I've never seen a prettier birdhouse. Can we go through the gate to see it?"

What could she say? It occurred to her that it had always been dark when Mr. Scott walked her home. After the first time, she'd never thought to worry that he would notice them.

"We can go in the backyard. They aren't anything special, but if Stella wants to see them . . ." She pulled the latch on the gate.

There were four of them in total, each from a different century of design. Leo paid no attention to them but chased Olive's cat, which disappeared into the butterfly bushes. Stella pointed and squealed at the birds as they swooped from house to tree. Nothing would have been remiss except for the fact that Mr. Scott was noticing the houses. Not noticing—inspecting.

"I've never seen such fine workmanship on a birdhouse," he said. Without warning he stepped up onto an iron bench to get a better view. "The detail is impressive."

Well, that's what one did when she liked to design but would never get a chance to see her work at full scale.

"Hello there." Olive's father opened the kitchen door and came outside. First smiling at the children, he then extended his hand to Mr. Scott. "I thought I heard someone back here. I'm Oscar Kentworth."

"Maxfield Scott. Forgive us for trespassing, but I compelled your daughter to allow us to see these remarkable birdhouses. Where did you get them?"

Her father wisely kept from looking her way. He knew the tight-rope she was walking. Smiling his affable grin, he said, "They are one of a kind, special order."

"Pass on my compliments to the artist. They are very clever."

Her father's face showed all the pride that she felt but couldn't display. "The artist will be pleased to hear praise from a renowned architect as yourself. Won't you all come in?"

Olive had been dragged along so far already. She had to stop this madness. "No, Father. Mr. Scott was just doing the courtesy of walking me home. He didn't intend to make a social call."

"Nonsense," Mr. Scott said. "We'd be delighted, Mr. Kent-worth."

"Please, call me Oscar."

"Only if you'll call me Maxfield."

Olive felt a twinge of jealousy. She'd spent hours in Mr. Scott's house, caring for it and his children, but two men could meet and be casual with each other in minutes. So distracted was she by hearing Maxfield addressed by her father that she almost forgot the danger that was looming ahead.

"Wait." She lifted her skirt and hurried to the door. "There might be something amiss. Let me go through the kitchen first."

"You keep the kitchen spotless," her father said. "I don't know what you're worried about."

"If you'll please let me pass . . ." She darted between them and ran through the kitchen. On the corner of the cabinet was a neat stack of her books. She swept them up and ran into the parlor where her plans for Mr. Blount's house were unrolled on the coffee table. Gathering everything in her arms, she dashed to her bedroom and threw them inside. She spun around to reenter the parlor and was faced with Mr. Scott.

"Is something wrong?" he asked. Although still subdued from his normal buoyant personality, the curiosity in his eyes showed that his spirits were on the rise.

Olive smoothed her hair. "Welcome to my home." It was then she spotted the soft-leaded pencils that she used for drafting. Squeezing her way between Mr. Scott and the coffee table, she said, "I'd better move these things before Stella hurts herself."

He took a step back, surprised by her proximity. He gave her only enough room to turn her back to him and sweep all the pencils together. "I'll be right back," she said.

Maxfield Scott was at her house, visiting her father like they were old friends. What would he think of her bare decor? She wished she could tell him that it reflected their lack of finances more than her lack of taste. After tossing the pencils on her bed, she turned and nearly ran over Leo, peering around the doorframe.

"Oh, you have giant pieces of paper like Daddy does. Do you draw buildings on them too?"

Hustling him out of her room, she closed the door behind her. "Let's see if we have any cookies in the kitchen, shall we? If not, I can make some."

This was a disaster. If she weren't already home, she would've run away.

"We really can't stay. My only intention was seeing that Miss Kentworth made it home safely." Maxfield hadn't intended to come inside, and he hadn't meant to take a seat, but here he was, on a comfortable old sofa across from a scholarly-looking gent who seemed content with his company.

Speaking of unintended, Maxfield also hadn't intended to admire Miss Kentworth so openly. She was a beautiful lady, calm, self-possessed. If it weren't for the fact that she'd spent the last month tiptoeing around him, he might have noticed sooner. How would she feel if he noticed now? He looked over his shoulder toward the kitchen. One wrong move and she'd never come back to his house again.

He'd be cautious, but he didn't want to go home. While Maxfield rarely found his own company satisfying, neither did he want the pressure of having to be jovial and entertaining. It really wasn't fair of him to be here, now that he thought of it. He had no right to trespass against Mr. Kentworth's hospitality when he was in such a foul mood. He scooted to the edge of his seat. "Thank you for inviting me into your home. . . ."

Here was where the host would stand to help you to your feet, while spouting assurances that the visit was just what they wanted. Instead, Oscar Kentworth stayed seated as if he already knew that Maxfield was going nowhere.

"Daddy, we're going to get cookies. We have to stay here." Leo dashed back to the kitchen.

Maxfield felt his heart stretch to encompass the happy chatter of his children in the kitchen. Leo had been Stella's age when Georgia died. Stella didn't remember. . . .

"Your children are very special." Oscar leaned back in his easy chair and propped his ankle over his bony knee. "Olive adores them."

"We are very lucky to have her help. She's been a godsend."

"Where people are hurting, that's where Olive is usually found. I worry for her. She's had to bear a lot of suffering in her life. I guess we all have, haven't we?"

Maxfield's chest tightened. The happy voices of his children assured him that all was well. They weren't in danger. No one was in danger. The sky wasn't falling, and he didn't have to talk about himself. He didn't have to reveal anything. He could listen instead.

"Tell me about your family, Oscar. I understand you have two daughters." Let Oscar do the talking and free Maxfield from having to carry the conversation.

"I do—Willow and Olive. Naming them after trees was their mother's idea. Myra loved to sit beneath trees and enjoy the breeze on warm days when she was feeling up to it. She had tuberculosis since she was a young lady, even before we got married. I knew the road ahead, but I was in love. I didn't want to think about the future. I only wished I hadn't brought so much pain on my girls."

"You married her, knowing that she wouldn't live?" Maxfield wiped his palms on his pant legs.

"We're all going to die. It didn't make any sense to give up on love because of pain down the road. Love meant being there with her through it."

If Maxfield knew Georgia's fate, would he have married her? Would he have started down that road? The voices in the kitchen told him that he couldn't change anything. He wouldn't have.

"How long ago did you lose your wife?" Max asked, relieved to delve into someone else's pain and ignore his own.

"It's been nearly a year. The girls had always helped their mother during her bad spells while I was away at work, and then Willow took a job out of town to help pay for the medical bills. Over the last few years, as Myra declined, it fell on Olive to take on most of her care."

He could well imagine how gently the caretaker of his children would have cared for her mother. To think she'd suffered loss even more recently than he and hadn't said a word. Then again, neither had he.

"I worry," her father said, shifting uncomfortably in his chair to cast an eye toward the kitchen, "I worry that I failed her as a father. That she didn't get to have all the experiences young ladies of her age normally do. I think she's too content hiding from the world."

Max laced his fingers together. Thoughts of Blount's house had faded in light of the bigger issue. Other people had losses. Other people had suffered. How did they handle their grief? Obviously

Miss Kentworth didn't do it by socializing every spare hour of the day. What had she done? Was she better off?

"Let's share the cookies with the gentlemen." Miss Kentworth herded the children before her and into the parlor. Stella ran straight for Oscar and lifted her hands.

His thin eyebrows raised with his smile. "You want to sit with me? It doesn't seem like that long ago I had a couple of little girls your size."

Miss Kentworth's cheeks pinked as she presented a plate of cookies. "I'm sorry this is all we have. I didn't have anything prepared."

"No need to apologize. I didn't expect to be entertained, much less fed." Max tried to catch her eye, but she wouldn't look in his direction.

"Well, if you all are settled, I'm going to bring in the laundry. It was still damp when I left today." She spoke over her shoulder as if fleeing a dangerous scene. He never saw her move so quickly at his house.

"I could help you." But she had already disappeared through the kitchen. Max looked at her father. "I could help her. The laundry. It could be heavy."

"I think these rowdies and I will do just fine if you want to give her a hand." Stella clapped her hands as Oscar bounced her on his knee.

Max had teased and pried, but this was his chance to listen to her just as she'd offered to listen to him. Yes, he was angry over the mess at Blount's, but that wasn't Miss Kentworth's fault.

After hearing more of her story, he wanted to offer her any support he could give.

CHAPTER

12

Olive hurried outside into the cool air. He would leave soon. What possible reason could he have for staying? But she had to escape. She'd heard the conversation between him and her father. That was personal. It was a part of her that someone like Maxfield Scott didn't need to hear about. He'd only discover another way that she was sad, dreary, and broken.

Maybe she could stay outside until he left.

Olive reached up and snagged the clothesline. She pulled the pins off her father's shirt and dropped it in the basket, moving it along with her foot to the next garment. She was so focused on her work that the opening of the kitchen door barely registered. It was her father coming, no doubt, to tell her that her company had departed.

"Sorry about that," she said as she removed a clothespin from her bloomers on the line. "I had no intention of him coming inside."

A finely cultured yet very masculine hand reached over her head to remove the second pin. "I was afraid I was an imposition, but your father insisted."

Olive spun around. With her bloomers bundled against her chest, she gaped at Mr. Scott. "What are you doing out here?"

"I came to help."

She was rolling her bloomers against her stomach, trying to make them into a smaller, tighter ball. "I don't need any help."

"Then maybe I came out to talk." The warm light from the kitchen window reflected in his eyes. "I'm not ready to be home alone."

Why did he have to look at her like that? She didn't know what had changed, but she felt the difference keenly. Oh, this being alone outside was worse than sitting in the parlor. With shaking hands, Olive tossed her undergarment into the basket. "You can talk while I gather the laundry," she said.

She darted down the first line of clothing, snatching any garments that she didn't want Mr. Scott to handle. It was her bad luck that she'd washed the whites that morning.

He busied himself with her father's shirts. "I'm glad tonight turned out the way it did," he said. "You don't know what a relief it is to be able to just *be* tonight. Without a facade, without having to entertain. Sometimes it's just too much."

"If you're tired of entertaining, why don't you go home?"

"Is home the only place I can be honest?"

Olive's heart twisted at his words. Beneath the jovial manners were unplumbed emotions, and they were emotions that he'd never felt safe to express to her before.

"I'm sorry," she said. He deserved her attention, however uneasily she gave it. "I want your honesty above all."

"Then you are the exception."

Another lock came undone. Her idol's pedestal lowered another inch. Not that he was anything less in her eyes—he was more. More of a man, more of a friend, and more desirable.

Ashamed of her thoughts, she hurried to the next line of laundry. She wasn't looking for a mate. Or was she? She could pretend that what she wanted was his expertise, his mentorship, and his experience in architecture but, if she was honest, she knew that her first inclination tonight was nothing along those lines. It was from the feminine side of herself that she'd kept in check.

"I didn't know that about your mother. Maybe I should've guessed from your conversation with the doctor, but I had no idea." He worked his way down the line of her father's shirts. "It's no wonder you're so . . ."

Olive swooped beneath the line of sheets to put some distance between them. He said he found people exhausting, but she found him terrifying. She'd stay there, cocooned between the swaying linens until he'd said what he'd come to say. She drew in a lavender-scented breath that reached her toes and listened as he extolled her virtues.

". . . patient and calm with the children. And with me. I'll admit I've tried to ruffle your feathers, but you're undaunted by any challenge I throw your way. It's no wonder. You've faced tragedy. Me showing up in a drenched suit doesn't bother you in the least."

But it had bothered her. It'd bothered her in ways that a lady didn't admit.

While her sister and cousins had been finding romance, she'd told herself that she was looking after the greater good at her mother's bedside. That she would give up on the romance. Taking this job as a nanny should've kept her safely away from any bachelors. Safe from having her heart engaged.

But Mr. Scott wasn't safe. He ducked beneath the sheets. "Why are you hiding?" he asked. He was too close. It was too private. His hair still had curl in it from his recent dunking, making him less of the professional that so intimidated her and more of a handsome man, who also intimidated her.

"I want to hear you," she said. "I want to share your sorrow, if it helps you, but I'd rather keep mine to myself."

"And yet you have compassion on me."

"Maybe I find it easier to help you than to help myself." Why was she saying this to him? She was losing control of this encounter.

"It saddens me that I didn't know you earlier, when you were going through that with your mother. I would like to think that I would've been a good friend to you."

The wind billowed the white linen sheet against her, enveloping her. She pushed it down. "You're good to me now," she said. "You don't owe me anything further."

"Maybe I would've tried to cheer you up. Tried to distract you. Tried to take your mind off the suffering and give you some relief." His words slowed as he came nearer. "That's what I've tried myself, but I'm realizing that it's not a cure. I've also tried staying home, sitting in the silence, but that hasn't brought me any comfort either."

"I've found no way to hurry grief." Brave words from Olive, but she was transfixed, her eyes intent on his face. "It comes and goes, day by day, without reason or warning. I never know what to expect. I can only endure. If you know of some way to leave it behind . . ."

"How did I not see it? Your pain." Now the sorrow in his eyes was for her.

She forced herself to hold his gaze, even though it taxed her. How was it that she couldn't see the structures taking shape, the bonds forming between them, but she knew they were being constructed just the same? The sheet flapped against her back. It filled with air, crowding around her. Mr. Scott brushed it away from her face. His eyes searched hers as his fingers traced across her cheek. Olive was intoxicated. She had thought she knew this man—she'd thought she knew herself—but the two people standing there were both mysteries to her.

With a gust of air, the sheet again covered her face, and this time Mr. Scott wasn't slow in removing it. With a growl, he thrust it aside. Blocking the sheet with his arm, he threaded his hand into her hair. He turned his head just so and brought his lips against hers.

Olive's heart pounded against her stays. He was kissing her. A completely romantic act that perhaps had caught them both by surprise, yet somehow Olive knew what to do.

Her mouth was moving beneath his. Her hands gripped him on either side, then slid down to his waist. Feeling the strength of his hips beneath her hands, she pulled him tighter against her and let the kiss deepen.

Now there was fire. A thrill ran through her core, and Mr. Scott felt it too. The next kiss was savage, robbing her of breath, flooding her senses, but then . . . nothing. He'd yanked away from her and was floundering in the flapping sheets and the coolness of the night air.

Olive gasped at the sudden change and grabbed at the clothes-line pole since everything else was spinning. Mr. Scott pushed a sheet away from his face and his eyes flashed to hers. He looked afraid. Afraid of her.

"It was an accident," he gasped. "I didn't mean to make you do that. To respond like that." He blinked as if pleading with her. Distraught.

Olive's hand went to her stomach. "Excuse me? Respond like what?"

"Make you . . . you know." His eyes roved the sky, looking for an answer "Do things I didn't expect. I should've known better. With your lack . . ." He stopped himself, but it was too late.

"Lack of experience?" Her eyes smarted. She'd received her first kiss and she had failed, even at that.

He hung his head. "I led you astray. It's my fault and I'm sorry. It's been a bad day today. A very bad day. You're not to blame, but I should go. Have a good evening, Miss Kentworth." Then he took off to the house, most likely to gather his children and get away before she could make his day worse.

"What is it that can't wait until I get to the office?" Eric dragged his straight razor over his face and rinsed it in the basin. "I've never seen you this flustered."

Max had called Mrs. Wester while it was still dark that morning and begged her to come to his house early. When she came with her hair still in rags, he'd slipped out and went to his draftsman's doorstep. He'd paced the porch until the first dawning, and then he'd decided that he'd waited long enough. Eric would forgive him for costing him an hour of sleep.

Now in Eric's washroom, Maxfield stretched his legs out before him and gripped the sides of the washtub. "I have a real problem. I kissed the nanny last night," he said.

Eric froze with his razor against his neck and caught Maxfield's gaze in the mirror. "Miss Kentworth?"

"The same."

Eric lowered the razor, dropped it in the water, and turned to face his friend. "Congratulations?" He shrugged.

"No. I'm still courting Ruby Dennis." Maxfield hated saying it aloud. Not when he'd betrayed the lady.

"I see." The judgment on Eric's face was well-deserved. "Your actions aren't that of a gentleman. I assume Miss Kentworth reacted appropriately to your bad behavior."

Maxfield bounded off the tub. Talking about it meant reliving it. Reliving it . . . well, he couldn't just sit and chat like they were discussing where the electrical lines should be installed on one of their projects.

"You would assume that she would be outraged, but no. I was the one shocked. I'm no provincial. I studied in France before I was married." He twisted his ring. "I kept company with a couple of lovely girls while there."

"Olive Kentworth isn't French."

"But her response . . ." Maxfield's neck warmed. "It was the most French response I've had since leaving the continent."

Eric's eyes widened. "Olive Kentworth?" He tried to hide his smile but failed. "I'm astonished!"

"I must speak to her, but I don't know where to start. I'd been talking to her father about her mother's death. Then when I saw her alone in the garden, I was moved with such compassion for her. I wanted to thank her for being so understanding to me. I wanted her to know she wasn't alone."

"There are ways to offer companionship besides that."

"It got out of hand, and I responded poorly."

"You kissed her and then you responded poorly? Add onto that, you are her employer, a gentleman, and a gentleman who considers himself bound to another woman. Sounds like you need to start with an apology," Eric said.

"But the way she kissed me—" Max drew a deep breath to steady himself. "How do I say I'm sorry? How do I make amends without insulting her?"

"You've already insulted her, Maxfield."

"Perhaps it'd be best to pretend it never happened. Allow her to maintain her dignity."

"Are you sure you're making the right choice? What if Miss Kentworth has more to offer than Miss Dennis?"

Was it possible? As frustrating as Ruby was, Maxfield wanted to marry someone who shared his view of the world. Someone who had broad horizons and worldly knowledge. Poor Miss Kentworth had barely left her mother's sickbed. As far as experience was concerned, she was a child, albeit one who was less innocent after last night because of him.

It was better to stay the course. He'd been off-kilter lately. That was all. Shouldn't make any rash decisions.

"I know what I want," he said at last. "And I want Miss Kentworth to keep watching Leo and Stella. They need her."

Eric lifted his shaving mug and scrubbed the brush against the soap. "Then you've got quite a balancing act before you."

It'd all started when he'd heard that Mr. Blount was letting an unknown, uncelebrated builder meddle with his design. That confrontation had led to a falling out with Ruby, which led to him coming home too early, which led to him imposing his company on Olive's family, which led to him sympathizing with her when he was already in a vulnerable state.

It had been wrong of him to kiss her. He'd wronged Miss Kentworth, wronged Ruby, wronged Mr. Kentworth who had been sitting inside playing with Maxfield's children. Miss Kentworth should've slapped his face and exposed him to her father. Instead, she'd kissed him back with a passion he didn't know her capable of.

"This doesn't change anything," Max said. "Mistakes happen. I have to forge on from here. I'll find a way to make amends." But he couldn't help but wonder if trying to ignore what had occurred might be the biggest mistake of all.

CHAPTER
13

Olive would finish the design on this fireplace. She had to. She'd spent a few days going through receipts and paying bills on the project, but tomorrow Amos had a meeting with the mason and was going to show him the detailed plan, so she had to get back to the drafting board. Although the furnace in the basement heated the house, the fireplace set the tone for the room. Kneeling against her sister's bed, Olive blinked at the sheet of paper she had laid out across a board. It might as well have been blank for all she could see.

Mr. Scott had kissed her last night. At first, she'd been flattered, swept off her feet, imagining a whole other future from what she'd ever considered before. But standing alone in the dark with her laundry, the cold reality struck.

He hadn't meant anything by it. He didn't love her, didn't cherish her. It had been an accident—one that clearly horrified him. Olive switched her pencil to her left hand and wiped her palm against the blanket to ease the knotting. But could things just happen like that and not mean anything? How could he forget that moment? How could she?

Anger at him, frustration at herself, but beyond that, a pulse-racing realization that there was something powerful between the two of them. Olive dug her elbows into the mattress and rested her chin on her hands. It wasn't always like that between men and women. According to what she'd observed, some kisses were light and forgettable. People pecked a kiss now and then with ease. But as confused as she'd been, as turned upside down and inside out, something was undeniable—Mr. Scott had been as shaken as she. He hadn't tried to deny it, he couldn't hide it. He felt what she did, and whatever it was, it was uncommon.

But back to the fireplace. It would be the centerpiece of the great hall and her opportunity to show her skill. She'd decided to go with dark rusticated stone for the firebox, but she was still undecided for the overmantel. She had to focus. It'd be better if she never saw Mr. Scott again, because finishing Mr. Blount's house was essential. It was the one part of her life she hadn't messed up.

"I'd like to see Mr. Blount, please. No, I don't have an appointment, but I was hoping he would see me." Maxfield had to speak to the man. Getting Blount to stop destroying his house was the only thing he knew to do.

The secretary disappeared down the carpeted hallway to Mr. Blount's office. Maxfield hadn't been in this office since he'd finished Clydell Blount's house, but he'd always enjoyed his time there. It'd been heady working for Mr. Blount, one of the richest men in Joplin. Not only was Maxfield free to utilize every extravagance without concern for a budget, but Mr. Blount was just as openhanded with the latitude he gave Maxfield on his creativity. Unlike other clients, Blount didn't come into the project with a list of demands and opinions. He seemed delighted with everything that Maxfield suggested, even as he corrected and perfected his earlier drafts. Even though he was rough around the edges, Mr. Blount had been wonderful to work with, which made his sudden decision to revamp Maxfield's work so confusing.

Also confusing was what had happened the night before, but as the day had worn on, clarity grew. He was a cad. Miss Kentworth was not a lady to be trifled with. She wasn't flighty, flimsy, or flirty. She was strong, solid, and steadfast, and he'd trespassed against her. That was the only part that he understood.

Maxfield wandered to the glassed-in bookcase showcasing Blount's awards and achievements. There was a plaque that Blount had no doubt made for himself celebrating the mining of 100,000 tons of ore from his mines. He also had a dented and stained hard hat and corroded pickax lying on a velvet-lined shelf. Maxfield didn't have to read the placard to know those were Mr. Blount's only possessions when he first arrived in Joplin, just a failed farmer looking to make enough to feed his family. He'd struck it rich, but no amount of money could turn him into a cultured gentleman, despite all the newspaper articles celebrating his philanthropic deeds.

And there among the newspaper clippings was the article that ran when the Blount home was completed. Maxfield could quote passages of it from heart. It listed all the modern amenities in Joplin's largest private residence—the electricity, the elevator, the vacuum system. Mrs. Blount had been embarrassed when the specifics of her water closet were published in the local paper, but such press had helped Maxfield land the Dennis account. And from that, he'd met the charming Ruby.

What was he going to tell Ruby? Was he going to tell Ruby? They already had one fight they needed to smooth over. How would she respond, knowing that he'd left her angry and taken up with another woman? Ruby wasn't the jealous type. She wouldn't be mad. Knowing Ruby, she'd laugh. She'd mock him for taking up with his nanny after leaving her. In fact, she might ridicule Miss Kentworth. Perhaps it'd be better not to mention it at all. As long as she and Miss Kentworth never crossed paths—

He'd check on Ruby today. After he'd confronted this travesty of a construction project, he'd be better shored up to appreciate Ruby. As for Miss Kentworth, he had no idea what to do about her.

The secretary returned with Mr. Blount on her heels. He was coming to meet Max instead of the other way around? That meant that he didn't want to take a chance on Maxfield overstaying his welcome. Max could expect this meeting to be curt and to the point.

"Maxfield, nice of you to stop by. How are those kids of yours doing?" His face twitched, evidence of the constant energy the man possessed. If he wasn't walking, the movement had to come out somewhere.

"They're getting bigger every day."

"Glad to hear it. Now, are you going to tell me why you're here, or should I guess?" He pulled his pocket watch out of his vest pocket and swung it by its golden chain. "Not that I need to guess. It's painfully obvious."

"Why are you altering your house?" Maxfield wouldn't waste their time. "Are you dissatisfied with it already?"

"Yes, I am. After living in it for a few years, I found that the floor plan needs improving. Some alterations should fix the problem."

Alterations? To his design? Whatever Maxfield had expected him to say, he didn't think it would flare his temper so to hear it.

"If you found a problem with the design, why didn't you come to me?"

"Do you think there's anything wrong with the house?" Blount asked.

"No, I don't. It's perfect."

Blount tossed his pocket watch into the air and caught it in his fist. "And that's why I couldn't trust you to do the remodeling. I didn't want to argue."

Maxfield winced. He'd walked into that trap on his own. "That's not the point. If you thought my design wasn't good enough, why not hire Austin Allen? Why not consult with someone who is a trained architect? I don't know what your builder's credentials are, but I'd never heard of him before this."

"His credentials are that he built my miners' center and finished it on time. Also, he gave me some good plans for how to change my parlor into a living hall and add . . . oh . . . a ladies' parlor? I don't remember what we decided to go with, but I remember that I wholeheartedly approved at the time."

"You don't remember what the changes are? How long did you contemplate this project before letting Amos Kentworth tear down my wall?"

"Don't take it to heart, Maxfield." Mr. Blount tucked his pocket watch into his pocket, then twisted his vest around so the buttons aligned correctly. "Next time I undertake a change, I'll give you another shot at it. Good day!"

Maxfield watched as Blount hurried down the hall, his footsteps muffled by the thick carpet. Next time he had a change? He hadn't expected the conversation to be easy, but he hadn't expected it to be so frustrating.

As long as he was working through his list of things he was dreading, he might as well get his apology to Ruby behind him. He walked out of the Blount mining offices and down Fourth Street toward Ruby's hotel. It wasn't that he was dreading seeing her. It was just that he'd gotten off track. They had quarreled, he'd been angry, and then . . . Well, he needed to get back to Ruby. There was safety in her prattle and cheer. Besides, as of late, he'd enjoyed his routine. Coming home to the children after work. Spending some time with them before going out for entertainment with Ruby, then coming home to a quiet and peaceful house, followed by a peaceful walk through the neighborhood to take Miss Kentworth home before retiring for the night.

Miss Kentworth. What had gotten into her? Max thought he was a good judge of people, but he never suspected that she would respond to his kiss as she had.

Could she have feelings for him? He regarded her highly, but never considered that she might feel the same. She must be better at hiding secrets than he'd have credited her for. Or maybe she hadn't meant to respond so enthusiastically. Maybe they'd both made the same mistake. Either way, he had to stop thinking about it.

But that wasn't so easy.

Maxfield walked through the lobby of the hotel and was immediately spotted by Mrs. Dennis as she exited the elevator.

"Mr. Scott, are you here to take me to my new house? The suspense has been my undoing."

"You can't mean you haven't seen it? I know you and Ruby walk by daily."

"But I haven't been inside. When will you think it safe enough?"

Safe enough? Until there was nothing undone above their heads that could fall, nothing underfoot they could trip on, and nothing being hauled around, it wasn't safe. "The time is coming," he said. "The interior doors are being hung and the woodwork is getting completed. Once we have the tools out of the way and all the debris removed, it'll be a much more pleasant experience for you ladies. I don't want your first impression to be a bad one."

She waved a graceful hand. "Be sure to let me know when you can. I'm headed to the upholsterers to pick out fabric for our new furniture. Every day that I can't see the finished product makes me question my decisions more and more."

"It'll be worth the wait, I promise." Then, looking to the elevator, he added, "Is Miss Dennis at home?"

"She is going to Dellmar's to check on a sideboard I had ordered. She'll be down in a minute if you'd like to wait."

"Of course." Here was a task he felt he could help with. Women didn't usually visit Mr. Dellmar's woodworking shop. It'd be nice to do something productive with Ruby. Life didn't consist of only concerts and theatricals.

When the elevator doors opened, Ruby strode out with a glum expression. Arms swinging as she marched forward, she walked right past him. Spinning on his toe, Maxfield fell into step with her.

"I would like to apologize." Better to cover a host of offenses without specifics.

Ruby spared him only the quickest glance. "You should've seen the commotion you caused. By the time I reached the shoreline, you were a legend and I the harpy that drove you to such desperate measures."

"I was trying to protect you from my bad mood. You deserve only the best of me, and I didn't have enough of that to offer."

With a jut of her chin, she looped her arm through his. "Honestly, if you weren't going to cheer up, I'd have rather you jumped into the lake. You weren't mistaken."

With Ruby's high spirits, one might think her as volatile as a spring storm, but in truth, she was steadfast. You could always count on her if you were looking to have a good time. A good time without anyone taking anything seriously.

Time to reengage and thus protect innocent governesses from his escapades. "Well, I'm over my sulk, so you no longer have to worry about me undertaking any alarming escapes."

"I'm glad to hear it. To celebrate, why don't we ride the trolley out to the Crystal Cave and see that again? I can't get it out of my mind how beautiful it was. Also, the pecan cookies were delicious. I could use another of those this morning."

"I thought you were checking on a sideboard your mother ordered?"

She waved her hand before her face. "She won't mind—she can do it herself—but we have a chance at an unexpected treat. You're never free on a workday in the morning."

Neither should he be free now. If he wasn't helping Ruby with her errands, he might as well get back to his office and work on drafts. Any time spent touring would be time wasted.

"I don't have time to go to the Crystal Cave, but I'd enjoy seeing what you ordered for the house. Besides, I can't bear the thought of you having to do that tiresome chore alone."

That brought the flush of gratitude to her cheeks. "Alright, then. Seeing that there's no lake for me to throw you into, I suppose I don't have a choice."

The furniture was being constructed by the same woodworker who created the jigsaw work adorning the house, a decision that Mrs. Dennis had made early in the construction. The shop wasn't the kind of place that a lady frequented, which was why Maxfield was surprised to see Miss Kentworth at the counter.

"Yes, you have a nice collection," Olive said to Mr. Dellmar as she walked the length of his display rack. "Can I pick out five or so different cuts and then bring them back?"

He wiped the sawdust and sweat from his bald head. "Can't make up your mind, darling?"

Olive eyed the different choices. "It's the builder who needs to see them. I'll take them to him and the owner, and they'll decide." She'd take them to Mrs. Blount, and she and Mrs. Blount would decide on what braces they wanted to include in the fireplace mantel.

"You bet. Pick out what you want, while I help Miss Dennis."

Olive took two brackets off the display rack and turned them in her hands, comparing them. Which was closest to what Mr. Scott had used on the rest of the house? Had she been paying attention, she would've registered the name that Dellmar dropped. Instead, she was completely caught off guard when Mr. Scott stepped into view.

"Miss Kentworth. What brings you here?" His suit was sharp and crisp and his face clean shaven. And the lady on his arm glittered like new pennies.

Olive searched his face. Gone was any connection they'd shared earlier. Another look at the curious woman and she realized why.

The two brackets in her hands required an explanation. "The birdhouses," she stammered. "I'm building another birdhouse."

Mr. Scott raised an eyebrow. "Building another? You didn't build those, did you?"

Why hadn't she said that something on her porch needed repairing? Because her porch wasn't in disrepair and now that he'd been in her front and back yard, he knew that.

"I'm . . . I'm . . ." She couldn't take her eyes off the gorgeous woman on his arm. "I'm Olive Kentworth," she said. "You must be Miss Dennis?"

"Call me Ruby." She grabbed Olive's hand and shook it vigorously. "Everyone else does." She looked to Mr. Scott and then to Olive. "Max, she beat you to the introduction. That's so unlike you."

He obviously had other things on his mind. They both did. "My apologies. Miss Kentworth watches Leo and Stella in the evenings when Mrs. Wester goes home."

"Rea-lly?" Her smile went even brighter, too bright.

Olive didn't like the forced gaiety. She also didn't like that Ruby didn't seem the least threatened. Ruby didn't know. He hadn't told her. Why would he? What happened had meant nothing.

"Without Miss Kentworth, I wouldn't be free to escort you in the evenings." It was uncharacteristic of Mr. Scott to explain himself, but it was a peculiar situation.

"What do you do when you aren't watching children, Miss Kentworth? Is building birdhouses a hobby of yours?"

Olive hated being the center of attention and she particularly hated this type of attention. If her cousin Calista were there, she'd put this girl in her place with a cold stare. Her cousin Maisie would do it with a right hook. Olive's only weapons were perseverance and a knack for discernment.

"I like to read," she said. "And I keep the house for my father."

"She likes poetry," Mr. Scott added. "She's kept a volume of poetry from my library for a month now."

Uh-oh. She'd forgotten the book she'd taken as an excuse to browse through his library. "I'll bring it back. I didn't mean to keep it so long."

"No need. Keep it as long as you like. I'm not missing it."

"I never knew you to be a connoisseur of poetry," said Ruby.

Her eyelashes actually fluttered as she elbowed Mr. Scott. "Who is this poet that you two are sharing?"

"Miss Kentworth found it on my shelf. What was it?"

Olive closed her eyes. In vain she tried to summon up the cover and see the name. It started with a W? Or was it a collection of poems? She didn't know. She'd never looked beyond the cover. "I don't remember. Browning, maybe? Something about the Portuguese? I'm sure they are excellent poems. It's just that I don't remember."

Ruby cleared her throat and began quoting,

> "Take, O take those lips away,
> That so sweetly were forsworn;
> And those eyes, the break of day,
> Lights that do mislead the morn:
> But my kisses bring again;
> Seals of love, but seal'd in vain, sealed in vain."

Olive's eyes flashed to Mr. Scott's in a panic. He looked twice as alarmed.

"That's not Browning." His lips were pulled tight. "I'm confident that's neither of the Brownings."

Ruby giggled and hugged his arm. "I don't remember where I heard that, but it stuck with me."

"I'm sure Miss Kentworth has more important things to do besides listen to poetry," he said.

"Yes, if you'll excuse me." Forgetting about her brackets, Olive moved toward the door, kicking up a cloud of sawdust in her hurry.

"Wait, Miss Kentworth," said Ruby. "I'd very much like to get to know you. Perhaps you and a beau could accompany me and Maxfield to a concert this weekend? Even if the concert is dull, I'm very entertaining, and the Schifferdecker Electric Park is superb."

Olive studied her. Was she mocking her or was she sincere?

Did she know more than she was letting on? Olive shouldn't let her own fear cause her to attribute bad intentions to someone unjustly. But from the terrified look on Mr. Scott's face, his fear was greater than her own.

"Your offer is generous, but it would mean leaving the children unattended, so I'm afraid I'll have to decline," she said.

Giving herself a moment to appreciate the disaster she'd avoided, Olive took to the exit when she heard Miss Dennis again.

"I imagine Max could find someone to mind the children for the night. I'm sure he'd like to show you his appreciation for the work you've done." She elbowed him.

From his wide-eyed stare, it was clear that Mr. Scott's unease had only grown. "Yes. Of course. You should come with us. I think you and Ruby would enjoy each other's company." His hand, the one on the arm not being hugged by Ruby, was balled with his knuckles showing white.

Oh, why couldn't she forget how he'd lingered at her house, as if he loathed to leave her father and go out into the dark with his children alone? Why did she have to feel sympathy for this man who had everything she wanted?

Why couldn't she forget what it felt like to be kissed by him?

But perhaps the best way to move forward was to do it quickly. No avoiding, just put it in the past and move on.

"I'll think about it," she said. "No promises."

His hand loosened. "Splendid. I'll send you information when our plans are firm. Good day."

No, it wasn't a good day. He'd nearly discovered her secret and now she might be obligated to do a social event with him and his lady friend. And on top of that, she'd left Mr. Dellmar's without her brackets.

It wasn't a good day at all.

CHAPTER
14

It would be nice to treat Miss Kentworth and a beau to an evening of entertainment that they might not otherwise be able to afford. It would also be nice to remind Miss Kentworth that he had a serious relationship with Ruby and that what had happened between them had not affected it at all. Maxfield waited outside the dress shop for Ruby. She'd spotted a reefer jacket with leg-o'-mutton sleeves that she wanted the first time they'd visited, but then she had to go to every other store to ensure there wasn't another coat she liked more. Now they were back at the first shop, finally ready to make her purchase.

Ever since he'd talked to Oscar Kentworth, he couldn't stop imagining Olive at her mother's bedside, caring for her while other friends her age were socializing and moving on in life. That explained her awkwardness in social situations. That had always been his motivation in teasing her—to prod her out of her cocoon. Mourning had a way of changing a person. Perhaps Olive Kentworth wasn't naturally reticent.

She hadn't been reticent when she'd kissed him.

He had to forget that.

He traced the engraving on the brass plaque that graced the

corner of the store and noted the builder as he waited for Ruby. She seemed determined to keep him entertained. There was nothing wrong with entertainment, but was he entertained? Regardless, Miss Kentworth deserved a night out. An invitation was the gentlemanly thing to do, if he could still lay claim to the name.

His greatest concern about his invitation was that she didn't have a beau and would be embarrassed to admit it. Or maybe he was more concerned that she did have a beau and that he wouldn't be able to endure him. Oh well. It would only be for one evening. He could do that much for Miss Kentworth. He owed it to her.

With a flash of sunlight that reflected off the brass bar, the door to the shop opened and Ruby hurried out.

"I decided against it." She crossed her arms over her chest. "The coat wasn't as dear the second time seeing it."

"That's too bad. Say, I need to get to the work site and check on some things with your house. I've been away too much today, and I know you don't want there to be any delays."

"I'll come with you." Ruby started down the sidewalk. "How can we keep ordering furniture if we haven't seen the interior?"

"You aren't stepping foot on the property. Not until it's safe. I'll take you to the hotel—"

"I don't want to go to the hotel. I want to see the house you are building me. If you're worried about me trespassing somewhere I shouldn't be, then give me a tour yourself."

He felt the sadness and futility creeping up on him. The house was nearly finished, and he knew she and her mother came by after hours to snoop around, yet it made a difference. If he'd done everything in his power to dissuade them, then he didn't feel responsible. Taking her there himself was out of the question.

"I'm taking you to the hotel. What you do after that is your business." He'd wait and talk to her father later. He could go home and work on his drafts for the department store and eat lunch with Leo, Stella, and Mrs. Wester.

"Don't be a baby, Maxfield. It's unbecoming."

"You don't understand my reasons."

"And I don't want to. If the final result is illogical, what's it matter what your reasons are?" She stood at the corner that split their paths, either to the hotel or to the Murphysburg neighborhood where her house was being constructed. She was unyielding, but he knew that as soon as he folded to her demands, she'd reward him with sweetness and glee.

But his opinion was not for purchase, even with smiles and laughter.

Reading the decision in his eyes, Ruby pouted. "You used to be a lot of fun."

"We had an agreement on the house." What was happening? It wasn't just about her visiting the house. He was growing tired of keeping up a suitable level of inanity. Or perhaps he was still in a bad mood over Blount's house, and he was taking it out on the one lady who had the power to get him over his bad moods.

He stepped forward and took her by the hand. "Go home," he said. "It's not worth fighting over. Give me one more week, and then I'll give you a tour. You'll see everything ready the way you want it." He leaned in and kissed her cheek. Surely that was still a safe gesture. "Can you give me that much time?"

Her eyes were like glittering sapphires. "One week. If you won't take me on a complete tour then, I'll have Father fire you and we'll take possession as is." Her smile softened her threat.

"Sounds like a deal. Now, where can I take you?"

Ruby turned back toward the shops lining Main Street. "There's more shopping I could do. Why don't you find Father and get your work done?"

Relieved that she wasn't going to sneak to the house, Max nodded. "That sounds like a good idea. Perhaps I'll see you tomorrow night."

She nodded, although he couldn't help but notice that she looked as worn as he did. "Good day."

Satisfied that his personal life was on the mend, Max headed toward the Dennis home. His plans had been followed and the details could easily be handled by his construction crews. If it weren't for his personal connection to the Dennises, he would've moved on already. It was hard to stay focused on the placement of fixtures and application of varnishes when new plans were underway—especially plans as brilliant as those that Christman had commissioned from him. The man had been delighted with the open floor plan and the custom columns. It was the columns that had won the bid for Maxfield, and he was anxious to devote more time to the job. Finishing an old project wasn't nearly as exciting as starting on a new one.

One week. There'd be no problem meeting that deadline from the looks of the house. The crew had already removed all the lumber and bricks from the yard so the landscapers could begin their tasks. From the outside, it looked completed. Even the front entry hall wasn't far from being finished. Max followed the sound of his workers until he ran into Mr. Dennis.

"I've been looking for you." Mr. Dennis pushed up his sleeves and rotated the ring on his finger. "We need to make a change."

"A change?" Usually it was the ladies who had trouble making up their minds about the decor. Max looked past Mr. Dennis into the dining room. "What is it that you don't like? The chandelier? The wallpaper?"

"We need to make it bigger."

Max's blood ran cold. "What bigger?"

"The house. I told you I wanted the biggest house in Joplin. That's what you promised me." From the pouting daughter to the pouting father, though Mr. Dennis didn't look nearly as appealing with his bottom lip extended.

"This is the biggest house in Joplin. You're getting what you asked for." What was it about rich men that made them so paranoid?

"Not anymore. Have you seen what Blount is doing?"

Blount. Just like that Maxfield had the air knocked clean out of him. "Blount? I have nothing to do with that. What he's adding is going to mar the beauty of that house. You can't add square footage to a structure willy-nilly and come out with any sort of balance."

"What he's doing is making his house bigger than this one, and I refuse to let him win."

By George, Mr. Dennis was right. Maxfield had agonized over Blount's decision, trying to make sense of why he would be unhappy with his house now, but his new addition would secure his title as owner of the largest house in Joplin.

It took a man like Mr. Dennis to understand Mr. Blount.

Maxfield stretched his hand toward Mr. Dennis. "Let's be reasonable. Just because Mr. Blount has decided to befoul his floor plan doesn't mean you should too. Your house will be the most beautiful and well-crafted—"

"But not the biggest. I wanted it to be the biggest. I understand that we agreed to a price and design, but I'm willing to pay for the change. Otherwise, I'll find out who Blount hired for his addition and have the same man design mine."

"You can't do that." Maxfield grabbed him by the arm. "Promise me you won't turn my plans over to some unknown hayseed posing as an architect."

He'd found Maxfield's weakness, and he knew it. Mr. Dennis's brows lifted. "It won't take much to knock out a wall and extend it a few feet, will it? Who will know the difference?"

Max looked at the completed interior, the tarps protecting the new wood floors, the workers languidly applying finishing touches. Start over? Scratch out the blueprints and redesign? And what about Christman's department store? In his mind, he was already free from the Dennis project and moving on. He couldn't let Mr. Dennis set him back, but neither could he allow his vision to be corrupted with another's fingerprints.

She hadn't gotten the samples she needed, but even worse, Mr. Scott had invited her to socialize with him and Miss Dennis. Olive rubbed her eye with the back of her hand. She should've politely declined his invitation. Why would she want to spend an evening with Miss Dennis? And why would she want to be with Mr. Scott? She could only hope that he was thinking the quickest way past their embarrassing encounter was to throw themselves together and prove that it would never happen again.

The real problem was who she should take. It wasn't as if there were men lined up requesting her company.

Turning on Moffat Avenue, she could hear the hammers ringing before the Blounts' house came into view. The walls were up. The extension on the roof was framed. She walked the length of the yard, passed the house, then came back from the other side, observing how the new portion would look from every angle. Stopping beneath the magnolia tree, she crossed her arms and watched the men work. They were following her directions. So far everything looked just like Mrs. Blount wanted it to.

After looking at the framing they were constructing, she wondered if the house would look better with the newly revived Palladian windows that she'd seen in Mr. Scott's architectural journal. The three panes of glass would give a better view of the garden and the unique shape would add some interest from the inside. Yes, it wasn't too late to make that change. She'd get the plans amended and explained to Amos so he could tell Mr. Flowers.

Speaking of Amos, where was he?

Olive picked her way through the site, careful not to get in anyone's way. She stepped up on the new foundation but didn't see Amos in the new portion. From behind a thick canvas hung to keep dust from spreading to the rest of the house, she could hear her cousin's voice. She could hear several cousins' voices, actually.

"Amos, are you in there?" Olive pushed aside the canvas and stepped into the Blounts' parlor. There sat Amos in Mr. Blount's easy chair with a cob of corn in his hand and a bottle of soda at his feet. Not to be outdone, his sister, Maisie, was sitting at Mrs. Blount's pump organ with her dinner spread across the keys.

"What are you doing?" Olive lifted a paper wrapper of fried potatoes off the ivory keys. "Do you have permission to be in here?"

"Mr. and Mrs. Blount are out of town." Amos turned the corn until he found more untouched kernels. "I've got to be here supervising, so I might as well be comfortable."

"I'm here as a witness so if anything gets broken or damaged, I can swear that Amos didn't do it." Maisie reached for another potato piece, but Olive swung them out of the way. Maisie hadn't lived in her new husband's mansion very long, but one would still expect her manners to have improved by now.

"Nothing had better get broken or damaged. It's my reputation at stake." Olive relocated Maisie's grub to the coffee table.

"Welp, now that you mention it, it's my reputation at stake, not yours." Amos gnawed on the cob. "It's my name on this project. If something goes wrong, you can keep hiding at your house and pretend that you had nothing to do with it."

He was right and that was precisely why she bothered going through with this ruse. Deniability in case she made a mistake. The danger was that Amos was one hundred times more likely to do something wrong than she was.

"I want to talk to you about the windows," she said. "I've changed my mind. The newest trend is to use Palladian windows, and I think they would enhance this room considerably. Where are the plans?"

Maisie left the organ to follow her food to the table. "You should've hired me to represent you," she said as she tossed her ginger braid over her shoulder. "I do a great job talking to the press about the Crystal Cave. I'm better spoken than Amos."

"What good would it be to have another lady pretending to be the architect? I need a man to do it."

"You're not going to challenge her claim to be better than me?" Amos sniffed. "I'm devastated."

"The way you can be better is to look at these plans, memorize the changes, and explain them to Mr. Flowers so the support for the windows is correct." Olive took out her pencil and ruler, then spread the roll of paper on the coffee table and knelt, wishing Maisie's fried potatoes didn't smell so delicious.

It took a few times of reciting the exact words for Amos to get it down. He kept getting the type of window confused, but when she wrote the measurements on a scrap of paper, he was confident he could explain the numbers to the crew and get it done correctly. Had her visit ended then, she would've been satisfied with her progress, but her escape was thwarted by the arrival of three more kinfolk.

"Olive, I've missed you so much." Her sister, Willow, held out her arms.

Olive rushed into her embrace. It was the first time Olive had seen her sister since their mother's funeral. Now married to a railroad tycoon, Willow traveled from coast to coast maintaining her husband's family empire. Every trip through the heart of the country would always involve a stop in Joplin, naturally.

"I thought we'd find you here." Calista stood aside with Willow's husband, Graham. "When I heard that Mr. Blount was expanding his house, I knew you had to be the one building it."

"You mean I'm the one building it," Amos said. "Give credit where it's due."

"Then you need to credit me with more intelligence than that," Calista replied. "You wouldn't know bargeboard from belvederes. Of course it's Olive who's doing the work." Although Calista had darker coloring than the other Kentworth offspring, she was cut from the same cloth, no denying it.

"I might as well go back to the farm, where I'm appreciated," Amos groused, but he didn't move off the wingback chair. "All these insults are eroding my self-respect."

Ignoring him, the female cousins had more important things to talk about.

"Calista told me about you working for Maxfield Scott." Willow's eyebrows rose in speculation. "Isn't he a widower?"

"Of course he is," said Calista. "Don't you think I researched that before I sent her to his house?"

"You missed one detail," Olive said. "He has a sweetheart."

"Is he devoted to her?" asked Willow. "Enough that he hasn't noticed how beautiful you are?"

"What she's asking is has there been any hanky-panky," Maisie said.

Olive thought of ice-cold snowbanks and fingernails on the chalkboard. Surely that would give her a chill to keep her face from flushing. Although hanky-panky wasn't how she'd term their encounter. More like . . . never mind. Snowbanks and fingernails. That's what she had to ruminate on.

"I'm tending his children," she said. "That's all."

"Awww . . ." Willow, Calista, and Maisie moaned in disappointment.

"Does he know about your hobby?" Willow asked. "Does he know about this?" She motioned to the canvas that shielded them from the portion of the house under construction.

"He can't know. Not now."

"Why?" Maisie asked. "It might put some shine on you. Show him that you have more going on than he expected. Then maybe he'd give you a second thought."

"I don't want him to think about me." Why couldn't her kin believe what she was telling them? Maybe because she didn't believe it herself. "He's already prying into my personal life. Just this week he brought his children to our house and visited with Father all evening." They would find that out even if she didn't tell them. "Now he's asked me to go with him and his lady friend on a date to a concert at the Electric Park."

"I'm glad you have no interest in him at all," Maisie said, blinking wide pseudo-innocent eyes. "Otherwise that would be awkward."

"How can the three of you dance together?" Amos asked.

"He expects me to bring my own escort."

Willow grabbed Calista by the arm. "She needs a beau. Calista, we've got to help her."

Amos rolled his eyes as he stood. "First you want me to pretend to be an architect and now you want me to pretend to squire my own cousin around. If it weren't for us being blood kin—"

"We are NOT asking you to go." With a well-placed hand on his chest, Maisie shoved her brother back down into his seat. "You stay out of this."

Calista took up pacing the room. "There are several prospects I could enlist and a few possibilities, but I haven't done complete investigations into their backgrounds yet."

"Don't let Silas Marsh near her," Maisie said. "He's trouble."

"I've got better discernment than that," Calista said, "but we want the perfect person. Someone who would show Olive to her best advantage. Someone who would make Maxfield Scott realize what a gem he has right under his nose."

Olive threw her hands in the air. "He has a sweetheart! I work for Mr. Scott, nothing more. I have no interest in spending time with him and Miss Dennis."

"What about just him, minus Miss Dennis?" Willow asked with a smirk.

Olive let her eyes roll toward the ceiling. "I have work to do. You all keep on with your speculating. This house isn't going to build itself."

"Wait, before you go, we have a request." Willow motioned Graham to her. He took a folded piece of paper out of his pocket and handed it to Willow. "We have another project for you," she said. "We need a private railcar, and we'd like you to design it."

A railcar? Olive lit up with the possibilities, the challenges. She unfolded the paper and looked at the rectangular structure. The space was limited. No way to negotiate for more room, but that made the puzzle that much more fun to solve. Just think how satisfying it would be when all the pieces fit.

"Of course we'll leave it up to you to figure out how to fit all these rooms in there, as long as they are all included."

There in the corner of the paper was a list—*kitchen, parlor, dining room, bedroom, washroom, nursery* . . . Olive gasped. One look at her sister and she saw the joy in her eyes.

"Oh Willow, that's wonderful!" Olive threw herself against her for another hug. "I'm so excited."

Amos huffed. "Ain't that something? She didn't get that excited when I got her the job on this house."

"Shhh. . . ." Calista said. "I think there's something more going on here than a building project."

"Have you told Father yet?" Olive asked.

"We came to you first."

"Is this what I think it is?" Maisie asked. "Are you carrying a calf?"

Amos shot out of his chair. "Congratulations, Graham!" He grabbed him by the hand. "This calls for a party. Let's tell the workers they have the rest of the day off and we'll all go out to the ranch. It'll be a regular shindig."

"You are not sending the workers home," Olive said, "but a visit to the ranch would do me some good. I'll send word to Father, and we can meet out there tonight."

"I'll get Matthew and we'll go straight out," said Calista. "Give Granny and Aunt June some warning that we'll be there for supper."

"Let me hunt down Boone," said Maisie. "Don't want him to miss out on the fun."

"Then it's all settled," said Olive.

She was excited for her sister and Graham, excited for what another generation of Kentworths meant to the family. But contained in all that joy was also the peace of knowing that, at least for tonight, she would be at ease with people who didn't confuse her.

CHAPTER
15

Maxfield had the new plans written up. He didn't like them, he resented that they'd been requested, but he had them and he was going to present them to Mr. Dennis. Unfortunately Mr. Dennis was not in his apartments at the Keystone Hotel.

Coming down the elevator with his blueprints rolled beneath his arm, Maxfield's eyes let the gold-and-red carpet blur. Last night had been miserable. He and the kids had enjoyed a nice dinner out, but as soon as they were in bed, he had to get back to work. He was champing at the bit to get the finishing touches on the department store, but instead of moving on to something fresh and invigorating, he was revamping plans that had already been perfected and nearly finished. It was torture. But it was finished. If Mr. Dennis would approve them, then the wall above the porte cochere could be demolished and the drive-through patio would soon have a room atop it. Maxfield had never wanted a porte cochere with a room above it, but at least that solution didn't require the foundation to be expanded. Once finished, he'd never want to step foot inside that house, which, come to think of it, would be a sight awkward if his relationship with Ruby continued to mature.

The bell chimed and the doors to the elevator rolled open. Max worked his way through the busy lobby to the desk, where a line had formed. He'd leave the plans at the desk for Mr. Dennis to look over. Might be for the best if he had a cooling-off period before he had to talk him through the changes.

The man in front of him looked rich, well-groomed, and unfamiliar. "I'd like to reserve a room here for next week, please. Marlowe Buchanan is the name of the guest. He'll be staying alone."

Marlowe Buchanan? Could there be two men with that name? Max had met Marlowe in Europe while he was studying architecture. As the clerk recorded the information in a leather-bound ledger, Max stepped up to the counter.

"Forgive me for eavesdropping, but did you say Marlowe Buchanan?" he asked.

The clean-shaven man beamed. "I did. He's my brother. I'm Graham Buchanan." He extended his hand.

"That's splendid! I'm Maxfield Scott. Marlowe and I crossed paths in France."

"Maxfield Scott, nice to meet you. I've heard about you. If I remember correctly, you are an excellent architect." Graham Buchanan had the easygoing confidence of a man who'd been born to work and to be amply rewarded for his work. "I wasn't expecting you in Joplin. Then again, Joplin is gaining a reputation for its beautiful structures. No doubt you are playing a role in that."

"Thank you, sir. I hope my work contributes." Of course it did, but modesty was always the best policy. "Your brother contributed to my education when we were in Europe."

"I am filled with wonder on how that could be." Graham leaned against the reception desk.

"Maybe it wasn't an education in architecture, but he did teach me how to order French food and which theaters were unseemly."

Graham laughed. "Which I'm sure he learned through trial and error. Marlowe will certainly want to see you while here."

"I hate to impose if he's only here for a short visit."

"Oh, he'll stay as long as we're in town. We have some family business to attend to as well as getting specifications on my new private railcar."

"Designing a railroad car?" Max had never considered such a project. "A living space, I presume."

"Yes, without compromising any luxury. It's quite a challenge, but I want something that will rival Jay Gould's *Atalanta* car."

Max imagined the space, passageway so narrow that two people would be unable to pass each other in them, but the rooms feeling big enough that a tycoon and his family could travel without feeling cramped. Here he was building for people who wanted the most space wasted. It would be interesting to build where space had to be justified.

"I would love to see the plans," Maxfield said. "I've never thought to design something with these concepts. Who did you commission to design it?"

"A relative here in Joplin, actually. Willow has a family member who's a sort of amateur architect but can take my ramblings and put exactly what I meant to say on paper. Very gifted."

"Your wife's name is Willow?" Somewhere there was a connection with the name, but he couldn't quite pin it down. He was too curious about an amateur architect in Joplin.

"And just as graceful as her namesake. I'll tell you what, when my railcar is built, I'll invite you for a tour. In the meantime, good luck with beautifying this rough mining town. I'll have Marlowe call when he arrives."

"That would be wonderful."

Marlowe was such a droll fellow. He'd either sympathize with Max or he'd dismiss his doldrums with a wave of his hand and air his own grievances. Either way, Marlowe would take Max's mind off some of his bizarre and unfortunate circumstances.

When the Kentworths got together, the whole countryside knew it. Now that the younger generation was growing and settling in around town, the number of conveyances coming from Joplin to the ranch had increased. The dirt road had a continual plume of dust rising from it as kinfolk streamed in to jockey for the best seats at the table and the best cuts of meat from the hog.

Olive, her father, Willow, and Graham all rode in the carriage that Graham had leased. He wouldn't let their father pay for part of the wagon. He was going out to the farm anyway, but even Olive recognized that he could've gotten a smaller, less expensive rig if it hadn't been for them catching a ride.

"I only wish your mother could meet the little one." Her father's eyes filled with tears as they reached the family's property. "She would have been so happy."

Olive felt the weight of sorrow on her chest as she climbed out of the buggy. Would it always accompany joyful news from here on out? Every milestone, every celebration would be missing the most important person in their family. And what about her own milestones? Would there ever be any, and who would she celebrate them with?

"Mother will meet this child and all of our children." Willow took her father's hand in hers as they walked toward Granny Laura's house. "That's the promise of heaven. Not only will we see Jesus, but we'll see the ones we lost. Mother will see us all again, and we'll introduce her to the family that grew while she was gone."

Having Willow home brought back the loss of her mother afresh. Olive had forgotten how lost she'd been before taking the job for Mr. Scott. She'd forgotten the daily trip to her mother's grave, the hours spent grieving there. Guilt beset her that she wasn't grieving as she should. Was it right, was it decent that she looked forward to the morning? That she had hopes that moved on beyond the day her mother's hopes ended?

Olive shook the heavy weight of dread that had panged and

went to accept the greetings of all the family gathered outside. Working with the Scott children and working on Blount's house had revived her. Maybe the family had been right to push her, yet she didn't need any more pushing. She had taken on new challenges, and now things were fine as they were.

Granny carried a tub of cornmeal mixture for the fish fry out to where Amos was stoking up a fire, while Aunt June and Amos set the grate over the stones to hold the cast-iron skillet.

Only Calista's family, Olive's Kansas City cousins, were missing. It was the first time they had all been together since the funeral, but it was clear that for all of them, life had moved on. Even for Olive.

"You should've seen Mr. and Mrs. Bragg when they came to visit." Uncle Bill toted a bale of hay out of the barn for seating next to the fire. "They weren't sure what to make of all the shenanigans going on out here but, after a spell, they settled in and had good fellowship. It helps that Maisie has broken them in."

Maisie's society in-laws didn't know what to make of it when their recluse son married the fiery farm girl, but they'd learned to love Maisie. And she was fiercely protective of them.

"They ain't used to people carrying on like that but they are good folks." Maisie lifted a hay bale and tossed it to its place. "We're getting along just fine," she said as she picked a piece of hay from her hair.

"What I want to know about," said Willow, "is Olive and Mr. Scott. Do you have anything to report, Olive?"

Olive glared at her sister. Why couldn't Willow relent? "There's nothing to know. I work for him of the evenings while he's squiring his girlfriend about." She took her place at the folding table and began to coat the catfish fillets in egg.

"Has he noticed how beautiful you are?" Calista asked.

"Did you miss my mention of his girlfriend?" Olive slapped a fillet into the cornmeal mixture. "If he didn't like her so much, I wouldn't be at his house in the first place."

"I met the man today." Graham tried to dust off a place to sit on the hay bale, but seeming to realize the futility of the action, took a seat anyway. "We talked about you designing our railcar."

"You didn't!" Olive looked around the circle of her kin. She should've made each of them go to the Secret Tree and swear to never reveal her hobby.

"Whew!" said Amos. "Cat's finally out of the bag and I can stop pretending to know what I'm doing with construction. Now I can start pretending to know what I'm doing with farming."

"Your secret is still safe," said Graham. "I told him that it was a member of Willow's family designing it, but I don't think he thought twice about it. But you have to tell him. How can your relationship progress if you hide the fact that you're both working in the same industry?"

"Girlfriend. He has a girlfriend."

"That's right," said Maisie, "and he invited you to go on a double date with them to the Schifferdecker Electric Park. Who are you going to take?"

"I want to go to the Electric Light Park," said Amos.

"No!" chorused everyone present.

"What happened to that nice boy from church?" asked Granny Laura. "He was always sweet on you."

"He's married," Olive said. All the nice boys she grew up with had found love while she was sitting at home with her mother.

"Granny, we've already made arrangements," said Willow. "We weren't going to take any chances."

"I'm not going," said Olive.

"Yes, you are, and Marlowe is going to take you." Willow had a look of mischievous glee in her eyes.

"Marlowe Buchanan?" Olive looked to Graham for confirmation.

"My brother is coming to town anyway. He's the perfect choice. Suave, debonair, and fully capable of making another man jealous."

Forgetting that her hands were covered with raw fish and corn-meal, Olive tried to rub the lines out of her forehead. "What did you tell Marlowe? That I'm incapable of getting an escort on my own and I need a pity escort? That there's no one I know in the area who would agree to spend time with me?"

Her sister shrugged. "He's excited about the prospect of spending time with you. Marlowe will know exactly what's called for."

It was one thing for her adventurous sister to marry into the wealthy Buchanan family. That was Willow's decision, and she had adapted beautifully. But for another member of that family to be dragged down to Joplin to pretend to be the beau of quiet, retiring Olive was humiliating.

And yet . . .

When Mr. Scott had suggested the outing, she'd recognized it as the perfect opportunity to prove to him that she wasn't a sad spinster mooning over their one misguided kiss. It'd show him that the kiss meant nothing to her and that she wasn't too embarrassed to be in his company, watching his children, borrowing from his library.

But Marlowe Buchanan? Olive had worried that any friend of the family that could be hornswoggled into escorting her wouldn't measure up to Ruby's standards. They would only make Olive feel more inferior. Marlowe Buchanan, on the other hand, would impress anyone. She'd only met him once, at Willow and Graham's wedding, but if she had to go, it'd be good to show Mr. Scott and Ruby that she had options, even if the options she showed were counterfeit.

For the first time, Olive began to have some hope that she could put Mr. Scott in his place and out of her mind.

CHAPTER
16

Be grateful. That's what Maxfield had to work on. He had two wonderful children he loved dearly. He had a career that he found exciting and fulfilling. All of his financial needs were met. Yes, he'd faced sorrow and loss, but God had given him Georgia in the first place. It wasn't for Maxfield to dictate how long he'd been allowed to keep her in his life. Gratitude. Anything less was being discontented with the gifts God had given him. He would be thankful, even as he was demolishing the wall of the Dennis house in order to rebuild it a few feet over.

Because he wasn't perfect, because he had a propensity to wallow in discontent, Max had gone out of his way that morning to stroll by Blount's house. He had hoped to see Mr. Blount outside and pretend that the meeting was accidental. When the indirect approach didn't work, he'd knocked on the door, only to find that the Blounts were out of town. He'd have to find his information another way. He walked around the front of the house to the west side that was under construction.

Mrs. Wester was staying with the children while he, Ruby, Miss Kentworth, and a friend went to the Schifferdecker Electric Park that evening. If he was going to face bad news, it might as well be today, because he fully expected his evening to be delightful. Delightful enough to wash away any frustrations he exposed himself to. Tonight would be the spoonful of sugar to follow the medicine.

And the medicine was seeing a second home of his disassembled. The wall had been down for a time and now the balloon structure had gone up, framing what was to come in the future. He'd just begun to feel a small sense of relief that whoever was building hadn't done so in a manner that took away from the design, when that relief was squashed like an egg hit by a hammer. What was that framework for? With the distinctive grouping of three elongated windows, it could only be one thing.

"Excuse me. May I have a word with you?" He'd spotted Mr. Flowers and knew him to be the foreman of the construction crew. "Is it true that a Mr. Kentworth is the designer of this place?"

"Yes, sir. That's him over there." Mr. Flowers pointed, then whistled. "Mr. Kentworth, Mr. Scott wants to have a word."

Amos Kentworth marched across the lawn with his canvas pants tucked into his work boots and his plaid shirt untucked from his waistband. "Mr. Scott, it's an honor to have you visit. How may I help you?"

"Can you tell me what you intend to put in that space right there?" Maxfield pointed to the offending framework.

Amos hesitated before answering strongly, "Palomino windows."

"What in heaven's name are Palomino windows?"

"Palestine windows?" Amos scratched his head. "It's Palo-something."

"Palladian. It's Palladian!" Maxfield could feel his temper rising. "I am the only builder in this town who uses Palladian windows. It's my signature window. No one else in Joplin uses them besides me."

Amos lifted his chin and a dangerous mischievousness lit in his eyes. "I reckon there's two of us using them now."

"You don't even know what they are named. How can you use them?"

"It don't matter what I call them as long as they look right, and I reckon they do or you wouldn't have recognized them."

"You haven't recognized this building for what it is—a masterpiece. But you come in here and alter it as if you, in your juvenile understanding, could improve upon it some way."

"I think you mean to insult me." Amos pushed up his sleeves. "I'm a mighty fine draw-er of houses but even better in a tussle. If I ain't afraid to tear down the wall of this here house, just think what I'm willing to do to a man."

Maxfield took a step back. He was used to negotiating with his contractors and with city permit grantors. Occasionally arguments got heated, but Kentworth didn't even seem that angry. Kentworth seemed to want a fight like he wanted a second helping of pie after his possum stew.

"If you hope to have any manner of career, you should consider before you imitate another man's style." Maxfield eased off the property as he spoke, wanting to avoid an altercation before his evening out. "Once people brand you as a hack, you'll have trouble getting work."

"I reckon that's none of your concern." He looked disappointed that Maxfield wasn't challenging him. Let that be a small victory. Maxfield had disappointed him.

In the meanwhile, whether by design or not, Amos Kentworth was wrecking Maxfield's peace of mind as well as his building schedule. It was almost like he knew exactly where to strike to cause Maxfield the most angst. When Maxfield thought about it, both of those Kentworths were making him lose sleep . . . and his mind.

"Miss Kentworth, how extravagantly breathtaking you are tonight." Marlowe Buchanan stood on Olive's doorstep with a bundle of roses too large for any vase she and her father owned.

"You already had that speech prepared before you saw me." Olive stepped aside to allow the dapper gentleman entrance. "Father, you know Mr. Buchanan."

"Please, call me Marlowe." He removed his straw hat with the striped ribbon around the crown. "We're family, after all."

Because family were the only ones she could count on.

"Alright, Marlowe. Would you like some iced tea, or maybe some bread and apple butter?" Most people would feel self-conscious about their homes when a Buchanan entered, but that never occurred to Oscar Kentworth. Possessions didn't matter to him, and he couldn't imagine that they mattered to anyone else either.

"We have a schedule to keep, but I thank you for the offer." He held the roses out to Olive. "I had no idea how big this bouquet would be when I ordered it. I hope you have room for these."

"I'll take them." Her father stepped forward and relieved Marlowe of his burden. "You two have a good time." He winked, as if it were possible that Marlowe Buchanan had an interest in his daughter.

A good time wasn't in Olive's plans. She couldn't believe she was doing this. Stepping out with a stranger, although he was the brother of her brother-in-law, to impress her employer and his date? What had gotten into her? Ever since that day when Maisie sawed off the tree limb, her world had spun out of control. Tonight was just another revolution away from sanity.

"We should plan our campaign now," Marlowe said as they walked toward the streetcar stop. "The most successful endeavors don't happen by accident."

"What are you talking about?" Olive stuffed her handkerchief into the pocket of her gray skirt. "I'm not interested in accomplishing anything. We are in pursuit of entertainment."

"Not according to my orders. Graham and Willow were very clear on the fact that if Maxfield Scott hasn't taken notice of you by the end of the evening, I'll have failed at my task. And Buchanans never accept failure."

"Mr. Buchanan!" Olive widened her eyes as her jaw worked to find the words. "Mr. Buchanan, that is not the purpose of this evening." Maxfield Scott had had an opportunity to take notice of her, and he'd declined. "I am not setting my cap for Mr. Scott."

"I asked you to call me Marlowe, since we're intimate."

"We are not intimate."

"Of course not, but if you want to be intimate with Mr. Scott, then you should act intimate with me. It's a pardonable compromise."

His poise and certainty about an issue that did not concern him was infuriating. If Willow wasn't carrying Olive's new nephew or niece, Olive would throttle her.

"I am not striving to be intimate with Mr. Scott. You've been misled." She turned the corner to follow the trolley's tracks to the stop.

"You are misleading yourself." His eyes, which never appeared more than half opened, slid sideways to appraise her. "Why is your name Olive, anyway? It's such a drab color."

"The tree. I'm named after the tree." Her fingernails dug into her palms.

He scanned her from her gray hat to her cream-colored blouse to her gray skirt, then shook his head sadly.

She'd endured enough. She stopped in the street. "I'm going home. Share my apologies."

"You can't go home," he said. "I'm not sure I understand everything involved, but I do know that this is what your family wants."

And somehow the family always got what they wanted. If it weren't for Olive's irrational desire to impress Ruby and shun Maxfield . . .

"I'll go, as long as you're clear that there is no mission beyond"—why was she doing this again?—"beyond showing myself in a positive light."

"To a man you wish would notice you." When she gasped, he

175

only chuckled. "This evening might be more entertaining than I'd hoped."

And all this time, Olive had always thought her sister married into a family that was different from her own interfering clan.

"Tease me if you will, but there's one thing that you must know. All talk about my building projects and my family are *verboten*. Mr. Scott and my cousin nearly came to blows over a project. If he had any idea I was the one behind it, it would ruin everything." Particularly her access to his library.

"What's going to happen when he finds out?" The ringing of the trolley bell alerted them that their wait was nearly over.

"That's a very good question," Olive said. "But I have enough to worry about right now. I'm not going to borrow trouble from the future."

Despite her brave words, the two-mile ride to the Schifferdecker Electric Park gave her time to worry about the thousand things that could go wrong between Mr. Scott and herself. And the biggest worry of all was the question of why it mattered.

She spotted Mr. Scott standing by the trolley stop. He'd donned a white suit that she'd only seen him wear when taking a leisurely early afternoon outing. In fact, it was the same suit . . .

"Maxfield, it's been too long!" Marlowe extended his hand then pulled Mr. Scott in for a hearty embrace.

Olive's mouth popped open. What was happening? Why was Marlowe pretending to know Mr. Scott?

"Marlowe! I told your brother to send my regards, but I didn't expect to be honored with your presence today," Mr. Scott said.

They knew each other? This was a disaster. Why hadn't Marlowe or Graham warned her? She stood, mouth agape, as they recounted their travels from Europe and how they both came to be at the same place. Noticeably absent, she realized, was any mention that Graham had married her sister. Had he explained that, then perhaps Mr. Scott wouldn't keep looking from Marlowe to her as if amazed that there was a connection.

Ruby joined them, ice-cream cone in hand. A smile passed briefly over her lips as a greeting to Olive but, unlike Olive, she wasn't content to stand silently and wait for them to finish their reminiscing.

"Max, aren't you going to introduce me to your friend?" How could she look so enticing with ice cream dripping from her knuckles? How did she prevent it from dripping on her bold red-and-white-striped walking ensemble?

Olive looked down at her gray skirt and cream-colored blouse. Drab little Olive.

"Miss Dennis, this is Mr. Buchanan, a traveling companion of mine. We met when we were touring Europe. Mr. Buchanan, a particular friend of mine, Miss Dennis."

"Please call me Marlowe," he said, taking her hand and pressing it to his lips. "I'm enchanted to make your acquaintance."

An eye roll was imminent, but Olive resisted. Good thing, because Mr. Scott was watching her closely.

"I didn't mean to overlook you, Miss Kentworth," he said. "How are you doing today?"

"Please, Maxfield," Marlowe said. "You must call her Olive. I insist on no formalities among my friends."

If Olive had any strength in her legs, she would've walked away.

"How did you and Marlowe become acquainted . . . Olive?" Mr. Scott asked, no doubt thinking how drab a color olive was.

Of course he didn't believe that a man like Marlowe Buchanan was interested in her. She wanted to end the ridiculous charade. But how to do so without looking even more pathetic? Instead, she took another look at his suit and said, "I'm glad to see your suit bears no ill effects from your swim."

"Maxfield, you went swimming in a full suit?" Marlowe hooted. "There's a story behind that, I'd wager."

"What did you tell her?" Ruby glared at Mr. Scott.

"He didn't tell me anything," Olive amended, remembering for the first time that Ruby had been involved. "But of course I noticed that he was drenched. That and the fact he came home early."

If Mr. Scott was grateful for her defense, he was unable to express it beneath the ire of his beloved.

"Ruby wants to ride the roller coasters." He spoke over the heads of the ladies as if signaling to Marlowe that he required assistance. "Are you agreeable?"

"I'm the most agreeable man on Earth," Marlowe replied.

But Olive feared that claim would be tested.

CHAPTER
17

Had Olive Kentworth kissed Marlowe with the same abandon that she'd kissed him?

Maxfield shook his head and tried to focus on their path as he led them to the roller coaster. He had no business wondering about Miss Kentworth's personal life. He must stop thinking about that kiss. Push it from his mind. It was the gentlemanly thing to do. And yet, even a gentleman deserved a respite. Maxfield had been hit with one catastrophe after another.

Not only was one of his favorite designs being marred, not only was it being marred by a rube that knew nothing of structure and beauty, not only was that rube committing sacrilege against his favorite design elements, not only was his current project being reset because of that rube and his desecration against the first structure, but on top of all that a sophisticated tycoon was courting the lady Max'd hired to watch over his children. A lady he'd trespassed against, and who had the power to ruin him socially and professionally.

Had she told Marlowe what he'd done? What they had done? It'd be just like Marlowe to save that knowledge to reveal at a strategic moment, leaving Max on edge, waiting for the next shoe to drop.

"My dear, would you like a gelato? It would be refreshing." Marlowe Buchanan, of the railroad Buchanans, couldn't take his eyes off Miss Kentworth.

She pushed a lock of her hair behind her ear. Was her hand trembling? Maxfield stepped back for a better look. She kept her face turned away from him as if trying to hide her expression.

"A gelato? I don't know what you mean."

Whatever was causing her distress, it didn't seem to be Marlowe. She stayed close by his side, and he was the model of an attentive escort. Too attentive. Maxfield didn't like the naked adoration that shone every time he looked in Miss Kentworth's direction. He should show more decorum.

"It's Italian ice cream," Marlowe said. "My apologies. Having Maxfield here took me back to Florence. I forget where I am. Do you do that, Maxfield? Do you ever come to your senses, and it seems that the people you are sitting with are strangers and you can't imagine how you came to be where you are?"

"If you only knew," Maxfield answered.

"It happens to me every morning," Ruby said. "I wake up in a hotel apartment and I wonder why I'm not in my own room, in my own house. Why am I surrounded by furnishings chosen by a decorator that did not consult me? What happened to keep me in this situation for so long?"

Max had hoped to take a break from the stress of his work, but Ruby had brought it with them. He felt Miss Kentworth's sympathetic eyes on him. She understood Ruby's charge. She listened when he bemoaned the complications of his projects. Olive was on his side, or at least she had been until he'd breached her trust.

"I don't need ice cream," Miss Kentworth said. "I'm content as I am."

In response, Ruby bit through the last bit of her soggy ice-cream cone. Max checked his ire. He had no reason to question Marlowe's interest in Miss Kentworth. Why wouldn't a man of Marlowe's class find her attractive? Rich women had no monopoly on beauty. Miss Kentworth's delicate coloring was exquisite. Her soulful eyes intoxicating. And her demeanor, the quiet, thoughtful manner in which she conducted herself, rose above class. Her presence would be prized in any parlor.

"Why are we so quiet, when we should be enjoying ourselves?" Ruby squeezed Maxfield's arm. "Marlowe must tell us stories about Maxfield in Europe. He's alluded to his time there but gives scant details. Perhaps Mr. Buchanan could fill in the gaps to give us a fuller understanding?"

"That was years ago," Max said. "I was fresh out of the university." And he hadn't met Georgia yet.

"Were you the life of the party, or did you keep your nose in your books?" Ruby asked.

"Would either surprise you?" said Max.

She widened her eyes so they were unblinking. "I think you're capable of anything. You've always been the jolliest man about town, but that changed when Mrs. Wester stopped staying at your house in the evenings. Now you barely get to town before you're ready to go back. It's a battle to keep you away from home." Her grip was leaving sticky fingerprints on his sleeve.

Marlowe leaned over Miss Kentworth and all but whispered in her ear, "You didn't tell me that."

Miss Kentworth turned as red as a beet.

Maxfield could feel his mood settling in like fog over the Thames. He felt like he alone was excluded from understanding what was going on. Why would Marlowe be interested in how late he stayed in town with Ruby? What did he mean by it?

Noticing that his friend was eyeing him with suspicion, Marlowe straightened and addressed the group.

"Maxfield was always the responsible one of our set," said Marlowe. "His best moments seemed to be when everyone else was making fools of themselves. He'd sit back and laugh with whoever was sober enough to enjoy the performance."

"That doesn't sound like the Max I know, or at least the Max I knew," said Ruby. "He never used to sit back and observe. He was always on the run to somewhere . . . or from something."

"Then we know two different people." Marlowe returned Ruby's smile, because everyone smiled when Ruby did. "But since our pronouncements are so dissimilar, we must call in a third opinion to settle the matter. What say you, Olive? You've spent time with Max, with his family. What do you say about him? Is he a wallflower, or is he heedless and wild as Ruby claims?"

Maxfield focused on the white rails of the roller coaster that rose above the trees on the avenue. He had half a mind to halt her response. On the other hand, he'd always been a curious man. Why wouldn't he listen to what Miss Kentworth had to say? If she was going to speak at all. He was tempted to look at her but could feel Ruby's eyes on him and decided that silence was preferable to making a mistake like that.

"I'm afraid I'm no help," Miss Kentworth said. "You and Miss Dennis will still be at an impasse because I can't claim to know one way or another."

Just when he'd settled that her answer was going to be as uninteresting as the question, she continued. "What is the nature of a maple tree? Does it have leaves or does it have bare branches? Someone who only knew the tree in the summer would swear it was thick with foliage. Someone who saw it only in the winter would claim it was bare. That's what I think of this controversy. You have known him in different seasons."

Ruby frowned. "That's nonsense. It doesn't match up. Most people settle down as they mature, not the opposite. I can't believe he was dull and uninteresting when he was young."

Dull? Maxfield had never thought of himself as that, and neither had Georgia. But he had changed. Loss had changed him. Marlowe was telling the truth. He hadn't followed the mad pursuit of entertainment back then like he did now. Or at least like he had been until recently. So what had changed? Why had he acted like that in the first place?

His questioning couldn't distract him from the careful regard that Buchanan paid Olive. Even though Olive was clearly embarrassed by his extravagant deference, she maintained her poise. When Marlowe insisted on escorting her around a puddle she could have easily stepped over, she acquiesced after only one attempt to dissuade him. What was interesting is that Max noticed how she started angling away from the next puddle before they came near so as not to have a repeat of his performance.

Maxfield had seen Olive at work and in her humble house. He knew she didn't require the chivalry Marlowe was attempting to bestow. And she didn't seem to appreciate it, which gave him hope.

Hope? What was he hoping for?

They reached the ticket counter for the roller coaster. "Does everyone want to ride?" When they answered in the affirmative, Marlowe said, "My treat," and bought four tickets.

He wasn't hoping to replace Marlowe, he told himself. Ruby was a better match for him, and when he had started to doubt it, he had made a fool of himself with Olive. It was better to settle on Ruby and protect his pride.

But he still wouldn't be sorry when he saw Marlowe's train carrying him out of town.

Waiting in line, Ruby was her usual sparkling self. She had no problem charming Marlowe, especially as Marlowe seemed to be someone who expected to be charmed. She fanned her hand in front of her face as she talked about how spicy the gumbo at Connor's Restaurant was. She trilled a melody while describing the latest singer to perform at the Opera House. She swayed as she imitated a tightrope walker that had plied his art over Main Street during Founders Day. Marlowe watched with faint amusement. Once he tore his eyes away from the entertainment that was Ruby to look at his calm companion. Olive smiled at him in her serene way, then he returned his attention back to Maxfield's partner.

Something about the exchange irked Maxfield. Any other day he'd take center stage along with Ruby and gleefully entertain everyone, but today he felt like one of the adults in the room watching as Leo and Stella sang the songs they'd learned in Sunday school. When a child took the floor, no matter how charming they were, the adults had to wait for the performance to end before returning to their conversation.

"How are Leo and Stella?" Olive asked under her breath as Ruby continued telling Marlowe about the new symphony.

"They are well. Ever since seeing your birdhouses, Stella has been crazy over birds. She stands for hours in front of the window and watches them on the back fence."

"I should make her a birdhouse. She'd see more of them that way."

"I've been meaning to ask you about that." Max took a step closer so he wouldn't interrupt Ruby's monologue. "Where do you buy a kit like that? The detail is astonishing. How many have you made?" He hadn't meant to bombard her with questions, but she could choose the ones she wanted to answer.

"I've made a few, and if Stella wants, I'd be happy to give her the next one."

Maxfield was touched. Despite the fact that it was his industry, Miss Kentworth was the one willing to build something for his daughter. Why hadn't he thought of that? Perhaps they could do it together and include Leo and Stella. He'd rather do that than whatever Ruby and Marlowe were conspiring over.

"What a perfect suggestion," Ruby said as they came to the attendant. "They are ignoring us, anyway. We might as well share a car."

"Excuse me?" Maxfield looked from Marlowe to Ruby. "What is going on?"

"Ruby wants to hear more stories about our time in Europe,

and I'm more than happy to oblige. With your permission, I'll accompany her in the first available car if you'll look after Olive."

Marlowe and his assumptions were too much. How dare he abandon Olive? Had he no concern for her feelings?

But Olive maintained her composure. "If it's alright with Mr. Scott, then I have no objections."

"Perfect. Wait until you hear what he said about the construction of the Eiffel Tower." Marlowe stepped aside to allow Ruby into the car before him. "No one is safe from criticism when Maxfield is around."

Ruby's reply was lost as she turned to take her seat in the small two-seater car before them. Maxfield swung open the door to the second car of the roller coaster and allowed Olive to slip inside on the bench seat. Even though the two belts were secured by a hook in the middle of the bench, Olive scooted as far away as she could, which wasn't far in the little metal car.

This was not how he'd planned the evening. He'd hoped to demonstrate to Olive that he was firmly attached to Ruby and that she could trust him as a friend. To assure her that he had no intentions of embarrassing her again. Instead, he was struggling to remember which lady he was accompanying.

"Have you ever ridden in one of these before?" he asked.

"No, but I've been in a wagon with my cousin Finn. It can't be any worse." She threaded the strap through the buckle and pulled it tight against her lap, proving how slight she was.

Max fastened his buckle as the attendant walked by and secured the door. "Keep your arms inside and your belts tight," the attendant called. "The Dazy Dazer travels at thirty miles an hour and makes sudden turns and drops. Your safety equipment is necessary to avoid injury."

The car jolted as the chain beneath it caught and began hauling it up the track.

"Whatever it is that Marlowe is telling Ruby, you shouldn't believe half of it," Maxfield said.

Olive's hair began to wisp around as they left the ground. "We all have our secrets."

He loosened his grip on the bar in front of him to turn to her. "What secret are you keeping, Olive?"

She was looking over the city of Joplin as it spread beneath them. Finally, in a voice so soft he wondered if she'd meant to be heard, she said, "I have many, but there's one we share."

Maxfield faced forward. "I'm sorry. An apology doesn't cover my offense, but—"

"She doesn't know?"

"Does Marlowe?"

"You can't tell him." Olive blinked wide. "He'll tell—" She clamped her mouth shut.

"He'll tell?" Maxfield was confused. Wouldn't her beau be the last person she wanted to know? Who could he tell that would care more than him?

"It's better if we pretend it didn't happen." Her full lips pressed together. "Let's move on."

"I agree. That's why I invited you today."

"I can't believe you already knew Marlowe."

Of all the bad luck. Marlowe was a fine chap, but not the sort of man one expected to court his employee. "I'm glad to see him, but you would've been fine without him," Maxfield said. "The invitation would've stood for you alone."

"What kind of girlfriend is Miss Dennis if she doesn't care if another woman tags along?"

It was on the tip of his tongue to say that Olive wasn't another woman. She was a friend who helped with the children. But he caught himself before uttering such a ridiculous statement. With a nod at the car ahead of them, he said, "She's with Marlowe. She must not mind too much."

The clicking noise slowed as they neared the top of the ride. The view was spectacular. Max looked to see if Olive was impressed but found her messing with her belt instead.

With one hand clutching at the rail, she tugged at the end of the strap with the other. "This buckle seems to be bent."

"These rides are brand-new. They should be fine." But he couldn't help but eye the bent buckle that had cinched her skirts tight over her lap. Sure enough, the strap was sliding out every time Olive moved.

When she pulled the strap tight again, the prong on the buckle inverted. Now the belt was worthless. It wouldn't do its job at all.

He looked about but there were no attendants at the apex. Ruby and Marlowe had their backs to them and could offer no help in any case. The tension was building around them as the cars slowed, leaned over the crest, and the passengers saw the giant drop before them. Ruby screamed her playful cheer, oblivious to the fear that was crushing Maxfield.

Olive's knuckles were white as Ruby's car disappeared from view. Max covered Olive's hand as they topped the edge and looked down at a terrifying drop. Slowly at first, the car started to descend, but it quickly picked up speed. The tempo of the *clack-clack* sound from the wheels along the track increased until they were flying along. The force of the first drop pressed them against the backs of their seats, but that safety wouldn't last long.

The first turn came so suddenly that Maxfield couldn't keep her from slamming against the side of their car. He winced at the thought of the bruise it would leave on her arm. Then, without warning, the car swooped in the other direction, throwing her against him. She was like one of Stella's rag dolls being tossed around by Leo when he was tormenting her.

Maxfield felt a panic growing inside of him. Olive tightened her grip on the bar in front of them. She planted her feet against the floor in an attempt to brace herself but the whole front of the car was open. If her feet slipped, she could easily drop beneath the bar. Shouldn't Marlowe be here? Wasn't he supposed to be responsible for Olive? But Maxfield didn't trust anyone else with her. She was his responsibility.

They were roaring toward another turn. Maxfield gave his own belt a strong tug, and finding it secure, he wrapped his arm around Olive's back. When the turn tried to rip her away from him, he stretched his other arm in front of her and caught hold of her waist. His grip was stronger than any belt strap. Especially when it meant protecting this lady.

When she relaxed her hold on the bar, he was able to nestle her firmly against him. Finally, she was secure and not going to slam into anything.

"I hope you understand," he yelled over the rushing wind. "Who would watch the children if you fly out?"

She leaned her head back against his shoulder and tilted her face to the wind. "It's the only logical solution," she said.

Her hearty squeal at the next dip delighted him. He was caught off guard by her reckless exhilaration. Now that she was safely in his arms, she was enjoying the ride with abandon. Maxfield's heart skipped a beat. Should he be surprised? Wasn't that how she'd kissed him?

They were taking another turn, both on the ride and in his heart. He tried applying logic to the situation. These feelings were false, brought on by a dangerous situation and his instinct to protect, but couldn't he embrace falsehood for just a moment? Could he acknowledge how nice it felt to hold Olive and look after her when she'd done so much looking after him?

He shifted his hold so it was more comfortable for both of them, and allowed himself to appreciate the thrills. He lifted his head to share her exhilaration. He squeezed her closer as they slung around another curve. They were both breathless with laughter as they were hit with each unexpected turn. It would be the best roller coaster ride of his life.

As they approached the end of the line, the car jolted and her head knocked against his, smashing his lip, but it didn't dim his happiness. She rubbed the spot on her head as she looked up at him with shining eyes. Maxfield felt his heart drop to the bottom of his chest as the car coasted to a stop. How could she trust him again? Would she ever give him a chance?

He still held her tight, unaware of anything beyond happiness and contentment, but as the car slowed and people on the sidewalks came into focus, he realized that his happiness and contentment were decked out as a fetching woman being held in his arms, and there would be some who would not appreciate his discovery.

With a guilty look at the car in front of them, Maxfield lifted his arm from around her. "We made it back safe, didn't we?" He was still buckled in place while she was sitting in the middle of the bench.

"Not entirely unharmed," she replied. Again she looked up at him, not having moved back to her spot. "I'm afraid your lip is going to swell." She leaned closer, her eyes on his mouth. All he could think about was the last time she'd come so close.

Now it was Maxfield who had white knuckles on the safety bar. He couldn't release it, for who could say where his hands would go? He felt like he and Olive were still racing through the clouds in the runaway roller coaster instead of sitting in the terminal as people disembarked around them.

"Miss Ruby, look over there! I say, I think that's a bear!"

Maxfield looked up in time to see Marlowe take Ruby by the arm and swing her away from them. He straightened in his seat as Marlowe cast a glance over his shoulder. The eye contact with Maxfield communicated his old friend's warning. Get away from Miss Kentworth before Ruby sees you.

Max unfastened his belt, stepped onto the platform, then reached back for Olive. She swayed a tad as she reacquainted herself with solid ground. Max reached to steady her, a quick hand on her waist before it could be noticed, then drew back. He bit his lip then winced in pain. The sooner he could get Marlowe with her and get safely at Ruby's side, the better. Else he was going to make a mistake and give his heart to the wrong woman.

CHAPTER
18

"I never thought Joplin would have a venue to rival the streets of Paris but, when evening falls and these lamps are lit, it is stunning. The quaint streets, the majestic homes, the wide avenues, every care has been given to provide a natural environment for romance. A perfect end to a perfect evening." Marlowe had kept up a cheerful monologue on their walk from Schifferdecker's Electric Park, never requiring Olive to say a word.

What could she say? She was confused. Immediately after declaring their kiss a mistake and promising to never relive it again, Maxfield had held her in his arms, reminding her how his nearness felt. Now, her normally jovial employer was as silent as she.

He hadn't said anything about the magician performing at the gazebo. No comment on the dance troupe from Hungary. For their remaining time at the park, Maxfield had parsed out his words with caution.

Olive had to stop thinking about him. It was unhealthy. Having left the park behind, they were nearly to the iconic Keystone Hotel that anchored Joplin's skyline. With jokes, teasing, and finally pouting, Ruby had tried to pry some levity out of Maxfield, but he seemed as unable to concentrate as Olive. Thankfully Marlowe pretended not to notice that two of their party were uncommunicative and the other was growing bitter.

"We might as well call it a night," Ruby said as they walked to the front of the hotel. "After that dinner at the biergarten, I don't have room for dessert."

"I'll see you up. Good evening, all." Without a glance at Olive and Marlowe, Maxfield took the brass handle of the glass door and swung it open for Ruby in haste to make his escape.

Instead of taking his cue, Ruby paused in front of Olive for a moment before settling on her words. "You should bring Marlowe around again sometime soon. He is a lovely companion. You'd be a fool to let him get away."

Olive felt sick to her stomach. Marlowe had been a lovely companion, but he wasn't the one who had caused the turmoil in her heart. She'd been so foolish to deny the attraction she'd felt for Mr. Scott. She'd thought she was too intelligent to fall for a man who was out of reach, but she'd been lying to herself. A few moments alone, a few awkward colliding gazes, and she was overcome with the roaring realization that she was hopelessly besotted by Mr. Scott.

"Thank you, my dear," Marlowe crooned. "Lovely of you to say."

Maxfield waited for Ruby to pass before following her inside the hotel without another word to Olive and Marlowe. He knew. He had to know how she felt, else why would he have been so quiet? And how could she live with the embarrassment? She'd go home, berate herself over the weekend, pretend to be sick to buy herself some time, and maybe by the next time he requested her help, she'd be able to trick herself into thinking that what she felt tonight was a fluke. That she'd experienced a temporary weakness brought on by the spinning roller coaster and too many sparkling lights.

It wouldn't be hard to convince herself that it was futile. If only she hadn't seen signs of interest in him as well.

Marlowe was watching her, a wry smile twisting his mouth.

"You look just like your brother when you do that," Olive said. She brushed her hair away from her face. "Come on. You have to walk me home."

"Just a moment." Marlowe was watching something through the glass doors of the hotel. "There. The elevator. It's gone. Let's go inside."

Olive propped her hand on her hip. "I'm not going to your room, Mr. Buchanan. Surely you know that."

His smile turned to disapproval. "You insult me, madam. I only wanted you to come enjoy the aquarium in the lobby."

"I've seen it before."

"But I have no familiarity with it, and I feel a sudden desire to have the fish identified." After an agreeable evening, her companion was demonstrating his wealthy, entitled expectations. No matter how Olive stared at his sudden change in manners, he refused to yield. "The fish?" he said.

"Very well," she said. "Let's look at fish, shall we?" Ignoring his offered arm, she pushed through the door and marched past the elegantly dressed patrons to stand in front of the lit aquarium. "I see some blue fish. That flat one looks yellow. And there's a seahorse." She turned to Marlowe. "I'm sorry. If they were perch or catfish, I might be able to help, but that's as good as I can do."

"Don't agitate the specimens, my dear." But Marlowe wasn't interested in the fish. He was still watching the elevator. "It seems I was mistaken. I thought our objective tonight was to get Max to notice you, but it appears that he's been noticing you for some time. Why have you hidden this from your family?"

Olive tapped her foot. "I'd go home by myself, but Graham and Willow would be furious with you for allowing it."

"Just another moment. It'll be worth the wait."

Worth the wait? She covered her forehead with her hand as Marlowe's purpose became clear. Why had she let Willow talk her into this? Marlowe Buchanan was just as treacherous as the rest of her family. "He's not coming back," she said. "He's walking his lady to her apartments. He'll stay and visit with her parents. He'll reminisce about the day and probably laugh at how we ruined their evening alone. He'll do anything to spend more time with her and will only part reluctantly . . ."

Ding. The elevator doors opened.

Olive and Marlowe both turned to see a worn and weary Mr. Scott holding his hat by the brim in front of him.

"That didn't take long," Marlowe said.

Mr. Scott looked uneasily at Olive. "I didn't expect you'd still be here."

"I prevailed upon Miss Kentworth to appreciate the fish with me. We hated to end the evening so early."

She was Miss Kentworth now? Why was Marlowe treating her like a stranger?

"It's not early," Olive said. "I'm ready to go home."

"Are you?" Marlowe adjusted his bow tie. "I was going to order some refreshments and enjoy this fine hotel where I'm staying. I suppose by the time I walk you to your neighborhood and sally back, the restaurant will be closed, though. It's a pity."

Olive glared at him, but Marlowe was unabashed. "Take me home, first," she said through clenched teeth. "Skipping a meal won't kill you."

"I'll take you." Mr. Scott put on his hat. "I can walk by your house on my way home." He kept his eyes on the door, refusing to look her direction and making it clear that she was being pawned off on an unwilling escort.

"You would do that?" Marlowe grabbed Mr. Scott's hand. "Thank you, sir. It's not that I want to abandon her company, but since I'm staying here at the Keystone . . ."

"Don't mention it," Mr. Scott said. "Are you ready?"

Ready to throttle Marlowe Buchanan and all the Kentworths that put him up to this. Olive gripped her skirt to keep from swinging a fist at him. "Fine. You can walk me home."

"Thank you for a delightful evening," Marlowe called.

Olive didn't respond but slammed into the door of the Keystone, flinging it open, as she marched outside. She'd never felt as inadequate as she had tonight next to Ruby. And if, by some miracle, Mr. Scott had some interest in her, it would surely be squelched by Marlowe's ham-fisted behavior.

The tepid air did nothing to cool her ire. Mr. Scott probably thought her escort didn't care for her at all. Or even worse, he thought that she and Marlowe had conspired to arrange this time alone with him. Which was the furthest thing from the truth. She'd rather be anywhere than walking with Mr. Scott right now.

"How long have you known Mr. Buchanan?"

Olive turned. Mr. Scott stepped into the circle of light thrown by the electric streetlamp on the corner. His worn smile had softened after an evening of moodiness, but he watched her intently.

"We've met once before. I can't believe he came with me tonight."

Mr. Scott blinked. "Only once? You can't be serious. What is this all about?"

The night air swirled around her, cooling her damp neck. "I wanted to have a day out and didn't want to be a third wheel. He was in town, so . . ."

"But Marlowe Buchanan?" He laughed. "Do you know how many women would give their eyeteeth to spend the day with him?"

"Look, I can walk home from here by myself. Thank you for your offer, and I'm sorry that Mr. Buchanan put you in this position."

"It's Mr. Buchanan now?"

"Yes, Mr. Scott, it is."

"Call me Max. I thought we settled that, Olive."

"The only thing that is settled is that I shouldn't have presumed to accompany you and Miss Dennis. We have nothing in common. We don't have the same upbringing, we don't have the same manners, we don't have the same understanding of the world. If it was as painful for you as it was for me, I'm sorry to have submitted you to it."

Mr. Scott tucked his chin and looked up at her. "'Forgetting those things which are behind and reaching forth to those things which are ahead.'"

"Then let's press onward. And home." Quickly, before either of them said something they would regret.

Olive didn't like this. She didn't know how to interpret his mood, which had swung wildly all evening. All she knew was that she didn't want their association to end. It couldn't end. Every uncomfortable encounter and misunderstanding damaged their relationship. She valued him too much as a friend, as a possible mentor, to risk losing him because she'd hoped for more.

He moved past her on the sidewalk, walking slowly. Olive stepped to his side.

"How's your arm?" he asked. "Is it sore?"

"More than likely it will be." She took a deep breath before asking, "And yours? Did you sustain any injuries?"

"Me? Nothing of importance. I was happy to be of service." He looked at the stars, then said, "I hadn't seen Marlowe in years. The two of you seemed to complement each other well."

They were back to Marlowe? Why couldn't he find something else to talk about? The dangerous streets of Joplin didn't seem as dangerous as this. "He seemed to get along with Miss Dennis as well," she said. Then clutched her fist against her stomach. "I shouldn't have said that. It was uncouth. I didn't mean any-thing—"

"But it's true. Marlowe has the happy ability to make anyone feel comfortable."

"As do you."

"But I might have wished that my date hadn't found him so charming."

"You're jealous?"

"No, and that's what concerns me."

196

Olive couldn't see his face, but he said it with a nonchalance that confused her. They'd reached her house. Forgoing the front porch, Mr. Scott walked to the fence and looked over it into the backyard. He pointed at her Tudor birdhouse. "So you made that?"

Olive had had enough of subterfuge for one night. "Yes, I made that, and it's not a kit."

"You designed it? That's incredible. If you'll allow me, I'd like to get a better look." Without waiting for her answer, he opened the wooden gate and went into the backyard. Olive paused before following him on the rock pavers.

Absent were the white sheets that had rolled in the wind like ocean waves. Instead, the clotheslines slashed through the night sky bare and ugly. Still, she couldn't help the shiver that ran through her at the memory of what had transpired there.

The silence cloaked both of them, and she wondered how he had the nerve to return to the scene of the offense. He walked beneath the lines and across the exact place they had stood, yet never hesitated. If one got goose bumps when someone walked over their grave, what happened in this case? Nothing, by looking at Mr. Scott. Just another sign that it hadn't meant anything to him.

With his gaze fixed above, he walked around the pole supporting the birdhouse. Finally. Olive had felt unequal to the vivacious Ruby at entertainment and felt like a dolt next to Marlowe and his sophistication, but there in her yard, looking at her work, she felt a sense of accomplishment.

"I didn't notice how perfect they were the last time I was here."

"I'm not surprised. You were otherwise engaged." Olive couldn't help the saltiness of her answer. Her patience was at the breaking point.

"And there's a Gothic church." He wandered to another of her creations, standing at an angle to the birdhouse so the moonlight aided his inspection. "Did you adjust the proportions to affect the view from the ground?"

"Of course. No one wants to see the bottom of a church. By building the upper levels larger, it made it look more balanced." For the first time since getting off the roller coaster, Olive felt steady. She remembered discovering the miniature finials and brackets at Mr. Dellmar's, which was when she decided to build some of her designs in miniature—a hobby that would use her skill while not destroying her budget.

It was good work. She knew it. With her confidence returning, she evened her gaze, but when she saw Mr. Scott watching her, she felt dizzy again.

"Olive, we need to come to an understanding." He ran his hand up the pole that held her birdhouse. "An understanding that puts our relationship somewhere between what happened here and the formality of every other day."

"Mr. Scott, I don't—"

"Max." When she shook her head, he repeated, "Max. Say it, please."

"Maxfield," she managed, "I don't know how a closer relationship would benefit us."

"I think of you as more than an employee. More than an acquaintance. I can't hide that. It should be acknowledged."

"It would bring suspicion on us. Ruby wouldn't approve."

"I wouldn't approve if I were her." He drummed his fingers against the pole. "And I intend to be fair. She'll need to know immediately."

"Know what?" Olive grabbed the pole, her hand landing next to his. "What do you have to say to Ruby? Would you tell her about . . . ?" Even still she couldn't believe it had happened.

"What I would tell Ruby is that I'm not as sure as I once was. That she has no obligation to me." With each word, the doubt that had troubled him earlier seemed to be fading. His countenance brightened. "Ruby is a good friend and a lively companion, but she should know that there's nothing else between us."

Olive felt like she was drowning. She stepped away. "Don't. Don't do anything on account of me. I can't take that responsibility. Ruby is lovely. She will make you happy."

He raised an eyebrow. "You don't really think so. Marlowe was right. I have changed, and not for the better. There's so much that I'm not sure about right now but time will tell." His gaze softened, making Olive wonder if he was considering a repeat of his offense. Then he blinked and said, "I'll see you inside so as to not trespass against Mrs. Wester's generosity with her time. Thank you again for braving an outing with Ruby and me. And it truly was ingenious bringing Marlowe Buchanan along. You might not have intended it to happen this way but I'm glad it did."

He motioned her around the house and ushered her to the door. "Good night, Olive. Next time we meet, I hope we can start afresh."

Olive couldn't get inside quickly enough. She pushed the door closed and fell against it. Of course she had dreams of Mr. Scott noticing her. Of course she imagined them sitting in the library discussing the plans for the new department store or her remodeling of the Blounts' home. That was as far as she'd imagined, and, frankly, that was what she wanted more than the romance. How could he admire her when he didn't know what she was, what she aspired to be?

"No, no, no . . ." She hurried through the darkened house to her room and shut the door, blocking out the sounds of her father's snoring. She had to convince Maxfield that he was making a mistake. That she cared too much for him to let him hang all his hopes on her.

Next time, she resolved. Next time she saw him she'd have a clear head and a steady heart, and she'd tell him that she had no interest in a love affair.

That would give her time to mourn her decision and to wonder what could have been.

CHAPTER
19

Would there be unpleasantness? Max couldn't predict how Ruby would respond. He gave Stella a hug at the door before handing her off to Mrs. Wester. He called up the stairs to Leo, but Leo was too busy playing with army men to answer. Ruby was a notoriously late riser, and Max had a mess at her parents' house to sort out. His plan for a room over the porte cochere had been approved by his engineer, who'd found the supports strong enough, but the furnace would have to be rerouted to get heat to the room, and that was going to be complicated. In the meantime, the siding and wall of the house had to be removed so construction could begin.

It was ridiculous and unnecessary. Why did people want things built, only to have them torn up and built again—in this case, before they had a chance to live in the home?

And maybe that was another reason he was willing to part ways with Ruby. When he first met her, she'd seemed everything that he was missing—light, laughter, outrageous fun. But too much time in the light could ruin your vision. As Marlowe pointed out, Max had never been the frivolous, eternally-needing-to-be-entertained man he'd become. Why now, when he had children to consider? Shouldn't he be more mature?

He was running from his pain. He was running from the quiet house and the sadness, and it was Olive's presence that had made it bearable. In fact, his primary reason for spending time with Ruby lately was that it allowed him to see Olive. He found himself watching the time, waiting until the earliest hour he could return home, so he'd be rewarded with a quiet conversation along the street as he walked her home. Knowing that, he had to set Ruby free.

But as bold as Ruby was, he could imagine her laughing in his face if he used careful words and apologetic phrases. Perhaps he hadn't meant anything more to her than a cheerful escort. He hoped so. The less drama, the better.

As he approached the property, the ringing hammers told him that the work was going on. Usually Max looked forward to seeing the progress. In this case, he dreaded it. This change was moving his deadline back. It was keeping him from procuring new accounts.

Before giving his whole attention to the site, he nodded at a neighbor standing across the street. Probably not a neighbor. Men who lived in this neighborhood didn't wear canvas pants, plaid shirts, and cowboy hats. Did he belong on Max's construction team? He turned for a better look and came eye to eye with Amos Kentworth.

"I thought I might see you here." Amos had his thumbs hooked in his pockets and was rocking heel to toe.

"Remove yourself from this property," Max said. "You aren't welcome at my site."

Kentworth looked down at his boots. "I reckon I have as much right to stand in the street as any. I came to be friendly. No reason to get your hackles up."

"You came to steal more of my designs. Were the Palladian windows not enough for you? Are you going to add a room above the porte cochere of Blount's house now?" It was especially irritating that the uncouth rancher had managed to masquerade as a talented architect, and no one was the wiser. Why had Max gone to school and studied if someone like Amos Kentworth, who couldn't even name the features he was building, could do the job?

"I just might add a room up there. Nothing illegal in it. Especially since Mr. Blount is sick and tired of living in the house you built."

Max took a deep breath. He had to cool down because this man didn't seem to fear an altercation. And he was some relation of Olive's. That could mean something in the future.

"Fine, stay and watch if you'd like, but do it from there. Don't come any closer."

"Max?" Ruby called. She nearly skipped down the sidewalk to join them. Wonderful, another person he didn't want any closer to the construction site.

With a nervous look at the work on the top of the drive, he intercepted her on the street. "I thought we'd agreed that you wouldn't come here."

"Mr. Scott is in a habit of telling people where to go, it seems." Kentworth tipped his hat at Ruby. "Amos Kentworth, ma'am."

Why did Ruby have to be so charming? She extended her hand and walked around Max to greet the interloper. "I remember you from the cave tour. I'm Miss Dennis and this is my house he's building and still he won't allow me to see it." She smiled at Max. "How do you two know each other?"

"We're both in construction," said Kentworth. All signs of anger had magically disappeared. He looked as harmless as if he were helping his granny knit. "Sometimes I finish up on work that he failed to complete."

Max groaned.

Ruby responded with her own dig. "He's taken so long to finish our house, perhaps we should look into hiring you."

"Ruby, don't talk to him," Max said. "He's a troublemaker."

"First he tells me where I'm allowed to go, and now he's telling me whom I'm allowed to talk to." Ruby turned her full attention to Kentworth. "You must be a very dangerous man."

Kentworth smiled a crooked smile that would melt the varnish off new wood. "Don't believe the half of it. As long as you're not slapping up sketchy work and passing it off as unique, you have nothing to fear from me."

He'd gone too far. Max bullied up to Kentworth, not liking the hard glint beneath the cowboy's humor. "You'll apologize or we're going to fight. I won't stand for the insult without satisfaction."

"What have we got here? An educated man but, when push comes to shove, he'll forget about the books and settle it with his fists," Amos said. "I like it. Too bad I have to whup you, because you might be a decent fellow."

"No one is fighting." Ruby shoved her way in between them. "Mr. Kentworth, you will remove yourself from my property, first of all. Maxfield is my friend, and I don't want to see his nose broken."

"I can handle myself," Maxfield said. "My nose is in no danger."

"Regardless, Mr. Kentworth surely has places to go, and you have a house to complete. No time for fisticuffs for either of you."

Kentworth winked at Ruby. "I admire a lady who speaks her mind."

"And I admire a man who is willing to stand up to Maxfield Scott." To Max's horror, Ruby beamed at Kentworth. "Maxfield, you insisted that I can't stay here, so I'll go."

"I need to talk to you," Maxfield said. "Friday didn't go as planned, and I'd like to iron it out. Can you stay?" Although, telling Ruby that he was considering seeing another woman might not be the most prudent thing to do while Amos Kentworth was circling like a turkey buzzard.

"We'll talk later. Work, remember? I need a house to live in." Her eyelashes fluttered at Kentworth. "And since he isn't allowing me to stay, I might as well ask which way you were heading."

Amos placed a hand on his chest and bowed from the waist. "However I can be of service to you, Miss Dennis."

Ruby grinned at Amos as they sauntered away without a backward glance. Maxfield was stunned. He'd thought through several different ways the conversation could've proceeded, but Ruby's departure with Amos Kentworth was one possibility he'd never considered.

He wouldn't be home. Not at this time of day, but not knowing where else she could find him, Olive headed to Mr. Scott's house, trying to smooth her hair for the hundredth time that morning.

He couldn't become romantically involved with her. It wouldn't work. Whatever strange spell Marlowe had put on him, it wouldn't last a week. He'd come to his senses, realize what a boring little bird she was, and then despise her. He would be ashamed every time he saw her, and Ruby would become her mortal enemy.

On top of that, Olive would never get to use his library again. If she ever did get the courage to do her architecture professionally and publicly, just think of the rumors that would spread. She'd be discredited as someone who was relying on her connection to Maxfield Scott instead of making her own way. She had to maintain her distance from him no matter how alluring the possibilities were.

Olive hadn't worn her black dress since her mother's funeral, but with the somberness of the message she bore, it felt like the right outfit. The stiff taffeta pulled against her shoulder blades, reminding her that she should slow her pace. How she missed her sweet mother! What would she say about Olive's predicament? It was impossible to imagine because if her mother was still alive, Olive would be by her bedside and not in this mess. This was exactly the kind of drama she always worked to avoid. So much for listening to her family's advice.

Olive stiffened her spine as she turned onto the walkway in front of Maxfield's house. She'd be kind, but firm. While she was flattered by his attention, she preferred to keep their relationship professional. Her job was too important to risk on the unpredictability of love. It would be too complicated. At her family's bidding, she'd agreed to go out and get a job, not to start a romance.

With her heart pounding, Olive knocked on his door. She'd tell him why she was there, encourage him to patch things up with Ruby, and then leave. No need to go inside. No need to draw things out. The less said, the better. That way when he did take Ruby out for a date and she came to watch the children, everyone would understand where they stood.

There was movement inside. Olive took a step back and waited on the second step. What would happen if she didn't reject him? What if they could have had a future?

No. It wouldn't happen, and she was wasting her time even thinking about it.

The door handle clicked, and Mrs. Wester swung open the door. Before Olive had time to appreciate her relief that it wasn't Maxfield, Mrs. Wester took her by the arm.

"Praise the Lord. I had no hope. I was praying and praying and now here you are. God sent you, sure as shootin'." She reached for her hat and secured it in her graying hair with a hatpin. "I was just writing a note to tell Mr. Scott that I had to go, but with you here, that'll save me the trouble."

"I can't stay," Olive said. "I'm looking for Mr. Scott. That's all."

"You'll see him tonight, I suppose. I tried telephoning his office, but he's out. If you send a messenger, they might find him."

"I can't stay with the children. These are your hours," Olive said. Stella's cries could be heard upstairs, while Leo was suspiciously quiet. "I've got important things to do."

"Not more important than what's befell me. My husband's manager called to tell me that he was injured at his mine. His arm got caught between two ore cans. They are going to operate, and I have to get to the hospital. Without someone to speak for him, they just might remove the arm. I can't stay here." She had already squeezed past Olive and was going down the steps.

"Wait . . ." Olive couldn't stay. She and Mr. Scott had a difficult discussion ahead of them, and she didn't want to be trapped in his house waiting for it. But she'd seen the anguish on the older lady's face. It was akin to the anguish she felt at her mother's bedside.

"Miss Kentworth?" Leo stood at the top of the stairs, pulling her back to the present. "Stella has a dead bug in her pocket and she's crying."

"We'll pray for your husband," Olive called after the retreating Mrs. Wester. Closing the door, Olive jogged up the stairs, bringing her scattered thoughts around to the children who needed her. She still had to see Maxfield, but the children came first. "If Stella is afraid of bugs, why did she put one in her pocket?" she asked.

Stella's cries were less from fear now and more from anger at being ignored.

"I put it in her pocket." Leo covered his mouth with his hand. "She didn't even see me do it."

Olive rushed into the nursery, stepping over toys and books. The offending bug lay feet up on a baby blanket. Seeing her rescue at hand, Stella began crying afresh, producing new tears to roll down her fat cheeks.

"Shhh . . ." Olive swooped her up. Olive wished she could express her own frustration as clearly as a two-year-old. She, too, would benefit from a screaming fit on the bedroom floor. "Leo, put that bug in the wastebasket."

"But it's pretty. Look how shiny the black is on its shell."

"If you wanted to keep it, you shouldn't have put it in your sister's pocket." Showing a stern face wasn't difficult under the circumstances. "Why did you do that?" she asked as he dutifully dropped the bug in the can.

"To see if she'd cry."

"That's the worst reason to do something." Olive kicked toys out from under the rocking chair before sitting in it. "Get your shoes. We're going to look for your father."

Leo dug under his bed while the little girl nestled her head against Olive's shoulder. Olive rocked as wildly as an open shutter during a windstorm. But then she heard Stella's deep breathing.

Her sobs had ceased, and she had stilled against Olive. Her soft warmth soothed Olive as well, and the rocker slowed.

Things weren't happening willy-nilly. There was a purpose behind all of this. God was the designer of her life, and His plans were perfect. She could rest as securely as Stella and know that despite the sadness and grieving in the world, God would bring her through it. Yes, she had to think, to plan, to act, but everything wasn't resting on her shoulders.

Stella was heavy in her arms, but Olive's heart felt lighter. Maxfield would understand. He would want her to look after his children even if she wasn't interested in a more personal relationship. Besides, he was so considerate, he wouldn't want her to feel uncomfortable. She could pretend to think he'd been kidding. And that was probably the best tack to take. Laughingly insist that she understood the joke. It would allow both of them to retain their dignity.

"I got my shoes." Leo had even tried to tie them on his own.

Planting both feet on the ground, Olive rose and jostled Stella. She really didn't have the time to stay with them. Today, Mr. and Mrs. Blount were to return to town, and they would undoubtedly have something to say about the progress on their new addition. Amos was supposed to be on-site to watch over Mr. Flowers and the construction crew, but it would be nice if Olive could inspect their work before the Blounts saw it.

As she retied Leo's shoes, then got Stella ready, the sense of peace she'd found earlier remained, and so did her determination to face her giants immediately. They'd go find Maxfield. There was no reason not to. She didn't know if Stella had a stroller or where it would be, but she'd carry her if needed. Having this settled couldn't wait. She grabbed a house key and herded the children out the door.

Maxfield could be at the Dennises' home, his office, or the Christman site. She'd pass by the building lot and his office on the way to the Dennis house, so she'd go there first. As soon as she handed the children off to him, she'd be free to go to the Blounts, and going by there was necessary.

At first, she let Stella chase after Leo on the sidewalk, but when they crossed through the business district, she took both of them by the hand and slowed her steps accordingly.

"That's Daddy's office." Leo pointed as they approached the redbrick structure. But his daddy wasn't at the office. Neither was he at the empty lot where the department store was going in. The tall grass jutting out around the rocks showed that nothing had been started yet. Shouldn't his crew have the lot cleared by now? Olive tugged Stella closer. If anyone understood the frustration of a slow start on a project, it was her. Hampered by her desire for secrecy, it seemed she'd waited forever to get Amos to push the right people and get ground broken. If even Maxfield Scott had trouble keeping to a deadline, how was she supposed to do it? It made her feel better.

From the street, the Dennises' house looked complete. The impressive Second Empire mansard roof with patterns made from slate looked fitting for a lady like Ruby Dennis. The lawn had been cleared of debris and landscapers were installing roses. She recognized the shadow of scaffolding from the front of the house. What was going on there? Why would he have left the scaffolding up?

"Let's find your father." Olive swung around the side of the house, careful not to trample any of the new greenery that was going in. Above the entryway and over the protected drive the new wall and siding had been removed and was leaning against the house, ready to be reinstalled when the expansion was complete. Lumber crashed to the ground as the workers tossed it over the edge of the porch. A pile of debris formed on the opposite side of the drive.

Why did Mr. Dennis want this done? The porte cochere looked elegant extending over the curved drive. The effect would be wasted by putting another bulky story atop the porch. Olive stepped back to get a better look at it. Surely Maxfield would figure out how to

209

make it look splendid, but it was a pity that Mr. Dennis questioned his original design. This really wasn't an improvement.

But, as was her practice, if she looked long enough, she could come up with some options that would alter the effect. Maybe it was a matter of preference—no clear better or worse—but she would've done things differently.

No sign of Maxfield. She'd take the children around to the side entrance and knock on the door. Surely the foreman would know where he was. But where were the children?

Her gaze traveled down, below the porte cochere, to where Leo straddled the lowest bar of the scaffolding with his little arms stretched as high over his head as he could reach. Stella lay with her stomach across a bar, putting a crease into her soft tummy.

"No, no, get away from there." Olive checked to see that the falling demolition materials weren't close. Then she ran toward them, but before she could reach them, a furious Maxfield came running out of the house.

With an ashen face and pounding feet, he snatched both children away from the scaffolding. So quickly did he grab them that Stella's head bumped against a bar, though she was too stunned to cry. Olive was too stunned as well. Especially when Maxfield raced past her and onto the sidewalk before stopping.

He hugged the two children tightly to him. Olive looked back at the scaffolding. Had she missed something? It was secure and in no danger of collapsing. Her main concern had been the boards being tossed from above, but the children were nowhere near that peril.

"What are you doing here?" He wasn't yelling, but his voice strained with passion that drove less angry men to break things.

"I was looking for you." Olive didn't come too close. His response confused her.

"Ladies and children are not allowed on my construction sites. Never. Is that clear?" He moved Stella's hand to kiss the bump that was forming on her forehead.

"It wasn't ideal to bring Leo and Stella, but certainly you aren't upset that I'm here."

"I am." He kept his gaze steady even though it was evident he was fighting strong emotions. "No ladies are welcome at my construction sites. That means you. Especially you."

Olive straightened. Did he know about her career? Is that why he didn't want her looking at his work? But he seemed more focused on the children. Either way, for someone who rarely crossed lines, she resented being scolded over one she didn't realize existed.

"I apologize for the children getting out of hand, but why wouldn't I—"

"Where is Mrs. Wester?" He was kneeling with both children within his arms.

"Her husband was injured at the mine. She asked me to stay with—"

"Why didn't you keep them at home?" The first signs of panic were fading but he was still being obstinate.

"I wanted to see you. We need to talk."

He stood and reached for her. Cupping the back of her head, Maxfield pulled her under his arm and against his chest. Stunned, Olive didn't know what to do.

With the same harsh kiss he'd dropped on Stella's head pressed against hers, he released her and passed Stella into her hands. Taking Leo's hand, he started down the street. "We're going home," he said.

"You're taking them?" Olive looked at Stella, who was still rubbing her head. If he was going home, then why did he need her? But there was still a conversation to be had. That was her whole reason for finding him today.

"You come too."

She'd follow. She had something to tell him, but perhaps what he needed to share was just as important.

CHAPTER
20

Things hadn't gone the way he'd planned. Maxfield had to control this irrational fear that spiked whenever he thought of someone vulnerable, someone he was responsible for, at one of his construction sites. Why was he going home? He could've sent Olive with the children alone, but he still felt that need to protect. He couldn't think of the next step until he'd seen with his own eyes that they were safely home.

Going through the business district was the worst. "Hiya, Max. You got your boy with you today?" Maxfield sidestepped the city councilman and kept going.

"Mr. Scott, any idea when you're going to break ground on the department store?"

"Sorry, no time." He plowed ahead like he was fleeing a pack of wolves.

"Slow down, Daddy," Leo said.

Maxfield had reached down to pick him up when he realized that Olive was falling behind too. He couldn't carry all three of them.

"Okay, Leo. We'll slow down." He waited for her to catch up and that's when he saw them.

Amos Kentworth stood amid the café tables on the sidewalk in front of Connor's Restaurant with his arm raised over his head. His legs were spaced wide, and he rocked as he circled his hand high in the air, mimicking a cowboy lassoing a cow. With a straightening of his arm, he pretended to toss the rope over one of the small round tables. And who did he catch in his pretend lasso? None other than Ruby Dennis, who was clapping her hands and laughing hysterically at his antics.

Splendid.

Olive saw it too. "Oh no." She sounded heartbroken. "I've got to stop him. He'll ruin everything."

Maxfield didn't relish another confrontation with Amos. Not now. "Let's just get home."

Why did he think everything would be better, all his problems solved, if he could just be at home with Olive? A few weeks ago, home had been the last place he wanted to stay. And how he wished he'd talked to Ruby already. He'd meant to notify her that his heart was becoming engaged with another. Was he still obligated to her? From the way she was acting with Kentworth, it seemed that she would be fine with the loss of his affection. Everything was such a mess.

They reached his house. Maxfield tried to walk in, only to find the door had been locked.

"Sorry." Olive stepped forward, pulling the key out of her pocket. "I didn't want to leave the house unsecured." She crowded in next to him to fit the key in the lock, then gave it a turn. She opened the door and motioned him inside, as if it were her house. There in the entryway, beneath his own roof, he could breathe again.

"You must be thirsty," Maxfield said to the children. "Let's get some water." Now the reckoning was coming. He'd acted without thinking, and while Olive had patiently gone along with his demands, she hadn't forgotten them. She watched him thoughtfully as he turned on the faucet and filled cups for each of them.

He hadn't acted irrationally, not given his history. But it wasn't something he relished talking about.

"My head owie." Stella tugged at Olive's skirt, wanting even more attention. Maxfield felt the same way and was jealous when Olive knelt to give her the attention she was seeking.

"Why don't we go upstairs and read a story?" Olive said. She collected the children's cups, then took his out of his hand. "Will you be here when I'm finished?" There was no coquetry in her steady gaze. Just concern.

"I'll be here."

She set the cups in the basin and took the children upstairs. Maxfield pushed the chairs in around the table, then headed to his library. His sketches had been left at his office with the expectation that he was going to return there before evening. He had nothing to work on. He picked up an architectural journal that he'd gotten last month but hadn't had time to read through. Unable to concentrate on words, he looked at the sketches of completed houses and the plans that were available for purchase.

Like the needle of a compass swinging wildly, then settling into true north, Maxfield's course was becoming clear. The last few days had been eventful and unsettling, but, after a season of drifting, he felt like he'd finally found his North Star.

He was still ambitious. He was still fiercely protective of his charges. He was charming and enjoyed giving people enjoyment, but that wasn't all there was to life. Life also included pain and loss, and if he wanted to get back to living, he had to face that.

He turned the page of the architectural magazine and stopped. Max folded back the opposing page so the illustration was visible to the binding, then held up the journal to see it better. He'd seen that particular window setting before. Somewhere in Joplin. It wasn't finished yet, but he knew now what the builder had intended. Who was it? He racked his brain before finding the answer.

Amos Kentworth.

How was Amos Kentworth, the rancher who was even now

clowning around, pretending to rope Ruby Dennis at a café, familiar with the latest innovation in Palladian windows? Max flipped the magazine closed and scrutinized the cover. Did Kentworth subscribe to architectural journals? He couldn't imagine that he did, but neither could he imagine that Amos Kentworth did any of the work that was ascribed to him.

It was also hard to imagine that the hot-tempered maverick was any relation to classy and calm Olive Kentworth. On the other hand, despite how staid and proper Olive looked, there was a wild side to her that surprised him. In a way, she was Max's negative image. Everyone thought him to be colorful and engaging, but he longed for peace at home.

Now he was home, and he wasn't feeling peaceful at all. He was more jittery than he'd been before, and he knew he would be until he'd talked to Olive.

He heard the bedroom door click as she eased it closed. He fanned himself with the journal before dropping it on his desk. The ticking clock echoed through the quiet house as she made her way down the staircase. Instead of her normally hesitant pace, she was rushing toward him and appeared before he'd prepared himself.

"Leo and Stella?"

"Asleep." She stood in the doorway, as if in a hurry.

"Thank you for keeping them today. I know you hadn't planned to." Seeing her in her mourning gown reminded him of her strength.

"There are things I need to do today, but first we must talk." Obviously this talk was going to proceed at a rapid pace, because she forged ahead. "This weekend at Electric Park, I feel like there was a misunderstanding. You and Ruby have known each other for some time now, and—"

"I don't want to talk about Ruby. I'd rather talk about you." There. He'd just say it.

There was a flash of fear in her eyes before she got it under control. Max didn't know what it meant but he was pleased that he had the ability to provoke such a strong reaction in her. Indifference would be the worst.

"About Ruby," she said. "You and she are perfectly suited. She's sophisticated and lively, and she obviously adores you."

"Does she? She seemed to like Marlowe well enough."

She rested her hand against her hip. "Is that what this is about? Did Ruby make you jealous? Are you using me for revenge?"

"Do you think I'm using you?"

She colored at that. "The seat belt was broken and that was the only reason you acted the way you did. I'm not reading anything more into it, and neither should you. Apparently we don't suit at all. The mere sight of me at your construction site was unacceptable to you. How could you think you care for me if you don't want me to share any part of your career?"

The intensity of her question surprised him. He'd hurt her feelings and not just from his outburst. Max had the feeling that even if he'd have calmly requested her to leave, it was the leaving that she opposed.

"Have a seat," he said.

"No, thank you. I don't intend to stay for long."

"I wish you would, because it might take me some time to find the courage to say what I need to say." He sat on the edge of his desk and crossed one leg over the other.

"You can tell it to Ruby. She's the one who needs a word from you." She tugged on her ear nervously.

"It's about my wife. My late wife. Her name was Georgia."

Olive's hand dropped. Her chin dropped. She took two steps and dropped into the chair.

"Continue," she said.

How do you tell a man that you aren't interested in his advances when you aren't sure he's advancing at all? That had been Olive's first concern. Secondly, she'd worried that if she didn't broach the subject, he would break off his understanding with Ruby, whatever that was, to pursue her. She hadn't thought that he might want to talk about the death of his wife, yet Olive, with her recent loss, could understand.

"I wouldn't marry a woman who wasn't brilliant, beautiful, kind, and lovely, so there's no reason to tell you all those things about her." Maxfield sat in the armchair next to hers. "Neither do I need to tell you how very much I loved her and our young family."

Olive leaned over the side of her armchair. "I'm sure you did." No longer lost in the landscape of courting and attraction, this was the familiar ground of grief and loss. She didn't need a guide here.

"I didn't realize how much I relied on her. How much I took for granted that I had a warm welcome waiting at home. That there was someone thinking of me throughout the day." His eyes ran over Olive and her mourning clothing. "I'd guess your mother was the same for you."

"She was." Olive's throat tightened. "For years she felt guilty because her illness kept her from doing all that she wanted, but knowing that she was there loving me was the biggest gift of all."

"Exactly." He'd rested his arms before him along the arms of the chair and now studied his fingers as they tapped. Two taps per finger down the line from index to pinkie and then back up. "I loved showing Georgia my buildings. I was always dragging her to a site to see the progress, even when it was barely changed from her last visit. I am a builder. That's who I am, but the reward for my work always included showing it to her. Without someone to celebrate with, it's not nearly as satisfying. Even that part of my life is less now."

The only completed project Olive's mother was able to see before sickness kept her bedridden was the miners' center, but she'd always shown enthusiasm for Olive's birdhouses and the designs she experimented with. Even when she was barely able to walk around the block, she'd stand in front of a new building and listen intently as Olive pointed out the features that were being planned. So many good memories as homes were created. Then why . . .

"You allowed your wife to go to construction sites but no other women? Was that always the case? Was she always the only one allowed?"

His fingers stopped tapping as his gaze drew away. "The porch cover wasn't finished. It was supported by temporary planks that were propped against the ground. It's standard, really." His voice was hollow, and it sounded as if he was reciting a story that he'd heard from a stranger and didn't quite believe. "She came with the children. Stella's stroller wouldn't make it over the loose gravel of the drive, so she left Leo and the stroller with one of my men just outside, then she walked to the door beneath the porch."

The hair on Olive's arms stood on end. She could feel the dread growing as he continued.

"There was a wagon from the lumberyard. It had delivered some paneling for the dining room and was loaded heavy for its next delivery. When it pulled away from the house, the back wheel clipped one of those supports. I heard the crash. . . ." He leaned forward and clasped his hands together between his knees.

Olive reached over and put a hand on his arm. "Was it instant?" she asked.

He shook his head. "We had a few days. Horrible, agonizing days. 'Time to say goodbye' is what people told me. But for the pain it cost her, it wasn't worth it. She shouldn't have had to endure that. I should've been more careful."

Olive hadn't known the man sitting next to her until now.

"You couldn't have prevented that accident," she said.

"But I could have. I could've insisted on a stronger temporary framework. I could've insisted that no deliveries were made in front. There were several things I could've done."

"But you couldn't prevent everything. Scaffolding falls, framework collapses, electricity shorts. If you weren't an architect, you might own a mine. Then you'd deal with cave-ins, explosions, and miner's lung. Or maybe you'd be a rancher like my granny and Uncle Bill. That poses its own risks. Life isn't safe, Maxfield."

He looked up at the sound of his name. Their eyes met and, despite her best intentions, Olive knew she was falling in love with him. She had come here to tell him that it would never work and here she was, doing exactly what she was trying to warn him away from. But this wasn't about her. It was about him finding the courage to put away the veneer of carelessness and show himself honestly.

He clapped his hands together. "Well, it's been a rule of mine since then that women and children aren't allowed in the buildings until all the construction is completed. The men who work there, they know the risks." He shrugged. "I have to try, don't I?"

Olive had always assumed that Mrs. Scott had died in childbirth, given Stella's young age. Imagining the young mother, knowing she was dying, knowing that she wouldn't see her children raised . . . Olive ached to go upstairs and take Leo and Stella in her arms and give them love on behalf of their mother.

"It's understandable that you want to try. It's admirable even, but women aren't children. They can understand and assess danger on their own. I'm sure your wife knew the risks. Seeing your work was important to her."

"It's terribly awkward to talk to you like this," he said. "Everyone has grief. There's no reason you want to hear mine, but I felt that I owed you an explanation. I wanted you to know why I acted like I did. I've enforced my rules to protect the women around me, all women, but until I saw you there today, I didn't realize the difference. You aren't just any woman. Not to me. Not anymore."

The house was so still and quiet, she knew he must be able to hear her pounding heart. What were the words she'd had planned? Something about that other lady—Ruby? Something about how he was so outgoing and merry and that someone like Olive would only slow him down. Now she saw the falsity behind his brightness, and she pitied Ruby because Ruby didn't know the caring man behind it. She also despised Ruby for demanding that he keep up the ruse instead of healing as he ought.

He straightened and brushed at an invisible spot on his knee. "Today, I tried to tell Ruby that I would be seeing her less often. That conversation didn't go as planned, but whether you allow me to court you or not, I think Ruby deserves to know that I don't see a future for the two of us. I don't blame her, but it seems that our association has been detrimental. It took Marlowe's observation to make me realize that I've become stagnant. It took hearing from your father to realize that I'm not the only one who has to live through tragedy."

She knew better than to make a quick decision. She knew not to change her mind on a whim, but if they were going to be honest with each other, could she pretend that she didn't care about him in that way?

"I don't expect any kind of answer from you, Olive. I didn't tell you this sad tale about my wife to garner sympathy or sway you, but I wanted you to know what I'd been through and why I reacted the way I did at the construction site. Also, I wanted to start our relationship out with no secrets between us. I've tried hiding how I was feeling, and it leads to misery. I want to be more like you, open and guileless."

Olive slid her feet beneath her chair where they hid beneath her skirts. Open and guileless? She might have another secret he didn't know about. How was she going to hide it if he continued to search her face like that?

"I'm going to do my best to improve, but now you can understand why I've kept my children away from my work, why it was so painful for me to be home alone until you came around"—he took her hand and squeezed it carefully—"and why I can never allow a woman to come anywhere near a construction site."

CHAPTER
21

"The roof on this addition needs to have a steeper slope." Olive pointed at the specifications she'd sketched on the blueprint. She had to lean around Amos's arm as he held the paper flat, so that anyone watching would think it was him explaining. "Without a better slope, rainwater will run back toward the house and get caught in that valley, so let's get the roof a little higher where it ties in."

Amos nodded. "I'll go explain it to Flowers. You stick around in case he has any questions. Be right back." He stuck a pencil behind his ear and ambled off.

Here she was at a construction site. What would Max say? As his nanny, she owed him no explanation for what she did when they were apart. And that was another reason, among dozens, that she should never become romantically involved with him. She'd owe him the truth. But what did she owe him now?

The night before, she'd come away with a better understanding, more sympathy, and a desire to help him any way she could. Their relationship had progressed from that of an employee and boss, to friends, but clearly he wanted even more. And she couldn't accept that until she disclosed everything. If she'd been worried what he'd think before she knew him, she was terrified now.

Olive picked up her compass and measured the angle on the roof again. With the increased slope she'd need more shingles, but she'd allowed for small deviations such as that. The sun reflected off the paper, whiting out her vision for a second, but when it focused, she was proud of the addition going in. It looked proportionate and, if she was allowed to boast, she thought it actually improved this elevation of the house.

Amos was standing inside the open framed area speaking to Flowers, then turned quickly, as if someone inside the house had called his name. The canvas that separated the Blounts' house from the outdoors moved and Amos ducked beneath it.

Olive rolled up the plans. Mr. and Mrs. Blount were home. She knew they'd returned from their travels, but she hadn't met with them and, as far as she knew, Amos hadn't either. What did they want from him? A report? Or maybe something simple like offering him an iced tea to show their appreciation. No. Her father had worked for Mr. Blount for years. He wasn't one for visiting unless there was a problem to solve. Olive had best get inside.

She picked up the plans and braced herself for what could be a difficult performance. Mrs. Blount was a smart lady. Mrs. Blount never expressed it, but she knew when she was talking to Olive that she'd gone to the top of the ladder. Mr. Blount, on the other hand, didn't pay enough attention to see who spoke the orders first, as opposed to who spoke them loudest.

Olive pushed the canvas aside and stepped into the Blounts' main parlor. Mr. Blount stood with arms across his chest with Mrs. Blount keeping her distance in the background. The look on Amos's face showed his opinion that whatever was being said was hogwash. When he was flustered, there was no telling what he'd do. Olive stepped forward before Amos could complicate matters.

"Amos, you left your plans outside." She shoved them at him. "Do you have any orders for me? Anything you want me to note?"

She held out her hand and motioned for Amos to take the pencil out from behind his ear.

Amos fumbled with the pencil. "We have to change our plans. Mr. Blount has new ideas about our addition."

Olive's hand closed around the pencil without feeling it. "Changed the plans? We've . . . you've already got the footings poured. The frame and window supports are finished. The fireplace—"

"It's not big enough." Mr. Blount was in his shirtsleeves, more casual than he dressed for the office but just as demanding. "I wanted this room to be bigger."

"We agreed . . ." Olive looked at Amos, cuing him for his next line. "We agreed . . ."

"We agreed on the plans, Mr. Blount," Amos said. "Any changes now would cost us in time and materials."

"Then charge me more. What do I care?" He shoved his hands in his pockets. "What good is doing something economically if it isn't what you want?"

But he did want it. Olive had made sure of it. Mrs. Blount caught her eye. With a disapproving shake of her head, Mrs. Blount mouthed, "I'm sorry," but she didn't contradict her husband.

Olive didn't blame her. Taking her notebook and pretending to be the secretary, she said, "What changed? I'll write down exactly what you want so that Amos will have it in his records."

"Yes, that's a capital idea. It's really simple. Write down that Blount wants the biggest house in Joplin."

Olive didn't move her pencil. "You had the biggest house in Joplin and now it's going to be even bigger."

"No." He jabbed his finger at her. "It *was* the biggest house in Joplin, but then Mr. Dennis made plans to build one even bigger. That's why I had this addition built."

Olive looked to Amos for support, but he wasn't understanding. "That's why you hired us?" he asked. "I thought you wanted another room."

But the pieces were all falling together for Olive. "He didn't care what the room was. That's why he let Mrs. Blount design it. He just wanted the square footage. And now Maxfield has expanded Mr. Dennis's floor plan."

Maxfield? Amos mouthed. Olive shrugged. It didn't matter. Not now.

"When I got back into town, I drove by to see how Mr. Dennis's house was faring and that's when I saw the room being added on the second story. The only reason I hired you was to have the biggest house in Joplin. If Mr. Dennis beats me, then we might as well stop what we're doing and move to Carthage in disgrace."

Mrs. Blount rolled her eyes, something Olive wished she could do without consequence.

"That's preposterous! That's going to throw all our plans awry." Amos didn't like being corrected, even when they weren't his plans being changed. He dropped his chin and shot Olive a look heavy with warning.

"How much bigger does the room need to be?" she asked.

Mr. Blount huffed. "I'm a mine owner and a leader in the community. Do you think I've had time to snoop around Dennis's house and measure?"

But he thought that she and Amos did.

"The house has to be bigger?" she said. "As long as the square footage is more than his house, you don't care about the design?"

"We care about the design," Mrs. Blount said. "I like the design as is. I liked the design before too. Maybe if you can add a little room without messing everything up?" She was addressing her comments to Olive, and no one seemed surprised.

Olive nodded her head at Amos. He raised an eyebrow. She wrinkled her forehead, making her signal even clearer. He coughed.

"I reckon we can fix this for you but it's going to cost a heap more." Amos rubbed the back of his neck.

Olive hated these talks, asking for more. This was one area that Amos and his nerve came in handy. She'd gladly sit on the sidelines for this portion of the discussion.

"The way I see it, we've already done all the hard work," Amos said, "and now you're asking us to start from scratch. Maybe even to tear down some of what we've already gotten put up. That's a heap more work, and I've got other projects waiting on me."

"Like what?" Blount was calling his bluff.

Never call Amos's bluff. No one dared more than him. "Bragg Industries is looking at building a new office building downtown. I'd hate to tell them I couldn't look after their building because Mr. Blount can't make up his mind on where he wants the wall to his lady parlor."

Bragg Industries wasn't building a new building, but since Boone Bragg was Amos's brother-in-law, he could make the claim with little fear of being contradicted.

"Fine," Mr. Blount said. "Get the measurements on the Dennis house and let me know what you're going to change to outdo it. I'll be generous if you can pull it off." He turned and disappeared through a doorway without a further word.

Mrs. Blount gave Olive a weak smile. "I don't know where this nonsense ends," she said. "I only hope it doesn't inconvenience you too much."

"It's not your fault," Olive said as Mrs. Blount passed, leaving her alone with her cousin.

"Inconvenience?" Amos blurted as soon as she'd gone. "I was glad for a break from the farm, but now Pa needs me to help sort the herd for shipment. Prices are high. If we don't get them loaded up, we're going to miss out."

"We don't know how bad it is until we see how much Mr. Dennis is doing." But she'd seen the extra room. It wasn't small. "We need measurements."

"You can do that while I'm at the farm. That'll give me one day off."

"I can't go to the Dennis house." Not after what Maxfield had shared. What would he say if he caught her there?

"Mr. Scott already ran me off once." Amos laughed. "Then again, when has that ever stopped me?"

"That's right, Amos." Olive saw her opportunity. "He can't keep you away. You take a measuring tape and get the measurements on that room this afternoon."

"And if he chests up to me again, we're having it out."

"Wait. Have you and Mr. Scott been feuding?"

"Yes, ma'am. He's no coward, I'll give him that, but I don't think it'll go well for him. He's too pretty anyhow. A broken nose will help him look more manly."

Olive rubbed her eyes. While she wanted to get the measurements, she didn't want to do it risking Maxfield's health and wellbeing—not to mention his handsome face. Besides, Amos was always one tussle away from being thrown in jail.

"What if I can get Mr. Scott out of the way for the afternoon? I could come up with some reason to get him away."

"I kinda cottoned to the idea of seeing what he was made of."

"He's made of bone and blood, Amos. But there's no reason for us to break or spill either. This battle between Mr. Blount and Mr. Dennis is a gentleman's war, and not Mr. Scott's fault. We're just the soldiers following orders."

And they were soldiers on opposite sides.

Olive pulled her hand away from the birdhouse and the shingle lifted off the roof, stuck to her finger.

It was too early. The birdhouse wasn't ready for Stella, but she couldn't think of any other reason to request Max visit her at her house in the middle of the day. She looked at the nearly completed Queen Anne. He would recognize immediately that the glue wasn't dry yet. Perhaps, instead of telling him she had it finished, she'd have to act like she needed his help completing it. She nodded. That made more sense.

Using her putty knife, Olive scraped off the carefully placed shingles and hid them in the trash bin. What kind of ninny interrupted a man's workday to ask his help gluing shingles onto a bird's house? Olive shook her hand wildly to get a shingle off her finger. Maxfield might think that she wanted to see him for more personal reasons. Would that please him? She knew it would.

Olive hadn't yet reconciled her secret role as the architect of Blount's addition with being a friend of Maxfield's. Those two parts of her life were kept in two different compartments. Very few people knew about her aspirations of being a builder. No one knew about the attraction growing between her and Maxfield, even if her family was hoping for something to develop. It seemed to Olive that as long as no one knew both pieces of the puzzle, then they could be kept separate until she figured out what to do about the mess.

The knock at the door shook her like a mine explosion beneath her feet. The hands on the German cuckoo clock read three thirty. He was early. Amos wouldn't be at the Dennis house until four. She'd have to keep Maxfield distracted for that long.

With another swipe of her glue-clotted fingers against her apron, Olive went to the door. A quick look around the house to make sure she hadn't left any plans or sketches out, and she opened it.

Why did he have to be so handsome? Why did he have to look so eager to see her? Usually Maxfield's greetings were delivered like petit fours to be admired on a fine china plate. This time he merely stood in the doorway, as if he was the grateful one receiving the gift.

"I asked you here for help on Stella's birdhouse," she said. "I hope I'm not taking you away from something important."

"Mrs. Wester's husband is back home and recovering. I didn't want to keep her past dinner, so I came early." His eyes roved her face the way an architect's did when they found a structure to admire. "I see you're not wearing mourning today. What should I make of that decision?"

She hoped Amos got his job done, and quickly, because she

didn't know how long she could handle the full attention of Maxfield Scott.

"I wore it yesterday because I had an unpleasant task ahead of me."

"Which was?"

Were her eyelashes fluttering? Olive blushed. And that was worse than the eyelashes. "It was telling you that you should remain with Ruby. That she was the right woman for you."

"If you really believed that, it wouldn't have been unpleasant." His dark suit looked formal for midday, but he was an important man. Too important to be gluing together a birdhouse.

"Today, I'm building a birdhouse. There's no difficult discussion involved in that, is there?"

Maxfield grinned. "One never knows when I might become difficult, but I promise to be on my best behavior."

He came inside, leaving Olive to close the door. Maxfield might claim to have been reserved when he was younger, but today he was his usual gregarious self. Or maybe he was trying to compensate for his sorrow from the night before. It hadn't been easy for him to be vulnerable. She shouldn't be surprised if he tried to smooth over the scene and hope she forgot.

She smiled fondly at him as she led him into the kitchen. She wouldn't forget. His sorrow had made him human.

"Thank you for calling on me," he said as they entered the kitchen. "I'm glad you feel comfortable requesting my help."

"I don't feel comfortable. I feel very foolish. You are a busy man—"

He turned to face her and the tenderness of his gaze caught her by surprise. Here, finally, was the emotion that she'd seen the night before and it stopped her in her tracks.

"I will always make time for what's important to me," he said. He took her hand and held it until the mood passed. Then he squeezed it playfully. "Now, what is it you wanted to show me?"

Olive moved a chair away from the table as Maxfield squatted so he could see the birdhouse at eye level. His eyes narrowed as he peered past the porch with the rail for the birds to sit on and into the actual house. He leaned to the right then to the left to get a better perspective on it. He shaded the window to look past the glass.

"There aren't actual rooms inside," Olive said. "The birds don't need a kitchen and parlor."

"It's exquisite." His eyes shone with awe. "How long have you made these?"

"Years. It's what I started practicing on before . . ." Olive bit her lip.

"Before?" He was too quick to have missed her slip. "What are you working on now?"

"Olive?" It was Amos calling from the parlor. He must have let himself inside.

What was Amos doing there? Olive's voice refused to work. She pushed away from the table. He wasn't supposed to be there, and he definitely needed to shut his mouth. "Amos—"

"I'm fixing to head over to Mr. Dennis's house to get the measurements." Amos's voice grew nearer. "Do we need the measurements on the new addition or the whole house?"

Max stepped in her path, preventing her from going to the living room. His face, she hated the pain on it. Betrayal. Confusion. But he wouldn't be confused for long. Not with Amos still gabbing.

"If you can keep Scott out of the way, then I'll be able to . . ." Amos stopped short at the door of the kitchen as his eyes fell on Maxfield. His lips curled into a dangerous grin as he sized up the situation. "Mr. Scott, I didn't expect to see you here. You're early."

"What measurements are you getting at Mr. Dennis's house?" Maxfield asked. His gaze shifted from Amos to Olive. "And what does your cousin have to do with it?"

"That's family business and none of yours." Amos winked at him, antagonizing him further.

"Amos, go home," Olive said. "I'll take care of everything."

"He's going to find out, sooner or later." Amos leaned both

hands on the back of a kitchen chair. "I don't know why you hide it. He's likely to be impressed."

"Go, Amos. Please." She grabbed her cousin by the shirtsleeve and dragged him to the parlor. "You've done enough damage."

"Don't blame me. He wasn't supposed to be here. Not until four o'clock. You could've left a signal at the door, or sent him away, or sent me a message, or something."

This was only getting worse. Pushing Amos to the door, she shoved him outside to the porch.

"Do you want me to wait here?" Amos asked. "It'd be handy to have me nearby if he gets cantankerous."

"Go." Slamming the door in his face, Olive dropped her forehead and pounded her fist against the door. She knew without looking that Maxfield was in the room. She tried to go over everything that was said and how it would piece together to him. How much could she deny? Was there any use in denying it?

"That's why you invited me here? Not because you wanted to see me?" Maxfield's voice was low and measured. "Preying on my fondness for you to help your cousin spy on my work?"

Olive turned, pressing her back against the door. "I'm sorry. I should've told you everything from the beginning, but I was afraid. I was afraid you'd laugh."

"You thought I'd laugh? This is my career, my calling, and you thought I'd laugh at you trying to sabotage it?" He shook his head with his eyes trained on the ceiling. "I thought it odd that designs from my journals appeared in Kentworth's work, but it was no coincidence, was it? I was paying you to watch my children and you were inviting my competition into my house, into my library. And what did he do with the information? Construct inferior designs that are a blot on the landscape of Joplin."

Olive felt like she'd been kicked in the chest. "No," she said, "they aren't bad. The designs are good." How could he say that about her designs? She was proud of them, but she wasn't proud of her behavior.

She leaned against the door, blocking his exit. "I was wrong, but not in the way you think. Amos didn't come into your house. I was the one reading your library. I wanted to learn. When I came to watch Leo and Stella that first day, I had no idea whose house I was going to. I couldn't believe my luck."

"You felt lucky because you could take advantage of me to help your cousin?"

Olive pushed off the door. "Amos works on my granny's ranch. Talk to him and you'd realize—"

"You pulled out all the stops, didn't you?" She'd never seen Maxfield's handsome face look so disappointed. "You gained access to my home, my resources, and then to make sure you could manage me, you gained my affection." He clapped his hands together slowly. "Congratulations, Olive. You put on quite a performance."

"That's not what happened!" She grabbed his hands to stop the awful noise. "Today, I was wrong. Place that on my account but nothing else. Everything before was genuine."

"Do you expect me to believe that Amos didn't get the window specifics from you?" He was gripping her hands now, begging her to tell him what he wanted to hear.

"This has nothing to do with Amos."

"It doesn't? I could understand if he swayed you to act against your conscience, but if you are taking responsibility . . ." Maxfield dropped her hands and took up his hat. "I hope Ruby isn't busy tonight. I'd rather be with someone vacuous but innocent, thank you."

Olive shivered as he walked past her and out the door. She'd known it was safer to stay home, to not strive, to not go forward. This wretchedness felt far worse than any she would've suffered if she'd have stuck to scrubbing gravestones. As much as she wanted to protest that Maxfield wasn't treating her fairly, her invitation that day had been a betrayal.

She stumbled to the sofa and sat. Maybe the reading material in his office was fair game and she hadn't purposefully used any features that he laid claim to, but all of her excuses would be pointless. The fact was that she'd used his regard to benefit her project at the expense of him and his client.

Curling up on the sofa, she made herself as small as she was able. Last night, Maxfield had bared his soul to her. He'd been truthful and authentic, and she'd accepted his regard. She'd been wrong to do so. Not until she was honest. But now he didn't care. He'd seen her designs on the birdhouses. He'd listened to her advice on the interior of his department store. He'd been around Amos enough to suspect that he was ignorant of everything but basic construction. Maxfield should regard her highly enough to know she was capable, but he still didn't suspect.

And he thought her work was a blot on the landscape of Joplin.

Olive covered her head with her arms and rocked, too drained for tears. How long did she lie there? Long enough to grieve her misdeeds. Long enough to acknowledge the death of Maxfield's friendship and to realize that she might never stop mourning the loss. Long enough to resolve that she would make amends, as much as was in her power.

And long enough to determine that her designs were as good as anyone else's. In that regard, Maxfield was biased against her.

CHAPTER 22

Maxfield clasped his hands behind his back and cringed at each bell tone that marked the passing of a floor in the Keystone Hotel's elevator. He was going back to Ruby. He felt like a turtle who had finally found the courage to stick his head out of the shell and, *whack*, a butcher's cleaver had sliced it right off. Despite the fact that a dead turtle couldn't go back into its shell, Max thought the analogy a fitting one and decided that an evening with Ruby was the same as forcing oneself into a dark, dismal place.

Why had he enjoyed Ruby's company so much before? He couldn't remember, but he desperately hoped it would come to him, and quickly. He wouldn't be able to pretend if the feelings weren't there. Surely the interlude with Olive was the aberration. Some laughs and a good time with Ruby would set him straight. He'd be back on track.

The doors of the elevator opened, and Maxfield walked the carpeted hallway to the Dennises' apartment. Already he could hear her ringing laughter. He steeled himself against the feeling of defeat welling up in him. He was back. This was moving forward. Things were how they were supposed to be. Or at least he had to convince himself of that.

He knocked on the paneled door. Although Ruby had complained that they didn't have any house staff besides the maids from the hotel, he hadn't expected her to open the door.

"Maxfield?" Her smile was as genuine as the ruby earrings that caught the light coming in from the window behind her. "Are you here to see my father?"

"No, I came to see you. I wondered if you would be available to go to Schifferdecker Electric Park tonight. I fear that we didn't do it justice last time."

Her smile hardened. "Are you inviting me only, or will Miss Kentworth and Mr. Buchanan be tagging along?"

Ah, yes. The piper must be paid.

"Just the two of us. Their company threw me out of sorts, and I'd like to make amends."

At this, Ruby stepped into the hallway while holding on to the doorknob behind her back. She walked forward until the latch clicked closed behind her. "I'm not being spiteful, Maxfield. I swear, going to the park with you sounds delightful, and I would gladly go . . . if only I didn't have plans tonight."

Plans tonight. The phrase reminded him that before he made any more invitations, he should find a new nanny for Leo and Stella, because he couldn't trust Olive inside his house.

A desperate sense of loss crested over him. Olive had betrayed him. He wanted to go back to her and have her explain it to his satisfaction. To explain how it was that she wasn't capitalizing on his success to help her cousin. If she'd asked him to mentor Amos, he would've been happy to assist the young man. They didn't have to be rivals. If only she would've been direct.

Then Max thought about Amos again and remembered that he didn't want to help him after all.

"Don't take it so hard, Max," Ruby said. "I think it's for the best."

He grunted in frustration. He'd been daydreaming about Olive while trying to pacify Ruby. What had happened to his oft-lauded social skills?

"I'm not dismayed." He felt like he was cranking the faucet to turn on the charm and the pipes hadn't been connected yet. "If your family has plans, then maybe another night."

Her lashes fluttered. "It's not my family. I'm going to town with Amos Kentworth. He came by the new house yesterday and invited me to accompany him."

"Kentworth?" Max stepped backward and bumped into the door behind him. "What are you doing consorting with the likes of Amos Kentworth?"

"He's so much fun, Max. You would enjoy his company, I think. He was walking by our new house when I saw him and he—"

"He was at your house?" After leaving Olive's house Max had tried to catch up with Amos to keep him from his goal, but he had failed.

"Don't be angry, Max. I know you don't want me to be with him, but I'm so desolate being in this hotel. Besides, now that Father has decided to add another addition, it's going to be even longer before we can move in. I've waited long enough, don't you think? And Amos was more than happy to make sure I was able to tour the home safely." She held up her hand. "Now, I know how upset this makes you, but you have to get over this superstition. Having a woman on a construction site is not bad luck. Besides, a builder like Mr. Kentworth knows how to protect a lady on the site."

Max felt like he was falling. Amos knew how to protect a woman but *he* didn't? It was a truth he couldn't deny.

"But I do want to keep it a secret," Ruby said. "My father won't approve of me going with Mr. Kentworth. Not since he's the one building Blount's house."

"Your father is the only person making any sense today," Max said. "Did it ever occur to you that he might have escorted you through the house so he could spy on it and steal the designs?"

Using romance as a subterfuge seemed to be the preferred strategy of these Kentworths.

"What does it matter?" she asked. "I don't care if there's another house in Joplin with some of the same features. They all have doors, windows, fireplaces, and staircases, don't they? Why would you worry about that?"

She didn't understand the first thing about him or his work. "I don't understand what you find interesting about Amos Kentworth." A public hallway was no place to have this conversation, but just like everything else that had happened in Max's life over the last few days, his preference didn't matter.

"Perhaps I'll find him less interesting after I get to know him, but I'm willing to risk it. Besides, Amos doesn't have all the responsibilities you do."

"He claims to be a builder, just like me." He narrowed his eyes as Ruby squirmed under his scrutiny. "Are you talking about my children?"

"It's good that you've wanted to be with them lately, but maybe you shouldn't be courting if you don't have time. You can't expect me to sit here in this hotel night after night. I don't even have a house to go to."

"My children need me."

"I need someone too. Tonight, it's Amos." Her unfailingly cheerful expression felt cruel and heartless.

"I'm disappointed that you feel that way, but it helps to know." It was like finding the splinter that had caused you pain. Digging it out was going to hurt, but now that he knew what the problem was, he could do something to remedy it. "Thank you for the time we spent together." She had been his friend. She wasn't responsible for his disappointment. "It was fun while it lasted."

He'd made it back outside before he could think rationally again. The problem was that he hadn't been himself lately. That person, the shallow version of him, was who Ruby enjoyed. He could keep her regard, or he could be the man God expected him to be. Once he framed his dilemma like that, there was only one path open to him. And it led to loneliness but obedience.

Without thinking, Max turned his steps to the cleared lot where Christman's department store was to go in. His personal comfort wasn't his greatest concern. He had to be more considerate of Leo and Stella. Without Olive, the house would feel too little, too dark, and too empty, but he didn't have to stay there every evening. He'd think of new things to do with Leo and Stella to entertain them. He would improve his fathering skills, but it'd take work. And time.

The sputtering engine of an automobile drew near and idled at his side. Max turned to see Mr. Christman in the driver's seat.

"Looking to get started, Mr. Scott? I'd like to see this going up."

Max shaded his eyes to survey the empty lot. He knew what he must do. It went against everything he'd always believed about a work ethic, and it went against his competitive nature. Here he'd just lost two women to a rival architect and instead of doubling his efforts, he was stepping aside. But he now saw what was at stake.

"Mr. Christman, I have some bad news. My current project is taking longer than I expected. I'm not going to be able to honor the dates I gave you."

Mr. Christman digested this information with a grumble. "How much time are you talking?"

"I don't know. Mr. Dennis keeps requesting changes to his plans. After agreeing to a plan, he wants it bigger. I don't know when it will end."

"I guess I don't stand a chance next to Miss Ruby Dennis, do I?" The portly gentleman pulled the cuff of his sleeve forward on the arm that was holding the steering wheel.

There was no use denying it. While Max would rather not have anything to do with the Dennises, he was too professional to base his operations on a lovers' spat. "Mr. Dennis has first dibs on my time. I have to finish his project. You'd want the same if I had started on yours."

"I do want the same. I want you to do it, but I can't wait indefinitely." He paused as a horse-drawn wagon inched around him on the crowded street, nearly clipping his brass headlamp with its back wheel. "You're forcing me to find another builder."

"Yes, sir. Go with my blessing. I'll return your deposit." It would cost him, but it was the right thing to do.

"What about your plans? I'd rather pay you something for them than start all over. You know no one is going to come up with a design I like as much as that one."

Max rested his foot on the running board as he considered. Let another man get the credit for his department store? That didn't seem right. But he and Mr. Christman had worked on them together. Now that Christman had seen the final design, he'd surely come up with something similar, no matter who he hired.

"You can use my plans for free. I'll request that you include my name on the design, though. At least it'll be there for posterity even if I'm not at the site supervising."

"Well . . ." Mr. Christman's fingers drummed against the steering wheel. "That's fair. I'd prefer to work with you but if there's nothing else to be done . . ."

"I regret it worked out this way but with my . . ."—what had Ruby called Leo and Stella?—"with my responsibilities, I must make choices."

If he wasn't mistaken, there was a new respect in Mr. Christman's eyes. "God be with you then, son. I'll have my lawyer send over a statement releasing us from your contract. Sign it and I'll move on."

He would move on while Max was stuck. But he was stuck with good things. He just needed to learn how to appreciate them better.

Let someone else have all the dross. Max would keep the real treasure.

CHAPTER 23

It'd been a week since she'd seen Maxfield. A week since he'd assumed that she was working for Amos and spying on him. A week since the second worst day of her life.

Coming home with a bag of vegetables from the market and a hunk of pork from the butcher, retiring Olive had done her best to be about town. Every day found another excuse to walk past the Dennises' home, but Maxfield was never outside. She'd gone to a dress shop for the first time since her mother died, just because it was on the same street as his office, but to no avail. She hadn't laid eyes on him since that awful day. Sleepless nights found her worrying about his welfare and wishing she could separate into two Olives—one who did the job she loved, and one whose only concern was caring about Maxfield and his children.

He'd been in her thoughts continually, but she hadn't expected to see a well-dressed man waiting at the door when she reached her house. Finally, she'd have a chance to present her case. Sensing her presence, he turned to face her, but it wasn't Maxfield after all.

"Marlowe?" Olive shifted the bag of groceries against her hip. "What are you doing here? I thought you were leaving town."

He gallantly took the bag from her, allowing her to open the

241

door to the house. "I am leaving, but I can't do it without saying goodbye and checking on my favorite Kentworth."

"Favorite? Even more than Willow?" Olive led him into the kitchen and motioned for him to set down the groceries.

"Willow is a Buchanan now. There's no controversy in my statement." Marlowe waved the wrapped pork at her. "But how are you? Did anything come of our outing? I could've sworn that Maxfield was besotted."

Olive snatched the chops from him and retrieved a frying pan. "Maybe he was, but he's not anymore. My client is competing with his client. Our projects make us rivals." Talking to Marlowe was strangely cathartic. "I should've told him from the beginning, but keeping him in the dark worked to my advantage, so that's what I did. I took advantage of him."

"You took advantage of the unrivaled Maxfield Scott?" Marlowe leaned against the icebox, his arm propped against the top. "I don't believe it."

"I did. I purposefully distracted him so Amos could spy on his project. It was wrong of me. I should've told him from the beginning that I was doing the building on Blount's house. I should've told him when Blount asked me to spy on him. Then maybe . . ." Olive shook her head. "It doesn't matter. It's too late."

Olive set the frying pan on the stove and dropped the meat into it. Maxfield's words about Amos being an amateur and a hack still stung. Amos's résumé was her résumé. Whatever credentials Amos lacked, she lacked. Telling Maxfield would only bring more scorn on herself.

"He doesn't know, and he won't guess," Marlowe said. "You have to tell him, and make it clear as day."

"And if he doesn't believe me?"

"He won't. Not at first." Marlowe picked at imaginary lint on his sleeve. "You can't imagine the snobbery, the elitism of those students in Europe. They strolled through the greatest cities of our civilization critiquing great architecture as if they were the superiors of the masters. Maxfield was no exception. While he knows a thing or two about architecture now, he'll have a hard time believing that someone who didn't study like him is qualified."

"So it's no use."

Marlowe's usually genial expression turned stern. "It's no use keeping it a secret, Olive. You've cleared the way, you've laid the track. Everything is ready for you. It's time to fire up the engine and chug forward. You might meet some resistance at first, but you're doing Max a disservice by not giving him a chance. You aren't doing yourself any favors either."

The hinges on the front door squawked. Marlowe raised his eyebrows in curiosity as Olive looked toward the parlor.

"Olive," her father called. "Are you home?"

"I'm in the kitchen," she answered as he and Amos walked inside.

"He's coming. He's coming to talk to you." Amos walked with a heavy tread to the kitchen. "I'm sorry. I tried to stop him, but he's got it all figured out. I could barely beat him here."

"Maxfield?" Olive asked as Amos dug a carrot out of the grocery sack. "What do I say?" she asked her father.

"Mr. Buchanan." Her father held out his hand. "Nice to see you again. I'm sorry to interrupt your conversation, but we have a rather urgent message for my daughter."

"Don't trouble yourself on my account," Marlowe drawled at a speed that infuriated Olive. "If there's something—"

"Who's coming?" Olive interrupted. "What's going on?"

Amos scrubbed the carrot against his canvas trousers and bit off the end. "It's not Mr. Scott. It's Mr. Christman. He's got plans for a department store, and he figured out right quickly that I wasn't the person he should be talking to."

This was something new. "Mr. Christman's coming here to talk to me? What did you tell him?" They'd been in this situation before. Not everyone was as obtuse as Mr. Blount. What would it take to convince Mr. Christman that Amos was the man to talk to?

"Olive," her father said. "This would be your fourth building project. When will you start taking credit for your work?"

"What does it matter who builds the buildings?" she asked. "It's just something I do. I'm not looking for attention."

"Sharing your gifts isn't boastful," her father said. "Your mother made the best pecan pies in the county. Everyone bragged on them. Did that mean she should stop making them? Withhold her talent from people because it was remarkable?"

It was on the tip of Olive's tongue to say that making a pecan pie wasn't the same as designing a building, but then she saw the pride in her father's eyes. Those pies and her mother's skill in making them meant as much to him as her job. As they should.

Maybe she was making too much of this.

Amos pointed at the door with his carrot. "He's about to knock."

Olive swore his senses were as fine-tuned as a bird dog's. She swung her hands into the air, then let them drop. "I'll see to this alone," she said.

"I'm here if you need me," her father added as a rap could be heard against the door.

"You know I'm listening to every word," Amos said.

"And I must depart." Marlowe grabbed her by the shoulders and graced her cheek with a quick kiss. "Be patient with Maxfield," he whispered. "He's as bullheaded as any man. Give him some time."

As Marlowe made his departure out the back door, Olive braced herself. If she was going to tell Maxfield the truth, she had to start being truthful with everyone.

Before Mr. Christman could knock again, she'd left the kitchen and opened the front door.

"Mr. Christman, I'm Olive Kentworth. Thank you for visiting. Won't you come in?"

"Am I in the right place?" He removed his driving gloves as he raised his gaze to the low ceiling then down to the homemade rugs on the floor. "This doesn't look like a builder's office."

"Tell me why you are here." Olive led him to a sofa and sat. She felt like she should've been offering him refreshments, but this was a business meeting. She wouldn't go back into the kitchen until she'd taken care of her first priority.

"You might have seen the empty lot on Main. I've planned to put a department store there."

"You hired Maxfield Scott to do that. I've seen his plans."

There was a question in his gaze, but he didn't speak it. "Well, Mr. Scott has run into difficulty. He is unable to start construction and he gave me leave to find another builder."

Olive eyed the papers rolled beneath Mr. Christman's arm. "What manner of difficulty did Mr. Scott encounter? Is there something wrong with the lot? Did the city rescind their permits?"

"Nothing like that. From what I gather, it was more of a personal nature. Said something about taking care of his first responsibilities."

Leo and Stella. Olive picked up a fringed pillow from the sofa and held it to her stomach. Mrs. Wester could care for them. Surely she hadn't quit too. This was because of what she'd done, though. It had to be.

"He left the plans in my care and signed them over to me. I have permission to use them, but I need a builder. It didn't take long to hear of the Kentworth buildings going up but when I called on your cousin, I found myself perplexed. He didn't have the knowledge that I'd expect from someone who was doing these projects. In fact, I found him more than a little ignorant of the designs."

"I don't appreciate your insinuations," Amos called from the kitchen. "I might be ignorant in a lot of things, but I'm exceptionally clever when it comes to recognizing insults."

"Amos, go on home," Olive said.

"Come on, Amos." She heard her father's languid voice coaxing his nephew. "Olive has got this under control. She doesn't need us."

Amos poked his head into the parlor. "She never needed me,"

he said. "She could've done this herself, and I hope you give her a chance to. I don't add anything to the bushel weight."

You never knew what Amos would say or do. That was part of his charm. He winked at Olive before walking out the door with an invite to her and her father for Sunday dinner at the farm.

"Now tell me more about what's ailing Mr. Scott," she said as the room quieted.

He wasn't angry any longer. Oh, Max knew he'd been wronged. There was no question about that. He knew that Olive had manipulated him and betrayed him on behalf of her cousin, but the anger was fading to hurt. How could she do that to him? Had all their interactions been counterfeit? And what if some of them were sincere? Did it matter? How could he ever trust her?

"Daddy, read this book to me." Leo held up a copy of *Five Little Peppers* and Max gauged the stack of books on the library's table. He should've brought a wagon to cart them home. He didn't know what the limit was for books one patron could check out, but the kids were going to find it.

"I can't read to you here. We have to be quiet, remember. You only get two books each, though. Put the rest of those back."

"Excuse me, sir." The rosy-cheeked librarian must have the patience of a saint. "I'd prefer they leave them on the table. I'll put them back on the shelves after you leave."

She probably hoped that would be soon, but Max had found a quiet place where he could work. The City of Joplin was taking bids on a new city hall, and Max wanted to have a design to submit. His crew wouldn't be busy with the Dennis house forever. He had to think ahead.

Coming to the library provided a nice change of scenery for the kids. This reading carrel sat at the edge of the children's section of the library. Surrounded by shelves of books, it shielded him from the public while giving him a view of the children's reading area.

They were having a wonderful time flipping through books, with Leo pretending to read to Stella. Stella laid her head on the little desk, getting sleepy. If only he didn't have to continually remind them to be quiet, he could accomplish so much more.

Who was he kidding? He wasn't sketching anything. He was only thinking of Olive—reciting his grievances against her while still trying to envisage some way she could be innocent in her duplicity.

"Miss Kentworth!" Leo dropped his book and darted out of sight. Stella lifted her head off the table and her eyes brightened. She kicked and squirmed to get down, leaving no doubt in Max's mind that her favorite nanny was within sight.

He forced himself to be calm as he rolled up his plans and set them aside. She hadn't come to see him. It was a chance encounter. She'd say goodbye to the children, then send them back to him. For one thing, she'd never cared about him. For another, she wouldn't have the nerve to show her face. Ashamed, as she should be.

All these things were going through his mind as he got to his feet, but his heart knew better. He wanted to see her. He wanted her to understand how much she'd wronged him. There were things he had to say, but once they were said, then maybe he could understand her actions better. Until then, he couldn't close the door. He might step away and he might always wonder, but he couldn't say never. Not until he knew.

"He's back here." Leo's voice grew closer along with the sound of his quick steps echoing through the silence.

Max braced himself, but the figure that stepped around the corner wasn't Olive. It was Mrs. Wester.

"Mr. Scott, we've been looking for you. I thought the children would be at Miss Kentworth's, but she didn't know where you were either. Thankfully Joplin isn't so big of a city that people don't recognize you and these two urchins." She patted Leo on the head. "It wasn't too difficult to follow your path."

He tried to hide his disappointment. This was good. Even if

she wasn't Olive, he needed Mrs. Wester if he was going to get any work done during the day.

"How is your husband?" he asked.

"The doctor said his recovery is progressing. Thank you for giving me the morning off. If I didn't go with him, I'd never know what the doctor said. He won't tell me nothing."

"Of course. If you want to take the rest of the day off, that would be fine," he said. "You might need to get him home and comfortable."

"Oh, he's home and just as rascally as ever. Once the doctor gave us the good news, I headed straight for your house. It's nearly Stella's nap time. I think she's out there with Miss Kentworth. I'll take them home and leave you two to plan the evening care."

"Miss Kentworth?" She was there after all. His skin pricked like he could sense her just out of sight.

Mrs. Wester took the stack of children's books off the study carrel. "I don't know if she's free to watch the children tonight, but you could ask. Come on, Leo. Let's get Stella."

Max placed his hands on the table in front of him and rested his weight with arms wide. She was helping Mrs. Wester find him, but she didn't want to see him. Only doing a favor for the older woman. It was for the best. He'd say words that he'd regret, and she'd hurt him even more. There was nothing left for them to talk about besides accusations and excuses.

Again his skin tingled. This time, he knew it was her. Max lifted his head, taking in the narrow leather belt around a trim waist, the flounce of the blouse with a roll of paper beneath her arm, and the practical set of her shoulders. He went no higher.

"Hello, Maxfield." Her whisper shook him. "May I speak with you?"

He lowered his gaze. There was a lot they needed to talk about. He wasn't sure he was ready to hear it.

"I understand how this must seem to you and while you probably have no interest in hearing from me, I wanted you to know that I'm worried about you. You can't quit your work. You are an asset to Joplin. Don't throw it away."

He could feel the flush rushing to his face. "I'm not ceding the field. This isn't a retirement. It's an acknowledgment of my responsibility to the children and my obligations to my current clients. I'm trying to restore some balance to my life. You shouldn't consider it a failure on my part."

"I . . . I didn't mean to suggest that you had failed, but I was worried when you turned this project down. I know how excited you were to get this commission."

"Maybe you should've worried before you tried to ruin my career."

She blanched. "Your career isn't ruined, Maxfield. I didn't hurt you."

"You used me to give your cousin an advantage. Now he's got my customer, my designs. He even has Ruby."

"Do you want Ruby back?"

"Maybe she'd be good for me." His eyes twitched at the lie, but he stood firm.

Olive had the grace to look hurt, or was that another act of hers?

"I apologize again for misleading you, but I wanted you to know that I never looked at your designs with the intent of stealing them." Her small, steady voice had gone back to discussing the practical issue before them. "I did avail myself of your library, however. I've already read everything this library has on architecture and design and have bought every book I could get my hands on—that's how I educated myself. I couldn't pass up the opportunity to look at the latest journals."

She still didn't understand. "But you knew that Amos was in competition with me. The moment he took the commission from Blount to redesign the house that I built, you should've realized that any help you gave him would be at my expense."

"That's what I'm trying to explain to you." She took the plans

249

from beneath her arm and dropped them on the table. Planting one hand on the edge of the paper, she rolled it out flat. "Do you remember showing me these plans? Do you remember when I suggested that you should have decorative capitals on the Corinthian columns? You were amazed at the suggestion. You were impressed. I could tell."

"If Amos wants to work for Mr. Christman, that's fine. I relinquished the design. It doesn't matter if you contributed to it or not."

"This has nothing to do with Amos." She was leaning over the plans with her arms locked against the table. Her eyes flashed. "Amos isn't an architect. He's barely a foreman on the construction crew. I'm the architect." She thumped her fist against her chest. "I'm the one who built the Lighthouse miners' center and the Crystal Cave visitors' building. Before I had the chance at a real project, I used to design and build those little birdhouses. You've seen my work. You've appreciated my work. Is it too much to ask that you could appreciate me?"

He stepped back. She couldn't be serious. He did appreciate her. But did he believe her? It was too incredible.

The look on her face set him back. What was wrong? Why were her eyes filling with tears?

"And that's why I didn't tell you. That's why I didn't tell anyone besides people who already loved me." She swiped at her eyes, gave a quick sniffle, then pushed Christman's plans at him. "Those are yours. If you want it built according to these plans, I'm willing to take the job, but it will be because you want me to do it. Otherwise, Mr. Christman can find someone else."

Maxfield's eyes slid closed as she rushed from the room. Let her build his building? Was it possible? Images flashed through his mind. Memories of the lectures he'd attended, the tours he'd taken, the exams he'd passed. How could she pretend to have done the same?

Or was she? Olive wasn't arguing that she'd had the same education. She was claiming she possessed the same skills. If she was telling the truth, he'd completely underestimated and insulted her, and that would make him a fool. A pompous, insensitive fool.

He couldn't be a fool. Not Maxfield Scott. Pompous, definitely. Insensitive . . . perhaps on occasion. But foolish? Max rolled up the blueprints. There were things that you couldn't believe, things that were hard to believe, and things you didn't want to believe. And even if he did start to believe it, what was he supposed to do about it?

Maxfield had no answer.

CHAPTER
24

Going to church had been a waste of Olive's time. She climbed into the buggy with her father and slouched on the bench next to him. She pulled her wide-brimmed hat down low as if to protect her complexion, but she knew it served like the first family's fig leaves . . . to hide her shame from God.

Usually Olive found the service refreshing. It was a time to look back over the week and thank God for His providence. To think forward and determine to do better, and to gaze upward and realize that the trials she faced were no match for God's power.

This week was different. Olive didn't want to look back at the week. Every time her family encouraged her to disclose her secret talent, they'd sworn that this wouldn't happen. They'd promised her that she'd earn respect, that people would be proud of her and that no one would mock her. They'd been wrong. Even in her worst nightmares she hadn't thought that Maxfield's disbelief would hurt so badly.

Looking forward? That was even harder. What did she have to look forward to? Either she forged on with her newly discovered path despite the mocking, or she folded up her plans and went back home. Neither option was encouraging.

Looking upward? Olive's eyes flickered to the brim of her hat. She'd made bad decisions. She'd practiced deceit and now she was bearing the chastisement. It was hard to imagine God wanted to hear from her. So going to church had only succeeded in making her feel like a hypocrite.

"Your granny is looking forward to seeing you. Ever since you started on Blount's house, you haven't spent much time at the ranch." Her dad had kicked his feet up on the dashboard and was cleaning his fingernails with a stubby pocketknife. The horse knew the way without his guidance.

"I miss my time at the ranch. I don't know that being an architect is worth it." Maybe she'd be better off hanging around there and keeping Granny Laura company. Granny Laura was spry for now but in a few years, she might appreciate having someone nearby to tend to her.

"You've had a rough time of it," her father said. "Keep going. You'll probably find that the worst is behind you."

They were coming up on Maisie and Boone's Crystal Cave. It was closed on Sundays, but the blue and red banners waving from the rock building announced the marvels beneath the ground.

World's Largest Geode

Best Tour in the Tri-State District

Her cousin Maisie had gone from farm girl to owner of Joplin's best tourist attraction. Her cousin Calista had gone from socialite to Pinkerton detective to pastor's wife. Her sister, Willow, had left home looking for a job to help pay her mother's medical bills. They'd thought she'd hit the jackpot when she landed a job as a Harvey Girl serving food at Harvey House Restaurants. That was until she met and married Graham Buchanan, the railroad tycoon.

All the ladies in Olive's family were scrappy and ambitious and brave. She was the only exception. No wonder they were disappointed in her. No wonder they couldn't leave her be.

Just past the Secret Tree, the road turned onto Kentworth property. As they came over the rise, Olive saw Aunt June walking over from their house carrying a large bowl of some delicious offering. Uncle Bill was probably already at the house frying the catfish that Hank and Hilda had caught for Sunday dinner.

Olive's cousin Hannah saw them coming. She unfurled a checkerboard tablecloth over the picnic table in the shade of the elm and called over her shoulder to the house. Amos was supposed to tell them that Olive and her father were coming but whether he did or not was anyone's guess. Olive had baked two pies—buttermilk and pecan—so even if they weren't expected, no one would go hungry on their account.

"It's the day of rest," her father said. "We might be busy visiting or cooking or whatever mischief you and your cousins get into, but at least you can rest your mind. Set aside your troubles for the day. They'll be there waiting to be taken up again on Monday."

Olive took his hand to climb down. "Good advice," she said. "I'm afraid it'll be swimming upstream, but I'll try." She walked to the back of the wagon to retrieve the pies, her shoes sinking into the soft green grass, then made her way to the house.

"Whatcha got there?" Hannah asked as she anchored the tablecloth with stones kept on the porch for that purpose.

"Buttermilk and pecan pies. Just headed to the kitchen with them."

"Can't believe you have time for baking pies. Not when you're so busy taking business from Maxfield Scott." Hannah beamed. The woman was genuinely proud of her cousin.

So much for a restful day. "I gave that project back to him," Olive said. "He's the one who should build the department store."

"You did what?" Amos stepped through the opened front door with his sister Maisie on his heels. "You can do better than old Maxfield on that store. Half the ideas were yours."

"No, they weren't." Olive never claimed that. "I just helped him with one little detail in the interior. The work was all his."

"Calista, come out here. Olive is talking about quitting." Maisie motioned inside the house and soon Calista and Maisie's husband,

Boone, had joined them. A whole audience there to confront Olive and question her decisions.

"Where are Matthew and Hank?" Olive asked. "Are you sure ganging up on me a dozen to one is enough?"

"They're helping Uncle Bill fry the fish, but now that you mention it . . . Granny . . ." Maisie's whistle split the air.

Olive sighed. The pies were getting heavy, so she set them on the table as Granny came out.

With one look at her assembled progeny, the tanned woman with the short-cropped silver hair shooed them back, giving her and Olive some room.

"Olive." She turned her weathered cheek to her granddaughter and Olive kissed it firmly.

"Hello, Granny. I just came for supper."

"And to see me. It's kind of you to take off your busy work."

"She ain't so busy," said Amos. "We broke our necks getting her these jobs and now she's wanting to throw them away."

"What's that?" Granny's clear blue eyes focused on her. "I thought everyone knew that you were the architect. Amos could come home and work on the ranch."

"People are hearing, but not everyone believes I can do it. I did what you all were after me about. I gave being an architect a shot but it's more than sitting in your office dreaming up plans. You have to line up workers. You have to deal with dissatisfied clients. And you have to tread carefully with your pride-filled competitors. But when it comes down to it, I have no credibility, and it might be impossible for a woman to earn it."

Turning to Granny, she said, "Granny, my dad doesn't need me moping around the house all the time. I thought I might come spend the days with you. Surely at your age you could use an extra hand keeping up with the house and the kitchen garden. Aunt June —"

"Don't you dare," Granny Laura said. "This farm is not a place for cowards to hide." Her stern but loving gaze softened her words.

"It isn't going to be easy to come into your own. You don't have your ma and you don't have the training, but you do have us. And you have God. He gave you this gift. Do you think He won't also give you the courage to use it?"

"Besides, it's too late to quit," Calista said. The package she pulled out from behind her was wrapped in a bow as big as the one that adorned her giant platter of a hat. "I've already gotten you this present, and I can't return it."

Why was everyone looking so eager? Olive took the package, wishing she could open it in private but knowing that wouldn't be allowed.

After carefully removing the ribbon—the bow was beautiful and she couldn't tie it that perfectly again—Olive peeled away the paper to reveal a white cardboard box. Holding the box in one hand, she pulled off the lid. The scent of new stationery reached her before her eyes focused on the embossed heading across the page:

Miss Olive Kentworth, Architect
Suite 108, Byers Building
Joplin, Missouri

"It's beautiful." Olive lifted the top sheet and moved it so the light caught the gold lettering. "Thank you, Calista. I don't know when I'm going to have occasion to use it."

"You'll use it for all your correspondence," Calista said. "Personalized stationery is the first step to respectability, whether personal or business." She fluffed up her leg-o'-mutton sleeves for full effect.

"I have to admit, it's so pretty it does make me want to write some official letter right now, but in no time, people would find out that I don't have an office in the Byers Building. I can't pretend that I do."

"No need to pretend." Maisie dangled a brass key on a leather strip. "You do have an office there. It's Boone's building, after all."

The small piece of metal looked more threatening than if it had been a knife. They couldn't be serious. But Boone, who wasn't one for joking around, was right there affirming what his wife had said. "I had a vacancy in the building. When I mentioned it to Maisie, she and Calista came up with the idea. You'll have a professional office on the ground floor. We'll even put your name on the directory out front."

Her name, somewhere public where Maxfield would see it? Olive pushed the key away. "I can't afford an office. As soon as I'm finished with the Blounts' house, I have nothing else lined up."

"What about the department store?" Maisie asked. "Amos said you were going to do that, and it'd be ten times more than an addition to Mr. Blount's house."

"I gave that job back to Maxfield. I can't take work away from him."

They might have thought they were hiding the disapproving looks being telegraphed around her, but Olive saw them clear as day.

"That's hogwash," Amos said. "He can't handle that job. It's up to you."

"Of course he can handle it. He's got the record to prove it." Maxfield might not like her anymore, but Olive couldn't stand to have him belittled.

"And don't worry about the rent," said Boone. "The first year is free. By then you'll have clients by the dozens. I might decide to build another commercial building myself."

"And when you do get clients, you can't have them coming out to your house. It's not professional." Amos elbowed her father in the side. "Besides, what's to keep me from walking in the front door and blurting out trade secrets?"

"He's like to do that," said Maisie.

"Something tells me he already did," said Granny Laura.

An office of her own? Olive took the key and held it in her open palm. It didn't matter to her whether she was sketching designs on her sofa or at a desk. And while it would be helpful to have the space for her paperwork and receipts, that wasn't what mattered most. What made this the most amazing gift was the people who had arranged it. They believed in her. They wanted to play a part in her success, and they did think she would be successful. They had faith in her even though she had no faith in herself.

All the care they'd put into their plans, all the conniving, was for one purpose—so she would have the tools to realize her dreams. They were giving Olive that, and the rest was up to her. How could she refuse?

"Thank you." She hugged the box of stationery to her chest. Looking around the circle, she thought of the unique relationship she had with each of them individually but also the strength of the bonds when they were combined. "I can't believe I have an office, with my own stationery. I never would've done this on my own."

"And that's what you have to remember," said Granny Laura. "You aren't doing any of this on your own. God is right there beside you in a hundred different ways. He's there in the provisions He's given you and He's also there in the family He raised up around you. We know how much you sacrificed for your mother, and we want to do some of the sacrificing for you now. It's your turn to get the help, and we aim to help you."

Olive's fear was turning to resolve. She couldn't let them down. Instead of burning her old drafts, it looked like she'd spend Monday moving into her new office. She could hardly wait.

CHAPTER 25

"When is Miss Kentworth coming?" Leo threw himself across Maxfield's lap, his elbows digging into Max's thigh as he squirmed. "I miss her."

"I'm sure you do," said Mrs. Wester as she set out a plate of veggies on the table. "But your pa has been home in the evenings for the past week, so Miss Kentworth hasn't been needed."

Maxfield had been home in the evenings and here he was, home for lunch too. Mrs. Wester was a wise soul. It hadn't taken her long to recognize his reticence when it came to the subject of Miss Kentworth, so she was quick to intervene when Leo had questions.

"What are we going to do tonight?" Max asked. "Would you like to go to the duck pond again? Or we could take a dinner basket to the railroad track and watch the train go by." He'd thought that Stella would be afraid of the roaring noise, but the terrifying cacophony had delighted her. She might have a wild streak like her mother. Or Miss Kentworth . . .

"Choo-choo!" She laughed and clapped her hands together. "I want choo-choo."

His confidence in his parenting skills was improving. He no longer felt overwhelmed taking the children to town. For one thing, he paid more attention to what activities were suitable for them, but it was more than that. He had trained them to the point that they were enjoyable. He only had to tell Leo once what they were going to do, and Leo knew that he meant it. Stella was more of a challenge, but when she showed signs of rebellion or exhaustion, it was a simple thing to swoop her up and remove the temptation.

"There you go." Mrs. Wester set a platter of cold beef on the table along with a pickle tray. "The children look forward to seeing you midday."

And he looked forward to seeing them. They bowed their heads as he offered thanks for their meal, then they turned to their food.

This was the kitchen and he felt at home here. No longer was he assaulted by the sinking dread he associated with parts of the house. He didn't avert his eyes from the rocker in the children's room. He could walk past Georgia's flower bed without regret. He even found himself checking his appearance in the mirror of her vanity without thought. Not that he didn't think of her, but he had reclaimed areas of the house that had been lost to him. He didn't have to hide from them or avoid the sting of pain that came with them. That made it easier to be home, and easier to enjoy his family. His children didn't have the same sad associations, and now that he realized he did, he did his best to shield them from them.

"Thank you for dinner, Mrs. Wester." Max carried his plate to the sink. "I've got to get back to work, but I'll be home before too long and then we can decide what we're going to do this evening."

"I want choo-choo," Stella said around a mouthful of food.

"The train hurts my ears." Leo picked up a piece of meat and pushed it onto the tines of his fork. "Let's go to the library. Maybe Miss Kentworth will be there."

He hadn't forgotten. Neither had Max.

After a last goodbye, Max headed to the front door. He paused outside his home library. Every time he thought about Olive's claims to be an architect herself, he redirected his thinking.

How many times had he come home and found her sitting quietly in the library? Reading poetry? Ha. She didn't know any poetry. So what was she doing? Could she really glean anything from his architectural journals? Could she learn enough to pass it on to Amos for it to be helpful? And what about Amos?

He didn't want to think about it. He turned his face to the door and had his hand on the doorknob when he stopped.

What was he doing? Again he was avoiding the areas of the house, of his life, that caused him pain. For a year and a half he'd shied away from the areas that reminded him of Georgia. He'd shut the doors in his mind that brought back memories or made him question his culpability. Now he was doing it again. Every time he thought of Olive in the library, he dismissed his questions and went back to his business. No time to wonder if Olive was telling the truth but plenty of time to recount how she'd hurt him.

So was she telling the truth?

With a last look at the library, he exited the house. He couldn't stay there. The children. Mrs. Wester. He could think better while walking to the Dennis house.

What did he know about Olive? He knew that she had been reading the materials in his library. He knew that the average person on the street would find those papers uninteresting and confusing. He knew that someone in the Kentworth family was responsible for constructing several different buildings about town. Everyone believed it to be Amos, but Max had always doubted that.

If not Amos, then who?

He waited for traffic to ease on Main Street so he could cross the business district and go into Murphysburg. How proud he'd been when he showed Olive his plans for the department store. He had expected her to ooh and ahh and make all those feminine sounds of approval that men sought. What he hadn't expected was for her to instantly understand what his drawing represented. He didn't expect that she would put her focus on the page instead of him trying to explain it. And he really was surprised when she came up with an idea for the interior that perfectly addressed his client's request.

How could the builder be anyone other than her?

"Maxfield!" Mr. Dennis waved his hand above the pedestrians on the sidewalk. "Maxfield Scott. Just the man I was looking for."

Not who Max wanted to see, but it was his job and right now it was his only job. "Do you have time for coffee?" Max asked. He might as well give Mr. Dennis his full attention, and a hot cup of coffee would make the time pass more enjoyably.

"My treat." Mr. Dennis led Max to the bakery and ordered two cups. Whatever it was that he wanted to say, he was already buttering Max up for it. This didn't bode well.

They'd just taken their seats at a round café table when Mr. Dennis broke the news. "I want to put a halt to the construction at my house."

Max gulped down a mouthful of hot coffee despite the scalding his throat was taking. He coughed into his hand, then looked up with watery eyes.

"Stop altogether? Why?"

"There's no reason to keep building until Amos Kentworth is finished with Mr. Blount's house. If my aim is to have the biggest house in Joplin, then I have to wait until the biggest house is finished and then determine how much bigger mine needs to be."

It wasn't Amos Kentworth building it. Max was coming to terms with that, but it didn't change Mr. Dennis's request.

"What's to keep Mr. Blount from adding on again when I start construction back up? This could go on forever."

Dennis tapped the side of his coffee cup. "I reckon it'll go on until one of us runs out of yard to build on."

"You already started adding to the second story. How high are you willing to go?"

"I hadn't considered that." He stared down into the coffee as he swirled his cup around. "But you see why it doesn't make sense for you to keep on. Not until we know what we need to do to beat that old dog."

Maxfield rubbed his forehead. He should've been done with this project weeks ago. If it wasn't for Olive getting involved . . . But it wasn't fair to blame Olive. She was doing what he did, accepting jobs to build whatever her clients wanted.

"If the house remains unfinished, will Mrs. Dennis and Ruby be content staying at the Keystone much longer?"

"I say let them move in. We'll close off the room that is unfinished. They might as well have the use of the rest of the house." Mr. Dennis eyeballed him suspiciously. "That is if you're going to approve the womenfolk coming on-site before the house is finished."

Maxfield was learning to let go. He was learning that a tragedy of the past didn't have to force him into more tragic mistakes, and insisting that Mrs. Dennis and Ruby avoid their home would cause hard feelings. He could overlook his fears for their ease.

"The house is ready for them," he said. "If we're not going to complete it right now, I'll have the materials removed tonight, and it'll be clear by the end of the day tomorrow."

Mr. Dennis beamed. "Thank you. That will thrill the ladies." He tapped the side of his coffee cup again. "And I'll settle up on whatever bills you have outstanding. We'll consider the house finished, and when Blount makes his final move, then we'll start a new project on the house. That way you're free to move on to the department store you wanted to work on."

Perfect. The department store that he'd already given to Olive. If he'd known that Mr. Dennis would close down his house, he would have kept Mr. Christman's project.

"I'm headed to the house right now," Maxfield said. "Are you?"

"No, I'll go back to the hotel and let the missus and Ruby know that it's time to start packing. They'll be overjoyed." He reached into his wallet and took out some coins. Dropping them on the table, he stood. "I'm sorry this turned out so messy. If it weren't for that Kentworth, we would've been done by now."

Max gave a courtesy nod even though he disagreed. It wasn't Olive's fault. It was men like Blount and Dennis who were to blame. They had no respect for the aesthetics that went into design. They didn't understand the balance of the elements that Max used. They only knew numbers, and in this case, it was the number of square feet. That's all they cared about.

Alone at the table, he finished his coffee and willed the kinks out of his shoulders. He'd given the department store away. If Olive decided to do it, would she allow him to be involved? Not that he'd want any kind of say on the project, but would she let him check in from time to time, just so he could share the joy of watching it go up? He took his hat as he exited the café. She shouldn't let him. Not after the way he treated her. She should expect nothing more from him besides disrespect and a power struggle.

If he was her friend, he'd advise her to keep him at arm's length.

He continued on down Virginia Avenue and every sight reminded him of Olive. A flash of blond hair caught his eye, but it wasn't her. A purple martin flew by, bringing to mind the birdhouses that she'd crafted. An advertisement for the Schifferdecker Electric Park reminded him of the roller coaster and how he'd held her tight.

And the sign going up on the Byers Building looked, at first, like it bore her name.

The workman held his screwdriver in the way, so Max couldn't quite see it, but he knew now that he was imagining things. There couldn't be a brass plate on the Byers Building that read *Olive Kentworth, Architect*. That was beyond ridiculous.

The workman polished the directory board with a soft cloth, and when he lowered it, sure enough, there were the words that Max thought he'd imagined.

She had an office? But why wouldn't she get an office? She was building Mr. Christman's department store. People with much smaller clients fancied themselves professionals. He stood before the sign, still in disbelief. This was his nanny. He thought he knew her. How could she have hidden something so important from him? Or had he been too blind to see it?

His nanny was an architect. Olive with clients, and him with none.

"Is there something wrong with the sign?" The workman held up his thumb and squinted toward the sign. "It's straight, isn't it?"

"Yes, it looks fine. Splendid. Superb." Max kept looking at the door to the office building. Was she inside? It'd been so long since he'd seen her. An eternity, it felt like.

"Room 108," the worker said. "You might as well pay your competition a visit, Mr. Scott."

Maxfield shot the man a second glance. He didn't know him personally but, more than likely, he'd worked on one of Maxfield's projects. And here Max stood in the street, as stunned as a painter who'd breathed in too many fumes.

"I will go inside," Maxfield said, "and wish her good luck. She's a friend of mine, after all."

"Oh, that explains it. I was wondering how a lady got started in the business. It makes sense you pulled a few strings for her." The man gave Maxfield a wink then took up his toolbox.

But he hadn't helped her at all. She'd done this without knowing anyone in the industry. She hadn't had the opportunity to go to the universities or the world tours he'd gone on. No one had helped her, and she'd managed to build two praiseworthy buildings for her family. When Maxfield thought back to all the people who had helped him along in his career, he had to wonder if he would've persevered without them.

"Wait." He turned, but the workman was already across the street. Maxfield darted after him. He should've looked first because an automobile swerved at the last minute, barely clipping Maxfield's leg with its front bumper. The driver blasted his horn as he rolled on down the street. Maxfield plowed on, despite the bruising pain, and caught the workman in front of the shoe store.

"Excuse me." Maxfield grabbed him by the shoulder. "I have something to say."

The man bristled until he recognized who had him. "Mr. Scott? What'sa matter?"

"I didn't help her," he blurted. "I cared about her, and if I'd been a better man, I would've realized that she had a gift, but I was too caught up in my own story to see hers. She did this all on her own. I didn't help her, but I wish that I had."

The workman's brow lowered. "I'm not a priest, sir. If you're looking for someone to confess to—"

"You thought something that wasn't true, and I couldn't have you leaving without correcting you. Especially as it gave me credit when it wasn't due and took away from Miss Kentworth's accomplishments."

"Sure, buddy." The workman had gone from a polite subordinate to a concerned peer. "I didn't think poorly of Miss Kentworth. It's okay."

"But you understand what I'm saying?"

"I understand what you're saying." He stepped backward and held his toolbox between them. "I don't understand why, but I hear you. Now, if you'll let me go, I've got another job for Mr. Bragg. Take care of yourself."

Maxfield let him go this time. He'd already made a fool of himself, but he wasn't going to stop. Not yet. He still hadn't talked to Olive.

Crossing the street took longer this time. He was more careful, and the limp slowed him down. He should get some ice on his leg. It'd be bruised, but he'd hurt feelings worse than he'd hurt his leg, and it was those feelings he should look after first.

She'd feared her office would look empty and forlorn, but Olive hadn't counted on her cousins' help. In the week that had passed since they'd told her about her new office, the family had showered Olive with gifts and advice. With Calista's newfound knack for being fashionable on a budget, they took drapes that Maisie's mother-in-law had replaced and sized them down for her window. Then Maisie and Calista had thrown together some knickknacks and family photos to populate the areas of her bookshelves that weren't full of secondhand architectural tomes.

Aunt June, who kept the records for Granny Laura and the Kentworth ranch, had come by to help Olive set up a filing system, as well as instructing her on accounting and bookkeeping techniques. Two desk drawers on the oak desk now contained files with divided pockets for holding receipts and time cards for her crews. The timing was perfect. She'd never done a project as big as Mr. Christman's department store and having the organization in place would be vital. The drafting board was a gift from Willow and Graham, and Olive couldn't believe she'd gone from spreading papers across her sister's old bed to this.

Although her sketches, books, and pencils were still in boxes, Olive knew what she wanted to do next. She took a framed needlepoint out of a box and held it against the wall to see where it looked best. Some might say it was too homey for a professional office, but she didn't care. The verse her mother had embroidered around a rendering of a log cabin was Psalm 127:1, "Except the LORD build the house, they labour in vain that build it." She wanted to be able to see it from her desk, so she'd always remember to give the credit for any success where it was due.

"Olive?"

She was on her tiptoes, pushing a tack into the wall, when she heard his voice. Turning her head, she saw Maxfield in the doorway. She pulled the sampler against her chest and faced him.

"Mr. Scott. I didn't expect a visit from you." Her heart leapt. Whether it was out of happiness or dread, she wasn't sure. Anything was possible.

"You should've known if you opened an office, I'd find my way to it eventually." He walked to her bookcase, but instead of admiring the knickknacks from Calista, he read the spines of the books, giving Olive time to fret over his intentions.

It had been so long since they'd spoken, even longer since they'd had a friendly conversation. She felt like they were starting all over. Was he planning to denounce her for lying about being an architect, to denounce her for spying on his work, or to beg her to return to watch the children, ignoring the fact that she had another opportunity available?

But addressing her wasn't his first priority. He continued to study the volumes, leaving Olive to wonder at what he might be thinking. She hung the picture on the tack as he released a quick breath, almost a chuckle. She watched as he reached for a battered copy of Alberti's *On the Art of Building.*

"How did you acquire your education?" he asked.

A calm descended over Olive. This was a sensible question, and she could give a sensible answer. "Mother was sick so often that I had time to read practically everything in the library. Once I read my first book on designs, I was hooked. After that, I was always looking at buildings when I walked to town or drove to the ranch. When I recognized something I'd read about, it was like greeting old friends. I read all the books the library had. I ordered some from a catalog when we had the money, and if I ever found a used book on the subject, I felt like I had found the pot of gold at the end of the rainbow."

Maxfield cracked open the book. The red cloth cover had worn thin on the edges, exposing the hard board beneath. He thumbed through the pages until he found what he was looking for. Turning the book around, he held it out to her. His eyes crinkled at the corners.

"These are my notes." He pointed at his angular annotation in the margin of the page. "I thought this looked familiar. I donated it to the church's rummage sale after Georgia died. I gave away a lot of my things then. I wasn't sure I wanted to build anything again."

"But you did."

"Staying home doing nothing proved an even worse idea, so instead of hiding *from* my work, I hid *in* my work."

"If that's yours, then you know this one too." Olive moved a picture of her mother and pulled out *A Book of Architecture* by James Gibbs. "I got this book at the same bazaar. I always wondered who it was that had such wonderful resources."

"They were dated by then, anyway." Then, seeing her expression, he hurried to add, "The textbooks contain excellent information, though. I've often regretted my impulsiveness because the fundamentals are sound. Thomas Jefferson kept a copy of Gibbs in his library."

"Ah, Thomas Jefferson. Another untrained, amateur architect." She found a particular box and pulled out volume after volume until there was a stack that reached from her desktop to over her head. She looked at all the titles. That day she'd felt like God had opened a door to her with the discovery of all these books. Without them, she wouldn't have had the knowledge or the confidence to do what she did. And she'd only gotten them because of Maxfield's grief.

"Here." She pushed against them, but they only slid an inch. "Take them back. How can I use them now that I know?"

He laid his hand atop the stack. "I want you to have them. They were meant to be yours." He moved his hand away from the books and buried it in his pocket. "Don't you see? You are doing what you're supposed to be doing. Maybe I was acting out of grief and despair, but God had a purpose. By throwing out those books, I gave you a chance. And look what you've done with it."

Olive's hands went cold. Did he finally believe her? He was there talking to her as if it didn't matter that they were rivals. In fact, for being a rival, he was quite complimentary.

"You don't have to say that." Her throat was tight with tears. "I mean, I know you don't have to say it, but it's so nice that you did."

The light in the room seemed to shimmer. She didn't want to cry but she'd been so worried about what he thought, so concerned

271

that she'd ruined her reputation, so fearful that he would mock her. His understanding was unexpected but so appreciated.

He reached for her hand, but she drew back. "I hope you're here about Christman's department store." She lifted her chin as she sniffed the last of her emotion away. He was her first professional visitor. A colleague in the industry. She couldn't behave like a sentimental weakling. "You still have the plans, don't you? It's your work, your design, and you should be the one to build it."

He had offered her respect. She wouldn't trade it for pity.

He read her intent and honored it by taking his place at the opposite side of her desk and giving her space. "That's not why I'm here. Actually I wasn't planning to come, but when I saw your name on the sign, I had to. The last time we saw each other, I behaved poorly. I should've apologized immediately, but I can be hardheaded."

"Marlowe warned me," she said.

His eyebrows raised. "He's not wrong. I was upset that you hid something essential about yourself but looking back, I realize why you hesitated to tell me. At the time, I refused to even let a lady visit one of my sites."

"Has that changed?" Olive asked.

He smoothed his lapel. "It has. I can't say that the thought doesn't make me nervous, but you were right about accepting the risk. I wouldn't allow another man to make that type of a decision for me. I have no right to make it for you."

"Not telling you was selfishness on my part too," she said. "If you disapproved, I'd lose access to your library . . . and I *love* your library."

His mouth twitched as if on the verge of making an impertinent remark, but he reined himself in. "You're welcome to come consult it whenever you'd like." The generous, expansive Mr. Scott had returned.

"Maxfield, you know I'm not going to drop in unannounced and peruse your collection."

His eyes widened at the use of his name. "What if you were invited? Would you come? How about tonight? Dinner with me and the kids. They miss you. You can read while I cook, then read while I bathe them and put them to bed, and then read while I sit bored in the next room wishing I had someone to visit."

Olive sobered. "I don't think that would be wise." He'd just learned that she had her own profession. She had her own office. As much as she missed the children, it was too soon to go back.

"I see." He sighed. "If you want to keep it professional, I'd love to see what you're working on now." Pointing to a sketch on her drafting board, he said, "Is that something you can show me?"

After months of waiting for any spare knowledge he might have dropped, any tidbit of wisdom he might mention, he was offering to look at her work. It was the opportunity she'd wished for all along.

Olive pushed aside the stack of books to see what he was pointing at. With a swish of her skirts, she swept around the corner of her desk to the board. She gathered her notes and pushed the clutter away from her plan.

"It's not final but it's getting very, very close," she said. "You'll see the unique challenges that a design like this presents. I guess that's why I enjoy this project so much."

His forehead wrinkled as he turned the paper to himself. "It's a very narrow space. . . ." Then his eyes lit up. "It's the railcar, isn't it? Mr. Buchanan mentioned that he had a local architect working on a design. I never dreamt it was you."

She ducked her head, afraid he would see how elated she was at his excitement. "They're family, so it's only natural they'd commission me."

"Nonsense. The Buchanans know dozens of architects. They have the world at their disposal, and they picked you because they know you have unique and creative ideas. Now, let me take a look at this."

She was doing it. They were doing it. They were talking about their projects together as peers. Olive moved from the center of the board to give him room. She traced her finger over the hallway. "The passage crosses from the left side to the right, midcar, and while that's not ideal aesthetically, it helps distribute the weight of the rooms and furniture across the axles of the railcar."

"There's a consideration I hadn't thought of. I suppose you can't have one side of the car weighing more than the other."

"Jay Gould's *Atalanta* has the hallway along one side, but I thought I could improve on the design. Besides, if the evening sun is coming in on one side, there will be cooler rooms on the other. Also, all the utility spaces like the food storage and the kitchen need to be in the front of the car. That way the servants can come and go from their railcar without passing through the family's private quarters."

"So this room at the very back of the car . . . ?"

"It's the family parlor, and for it to be at the back of the train is essential." She grasped the edge of the drafting board and stretched to her full height even though she still couldn't meet him eye to eye. "I didn't realize until Willow told me, but their private car is always at the back. Not only is it the safest, and the most private, but it also has the best view of the landscape that they're passing. See here, how the windows wrap around the entire room? Just imagine sitting on your sofa and seeing the countryside on three sides as you pass through."

"Sounds like the best way to travel."

Olive couldn't help but be a little wistful that he would stop studying her design and look into her eyes again. But he seemed genuinely interested, and that was amazing in itself.

"It's remarkable how spacious you made it feel, given how narrow the car is. Was the placement of the furniture part of the commission too?"

Olive nodded, still in disbelief that they were having this conversation. "Willow told me what pieces they wanted, and since most of them are built in, they have to be considered from the beginning.

Graham has the Herter Brothers doing the cabinetry, so I had to consider their style with my design. I think the artisans we have in Joplin are just as skilled, but the Herter name was important to the Buchanans."

"Knowing Marlowe, I understand." Finally, he was looking at her again. "The railcar, the Blounts' house, and the department store—you have a thriving firm. Congratulations."

Olive felt her cheeks warming at his praise. Absent was any trace of jealousy or censure, but she was too aware that some of her success had come at his expense.

"It's too much," she said. "I can't possibly do it all. That's why I'm going to tell Mr. Christman that he needs to rehire you. It doesn't matter what Mr. Dennis has going with his home. I know you're capable of doing both."

Max crossed his arms over his chest. "Our friends Mr. Dennis and Mr. Blount are preventing us from moving on to new, more profitable projects."

Olive leaned one elbow against the board. "And according to Mr. Blount, there's no sense in stopping until Mr. Dennis has stopped, because he's going to add on until his house is bigger."

"And according to Mr. Dennis, he will keep adding rooms until he has the biggest house in Joplin. The contest will last forever." He looked at her evenly, a friendly, fair gaze as if they were partners solving a puzzle together. There wasn't a touch of romance in it, just respect, and Olive felt more known and understood than ever before.

"What are we going to do?" she asked.

"Work together," he answered. "We can figure out a way to bring this to an end."

"But who will win? Mr. Blount or Mr. Dennis?"

"Neither. It'll be us who wins." His eyebrows raised as if daring her to argue. "You wait and see."

CHAPTER

26

When Max and Olive had parted on Tuesday, he'd asked her if he could visit her office again, as they had projects to collaborate on. It was no secret that she had misgivings. Now, as he pushed open the door to the Byers Building, he had to admit he understood why. He'd discredited her skill when she'd revealed it. In fact, he'd refused to believe her at all. Of course she was wary of him. He would have to prove to her that he wouldn't commandeer her projects. He had to prove that he saw her as an equal.

Perhaps working together on Christman's department store would give him the chance to reform. Despite his resolve, Max knew himself too well to think his mistake had completely humbled him, but he'd do whatever it took to change.

Whether he took the lead on the department store or she did didn't matter to Maxfield. He'd won the bid on the new city offices and was being queried about constructing an apartment building downtown but, more than anything, he wanted to be finished with Mr. Blount and Mr. Dennis. Though the competition between them had brought him and Olive together, now it was in the way. They had to come up with a solution.

The door to her office was cracked open. He caught a glimpse of Olive standing at her drafting board, leaning her weight against her straightedge to hold it firm while she whisked her pencil along its side. Not wanting to cause an error, Max waited until she lifted her pencil to knock.

How did her expression change upon seeing him? Was she relieved? Cautious? Her cheeks were already flushed from the warmth of the room. Her eyes fluttered back to her board.

"Good afternoon." She moved her straightedge around to make another line. She'd been professional taking care of his children. Why had he wondered how she'd act at her office? "I've been preparing for your visit," she said, keeping her gaze on her work.

"I would've come sooner, but it . . ." The only reason he hadn't come earlier was he wanted to give her time. He didn't want to seem too eager. Too suffocating. ". . . it seemed too soon."

Now she looked up. Her lips parted, then pressed together with a slight shake of her head. "I'm in the middle of something. If you'll give me a minute—"

"You're working on the railcar?" He motioned to the draft.

"Willow and Graham had some changes they requested. Their furniture makers have some definite ideas on the size of their pieces. I'm trying to accommodate them without jeopardizing the integrity of my design."

"People imagine that we sit alone in an office and construct fairytale castles out of the air. They have no idea all the input, all the opinions, all the compromises that have to be made."

"I have a lot to learn." Olive took a soft eraser and rubbed out an interior wall. "But I can't think of anything I'd rather be learning about."

"I can leave if I'm bothering you. Or I could wait. I'm in no hurry."

She didn't answer but returned to the sketch.

Max dropped the department store blueprints on the sofa and took one of his old books off the shelf. He stole a glance at Olive. She looked happy. Supremely happy. Then he was happy too.

He made himself comfortable, flipping through the textbooks.

While he rested his mind on the essentials of his art, he began to process through ideas for the apartment building he'd been commissioned to build. Would it match the tone of the neighborhood, or would it be the first of a new trend? Palatial welcome or a homey embrace? He knew the personality of the man commissioning it, but what kind of people would rent an apartment there? What were their preferences?

Slowly ideas were rejected, while others he set aside for more investigation at his convenience. The time spent relaxing in her office was beneficial. It was relaxing to hear her moving about, whispering to herself, while still giving him the space to arrange his own thoughts. The new space gave him fresh thoughts, and knowing she was near meant that his thinking was calmer and clearer.

"There." He looked up to see her stepping away from the desk with arms crossed over her chest. She reached down to straighten the paper one last time, then nodded. "I think that will do it. Thank you for waiting."

"I made good use of my time." He closed the book and placed it back on the shelf. "There's a direction I want to try on a new project. This helped narrow that down."

"Perfect. And now, what did you want to work on first? The department store or our two banty roosters?"

The description was perfect. Two cocky men who were fighting over who would rule the henhouse. "Are we agreed that we won't pick a winner? They both need to think they have the biggest house in Joplin?"

"Yes, and I think I have a solution." She reached for a roll of paper leaning in the corner. "We need to find some ambiguous footage. Some feature that one builder might count as footage, but the other wouldn't."

"Like a basement?" he asked.

"Did you count the footage in the basement?"

"Yes."

"Me too, so that's already off the table." She spread her plans of Blount's house on the board. "Here's what I've added. When you finish the upstairs addition, the Dennises' house will be fifty feet larger than the Blounts' even with this extension."

"Which is why Mr. Dennis won't let me finish until you are finished. I guarantee he'll make his add-on bigger once we know what we're aiming for."

She straightened the little bow at her collar. "That's why I decided to add a screened-in porch."

"For whom? Blount?" Maxfield asked.

"Yes. I'll tell him that I have exact measurements of Mr. Dennis's house and that we'll build this porch on to put him in the lead once and for all. But the windows will be screens, not glass."

"And some would consider that an outdoor feature, not part of the house." Again she had surprised him.

"That way, I can give Mr. Blount the number he's looking for, and you can assure Mr. Dennis that a porch is not included in the square footage by most accounts, so he can think he has the bigger house."

"It's inevitable that they'll find out what we've done and have a big argument over it." Max tried to look contrite. "I hate to confess that I really look forward to hearing about that fight."

She grinned, making all his trouble worth it.

"Me too," she said. "By then we'll be finished with these two projects and if they decide to hire someone to start up the construction again, it won't affect us. But we do need to get accurate measurements before we get started."

"The Dennis family has started moving in. It'd be easier to get it done before they leave the hotel for good."

"Tonight? We could do it while the Blounts are at the theater." She tilted her head to the side, waiting for his response.

"After dark, secretly sneaking around? That sounds like a very Kentworth thing to do."

A flicker of pride flashed in her eyes. "I might be the tamest of all the cousins, but I still have a wild streak."

Max adjusted his necktie. Yes, she did, and he was extremely grateful.

She should have known when her suggestion brought on a comparison to her mischievous cousins that it was a bad idea.

Olive hugged her knees to her chest as she waited in the shadows of a wheelbarrow. She didn't have a wild streak. Not really. Olive could have asked the Blounts for permission to measure—she was the builder, after all—but instead, she and Maxfield had dodged around trees and dived behind bushes just to prove that she had more mettle than he'd credited her with.

Keeping up the bravado, Olive had suggested they start measuring the footing even before the Blounts had left for the evening. She held one end of the measuring tape tightly as Maxfield dashed to the opposite corner of the house. As arranged, he tugged on the tape, letting Olive know he was in position. With a dread look at lit windows, Olive pressed herself against the brick corner of the house. To get the measurement accurate, they had to stand so the tape would rise around the porch steps and lie flush against the wall.

Maxfield emerged from the bushes at the same time she did, his face illuminated by the streetlight. He held her gaze—silent, patient. When she was close to him, she was guarded, unsure. Seeing him across the way reminded her of the good times. The exhilarating roller coaster ride when he'd taken a bruising for her sake. The peaceful neighborhood walks talking about their journeys through grief. Could it be that he was thinking the same? The wistful set of his mouth made her wonder.

Another tug. Oh, yes. They had a job to do. Olive cranked on the little handle to tighten up the slack in the measuring tape. The line went taut. She'd just marked the tape when the front door opened.

She only had time to see Maxfield's grimace before he ducked beneath the bushes. Olive ducked too, but there was no hiding the tape that was stretched across the porch. Quick as a wink, she tugged downward, forcing the tape hard against the threshold. Maxfield must have had the same thought, and just in time, because Mrs. Blount walked over it without a second glance.

Mr. Blount stepped on the tape and pivoted.

Olive caught her breath, waiting for his exclamation. But he'd only turned to lock the door, then follow his wife to the buggy.

She knew the minute Maxfield released the tape. With shaking hands, she rolled it up, and as soon as the buggy drove away, Maxfield was at her side.

"I don't think I've ever had so much fun taking a measurement." Gone were all the careful manners he'd adopted around her lately. This was the easy, sociable Mr. Scott that she'd first become comfortable with. "Did you get the measurement? I'll write it . . ." He felt in his coat pocket. "Did you bring paper?"

Olive pulled a pad of paper from inside her vest. "Of course." When she got her pencil in hand, she paused just to see if he was watching her with that wry look.

He was.

"It's the curse of the organized to always be rescuing those of us who aren't," Maxfield said. "Guard against that in your career, Olive. You have original ideas that will require your time and attention. Don't sacrifice your opportunities because others don't want to do the drudgery."

It was good advice, especially given her desire to help people. She hesitated, then pushed the paper and pencil to him. "You sketch the footing. I'll go to the next corner." Hooking her finger in the end of the tape and giving him the roll, she jogged away, but not before she saw the pride in his eyes.

Maxfield Scott was proud of her.

She hadn't realized her hands were shaking until she tried to hold the measuring tape against the corner. She took a deep breath, all the way to her knees, and let it out in a long sigh. He not only believed her, but he was proud of her.

With that, she began to hope again.

Between their crawling through landscaping and untangling a measuring tape, the laughter grew more frequent and the ease between them returned. But not too much ease. As friendly as they might be, there was a longing for more that Olive had to keep in check.

Once finished with Blount's house, it was time to go to Mr. Dennis's. After measuring the ground level, Olive waited outside as Maxfield crept through the second story of the unoccupied home. The second story was where the changes had taken place, and Olive didn't feel right sneaking through a former rival's house. He could do it on his own. Besides, she needed a break from the heady rush of whispering with him in the darkness. Olive was watching the windows, looking for the light of Maxfield's flashlight, when she heard voices that made her shrink back.

"I think it's Maxfield in there. We can't go in there until he's gone." It was a lady's voice. A young lady.

"It's your house. What's it matter?" Without a doubt, that was Amos.

Olive covered her mouth as if it made her even quieter and tucked in closer to the gardening shed.

"He wouldn't want me around if he's working. I don't know why, but it upsets him." To Olive's surprise, Ruby sounded sympathetic. Amos snorted and Ruby added, "He's a good man, Amos. No reason to vex him."

"I hate to bring it up, but I think your good man has an eye for my cousin."

Good thing Olive had her mouth covered or her gasp would've been heard. There was Amos pretending to know more than he did. And how rude of him to say that to Ruby. Olive winced, preparing herself, because whatever Ruby replied was bound to sting.

"I'm not surprised." There was an edge to her voice, but less than Olive expected. "I was always intimidated by her. She's so smart. Just like Maxfield."

Olive's hand dropped to her side. Ruby was intimidated by her? That made no sense. Not beautiful, fashionable Ruby.

"But you don't feel intimidated by me?" Amos asked. "I'm as smart as the next fellow."

"He's coming." There was a rustle as Ruby grabbed Amos, or Amos grabbed Ruby. "Let's go around the side," she whispered, and they ran away from Olive to duck out of sight.

She couldn't wipe the smile off her face. Four adults sneaking around at night. They weren't causing any harm, but neither were they ready to give up their juvenile escapades for dull adulthood. One look at Maxfield as he strode toward her and Olive was reminded that her adulthood was anything but dull.

Neither of them spoke until they'd turned the corner and the Dennis house was out of sight. If Maxfield had any suspicion that Ruby and Amos had been there, he didn't voice it. Olive decided that Ruby was right. He was a good man. No reason to vex him.

"How big does Blount's porch need to be?" she asked as they walked through the peaceful neighborhood.

"At least two hundred square feet enclosed. That'll do it."

"I'll write up the plans tomorrow and get him to agree."

"And I'll do my part to convince Mr. Dennis that I've seen your plans and he has nothing to fear. We can continue with the second-story room and he'll still have the biggest house."

Olive chuckled. "I only hope you aren't commissioned by someone to build a railcar next. If a Mr. Vanderbilt wires you, don't respond."

"And I'll hope you don't get a commission for an apartment building. Stay away from multi-family housing."

"At least until you're finished," she said.

Olive wanted their stroll to last forever. Then again, she couldn't wait to get started on the draft of Blount's porch. Life was good when you had so many things to look forward to that you couldn't decide which you wanted most.

Max's feelings toward Olive hadn't changed. If anything, they'd only grown stronger.

When he caught her helping Amos, he'd been devastated. But why had it bothered him so much? Because he wanted their relationship to be real. He wanted her to be real. He couldn't bear the thought that she'd orchestrated their interactions to her advantage. He couldn't bear the thought that the Olive Kentworth he knew would not be in his future.

Now he knew her better, and everything he knew—once he finally believed her—impressed him even more.

With Olive no longer hiding her skills behind her cousin, she wouldn't be available to watch the children in the evenings, so he wouldn't get more of these walks home. For a while, they could collaborate on the Christman store, but what happened after that? Would Maxfield constantly have to come up with business projects in order to see her? Or was there another way?

A whistle from the Fox-Berry Mine blew in the distance, calling the evening crew to work. Mrs. Wester had been generous to watch the children that night. Maxfield suspected that she wouldn't have been as helpful had he been going out with anyone besides Olive, but he didn't fault Mrs. Wester for her discernment.

"Maxfield, I need to apologize again."

They were nearly to her house. He noticed that she'd waited until she could escape before starting this conversation. Maxfield straightened his back and smiled as he prepared for the worst. "What evil have you perpetrated against me today?"

She dropped her gaze. Her lashes fluttered against her cheek. "Some of the things you accused me of were not true. I defended myself against those charges, but I didn't admit everything."

Max had put it behind him, but he understood her need for absolution. He took her hand. "I'm listening."

"There's something you don't know. The first time you hired

me, I didn't know whose house I was going to, so that wasn't planned. I didn't know you'd have books and journals available either, that just happened. But when I saw them, I really wanted to be hired again so I could learn more. In fact, I wanted to work for you so badly that I mailed you tickets to the Crystal Cave. I arranged for you to have an evening out so I could avail myself of your library."

"What?" She looked so stricken that he had a hard time not laughing. "You bought tickets for me and Ruby so you could come watch my children?"

"I didn't buy them. It's owned by my cousin, so—"

Maxfield tried to contain his smile and his relief. "That's a serious offense—encouraging me to spend more time with Ruby only to suit your purposes."

Olive clutched his hand. "I know! I feel so terrible. I couldn't have you forgive me without knowing the worst of it."

"You didn't arrange for the restaurant to delay our dinner, did you? To give yourself more time to study?"

"No, but had it been within my power . . ." She shrugged.

"And what about the time you asked for my help with the birdhouse? If it hadn't been for needing to get that measurement, would you have ever requested my company?" She'd made a confession, but it wasn't the one he wanted to hear.

At that she looked toward the street. "I can't imagine that I would ever need your help on a birdhouse. I've been building them for years."

"Would you have requested my company for any other reason?" It was the question he had to ask, even if he was unsure of the answer. She seemed unsure as well. Max touched her face, drawing her gaze to him. "There's a difference between pretending to need my help at that certain time and pretending to like my company."

"I wouldn't have asked for your company," she said at last.

He tried not to let the disappointment show, but she saw it regardless.

Pulling their clasped hands against her stomach, she spoke rapidly. "I would be too embarrassed to ask. Why would I presume on your time? Who am I to make demands of you?" Her ribs expanded with each deep breath, her eyes shining in earnestness. "That doesn't mean I don't enjoy our talks. That doesn't mean that I don't want you to ask . . ." She bit her lip, then ducked her head. "I apologize for everything." Taking her notebook from him, she turned to go to the house.

Maxfield's head was spinning. He'd thought he was going to have to endure needless apologies, and instead she'd inadvertently confessed her preference for him.

"Miss Kentworth," he called.

She turned warily, one foot on the porch. "Yes."

"Have dinner with me and the children tomorrow. We'll have a picnic."

"Are you asking me to watch Leo and Stella?"

"No. I'm not paying you, and I'm not leaving the children. You'll have to put up with me along with them."

He bounced on his toes, eager for her answer. She looked to the house, then back again. "Maybe it'd be a good idea. We need to iron out the Christman details."

"No, ma'am. No talk of business. You won't be able to read my books or pick my brain. We'll have to come up with something else to talk about."

Had he pushed too far? Surely his intent was clear. Or maybe he'd made it too clear.

Olive swung her arms. "Well, why not?" she exclaimed. "Everything is crazy nowadays." And then she went inside, only gifting him with a quick grin before she shut the door.

Maxfield laughed again. His nanny was not who he thought she was. She was so much more.

CHAPTER
27

Olive pinned her hair behind her head for the third time. The first time it had too many bumps. The second time it was pulled back too tight and slick. She'd never had trouble fixing her hair before, but maybe that was because she'd never cared. She slid the last hairpin in and held up her hand mirror. Why hadn't she learned how to fix herself up? Every other woman her age knew how to set herself to her best advantage, but it'd never seemed important to Olive until now that she was going to dine with Maxfield.

"What's it matter?" she asked herself in the mirror. "He already knows what I look like." But it did matter, so she pulled the pins out for the third time and ran the brush through again. If it didn't matter, she wouldn't have dug in the back of her closet for one of Calista's cast-off blouses that Willow had left behind when she moved away. The square neckline showed off her fair skin and made her look more like the fashionable ladies about town. But she couldn't dress fashionably and then leave her hair in the same wild state she usually did.

The parlor clock chimed a quarter till five, and Olive winced. Mrs. Wester would be leaving. Twisting her hair into a roll higher on her head than usual, she shoved in the pins. Then, ignoring the mirror on the desk, she picked up her birdhouse and hurried out the door.

It was starting like a typical evening with her caring for the children, but it felt like anything but. She wasn't freeing the man so he could court another. Instead, she was joining him and his family as their guest. What did that signify? She wasn't sure. Maxfield hadn't made any overtly romantic gestures since the discovery of her secret career, but he'd offered her his friendship. More than friendship, actually. Or was she imagining things? Olive was confused.

She'd thrust herself into a man's profession without understanding how the interactions and connections between those peers developed. Maybe he had other builders over for dinner with the family regularly. Maybe establishing friendship over other interests besides architecture was part of being savvy.

The birdhouse was heavy and catching the fine threads of her white blouse. She held it lower against her hip, where the heavier fabric of her skirt could take the abuse and save her blouse from snagging. Why hadn't she waited to deliver this at another time? Her effort was shortening her breath and bringing a dampness to her skin.

She set the birdhouse on the sidewalk and dusted off her hands. There had to be a better way.

"Don't take another step." Maxfield jogged across the street from an intersecting lane. "What are you doing lugging that around?"

"It's for Stella. I thought I could carry it."

"This here is the most beautiful thing I've ever seen." But his eyes weren't on the birdhouse.

Olive lowered her gaze even as she smiled. It was safe to assume he didn't say that to other architects. "Thank you. I worked really hard, hoping you'd say that."

"Wait," he chuckled. "I'm not talking about the birdhouse. Are you?"

She lifted the birdhouse with both hands and handed it to him.

"Perhaps the birdhouse took effort, but it didn't vex me as much as my hair did, so you'd better appreciate it."

Her answer pleased him. He held out his elbow, an offer for an escort, but Olive waved it away, knowing how heavy the birdhouse was and how close they were to his home.

"I heard from Mr. Christman," she said. "Now that the foundation is laid—"

"Nope. I refuse to listen."

Olive's eyebrow spiked. "It's important information. Why wouldn't you want to listen?"

"We already established that work talk is for the office. This is not a business meeting."

She'd thought he was just flirting. She hadn't realized he was going to stick to his guns. "If work is verboten, then what will we talk about?"

"I'm sure we'll think of something." He cut her a side glance with as much mischief as any of her cousins possessed.

When they reached the house, Olive held the door open for Maxfield, who had to turn sideways to slide in bearing her creation. The sound of the front door alerted the household that he was home. Quick thumps from upstairs sounded above their heads, along with Mrs. Wester's admonitions for them to not run down the stairs.

Olive wished she could wrap up the moment and preserve it so she could enjoy it over and over again. Their happy voices, the pure joy and love they had for their father, the homey peace of the household, and Mrs. Wester's guidance that had held it together while Maxfield healed. Feeling a sudden gratefulness to the woman, Olive forgot about the children exclaiming over her appearance and pulling at her skirts. Instead, she flung her arms around Mrs. Wester.

"I just want to thank you," Olive whispered beneath the excited jabbering of the children. "Thank you for taking care of them . . . and him."

Mrs. Wester returned the embrace. "I'm standing in the gap until the one who is supposed to be here realizes it."

Olive drew back, startled at her implication. Maxfield cleared his throat, his cheeks pink at Mrs. Wester's words. "I love these children," Olive said. "And you do a marvelous job filling any lack they have. That's really important to me."

"Of course it is, sweetie. It's natural you would feel this way. Don't let the strength of your emotions scare you off." She reached for her hat and her bag, which rested by the door. "No use wasting time here, now that the two of you are home."

It wasn't Olive's home, yet she felt the truth of the statement even as she prepared to deny it. But Maxfield intervened.

"Thank you, Mrs. Wester. It wouldn't have felt like a home for any of us without your help. Have a good evening."

"You too!" Mrs. Wester beamed a little too brightly as she walked out the door.

"It's mine, not yours." Stella pulled on her brother's sleeves, trying to establish her place next to the birdhouse.

"If it wasn't a good present, they wouldn't be fighting over it." Stepping around his squabbling children, Maxfield carried the birdhouse to the library and set it on an end table.

"The house is for Stella's bird friends, but you can both look at it." Olive knelt and drew Stella to her side. "See the door and the windows? They are all doors for the birds, but it's not like your house. There aren't hallways or kitchens. Each bird gets its own little room, though. They don't want to be together."

"And they don't need a water closet," said Leo, "because they poop while they fly. Isn't that right, Dad?"

Maxfield considered this carefully. "I have to agree with you. I've seen evidence to support this observation." Then, to change the subject, Maxfield began pointing out the different features that Olive had so painstakingly added. He showed them the eyebrow windows she used for dormers, the gingerbread work around the porch, and the tower. While he was occupied, Olive noticed something new on the bookshelf.

Leaving the gathering around the birdhouse, she was drawn to a picture of a smiling lady beneath an ornate streetlamp in a distant city. Olive picked up the lacquered frame to get a better look at the playful pose the lady adopted, with one hand on her hip and the other holding her platter hat on her head as she leaned to the side. The smile she was sharing with the photographer was personal and joyful. Without asking, Olive knew who was in the picture and who was behind the camera.

The room had grown quiet. Seeing what Olive held, Leo hopped to his feet.

"That's my mama." He stood on his tippy-toes until Olive lowered the picture to his level. "I remember her. Stella doesn't."

"She looks very happy." Olive put her hand on his shoulder and drew him closer so he could see better. "I bet she had the best laugh."

The boy shrugged. "I have a good laugh. Do you want to hear it?" He belted out an obnoxious outburst that Olive couldn't help but join. His eyes shone up at hers before returning to the picture. "I bet that's how she was laughing. That's why she's happy." Then, turning to his father, he asked, "When can we put the birdhouse up? I want to see the birds go in it."

"Not today. We're having a picnic, remember? And I'm hungry. Get your shoes and let's go."

Leo and Stella made a mad scramble for the stairs as Maxfield came to stand by Olive.

"I'd never seen this before," Olive said. "She's beautiful."

"It's my favorite picture." He lifted his hand but let it fall short of touching the frame. "I thought I was making it easier not to see it. Not to be reminded."

"She deserves to be remembered." Just like Olive's mother. Olive returned the picture to the shelf, feeling more drawn to

Maxfield than ever before. "I'd love to hear more about Georgia. Anytime you want to talk . . ."

"That beautiful smile shouldn't make me sad," he said. "I want to be happy when I see her picture and I want the children to be proud of her. I feel that life is finally reaching a sustainable equilibrium." The noise of those children coming down the stairs couldn't be ignored. "Now, I ordered a dinner from the restaurant. I knew if we stayed here, either you'd end up cooking or we'd end up with a mediocre meal by me. The restaurant is supposed to have the food ready for transport. So let's go!"

How could they be melancholy with an outing with the children planned? Olive took a small hand in hers, and they set off.

⊱♦♦♦♦♦♦⊰

It was going to be a good evening.

Before Olive, Maxfield had tried to pass time quickly like he was swallowing a bitter pill. Avoiding solitude, avoiding thought, avoiding planning for the future. He'd been stuck in a stagnant pool, hating where he was but not knowing how to move forward.

Now he knew, and it was all he could do to slow down and give Olive time to come to the same conclusion.

He loved her. He loved her quiet courage, he loved her steadfast goodness, and he loved her determination. Who else would've accomplished so much with so little encouragement? Even though she had her insecurities, she had pushed through them. And he wanted to be there to bolster her courage on the hard days when the doubts returned.

The four of them rode the trolley to Schifferdecker's Electric Park. Olive held Stella on her lap while Maxfield dug through the picnic basket to prove to Leo that it had everything they needed. Although the park had wild rides like the Dazy Dazer, it also featured sprawling green lawns, and the one he was aiming for overlooked the pavilion.

The band wasn't playing yet, but Maxfield figured when they

did, they could hear from the rise as well as anywhere. He handed the basket to Olive so he could spread the blanket and establish boundaries for Stella before she wandered off in search of the petting zoo.

"Stay on the blanket." Olive had the same idea as she set Stella on the old quilt and opened up the basket. "This is a special treat, isn't it? We've never eaten outside together before."

"We have," said Leo. "Daddy eats outside with us all the time now."

"Just lately," Maxfield said, "but only the three of us."

"Just the three of you?" Her eyes crinkled with mischief. "You felt the need to clarify?"

"You are pleased that I did, are you not?"

She pulled out the plates and the crock of barbecue that he'd ordered. Removing the lid, she took a deep breath of the savory meat. "I hope you brought more than a handkerchief. This is going to be messy."

"It'll be fine. I'm feeling reckless." Although he should've thought to pack napkins. Smeared barbecue wasn't romantic. Then again, neither were toddlers and children, yet Olive looked as content as he'd ever seen her.

Together they served the children and arranged them to make their meal as trouble-free and clean as possible.

"Ordering the food was a wonderful idea." Olive helped herself to some fried pickles. "I was hungry after work today."

"I've been ordering meals to carry away for a few weeks. Once I made the decision to spend more time with the children, I had to figure out what to do for dinner. Mrs. Wester was always happy to start supper, but they are ready to get outside by then." Stella leaned across his knee to grab a piece of bread. "And while they are becoming better at eating in a restaurant, this is much more relaxing than sitting at a table and waiting for our dinner."

"It's delightful." The flowering azaleas behind her framed her with riotous purple. "I would eat outside all the time if given the opportunity." She crossed her legs in front of her and smoothed her skirt over them before taking another slice of fried pickles and dropping it into her mouth.

Life was beautiful. This caring, intelligent woman had never looked happier than she did right now with his children around her. The breeze fluttered her collar against her creamy skin. Her one clean hand smoothed Leo's hair out of his eyes, then she stuck her barbecue-covered finger between her perfect lips and sucked it clean.

Those lips. He'd done his best as a gentleman to banish that encounter to the outskirts of his memory, but it came roaring back with a clarity that astonished him. Max looked at his children with alarm, with the suspicion that they had read his thoughts, but of course, they were unaware. He chuckled to himself. He was as jittery as a first-time beau.

"What's so amusing?" Olive asked, eager to be in on the joke.

He held her gaze, wishing he could create something as beautiful as the moment. Before long, he'd tell her how much she meant to him. He'd tell her everything. "I laughed in appreciation of God's sense of humor. Sending you, a skilled architect, to watch my children." That was the safest explanation he could come up with.

"It might be less miraculous than you think." Olive sighed. "I hate to admit it, but I think Calista arranged for me to take that job when she saw that it was the famous Maxfield Scott asking. God does have a sense of humor, and He proved it when He surrounded me with those crazy cousins of mine."

"So I have the preacher's wife to thank for all this mess?"

"You think you've suffered?" She rolled her eyes. "You have no idea what they've put me through over the years."

"I forgot about Amos. If the rest of them are anything like him . . ."

"It's a wonder I'm so levelheaded and reasonable." She passed an unopened soda bottle to Maxfield.

"I don't know about that. What levelheaded woman decides to become an architect and then carries it out beneath the noses of her clients without them having a clue?" He popped off the top of the soda bottle lid with his pocketknife.

"Only a levelheaded woman would be capable of succeeding," she said, then admitted, "although she had to endure a string of emotions that makes the Dazy Dazer look tame." Then with a shy glance, she added, "And I haven't quite put that exhilarating ride behind me yet."

"I hope there are more to come," he said.

The temptation to say more was building until it felt like a physical force. In fact, a physical force hit him right between the shoulder blades and bounced a charred rib off his plate and onto his fawn-colored trousers.

"Uncle Maxfield!"

There were soft little arms around his neck.

Reaching behind his back, Max grabbed young Norris, pulled him over his shoulder, and dropped him on the blanket in front of him. The squeals of the Vogel children joined Leo's and Stella's as they fell into a writhing mass of juvenile shoes, ribbons, and sweet barbecue sauce.

"Hey kids, I didn't say to jump in the middle of their dinner," Eric said as he and Elaine approached. Although he was talking to his children, both of the parents couldn't stop looking at Olive.

"I'm sorry, Max," Elaine said. "As soon as they saw their friends, they took off running. I should keep them on a shorter leash."

Maxfield set his plate aside, stood, and tipped his cap at Elaine. "You've come at the perfect time. I'd like to introduce you to my friend, Miss Olive Kentworth." He took Olive's hand to help her get to her feet. "Olive, this is Eric and Elaine Vogel. Old friends of mine, and Eric is the best draftsman I know."

Elaine smiled sweetly. "Nice to meet you, Miss Kentworth. I think your name has come up in conversation with Maxfield a couple of times. Remind me again, how do you two know each other?"

Oh, Elaine was a clever one. It was impressive how she pried without effort.

Olive wasn't quite as smooth. "I used to watch Leo and Stella in the evenings when Mr. Scott was entertaining. Lately I haven't been doing that as much. . . ." She looked to him for help, but Maxfield only grinned. He wasn't going to rescue her. He wanted to hear exactly how she defined their relationship. "Tonight, we're watching the children together."

"Is that so?" Eric beamed at Maxfield, making Max regret ever telling his friend about the kiss. "So it's purely a professional association?"

"Professional in more ways than I expected," said Maxfield. "It turns out that Miss Kentworth is also an architect—one with great skill, actually."

"An architect? How interesting." No one could fail to see the speculative look Elaine gave Eric, but Eric shouldn't have been surprised. He'd known for weeks that Maxfield was collaborating with someone on the department store.

"She's incredible," Maxfield said. "You've seen the Lighthouse miners' center, haven't you? And the Crystal Cave? She designed the visitors' center for that. Both are fantastic, creative works."

From their expressions, they didn't know what to think. Then again, neither had Maxfield when he first learned of her secret.

CHAPTER
28

Elaine and Eric were impressed, and Olive was embarrassed. Maybe it was on the strength of Maxfield's testimony, but the Vogels didn't question her skills. They didn't laugh or belittle her work. They beamed as Maxfield extolled her praises, almost as if they were proud of her themselves.

How could praise be so hard to hear and yet so wonderful? She knew she'd relive this moment a hundred times over. She'd quote to herself all the generous opinions he was sharing about her and her work. All of them would be stored away like flowers pressed between pages of a heavy book, to be treasured later.

But right now, they were painfully awkward. All the years she hid from sharing her passion, she'd told herself that it was because she would fail and be ashamed. Now she realized that even in success, she still felt pained. There was no winning. Would she ever grow used to compliments? Did she want to?

"If Maxfield is saying that you are good, then you must be the best," Mr. Vogel said. "He's very particular . . . when it comes to buildings, anyway."

His wife burst out with a sharp cough and a sharper look of warning. Mr. Vogel avoided his wife's gaze while winking at Maxfield. What was he talking about? She looked to Maxfield, who was sending his friend the same look of warning as Mrs. Vogel was.

The tussle of children was growing rowdier with every misunderstood jest. Leo and the Vogel children sped toward the stage, playing tag or some such game. Olive barely snatched Stella by the arm before she got out of range as well.

"I wanna go," she pouted.

"You're too little," Olive said. "Let's see what they packed for dessert." Then remembering their guests, "Would you like to join us?"

"Sure . . ." said Mr. Vogel. "That food looks—"

"It's a pity you don't have time," said Maxfield. "Or else we'd love for you to stay."

"I don't have time?" Mr. Vogel laughed. "That's news to me. I was hoping to get to know Miss Kentworth better and to make sure she knows you well enough."

"Now that you mention it, I just remembered that the children have been longing to spend time with their friends." Mrs. Vogel made a wide-eyed look at her husband. "Why don't we take Leo and Stella with us? They could stay as late as you want. In fact, let the children stay the night. You can pick them up in the morning."

Mr. Vogel wavered. He squinted at Maxfield. "I'm not sure I'm that good of a friend," he said.

"I knew there was a reason she was my favorite," said Maxfield.

Olive's arm tightened around Stella's waist. The children were her shield. She'd had the security of knowing that nothing too personal could occur with them as escorts. But if they were gone . . .

"My wife is right, I suppose. We've already had our dinner and were on our way home. We'll take the kids, but I don't know if it's a good idea to leave them all night. I wouldn't want you to be lonesome at your house all alone, Maxfield."

Now it was Max's turn to look uncomfortable. "I'll get them as soon as I walk Miss Kentworth home. It won't be past ten. I promise."

Olive handed Stella over to Mrs. Vogel. After the niceties of first meetings and promises of second meetings were performed, the Vogels left with the children, leaving Olive and Maxfield alone.

This wasn't what she'd planned. Not knowing what to do, Olive gathered their supper and stuffed it in the basket. She looked at the half-empty soda bottle and took a long swill from it. Suddenly finishing off the rest of the drink was all she could think of. It kept her from having to think of something to say to Maxfield. She'd lifted it to her mouth again when Maxfield pulled it away.

"You don't have to finish it all now."

"I thought we were tidying up here so we could go."

"Go where?"

"You said you'd walk me home."

"The music hasn't started yet."

Olive looked around them. They were at the edge of the green with hedges at their backs and a long rolling vista before them that stretched to the white gazebo where the bands performed. Not private, exactly, but definitely not where they'd likely be interrupted should anything occur. And all she could think about was what might occur and how badly she'd botched it last time.

"You want to stay for the concert?" She felt a nervous belch working its way up.

"That's what we came for."

"Even without the children?"

"Especially without the children." His eyes sparkled.

"I don't think I can sit through a concert. I feel like walking."

"You aren't happy to be here?" Seeing her shrug, Maxfield picked up the blanket. "What do you think is going to happen to you?"

Olive lifted the picnic basket. "Nothing is going to happen. I'm sure of it."

"And yet, you're worried. Could it be that you agreed to come only so you could see the children? I'm sure you've missed them." He folded the blanket beneath his arm.

"I have missed them. I didn't expect that they would go home and leave us here alone."

"You weren't this nervous in your office."

"We were talking business there. You already said that there'd be no talking business tonight. I'm not sure what else we can talk about."

"We can talk about us." The tuning fiddle alerted them that the band was about to commence. Olive watched the figures finding their spots on the lawn beneath them. The people's shadows were longer than they had been before. The sun was going down, and she was alone with Maxfield.

With a tilt of his head, he motioned her to a path, too new to be more than some trampled grass leading toward the water. Olive fought her fears. She'd been brave of late. Why shouldn't it continue? She could do this.

The music started in earnest, growing louder even though their steps took them away from the venue. Olive looked both ways on the water. The boats had been tied up for the evening and the park-goers were enjoying a lively tune on the other side of the rise.

"Do you know why Mr. Vogel was teasing about me being picky?" Maxfield waited for her to come over the crest before pointing to the dock and starting that way. "He never liked Ruby. Neither did Elaine. They thought she was cold and shallow."

"Cold?" Olive shook her head. Her footsteps echoed on the boards of the dock. "Ruby is energetic and charming. I don't see how anyone could call her cold."

"She wasn't you. Now that I know you, I know what I was missing, and no one else will do." He took the basket from her and laid it on the bench alongside the blanket and soda bottle.

Olive looked out over the smooth water reflecting the last light of the sun. She'd risked so much in stepping out with her career. Was it greedy to hope for two miracles?

"Somehow," she said, "when I look ahead at what I think the future is going to hold, all I ever see is disaster." He took her hands, sheltering them inside of his. "For years, I knew that my mother was going to die. Every morning I woke with the reminder that there was great, unavoidable sorrow awaiting me and my family. Now that it's happened, it seems like there should be another great sorrow amassing to take its place. I can't imagine life without imminent disaster waiting around the next corner. It makes me hesitant to plan for tomorrow. Afraid to step out."

"None of us are guaranteed a life free from sorrow." Giving her a look of warm encouragement, he said, "Whether you know there's sorrow ahead or not, we can't prevent all of it."

Max had had little warning when his wife died, and the shock of it threw him off-kilter. Which was better? To dread an event for years or to have it suddenly come upon you? Maybe her experience wasn't the worst and maybe she shouldn't always expect the worst.

Despite her nervousness, his hands felt secure. With all the potential future disasters, all the imaginary scenarios she could dream up, his touch was real and anchoring. She closed her eyes, noticing that the band had started a languid ballad and the birds were in the trees, chirping to each other as they settled in for the night.

Settling in. She should stay here, in this moment, and not get carried away by what could happen. Was that possible? Surely other people did it, but Olive could never quite grasp the skill.

"Think about right now," Max said. He released her hands and pulled her next to him. Lulled by the lapping waves against the dock, Olive allowed her body to rest against his. "Listen to the music, listen to the birds. I would say smell the roses, but there aren't any roses in this part of the park, so smell the fishy water. Feel how the air is starting to cool. There's a touch of dampness in it. Before too long, it might have a touch of chill."

For this moment, she'd stop questioning and she'd obey. She let her mind be led as he described the things they were both experiencing. Her hands were tucked between them against his chest.

"There might be a chill but not here between us. Feel how nice this warmth is next to me. Feel how precious it is to be held, to belong, to occupy a space where so few are admitted. My children—Leo and Stella—I would let them share this space but no one else. It's reserved for you."

She had feared words of romance, but this was different. This wasn't about loud declarations and prideful public appearances. It was about belonging, companionship, and something that could be enjoyed privately in the security of home.

"Would you like to be a part of this, Olive?" His hand wrapped around her waist. "Who knows what can happen? We can only control our decisions, and I'm asking you to help me decide my future. Please tell me, does being a part of my life, my family, appeal to you?"

That's what it came down to, wasn't it? Her family would tease her endlessly, but if people could grow used to the idea of a female architect, surely they would cease to wonder at Maxfield Scott wooing Olive Kentworth.

She was tired of the fear. Tired of denying what she wanted just to spite herself. There was no one against her. Nothing that stood in her way besides her own feelings of inadequacy. She was ready for another step forward.

"This . . ." she said, "this is how I want to spend the rest of my life."

He tightened his grip on her waist. His chest stretched with a breath he held and held until she wondered if he'd ever breathe again. But when he spoke again, it was she who stopped breathing.

"It may seem sudden, Olive, but I know my mind. I know how I admired you from the beginning. I know how hard I tried not to think of you in a possessive sort of way, how hard I tried to keep Ruby at the center of my thoughts. But the more I was around you, the more untenable it was to consider her.

"You're young," he said. "You haven't been married before, so I'm going to give you the experience you deserve. I'm going to court you and woo you. I'd work fourteen years for you like Jacob did for Rachel if I needed to, because you deserve that. But . . . just so you know . . . I love you and that's not going to change. It might grow stronger, but I want you in my life and in my family. Take all the time you want in making your decision, but as far as I'm concerned, my decision has already been made. But that's not to pressure you. You take . . ."

He was rambling, bouncing back and forth between assurances of his enduring affection and apologies for having his affections settled before giving her a chance to know her own mind. There was nothing for Olive to do besides watch, listen, and find his discomfort endearing.

"For now, just this is what I want." He looked over the water and the shore in the distance, giving Olive a chance to hide her smile. "What I want is the ability to spend time with you, to work with you if you'll allow it, the privilege of letting my children get to know you better. That's all I'm asking for. You've been kind . . ."

Oh no. He must have seen her mouth twitch because he stopped abruptly. "Are you laughing at me?" His mouth quirked sideways, and his shoulders relaxed.

"I don't know what else to do," she said. "You're telling me that you love me, and I think you're telling me that you're going to ask me to marry you someday. I don't know if that qualifies as a proposal, so I'm uncertain how I'm supposed to respond." Funny how delightful it was to look him in the eyes now that she had nothing to hide. "The best thing for me to do is to stay quiet until you finish your presentation and see how you're feeling after that."

"Oh, Olive. I'm feeling like I want to kiss you."

Now that was a statement that she understood. His eyes traveled to her lips and Olive sprang into action. It took a hand to his chest to halt what he intended.

"I can't kiss you," she said. "You know that."

"I most certainly don't know that! Whyever not?"

"Remember last time? It didn't go well."

"I remember." He sighed. "I could live to be two hundred and I wouldn't forget that kiss."

"Then you have to understand why it's impossible. I can't kiss you again until I figure out the right way to do it." Her heartbeat was notching up, just talking about it. "Maybe there'll be some books on kissing at the church bazaar? That's how I learned architecture." She was spouting nonsense to stall.

"You gave me an amazing kiss the first time. So amazing that I was unprepared and failed to behave properly." The sun was down now but twilight lingered enough for her to see his eyebrow quirk.

Olive was finding it difficult to form words. She licked her lips, then remembered their dinner. "Oh no! I ate pickles. You can't kiss me when I reek of pickles."

He seemed entranced by her lips, leaning even closer, tilting his head in a way she now recognized. "I ate pickles too. I love pickles. Almost as much as I love olives." Maxfield paused long enough for her to reconsider, but Olive found herself stretching toward him.

She'd meant to keep her eyes opened, but as their lips met, her head tilted back, her eyes closed, and she felt herself being drawn into the whirlwind that had produced the last disaster. The music from the band turned into a roar in her ears. She remembered she should hold back this time, to let him take the lead, but she soon found that patience in this area was not one of her virtues.

Her only salvation was that he pulled away. At least his lips were gone from hers because now they were pressed against her head, flattening that hairdo she'd fretted over.

Olive clung to him as he gathered her up against him.

"This is going to be harder than I expected," he said. "I am undone by your enthusiasm."

"It's that bad?" Her senses were returning but they all called out for more of Maxfield. She disentangled herself, trying to restore the decorum they'd abandoned. "I'll try to be more subdued in the future."

"That's entirely unnecessary." He had adopted that nonchalant air again, but Olive knew the truth. He was as enthusiastic as she. "I'm not offended. In fact, I'm enchanted, but I never got to finish that presentation. The one where I ask you to marry me."

Olive fanned her face as she turned toward the gentle lapping of the lake. Being the wife of Maxfield Scott, a man whose name she'd revered for years, was a ludicrous idea. The girl who read the secondhand architecture books at her mother's sickbed would say no. She'd be alarmed at the prospect. She'd do everything in her power to avoid such a prominent role.

Her gaze traveled across the lake to the gently sloping hills on the far side. That girl would say no, but Olive wasn't that girl any longer. She was a woman who met with investors, hired construction crews, and directed them to build her creations. She was a woman who could appreciate a man like Maxfield and all that he had to offer. A woman who would love him ardently and tenaciously.

She would be a better woman because of him and, in her opinion, he was already a better man because of her.

Olive turned. She couldn't hide her heart's decision. He read it on her face and dropped to one knee on the dock. He took her hand, and the rest was easy from there. In fact, it was the easiest decision she'd made in her life.

It was Mr. Blount's final walk-through of the newly finished addition, and Olive was holding her breath. He'd walked the construction every day, but this was an inspection and, as a mine owner, Mr. Blount knew the importance of thoroughness. He stuck his head inside the fireplace in the great hall and commented that he didn't see any light shining through. He bounced on the floor, making sure it didn't give any more than it should. He flipped the light switches, grunting his approval when the lamps responded, and then he slid open the pocket door that led to Mrs. Blount's enclosed porch.

"Are you happy?" he asked Mrs. Blount, who was bent over a massive potted plant.

Hugging the pot with both arms, she scooted backward, pulling it toward the screen and the indirect sunlight. "I'm happy if you're happy," she said.

Of course Mrs. Blount was happy. Her new rooms were perfect, and she was constantly sharing her delight with Olive as she arranged and rearranged the new furnishings. But with a husband like Mr. Blount, Olive understood her answer. Thankfully Olive's husband was nothing like him.

"I'm only happy if this is the biggest house in Joplin." Mr. Blount raised an eyebrow at Olive. "What did your cousin Amos say about that?"

Despite the fact that Olive had an office with her name on it and Amos hadn't shown up at the construction site for weeks, Mr. Blount still pretended not to understand who the builder was.

"With the addition of the enclosed porch, your home is the biggest in Joplin." She looked about the beautiful room. Too bad it represented a selfish pride. Maybe someday someone would own it who appreciated it for the design instead of the square footage.

"It's perfect," said Mrs. Blount. Maybe somebody already did appreciate it.

"Then we can close the books on this deal." He pulled an envelope out of his pocket and handed it to her. "Here's the remaining balance on the project. I'll be sure and recommend your boss for the work he did."

Olive couldn't help but grin as she took the check. "Thank you. Amos will be grateful." She dropped it into her bag and snapped it closed. Just in the nick of time. Olive's day had been full between visiting her mother's grave and packing her bags, then there was that short appointment they'd had with Pastor Matthew that morning. Now there was so much to do before the train left.

She walked with her head held high, more concerned about accomplishing her tasks than who was looking at her and what they thought. Her office would be neglected for the next two weeks, but her clients were aware of the situation. The department store, the railcar, and Boone and Maisie's new house would wait until she returned.

It was no longer a surprise to see Maxfield sitting behind her desk, although he was always quick to jump out of the way when she entered. Or maybe he was quick to jump to her. In unison, they pulled out slips of paper and presented them to each other.

"Mr. Dennis is satisfied?" she asked as she scanned the amount on Maxfield's check.

"He agrees that no one counts the square footage of their porches so in reality, his house is the biggest. How about Mr. Blount?"

"His porch is so wonderful, of course he's going to count it. It would be a disgrace to ignore it." She looked again at the amount. "That is all you were paid? You didn't charge enough. The great Maxfield Scott shouldn't work for peanuts."

"Don't you worry, sweetheart. That was just for the addition. But now that you mention it, I hope your check was only a partial payment too. My wife's time is worth more than this."

"Absolutely." She lifted her chin, daring him to repeat the kiss he'd bestowed that morning in front of family and friends.

Maxfield complied, short and sweet. "Regretfully we have a deposit to make and a train to catch, but there'll be more kissing before the day's done. Don't you worry."

He handed her the check, then picked up the two bags of luggage that waited by the door. From there, everything was done in a rush, from the deposits at the bank to the instructions for Eric to carry out while they were gone. Leo and Stella had already been taken to Granny Laura's farm to stay while their parents honeymooned, and Olive had no doubt that they would be as wild as March hares by the time they returned.

They'd reached the train station and boarded the private car her sister had arranged for them before she thought to tell Maxfield, "Did I mention who I saw while you were meeting with Mr. Dennis? Amos and Ruby. He had her trying to ride a unicycle on Main Street."

"I wish him all the luck." He took her bag, set it on the dresser next to the bed, and removed his hat. "Did I mention to you that our bid on the residential lot was accepted?"

Olive's jaw dropped. "The bid for our lot?"

Maxfield smiled as he pulled at the ribbon holding on her hat, then lifted the hat and dropped it atop her luggage. "I gave them the earnest money and we'll close the deal when we return."

Olive squealed like the carefree child she never got to be. "Our

311

house plans. We have to finalize our house plans." She dug through her bag until she located her sketchbook. Flipping over the cover, she paged through until she found their latest project. "I can't wait to get these done," she said as she sat on the bed.

"I can think of other things I'd rather do," grumbled Maxfield.

"Our offices," she said. "We haven't finished planning them." With both parents working, having an office at home with the children made sense, but the Scotts were going the extra mile and designing an office each for Maxfield and Olive. Two independent architects, two separate doors, two distinct creative styles—all in one family.

"I don't care much about my office right now," Maxfield said. He dropped a kiss on her neck and sent shivers through her bones.

He was trying to distract her. "Good, then you won't mind if I scoot this wall here and then we're settled?" Olive held the plans out with hands that couldn't help but tremble.

"I don't mi—" Max straightened. "Wait. Why would you do that? That makes your office bigger than mine. No, it'd look better if the wall were here." He tapped an empty space in the middle of her office.

"Nice try. That gives you nearly fifty square feet more while I'll be scrunched up in a corner." She couldn't speak until the chill from his next kiss passed. "If we moved your window here and the wall there, then that would give me more room."

"My legs are longer than yours. They'll never fit, not with all my books and shelves." He shrugged, then found a place beneath her ear that he'd hitherto missed.

"What if we attach a screened-in porch to your office?" she asked. "Would that satisfy you?"

"Hmm . . . I'll have to ask Amos. He's going to be the designer of this house if you don't cooperate."

Another kiss, but this one more than a peck. Olive sighed. "I guess if Blount and Dennis could work it out, we can too. Do you ever wonder what would've happened if I hadn't let Calista talk me into watching your children?"

"It was only a matter of time," Maxfield said as he took her sketchbook and laid it aside. "Your talents wouldn't have gone unnoticed for long and once I discovered what a beautiful, accomplished lady you were, I wouldn't have stopped until you noticed me."

The room swayed and the Joplin depot slowly slid past the window. In a matter of minutes, everything she knew, everyone she knew, would be left behind. But she'd be back. She'd found the one piece of the puzzle that her family couldn't provide, and he fit perfectly into her life in every way.

A Note from the Author

Dear Reader,

I can't believe we're at the end of THE JOPLIN CHRONICLES (at least for now). Thank you for spending time with the Kentworth cousins. They were so fun to write. I have dozens of ornery cousins, and they are more like the Kentworths than you might imagine.

Once again, I'd like to thank the generous Joplinites who helped me with my research and local connections. In particular, we should celebrate the members of Historic Murphysburg Preservation. It was a walk down the streets of Murphysburg that convinced me to write about an aspiring architect and the type of people who would have commissioned those impressive homes.

As usual, when naming my characters, I used the family names of Joplin's early citizens, although it's only to honor them, not to suggest they were involved in any of my fictional shenanigans.

A real Joplinite mentioned in the book is the acclaimed architect Austin Allen. Maxfield's fictional career was modeled after Allen's, but forgive me for moving his timeline up, as Allen would have just graduated high school in 1899. Despite dying at the young age of thirty-six, Austin Allen made rich contributions to the beauty and culture of Joplin.

Another Joplin architect you should know about, especially since she was untrained like Olive, is Matilda Weymann. Around 1890, Mrs. Weymann designed her sprawling Queen Anne at 508 South Sergeant Avenue. The house contained such modern conveniences as speaking tubes and a central vacuum system. You can still see that home today. Another connection the Weymanns have with THE JOPLIN CHRONICLES is that Matilda's husband was the zinc miner who discovered the Crystal Cave just three blocks from their house. One couple whose lives inspired two different storylines—impressive!

Thank you again for reading my stories. Without my readers, this pecking at a computer would be pointless. If you want to connect, you can find me at reginajennings.com or on Facebook.

Blessings!

Regina

Regina Jennings is a graduate of Oklahoma Baptist University with a degree in English and a minor in history. She's the winner of the National Readers' Choice Award and a finalist for the Christy Award, the Golden Quill Award, and the Oklahoma Book of the Year Award. Regina has worked at the *Mustang News* and at First Baptist Church of Mustang, along with time at the Oklahoma National Stockyards and various livestock shows. She lives outside Oklahoma City with her husband and four children and can be found online at www.reginajennings.com.

Sign Up for Regina's Newsletter

Keep up to date with Regina's news on book releases and events by signing up for her email list at reginajennings.com.

More from Regina Jennings

Left to rue her mistake of falling in love with the wrong man, Maisie Kentworth keeps busy by exploring the idle mine nearby. While managing his mining company, Boone Bragg stumbles across Maisie and the crystal cavern she's discovered. He makes her a proposal that he hopes will solve all their problems, but instead it throws them into chaos.

Proposing Mischief • THE JOPLIN CHRONICLES #2

You May Also Like . . .

Assigned to find the kidnapped daughter of a mob boss, Pinkerton operative Calista York is sent to a rowdy mining town in Missouri. But she faces the obstacle of missionary Matthew Cook. He's as determined to stop a local baby raffle as he is the reckless Miss York, whose bad judgment consistently seems to be putting her in harm's way.

Courting Misfortune by Regina Jennings
THE JOPLIN CHRONICLES #1
reginajennings.com

Caroline Adams returns to Indian Territory craving adventure after tiring of society life. When she comes across swaggering outlaw Frisco Smith, his plan to obtain property in the Unassigned Lands sparks her own dreams for the future. When the land rush begins, they find themselves battling over a claim—and both dig in their heels.

The Major's Daughter by Regina Jennings
THE FORT RENO SERIES #3
reginajennings.com

Confirmed bachelor Lieutenant Jack Hennessey is stunned to run into Hattie Walker, the girl who shattered his heart . . . and she's just as surprised to find her rescuer is the neighbor she once knew. But his attempts to save her from a dangerous situation go awry, and the two end up in a mess that puts her dreams in peril—and tests his resolve to remain single.

The Lieutenant's Bargain by Regina Jennings
THE FORT RENO SERIES #2
reginajennings.com

⬩ BETHANYHOUSE

More from Bethany House

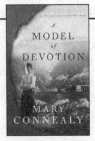

A brilliant engineer, Jilly Stiles sets her focus on fulfilling her dream of building a mountaintop railroad—and remaining independent. But when a cruel and powerful man goes to dangerous lengths to try to make Jilly his own, marrying her friend Nick may be the only way to save herself and her dreams.

A Model of Devotion by Mary Connealy
THE LUMBER BARON'S DAUGHTERS #3
maryconnealy.com

After years of being her diva mother's understudy, it's time for Delia Vittoria to take her place on stage. Attempting to make amends for a grave mistake, Kit Quincy is suddenly pulled into Delia's plot to win the great opera war and act as her patron and an enigmatic phantom. But when a second phantom appears, more than Delia's career is threatened.

His Delightful Lady Delia by Grace Hitchcock
AMERICAN ROYALTY #3
gracehitchcock.com

Longing for a fresh start, Julia Schultz takes a job as a Harvey Girl at the El Tovar Hotel, where she's challenged to be her true self. United by the discovery of a legendary treasure, Julia and master jeweler Christopher Miller find hope in each other. But when Julia's past catches up with her, will she lose everyone's trust?

A Gem of Truth by Kimberley Woodhouse
SECRETS OF THE CANYON #2
kimberleywoodhouse.com

◊ BETHANY HOUSE